BRANCHING OUT

FALL OF THE CITIES – BOOK III

BY
VANCE HUXLEY

© 2016 Vance Huxley

Published by Entrada Publishing.

Printed in the United States of America.

TABLE OF CONTENTS

DEDICATION

To my Noeline and to the Joy of my life

Acknowledgements

Thank you to my editor Sharon Umbaugh,
for turning my words into a book worth reading.

My thanks to Rachel at Entrada
for all her hard work and encouragement.

Chapter 1:
Drizzle and Gunsmoke

Across the globe, chaos reigned, while the cabal, the conspirators who had triggered the whole disaster fought to control the consequences and shape the new world. Their aims, to generate all electricity by renewable means, to reduce oil consumption, and to ensure that every region of the world produced enough food for their population, seemed admirable. The methods were draconic.

In 2016, the top ten oil refineries worldwide processed ten percent of world's oil production, scattered around the world among the hundreds of smaller facilities. Within years, the new Gulf States refineries alone treated ten percent, while the Chinese and Russians built similar facilities, driving smaller refineries out of business. The cabal attacked in only thirty places, destroying almost fifty percent of the now concentrated global oil refining facilities. Their attacks used the cheap simple sugar rockets perfected by groups such as Hamas, while messages on social media claimed responsibility on behalf of dozens of terrorist organisations. Unfortunately, all over the world, groups of terrorists and militant eco-groups copied them, launching their own attacks on pipelines, wells, fuel storage tanks and smaller refineries.

The resulting chaos helped the cabal in virtually destroying or taking over major governments, and specifically seizing control of major naval and air forces at a government level. On the oceans, as refined oil stocks dwindled or were destroyed the ships delivering food ran out of fuel, and large areas of the world faced starvation. In Europe the cabals planned to extract the smaller population they needed from the cities, then pen the rest of the people inside to die. They failed, in the most part, and starving mobs swept west to the only country growing a surplus of food, France. There they fought over what remained.

In the UK, the generally unarmed population were penned in their cities, while the Royal Navy stopped the starving European mobs from crossing the channel in their search for food. The UK cell of the cabal choreographed a series of riots to reduce the trapped populations of UK cities one at a time.

Mobs tens of thousands strong roamed the cities, smashing and killing, their rage turning to panic and starvation. Hastily fortified housing estates were swamped, shopping centres burned, and anyone in their path died. When the cities no longer provided enough food or victims, the mobs tried to escape and met armour and soldiers, dug in and waiting for them around the perimeters. In city after city the tanks and machine guns drove the survivors back and killed most of them. The army retreated to their positions on the perimeter, and the armour moved to the next city.

Amid the ruins of the cities, small groups of friends or even strangers gathered together, found similar minded groups, and coalesced into enclaves. Some found a strong building or one with resources such as food, parkland for farming, steel, fuel or clothing, or just houses with water and electricity. In many places, the second-rate criminals or unscrupulous took their chances, forming gangs and carving out little empires by using threats or violence to subdue other survivors. Elsewhere, groups of ordinary citizens found a leader or leaders and a place to defend; sometimes they simply decided to stop running, exhausted or losing the will to continue.

The cabal seized the reins of power but still didn't have the resources to finish culling the population. The new rulers' grip on power was shaky, and they dare not order British Army to massacre civilians. Instead, a system of coupons and marts, huge superstores replacing all the other shops, kept the survivors fed while paramilitary contractors swept the rest of the country clean of undesirables. Coupons were only issued to stable groups within the cities, named enclaves, which forced the surviving population to join an enclave or form their own. Although some of the enclaves tried to maintain civilised rules, even the pacifists had to fight roaming gangs or other enclaves just to survive.

Three years after the crash, in late January, one such peaceful enclave calling themselves Orchard Close seemed to have found a balance with their neighbours. Much of their survival depended on the reluctance of neighbouring gangs to go up against their leader, Harold aka Soldier Boy, an ex-soldier. Harold had led a small band of survivors to a group of intact houses and the disparate group had built defences and survived the initial chaos. Now they had trade deals with other gangs to bring in a few extra coupons, as well as extra food planted on land reclaimed from the rubble.

*   *   *

Six miles across the ruins from Orchard Close, the SIMS were being forced to defend their way of life. A young man called Stevie crouched among derelict buildings, peering through the rain at the advancing group of armed men. "Are you sure they'll work in this rain, Julie?" He glanced back. "The Men in Black are reversing a van to protect their fighters." The invaders were coming from left to right across Stevie's line of sight, aiming at the rough-built brick wall and group of houses registered as the SIMS enclave. "If we can't stop the van they'll get over the walls."

In response a young woman's head showed briefly above the rubble nearby. "Bert and the rest said they'd work. They're under a roof so the rain won't matter. Has the van reached the marker yet?" The woman crouched back down into a nearby manhole, out of sight yet still clear of the water in the pipes beneath. She held a box sealed inside a plastic bag and attached to an insulated wire running down into the water and off along the drain.

Stevie kept up a commentary. "The van is past the rear marker but the fighters on foot are straggling. Bert and Maisie said get as many between the markers as possible." A savage grin crossed his face. "Those smart-arsed MiB bastards won't be making a bloody corporate takeover here."

"Just keep your head well down Stevie. They've got machine guns."

"Don't worry Julie. Right, the front ones are just coming up on the front marker. Send the signal." He brought up a target pistol and aimed as best he could through the rain.

Behind him in the manhole Julie pressed a button, holding it down firmly for several seconds. Moments later a green light showed through the plastic. "Message received. Get your head down." They both ducked and waited, and waited.

"Oh shit, it hasn't worked. Make a run for it Julie. I'll keep them occupied."

"You'll stop a machine gun for about ten seconds with that pistol. You stay down and we'll run together once the blokes with guns are past." She sighed. "There's rumours of a place to the north, some professors and students from the college."

"We could go east? I've heard of an enclave near an Army post, where the gangs can't attack with automatics. There's some big black woman in charge, and maybe an Orchard." His voice sounding despondent, defeated, Stevie put his head back up to let Julie know where the attackers were. "The last of them are past the back marker. Shit! Christ! Keep down!" Both of them cowered in cover as lines of smoke curved in and the column of armed men came apart under a deluge of explosives. Another line of smoke tore across the rubble from nearby and the van blew apart. More smoke trails arced in and more explosions rippled across the roadway.

"Yes! Nail them, Stevie!" Julie popped up out of her manhole with a bow and lofted an arrow towards the chaos.

"Aim at the ones in the front, Julie. We're supposed to drive them backwards." Stevie fired, reloaded, and fired again and again as fast as possible. He wasn't sure if he hit anything, but some men were falling. Another arrow arced over and a man pointed towards Stevie. "Duck Julie." Automatic fire lashed the heaps of bricks briefly. He peeked again. "They're running. Yee-ha! It worked! Go, go the SIMs!" He fired and then turned to see why there had been no answering cheer. "Christ! Hang on, I'll give you a hand."

"Keep shooting Stevie, it's only my arm." Julie looked sheet white, concentrating on wrapping a bandage around her upper arm. "We can sort this once they're gone. Keep them running." She ducked out of sight as shots whined overhead, emphasising that the enemy were retreating but not running. Stevie went back to shooting until two minutes later, as planned, another salvo straddled the rear half of the ambush box and the road beyond, breaking the last organisation. The remaining attackers turned and fled into the driving rain.

Julie's radio crackled. "Stay in cover everyone. Let those who have a clear shot deal with the wounded who still have some fight in them." Stevie kept watch, firing once at a moving figure. Single shots cracked out here and there, not many because their enclave didn't have many firearms, and feathered shafts flew whenever a target showed. Eventually a man stood up in the rubble beyond the roadway, waving a machete above his head. Other figures rose and closed on the dead and dying with machetes, clubs and homemade spears. Stevie went to help Julie out of the manhole, and to tend to her wound. The SIMS had survived again, and better still they now had the firearms and weapons on the bodies and dropped by fleeing gangsters.

*   *   *

An hour later seven immaculate young men in suits, wearing dark glasses despite the gloom and pouring rain, looked over a group of wounded and demoralised fighters. Beyond them a smoke-blackened van drove into the old warehouse, bringing the survivors who couldn't walk. The seven in suits all carried automatic rifles or pump action shotguns, and wore handguns and machetes. "That didn't go to plan."

"Hah bloody hah Jones. Fucking artillery. Where the fuck did that bunch of airy fairies get artillery?" The oldest of the group scowled. "How many weapons did we lose?"

"Not fairies Branson, the SIMs are commies, some sort of commune. They call themselves after that bloody computer game because they're all ordinary people. Yeah, right. We lost four automatics which is what matters, and two of the vans so ammo as well." He spat. "We lost crossbows and handguns as well, and machetes of course. At least we've got a fucking blacksmith to replace the machetes." Jones turned on another youth. "You, Scrooge, I thought you said the plate on the vans would stop whatever they'd got."

"We plated the back and then reversed towards them. The bastards got the vans from the side with fucking great rockets. We got ambushed." The youth shrugged. "It worked the first three places we hit."

"Yeah, I think that's the trouble. We've only got one trick. A fucking good one with all the automatics we picked up from the city centre after the crash, but this lot have something as good. Worse, they've got some bastard who can plan a fight." The older man looked over at the defeated fighters. "We'd better give these wounded heroes a drink and a woman each before they desert to some other fucking gang." He sighed. "We need an ally, someone with more men and some sort of experience with this shit."

"Someone who knows more about tactics and all that bollocks? Christ, do you mean the General? Risky, Branson, he sort of eats up allies." Jones looked at the defeated gangsters. "There's an enclave to the west that's not too strong, but they're in sight of the Army so we can't use automatics. These pussies haven't got the balls for a fight without heavy firepower."

"The General has a lot of men who are used to fighting with machetes, but we've still got a lot of really good weaponry and a shitload of ammo. More than him." The older man, in his mid-twenties, smiled. "Treat this as a miscalculation; we got a wee bit too ambitious and the opposition rejected our bid. First we'll snap up that small enclave to the southwest because they haven't even got a proper wall. That'll give the fighters an easy win. Then we'll open negotiations with the General. Very careful negotiations. After all, I'll bet he'd like those bloody rockets out of the way as well."

Scrooge sighed. "Right, give them a beer and a woman and explain about all the rape and pillage once their bandages come off. Oh, and smile." He plastered on a beaming smile before heading towards the despondent fighters. The other six leaders of the MiB, Men in Black, weren't smiling. It had all gone very well to start with, because the average peaceful enclave couldn't resist a few nutcases and automatic weapons. The leaders knew they were ex-business trainees, not military geniuses or even gangsters, who had got lucky in this bloody new world. They'd taken an opportunity and ended up with a shitload of automatics when nobody else had any. Now they had to work out how to make the most of them because the easy times were over.

* * *

Nearly three miles to the northwest another new enclave, the Professors, stood to their defences. An elderly man stood on the flat roof of a concrete multi-story car park with a pair of binoculars to his eyes. Behind him a group of young men and women frantically wound a cable onto a drum until a loop came near enough to slip over a hook. The elderly man glanced back. "Ten kilos, incendiary this time. Then wait for my word." Behind him a young man placed the sealed tub of liquid into the sling hanging from the home-made trebuchet, and waited with a cigarette lighter.

"Ready, professor."

The older man waited, watching something through the binoculars. "Fire." The young man lit a short fuse and stepped back. A young woman pulled a lever, releasing the loop on the cable.

The steel trebuchet swung up, the sling came over and the container arced lazily across the grey sky, trailing a thin line of smoke. The missile plunged down the other side of the partially cultivated parkland, splashing flame on and around a van. A group of armed men accompanying the vehicle scattered, then moved back in to rescue the occupants. The elderly man raised a fisted hand. "Hit, sound the attack!" A bugle blared, again and again.

Along the far side of the parkland where a line of bushes and trees had been preserved, loudspeakers blared out a section of the Nutcracker Suite. Gaily painted figures darted into view, launching arrows and javelins into the gangsters trying to rescue their comrades from a burning van. The figures turned in time to the music and leapt back into the greenery. A fusillade of shots tore through the leaves but as they stopped the music swelled. The figures sprang out again, loosing their missiles before turning as one and retreating into the greenery. A gangster waving a pistol started forward, shouting to the rest. "Come on, they're only fucking women and ponces in paint. Up close we'll slaughter them. Follow me." He fired into the bushes and charged forward.

Behind him thirty young men and youths followed, waving pistols, machetes and clubs. Those with handguns emptied them into the bushes as they ran, pinning the defenders. With a cheer the first few broke into the bushes before reeling back, blood spurting from long slashes. Even as the rest paused, ten tall, broad, black-clad figures stepped forward, wearing hooded helmets with hideous faces painted onto the front grill, and wielding long blades or staves. The figures struck out savagely and accurately. In moments over half the attackers were down, dying or unconscious. Even where the machetes and clubs hit back, they had no appreciable effect on the black armour. Meanwhile missiles flew out of the greenery wounding or killing more attackers. The tall figures stepped back into the bushes before any gangsters could reload to shoot at them.

Half a dozen attackers went into the bushes to the side of the Kendo fighters, but none came back. A few screams and some shaking foliage were the only signs of their fate. Even as the rest of the gangsters ran the music swelled again and the gaily painted figures darted out to launch more missiles. The rewound trebuchet dropped another firebomb near the stranded vehicle, driving back those trying to rescue men or weapons, and the surviving attackers broke and ran. On the car park roof the elderly man lowered his binoculars, smiling quietly. "Brains against brawn."

"Professor, did it work?" A willowy woman in a flowing dress ran across the roof. "Are my boys and girls all safe?" She put her arm round the elderly man and rested her head on his shoulder. "I worry about them."

"There are wounded but they are all alive, Celeste. Your students jumped in and out of the trenches just as planned. Their choreography is perfect." He hugged her. "You were right, they do have war paint to die for." Behind them the trebuchet crew cheered and chanted, four of them linking arms to high-kick in time. The professor glanced back. "We should resurrect the cheerleaders, though as the Tigers instead of the Pussycats?"

"Really? That would certainly keep everyone fit, and will be something normal for them all in this chaos." Celeste looked across the neat lines of crops, and the trees and bushes beyond. "Will that gang be back?"

"Not for a long time. Meanwhile we have gained more weapons and ammunition for when they do. We'd better get down there to welcome the conquering heroes home."

"Oh yes, but they won't want us old fogies at the dancing." Celeste looked a little bit shy. "I still have an unopened half-bottle of Riesling if you want to share? To celebrate."

"That would be lovely, Celeste." The professor turned to the trebuchet crew. "Well done. You can stand down now except for the lookouts. No lectures until tomorrow!" The crew cheered.

The professor walked down the stairs from the roof deep in thought. The move from the University had been a frantic scramble, as had initially fortifying the block of flats, the shops beneath and the car park. Now the last of the neighbours had been taught to leave them alone, which gave their enclave a breather. The remaining tutors would keep educational classes going, despite the demands of gardening and scavenging. When this nightmare ended he wanted his students to be ready for whatever followed, with an education and a decent set of morals. Though first they all had to survive so he must swallow his distaste and meet with the defeated gang to agree the borders.

*   *   *

Across the ruined city, seven miles south, a small group of young men ducked and ran away from a canal as shots rang out behind them. "Will the bridge go down?"

The short, slightly built youth in the front laughed as he swerved into a derelict warehouse. "Oh yes, as soon as enough of the twats get on there. Stop here and shoot at them, bunch the fuckers up. Then they'll bring up something to give them cover crossing the bridge." He grinned at the rest. "Let a few across before that, so we can collect the weapons from the bodies."

"Are you sure?" One of the others flinched from the glare. "All right Skipper, just saying, right?"

Another youth with a long-barrelled pistol topped by telescopic sights waved the gun. "Good idea, about the weapons. This is OK but at least one of them has a long gun, a rifle or shotgun."

"See, Smiler's got the idea. Don't worry, the bridge will go. Spread out inside here and shoot at the ones this side to encourage more to cross." The eight men crouched or stood behind the walls of the derelict building, shooting through the gaps. The men pursuing them scattered into cover and called out frantically for help. A few men ran across the bridge to join them before opening up on Skipper and his crew.

The return fire bit into brickwork and whined off concrete, while the shooting from Skipper's men made the bridge impassable. The stalemate didn't favour the attackers pinned against the canal, still calling back across the bridge for help. An engine started up somewhere nearby and started to come nearer and one of the attackers called out to Skipper and his crew. "Give it up. Once our tank is over you're all dead men. If you toss out the guns we'll let you join up."

Skipper laughed. "Yeah right. I stopped believing in Santa when he didn't deliver the blonde." He reached round a doorway, firing towards the voice, then spoke in a quieter voice. "Be ready. The twats will come across behind that motor, whatever it is."

The two groups exchanged occasional shots as the motor came nearer. "It's a transit van, Skipper, with a steel plate across the front."

"That'll float well." A ripple of laughter sounded in the warehouse. "Smiler, bounce a couple of shots off it to encourage the twats." The shots clanged off the steel, to be greeted by cheers from the advancing gangsters. "Remember, when you hear the fucker go, charge. They'll all be looking that way so don't shout until we're in close."

"It's on the bridge, Skipper." The youth known as Smiler watched as the van moved further onto the bridge. "It's halfway now, are you sure...?" The question wasn't completed since just then a screech of tortured metal split the air. Alarmed shouts followed and the van revved desperately but too late. A crackle of shattering timber and more tortured screeches were followed by screams as the bridge, the van, and a score of attackers dropped into the canal.

"Now." Skipper spoke quietly, almost drowned out by the crash, splash and the screams, and the other seven defenders surged forward out of cover in silence. The attackers on the near bank of the canal were looking back towards the bridge, some even half-rising from cover. By the time they realised they were under attack the eight men had closed in, shooting or chopping them down.

"Get down!" Smiler dived behind a partially destroyed wall as a flurry of shots rang out from the other bank.

"Fuck!" One of Skipper's men dropped his machete to work on another youth's bullet wound. "I think he'll live."

"Stay in cover and don't take chances lads. Any survivors that climb up this side, let them crawl right out onto the flat so we can strip the bodies after shooting them." Skipper laughed. "Smiler, you've got fancy sights on that pistol. Shoot any fucker climbing up the other side. We'll drag the canal for the weapons later."

A young man with a shock of reddish-blond curls peeked around a low wall, ducking back smartish as shots rang out. "Will they let us?"

"Too true they will Goldie. They just lost at least thirty men with their weapons, and their boss. It'll take them a week to sort out who runs the gang, even if they can hold what they've got." Skipper sighed. "That's it lads. There's only four ways across the canals and we've raised both bridges and opened the locks for now. We'll get everyone properly organised as an enclave and ask for a coupon bus, then negotiate with the neighbours."

"Good, once it quietens down I can get in some fishing." The laughter at that temporarily drowned out the cries of the wounded and those struggling to stay afloat.

Skipper smiled broader than most. He hadn't told his gang the whole plan, not until it was possible. If his men put nets across the exits from their area, and farmed the fish, this enclave would have a surplus of good protein for his mum and his sister's kids, all the kids. They could even sell some to the neighbours for extras, because buying would be easier for the gangs than trying to fight their way across the water. He headed back towards the habitable houses at the centre, making plans to fortify one of the steel houseboats as a trading vessel.

*　　*　　*

Five miles northwest, beyond a motorway patrolled by army vehicles, the enclave known as Precinct Nineteen were on the move. The man wearing a patched policeman's uniform crouched in the dusk and looked back at the line of silent vehicles. In a low voice he spoke to a young woman wearing a crash helmet and a stab vest. "Go back along the line and remind them to turn on the sidelights after the engine starts, with no revving until we start moving please, Sue. We don't want any noise yet so keep low, and move slowly and quietly."

"I will grandad. I still don't like it, we were safe here."

The grey-haired man sighed. "Not really safe lass because the gangs are wearing us down. We have to keep going to the marts but we're losing men and using up ammunition every trip. We need space to grow food, and although the flats make a strong fortress to live in they haven't got gardens." He reached out a hand to squeeze her shoulder in reassurance. "At the beginning we didn't think this would last so we chose strong position. Now the majority agree this is our best chance for the long term. Remind everyone about the lights and noise on the way back, and make sure you are on that bus."

"Sorry grandad. Don't worry, everyone knows what to do." She giggled nervously. "Should I call you sergeant or 33 tonight?"

"Scat, cheeky. In four minutes 15, or sergeant Koos to you, starts clearing the way. Off you go." He raised his G36 police automatic, using the night sights to inspect the streets ahead. No reaction from the neighbours yet but he didn't relax.

The young woman, girl really, took off her helmet and kissed him on the cheek before putting it back on. "Good luck grandad." She ran off back down the road, keeping low and stopping at each vehicle. The sergeant smiled, then settled his eye to the sights again.

*　　*　　*

Nearly four miles ahead another police sergeant also inspected the streets ahead through his night sights, ex-police really because he hadn't been paid since the Army sealed the bypass nearly two years ago. He watched as other ex-policemen in partial uniform, bearing a mix of modern and ancient weapons, slowly and quietly leapfrogged past each other to close on their objectives. In an upper window of one small block of flats a figure showed, leaning forward to check on a glimpse of movement. The sergeant stroked the rifle's trigger and murmured "15" into his radio, to let his men know who had fired. With less than fifty men left the sergeants used the last two digits of their old police numbers, and the constables used three digits.

The silenced rifle wasn't silent of course; it just didn't sound like a shot. Other heads came up in the buildings ahead as sentries tried to identify the sound. More muffled noises from other silenced weapons cut the first three down but one called out as he fell. The loud crack of a pistol shot echoed in the night and more shots followed as voices were raised in alarm. The men creeping forward accelerated, still silently except when their weapons had a target and still using single shots.

"Look out, someone's after the women!" The sergeant cursed at the chorus of voices answering the gangster because they came from off to his left, not in the two buildings his men were now storming. What information he'd had indicated the gang members slept in these flats.

Sarge spoke quietly into his microphone. "We've got flankers. Five-one-eight and 277, hold fire. Let them in between us and the objective." At least the gangs around here didn't monitor the bands his tactical radios used. Nobody listened to the police radios these days, not since the police left the city, a small mercy that wouldn't last once the locals saw the uniforms. Ahead the ex-policemen were already entering their target buildings. Gunfire and screams, interspersed with the loud cracks of flash-bangs, drowned out any more noise from the flank. The gunfire reached a crescendo then began to die back so there had been fighters in there, but not as many as expected.

Morse code flashed from an upper window and the sergeant replied on the radio. "Stand by 613." Shortly after a light flashed code from a top flat in the other building. "Stand by 229. Caution, gate-crashers coming left of backstop. Single shots. Mousetrap." Sarge saw the armed figures running up the street from his left. He switched channels. "Fifteen to 33, wagons roll." He switched back and hunched down deeper into cover.

*　*　*

Back at the convoy the older sergeant, 33, hobbled to the bus doors where willing hands pulled him inside. He closed the door as quietly as possible and pointed the barrel of his weapon out of the open window. "Start up. Wait until the last set of sidelights come on then don't mess about." He smiled, unseen in the dark. "It's only four miles and there's nobody out there with a speed camera." The engine caught, then grumbled quietly. In the wing mirror sarge watched the string of sidelights light up off around the gentle bend behind him as the convoy came alive. His radio clicked three times, a message from the last vehicle because he couldn't see them all from here. "Go!"

The bus engine roared, drowning out any other noise, and the steel-plated behemoth lumbered into motion. The plate fastened to the outside showed the repairs and scars from convoys to the Mart, because none of the gangs around here were willing to give Precinct Nineteen safe passage. Inside the single-decker bus twenty crossbows, bows, pistols or in some cases catapults aimed outwards, many with more determination than skill. Another, almost identical bus brought up the rear of the convoy. A convoy containing every man, woman, child, pet and remotely useful item from their old home.

Or everyone except their forty-three most experienced fighters, the experts with the best weapons, who were four miles away making a hole for the exodus. Though first this convoy had to smash clean through The Quarrymen's territory before the gang could react. A man reared up from behind a wall, firing at the oncoming vehicles until sarge put a short burst into him. "Faster. Lights." The bus headlights lit up the dark streets ahead, and sarge snapped a short burst at another man diving into cover.

*   *   *

Four miles away, the running gangsters slowed as shots from the captured buildings cut down the first of them to arrive. "You bastards are dead! You're trapped now you stupid shits." The speaker waved his arms to the gangsters following. "Spread out, take cover." The men used the houses and garden walls to spread out across the approaches to their target. "Give it up and we'll let you go."

"No thanks, we're settled in now and there's all sorts of home comforts." The hidden sergeant smiled because David, 613, just couldn't resist tweaking gangsters, but this time the reply might just pull the suckers in.

"You leave our bloody women alone!" The speaker lowered his voice. "I want that bastard alive. I'm gonna make him eat his own nuts. There can't be many if they got here without being seen so when I say, open up and rush them."

"But Currie, what about all the women?" The sergeant tensed at the voices in the street below. Damn. Now he knew why the incomplete info had indicated the gangsters slept here. These buildings were where they kept the women. The gangster below kept speaking when his boss didn't reply. "We might kill some of them."

"Then we'll get some new ones. Now shut it. Everyone creep forward a bit.

As soon as we're near enough, rush them." The gangsters, over fifty of them, began to creep forward though many were muttering unhappily about killing their women. Single shots from the flats began to drop the less cautious, bunching the men behind the best cover.

Sarge watched, but he also listened. As soon as he thought he heard approaching engines, the ex-policeman put down the rifle before picking up a pipe bomb and his lighter. He spoke into his radio. "Five-one-eight, 227. Three count then boom. Use auto to break them." He paused, giving the men time to prepare their own pipe bombs. "Three, two, one, boom." Sarge lit his bomb before throwing it into the nearest clump of gangsters. He picked up his G36 automatic, ducking and waiting for the explosions and hopefully the screaming. He kept down until after the third explosion because these things threw bits of metal erratically and sometimes a long way. Sergeant Koos came up even while the echoes were still dying and, using his night sights and short bursts, started killing as many of Currie's gangsters as possible.

Ahead the men in the flats shot targets of opportunity. Meanwhile 518 and 227 combined their firepower with sergeant Koos, using their automatics to break the attackers beyond recovery for tonight at least. By the time the last surviving gangster had run into the night Sarge could clearly hear approaching engines. "Six-one-three, take two squads ahead to make sure the road is open. Once you've taken the school send 261 to take the canal bank and bridge to the west. Two-two-nine? How many women?"

"Two-two-nine. Eleven in this place, I'll check the rest. What do we do with them?"

"Tell them who we are and explain they can come with us or wait for their boyfriends, because we won't be staying." Sometimes the gangster women were volunteers, and Precinct Nineteen wouldn't take anyone against their will. "Hurry because we'll want them on the bus. Tell them to grab any gear, sharpish. Send men to finish the wounded gangsters and search the bodies" The engines were coming nearer and 15 didn't want to stop the vehicles for long. "Five-one-eight, come here and watch for any of the runners coming back, 288 watch the back door once the convoy arrives. Use your rifles to pin down anybody trying to interfere before we're done." He broke off at a crackle of gunfire from the direction of the engines and switched channels. "Fifteen here. Convoy? Thirty-three?"

A familiar voice reassured him. "Thirty-three. We just broke through the border into Currie's territory. Only a few sentries and the survivors are running. The Quarrymen are still waking up behind us so we're clear. With you in two minutes max. Out."

"We have extra passengers if a bus pulls up. Two-six-one and 613 are clearing the road ahead but we've broken them here. Keep the hammer down and we'll be gone before anyone gets organised. Out."

Javed, 229, led most of his squad forward from the captured flats. The men used pistols or machetes to finish the wounded gangsters and stripped the bodies of weapons, ammunition, coupons and good clothing. The convoy roared up and through, the rear bus and a transit van pausing briefly. Nine women hurried out of the flats and into the bus, all carrying bags. Within minutes the remaining policemen climbed into the bus or van and the marksmen and sergeant ran to join them. The two vehicles set off and quickly caught up to the rear of the convoy.

*   *   *

As the front of the convoy reached a larger road, a T junction, Sarge climbed out and limped across the street. The bus and fifteen vans and cars swung left while other vans turned right, followed by the second bus. The rest, including the van with sergeant Koos, drove straight across the junction into the ruins of a school as David, 613, waved them in. He beckoned and both sergeants moved to meet him, and the four strangers. "These are the new neighbours, sarge."

One of the strangers looked back across the road as the last of the convoy came into the school grounds and men spread out in defensive positions. "How many of Currie's gangsters are following you?"

The older sergeant limped over and put out his hand. "Hello Abby, pleased to finally meet you. Nobody will follow tonight. We've just added up the scores and we killed up to forty and wounded a lot of others on the way through. How many fighters did Currie have?"

The stranger, a middle-aged woman, looked shocked. Then she looked at the automatic weapons and a savage smile split her face. "That's got to be a half out of action, at least. With those guns you could go back and finish Currie. We'll come and help?"

"No thanks, street fighting will eat up men and ammunition and we don't want a lot of ruined housing anyway. Tonight has already cost us four good men, and at least a dozen wounded. The vultures will be gathering behind us tomorrow. By the time Currie has either gone under or fought the other gangs off we'll have firm control of what we want, the arable land. The deal is still on?"

"Absolutely, especially if you just killed that many of Currie's bastards. He won't try to hold if we move now which means we can push him right back over the canal." Abby frowned. "You don't want any more housing?"

"No thanks. We will take over the area bounded by the canal on the south and west, and Cinder Bank and Highbridge Road down to your boundary on the east?" He smiled. "Nearly all parkland except that one estate and a few places where there's already some veggies conveniently planted."

Abby shook his hand firmly. "Oh yes, that is definitely a deal." She nodded at the automatic. "None of the local gangs have been able to hold the open ground, but those machine guns will scare them off. With those you can hold the canal bridges."

Beside him a constable answered his radio, and passed the messages. "Eight-one-four has secured the housing to the south. He's sent a patrol along the road to seal the bridge over the canal to the south. Two-six-one has secured the canal crossings to the west. Two-two-nine has taken the small industrial estate north, though he says the place is stripped bare and there's nowhere fit to live in. He wants to know where to set the northern boundary because there's a real jumble of warehousing along the edge of the open land?"

The injured sergeant, the man in charge, looked back to the woman. "You were going to find us a good boundary line there."

"If you've really broken Currie's gang, take his share of those warehouses and industrial units or maybe the lot." She smiled. "If you wave those machine guns at them the other two gangs will back off and you can take all your bank of the canal up to the dual carriageway. That would be a good northern boundary?"

"Are you sure? We don't want to stretch ourselves, or you, too thin." Sarge looked south where many of the non-fighters would be moving into the small housing estate. "We've got a full-time job on repairing those houses."

"Some of the warehouses are still weatherproof, just empty. You might find them easier to make habitable than houses. We'll have people to spare because our new boundary will be a canal and easy to defend, and with you to our north we won't need to watch the canal there." She sighed. "Christ, it is such a relief to see a civilised face, and get neighbours who won't be trying to steal our fillings in our sleep." She turned to her colleagues. "It's a go."

"They can attack now?" One man had his radio up, ready to call.

"Yes. Take Currie's share of the woodland as well then drop that footbridge into the canal to make a new boundary." The man grinned and started talking into a two-way radio. She turned back to the police officers, smiling happily. "We'll help patrol the warehouses for cladding and steel, and share our extra timber to make charcoal and arrows. We've just got our gardens inside the walls while the rest is woodland, so we'd like a bit of land for crops?"

"That sounds like a good idea. We'll have a meeting once we've settled in and get the details hammered out." He smiled tiredly. "We've got an extra nine women who have left Currie. Ask around your people for anyone who has room for some of them." The sergeant turned back to his colleague. "Koos, you heard that."

Sergeant Koos started talking into his radio again. David escorted the rest of the party to a building that, apart from two broken windows and some very fresh bodies, would provide housing. As Koos finished, Sarge nodded towards the man's automatic rifle. "How are we for ammo for the automatics?"

"We're getting short now, though we collected most of the brass. Unless we can find a source of propellant we'll be down to using the captured weapons and ammo. I wish I knew where the gangs get theirs."

"So do I, though we can probably hold our new home with the captured weapons and ammo." Sarge's shoulders straightened and he smiled. "Though ammunition might not be quite so important now because we did it! We've got someplace we can grow food so we can cut down on mart trips."

Koos laughed. "Even better, there should be plenty of rabbits here." The men set into unloading the vehicles into their new homes.

Despite the loss of men the ex-policemen were satisfied with their night's work. Their own enclave had evacuated without losing a single non-combatant, driving clean through two gang territories. Now, instead of the tarmac and bare concrete surrounding their old home, the Precinct 19 had acres of parkland to grow food. Better still, Abbey's small enclave were now secure allies instead of being slowly squeezed out of existence. With their combined numbers, and canals as defensible borders on two sides, both groups were as secure as anyone else in this nightmare.

*　　*　　*

Well over a hundred miles southeast of the city and Orchard Close a small group of men gathered in an old church inside London, next to a stone-built library Soldier Boy would have recognised immediately. None were laughing, especially the man wearing a white clerical dog-collar as he repeated his request. "I'm serious, we want an agreement with the Sinners allowing us to use this church."

"I'll agree if you don't try to tempt our people away when they want a marriage or to join the prayers. You'll carry out any ceremonies they want without any conditions." The speaker, a big brawny man with cropped blonde hair, looked around the church and frowned. "Is this place still fit for it, church stuff?"

"The church and churchyard are still consecrated, but better still from my point of view this is the only church nearby that hasn't been vandalised. Most of the others have had animals killed on the altars, or someone has shat on them, that sort of thing." The cleric smiled. "Which considering your gang name, is a pleasant surprise. I'll agree to carry out any ceremonies and let your people join ours, but won't try to get any of them to join my flock. In return we get to use the place for prayers and ceremonies." He hesitated. "Can we bury people in the churchyard? It matters to some of us."

Sinner, leader of the enclave known as the Sinners, looked interested at that. "No problem. We've buried a couple of ours here, the ones who'd said they preferred it, but without proper ceremonies. What sort of religious are you? We've got a few who worry about not going to confession and all that?"

"I'll do that, take confessions. I'm Church of England, but I'm adaptable so I've read up on the right ceremonies and responses for most types of Christian. Most people don't mind about exact wording as long as this thing is real." The vicar touched his white collar.

"Can we get to the rest now, unless you want to bring that bird of yours and get married right now, Sinner? Where is she anyway?" The short, slim black youth grinned. "How come you've been allowed out without her?"

"No marriage, Kermit. I prefer Sin." The mood lifted because everyone made jokes about the gang name, the Sinners. "How come you four want an alliance now? You've been raiding our farm for over a year now, all of you, and now suddenly everyone wants to play nicely."

"Not suddenly." The bearded speaker nodded towards the cleric. "We may not agree on some religious matters, but I agree with the Vicar about what the government wants. We were left to starve but we haven't, though we are killing each other over food. Every raid someone is injured or dies means we're doing their job for them. If our people going to die, we'd rather do it fighting when the soldiers come for us."

"I thought your lot believe in God's will and his lot in peace and love?" A tall slim white man waved a hand around him at the church and at the speaker, an Imam. "I'm surprised you didn't burst into flames coming in here."

The original speaker with the dog-collar laughed before answering. "The Imam and I believe in the same God, and in His will, but there's nothing that says we can't help Him to make his mind up." For an apparently mild man the Vicar's smile looked downright savage. "There's nothing wrong with striking down a sinner or two, present company excepted."

Sinner frowned. "You lot will just stop raiding the farm? I can't believe that."

"Yes, we will, though as part of a deal, a treaty. A lot of the gardens around here are waterlogged because the drains are knackered, so this bloody rain has no place to go. Your fields stay dry, either because there's no bloody drains under them or this bit is higher. If you let each of us have a small piece of the playing fields to grow our own food, we'll keep off the rest." Kermit leant forward. "At the moment you can't farm it all because of the raids, which means at least half that ground is wasted. Give us a third between us to grow our own." He smiled. "Then you can trade any surplus you grow on the rest."

"Seriously?" Sinner looked around a group of nodding heads.

"Too true." The tall man sighed. "I'd like a bit more than land if possible. How about some sort of mutual defence treaty to protect our crops? We'll all get raids from the surrounding gangs, but combined we can slap them down. Better yet, if we aren't shooting at each other we'll save our ammo for when its needed." He smiled at them all. "I can trade coke, or coal."

"We'll trade vegetables for coke or coal, Hans, because then we can mend our bloody machetes." The Sinner looked around the group. "You're all serious, aren't you?" Four heads nodded again. "I'll agree to you four sharing a quarter of the fields, if we can agree borders and trade as well."

"We'll discuss details later because I want to trade for knowledge, a chance to get hold of those books." The Vicar shrugged. "Not just the religious ones, there's got to be books about farming, medicine and nutrition, and a score of other things." The Imam nodded in agreement.

"Lending library only. Nothing leaves the premises and I'll have to OK it with the librarian." Sinner shook his head. "It's more than my life's worth to let anyone at those books without permission."

"Can you agree this here and now, without herself along to hold your hand? You never did say where she is." Kermit had a little smile again.

"She's helping with a birth and yes, there's a book about that. If we all shake hands now it'll stand. Then we can hammer out details later, in time to get planted up." Sinner smiled. "Now if you lot don't mind, all this godliness makes me nervous. I'd like to get back to Sin." The group broke up with handshakes, laughter and smiles, making arrangements for a proper meeting out on the school playing fields now they'd agreed in principle.

Sinner headed back to the library, pleased at both agreements. Nita at least would be really grateful for the chance to confess, though most of the Sinners owed her their lives and didn't think she'd done anything wrong. He wondered how many other enclaves were getting over the initial shock, and starting to draw together for mutual benefit. That would be more important here in London, where there were no marts so everything had to be grown or salvaged. Five enclaves stood a better chance at doing that than one. The Imam, Zaid, had hit the nail on the head. If the government wanted them to die Sinner wasn't inclined towards doing the job for them.

*　*　*

Nobody laughed in a bunker three hundred and sixty miles north, deep under the Lincolnshire countryside. The UK cell of the cabal that had triggered the global chaos didn't look at all happy about how their plans had turned out. The initial strikes again the world's major refineries had gone well, but the lunatics and terrorists who joined in had extended the destruction well beyond the planned parameters. At least that had accomplished one aim of the group, reducing the global reliance on oil.

Nearer to this group's home, the UK, the deliberately provoked uprising of refugees in Europe had succeeded well beyond anything the planners had expected. The local populations, starving in their cities when the food shipments from South America stopped, had joined the rampaging hordes. Worse, some military units had changed sides rather than shoot their own civilians. The sheer chaos and bloodshed had exceeded another target, the culling of two-thirds of the population, but hadn't always culled the right ones.

Now the weather itself seemed to have turned on the UK plotters, hampering their attempts to get the country organised. "Is this some more of our propaganda coming home to roost, Nate?" Owen, the chairman, pointed at the flat-screen on one wall which showed steady rain falling onto already flooded fields. Even more water poured over the banks of the nearby river. "That spiel about oil fires and nukes affecting climate was supposed to be just a convenient excuse when we wanted to cut down food."

"There really is nothing in that theory, even if India, Pakistan and the Israelis went well past a few nukes. The evidence after the first Gulf War showed that oil well fires don't affect climate except very locally." The big black man looked a bit embarrassed, because some of his propaganda hadn't been received well.

"In that case why are all the fields flooded? Fields that are meant to feed the population we actually care about, the ones not penned up in the cities like the animals they are?" Owen looked at the other ten people around the polished wood table and several nodded agreement with the question. "We daren't even starve the scum yet until we've thinned them out a bit more." He smiled. "Or until they've thinned each other."

Nate looked offended now. "I wouldn't distort information given to anyone in this room. This is just a wet winter. Last winter turned out to be colder than the average, this is a lot wetter than the average. Some of these fields flood about one year in four, the local farmers assure Henry." Nate indicated the stout man with a black beard who controlled the farming operations.

Henry frowned. "Don't expect miracles. The whole point of the exercise is to reduce the population to where the land can feed them. Until that is accomplished, we can't grow enough food."

"But regardless of reason, the expected food production won't happen? You promised to keep enough food coming to top up the frozen reserves while we reduced the population to self-sufficiency levels. That means until we've processed the populations trapped in the cities." Ivy, a middle-aged red-haired woman, frowned. Her responsibilities were processing food, then supplying and supervising the firms running the only retail outlets, the marts. "We've been planning the supplies to marts based on the original figures. Now there could be a real problem." She looked around the table, hopefully. "Unless we get another supply?"

"The increased crops will arrive Ivy, but later in the year. We can't work the land when it's underwater or even if the fields are waterlogged." Henry shrugged. "At least this reason is genuine, and Owen is preparing emergency measures anyway."

"True, but I hoped to avoid any more direct confrontation because the London problem is still tying up too many soldiers." The London problem meant the refusal of the Londoners to either kill each other over dwindling food supplies or starve after their only shops, the marts, were closed. Owen smiled. "The rains have helped there, because the flooding has destroyed some of their cultivation. Hopefully they'll fight over what's left." Owen clicked the screen through several pictures showing flooded areas of London. "Unfortunately not just in London."

The next picture showed a small, insignificant enclave called Orchard Close, but not in the centre. The view centred north of territory the overlay identified as belonging to the GOFS, Gods of Fire and Steel, one of the impromptu gangs seizing territory after the forces of law and order died or left the encircled city. A close-up showed frantic families trying to get their sparse belongings away as the waters rose while armed gangs tried to rob or protect them. The scene moved to the south of the city where water covered wider areas. Joshua, the man wearing an Army uniform, looked at a map in his opened file. "The Army posts will be alerted to watch for people like this trying to break out. York and Gloucester are a real problem, because their rivers will overflow if this keeps up."

Owen frowned. "The enclosures with the worst flooding must be reinforced to prevent the animals breaking out or they'll strip the farmland like a swarm of locusts. We don't want another loss of crops such as that on the Isle of Wight."

Joshua cleared his throat, so Owen stopped to look at him. "We're stretched for troops Owen, because there's small guard posts at all the wind farms and hydro-electric facilities and substantial units at the nuclear power stations. Reinforcing everywhere else can't be done. We managed to stop all the mass attacks the first time round by staggering the timings of the uprisings so we could concentrate troops, air and armour."

A voice broke in. "Ah yes, the spontaneous uprisings?" Everyone smiled.

"Perhaps there could have been more soldiers if there weren't so many B list civilians." Ivy looked pointedly at three separate people. "I found it remarkable that so many pretty young secretaries were deemed essential."

"Ivy has a point in one way. The thousands of middle class civil servants probably outnumber my soldiers. Perhaps the decision to cut down the armed forces was premature or not strictly necessary." Joshua looked around with a challenge in his eyes. "I made that point at the time but was overruled."

Owen answered. "Civil servants are essential to keep your soldiers paid, fed, and housed. We didn't reduce your soldiers until Vanna's paramilitaries had cleared the unwanted populations outside the barricades."

"But we kept most of Vanna's civilian contractors, who are also armed to the teeth but nothing like as well trained or disciplined. I hate the term paramilitaries because they are nothing like military." Joshua glared at Vanna, a slim Asian woman. "We could have kept more real military and got rid of those."

"But my civilian contractors have less qualms about conditions inside the cities, or dealing with surplus populations. Your soldiers won't do the dirty work Joshua, will they? They certainly wouldn't have manned the special facilities." Vanna shrugged. "Though maybe my contractors can help you out now most of those facilities are no longer fully utilised?"

"I'd rather have Vanna's men than some bleeding heart soldier guarding my work camps. The scum need a firm hand." Grace, a tall, aristocratic grey-haired woman, smiled at Vanna who nodded her thanks. "They are also much less fussy than the soldiers about their entertainment."

"Brothels again? Not in England! I will invoke my veto if it comes to that."

Owen rapped with his gavel as other voices were raised. "We hear you Nate. Your veto will be accepted if brothels are proposed as an official institution. You have a suggestion, Vanna? That would be a relief if only to stop the squabbling."

The Asian woman passed out sheets of paper. "Firstly, my special facilities forces shouldn't be put with Army units or something might slip in conversation. We can use them for distinct operations where a certain ruthless disposition is preferred. Secondly, I can thin out the mart guards. To be honest there are too many anyway now the marts are established. If I pull out the sympathetic ones to use against any attempted breakouts, that will blood them and harden attitudes. They'll stop joking with the scum once a few have tried to kill them." She smirked. "Better yet, the ones left at the marts will be even less sympathetic once a few of their friends die."

"Excellent. That's what I like about you, Vanna, always looking for the silver lining." Owen bent over his copy.

Joshua smiled. "I can see a silver lining or two as well. We can train them while containing any badly flooded areas, then once they're blooded we can use them as shock troops when London is finally cleared."

"Cannon fodder or at least bullet magnets." Everyone smiled again and relaxed.

Owen sighed. "That's the urgent business in the UK dealt with, what about the wider plan?"

Boris, the diplomat, smiled. "World-wide either the local cells have control of the major fleets and air forces, or have diverted them to fighting their neighbours away from anything valuable. While that continues no land forces can affect us in the UK, though we'll have to keep an eye on Europe."

Faraz the RAF liaison spoke up. "We are keeping flights over the continent down because of the fuel situation. We might need the fuel here. What the surveillance shows is that too many of the feral population including survivors from the refugee camps are surviving the winter. Worse, some are beginning to organise but we don't want to use the RAF against units technically belonging to allied nations. That will jar with the official line about rebels and terrorists and worse, some may still have viable anti-aircraft defences."

Owen frowned and glanced at Joshua, the Army man, who looked worried. "How serious is that, Faraz? Will they survive well enough long-term to be a problem for Joshua when we liberate Europe?"

"Some will, the ones based around portions of various national Armies and especially the remnants of armoured forces."

"Contact those groups to offer them sanctuary, then we can use them as shock troops, cannon fodder." The naval officer, Victor, smiled. "If they refuse, the warships blockading the coast can be given the coordinates for a fire mission without actually seeing anyone." He looked at Owen.

Boris spoke up again. "We can use the survivors of their own governments to get in touch. They are very grateful and relieved at the moment." He laughed. "Despite their objections, maintaining the credit card system in the UK until we had the cities isolated was a good idea. Our population could still buy food, right up until when we killed a good few and sealed in the rest. Their populations rioted when the money stopped, before they were properly controlled."

Owen smiled reassuringly. "If we can't tempt any it doesn't matter until we have dealt with the UK. Naval forces are the only ones that can reach us here now all the European airfields have been overrun." He passed out sheets of paper showing the dispositions of major naval facilities and airfields around the globe. A key showed which were held by allies, which were under control by a cabal-friendly government, and which were neutralised by supply problems or local threats. Friendly fleets such as the Australian, New Zealand, Argentinian and Brazilian navies were shown in better detail, with notes on their missions. Owen checked his notes. "If the cells in the USA, Russia and China lose control of the fleets, there are fail-safes in place."

"The submarines? Will a nuclear attack work if there's warning? Some ships may escape and just one of those aircraft carriers could screw everything up." The navy man looked at his own notes. "We haven't enough totally loyal submarines world-wide."

Owen shook his head. "No missiles, no warning. The rest is need to know, under local control. Those are not our concern, only in that they will not interfere." Everyone at the table nodded or otherwise signalled their understanding.

"Which means we can concentrate on the UK and South America, or south of the Amazon." Victor sighed and sat back. "That's a relief." From the relaxation and expressions around the table, everyone else felt relieved as well. The other conspirators would deal with their own parts of the globe, and none were likely to impact the UK. This cell of the cabal, the legally elected government as far as the rest of the country knew, set into the general business of running the UK. Or at least they tried to turn this mess into the sort of country they had planned for.

As the meeting broke up Vanna and Grace barely hesitated on the way out, except to answer Owen's raised eyebrow with faint nods and tiny smiles. The master plan had remained more or less on track, but a squeaky black wheel needed fixing and they had the people to do it.

*　　*　　*

Meanwhile, in the small enclave labelled Orchard Close, a hundred people continued trying to build some sort of life out of the chaos while protecting themselves from the neighbours. Their chosen leader, Harold aka Soldier Boy, feinted before smacking a wooden machete aside. Around him another dozen residents of Orchard Close prodded, feinted and thrust to practice for when they had to use a real machete. Harold knew the surrounding gangsters used machetes like clubs with a sharp edge in a fight. Harold's people, who generally weren't heavily-muscled homicidal maniacs, needed some finesse if that time came.

Doll, a twenty-one-year-old blonde, set herself to try again. Harold wondered how many of these trainees would freeze in the real thing, pull the stroke rather than kill a fellow human. He wondered the same about those who had learned to fire a pistol or crossbow. He worried because the city had descended into ruins ruled by armed gangs, so Harold needed people who really would shoot.

"Sorry."

"No Doll, that's good. I relaxed and got careless, so you nailed me." Harold rubbed his chest and smiled. "Being stabbed, even with a bit of wood, will remind me to be more careful." The blonde beamed and set herself again, with her wooden practice machete ready. All the trainees loved any proof they were becoming more dangerous. Doll for one really did intend serious harm to anyone else trying to kidnap her nineteen-year-old sister, Matti. Twice had been well past too many attempts. Patty the twenty-five-year-old demon knitter also wanted a chance to stick some unsuspecting scroat for real, but the local gangsters were too wary of her outsize crossbow to give her an excuse with a machete. They already knew Patty wouldn't freeze or even hesitate.

"You're lucky." Billy rubbed his arm. "Alfie hit me and he's got more muscles than Doll." Billy smiled hopefully. "I'd rather tussle with Doll?" As one of the men in their late teens Billy definitely meant that.

"No, you'll learn to defeat a stronger attacker by using his brute strength against him." Harold looked round the rest where all the trainees were mismatched to represent facing the usual gangster attackers. "Remember, the smaller of the pair must be faster, more agile, sneakier."

Billy scowled. "But you've taught Alfie all the sneaky stuff and he's stronger than me as well, which is embarrassing because he's only sixteen."

Harold looked round the rest and they chorused, "Try harder."

"I know, so when I meet some scroat who doesn't know this stuff he'll be dead meat." Billy sighed. "I wouldn't mind, but Alfie can get his bruises kissed better and I can't. I know, try harder. I could move into Cherry Tree House?" Alfie blushed scarlet while the rest teased Billy about who in Cherry Tree House, a block of single flats, might kiss his bruises. Then they set into bruising each other.

*   *   *

On the way home after practice Harold answered greetings from several of the latest arrivals coming out of unexpected houses, houses containing longer-term residents. The new refugees and those in the initial mad exodus from the chaos of the city centre were mixing, becoming one group. Louise, a reclusive graphics designer in her thirties, had asked two younger single women refugees to move into her house when Celine moved out. Celine, in her late twenties, felt that she would hasten her mental recovery from rape by taking a single flat in Cherry Tree House to be more independent.

Other residents had moved about to get a better fit for house-share as more refugees trickled in, escaping from the gang-controlled enclaves that had sprung up. Any refugees came past the main gates, headed for the Army post sealing the way out of the city. When they were turned back someone in Orchard Close would ask if the rejects wanted sanctuary. At least the numbers of single women wanting sanctuary had dropped because the Army asked some women if they wanted help. Those who accepted were taken away in mini-buses, for treatment according to the TV.

A voice interrupted Harold's musing. "Harold, just the right person. Could I have an air pistol please?"

"Of course Alicia. I thought 003½ had taught you to use a real pistol? You can have a nine mill once you show me you're accurate?" Harold smiled. "It'll stop them better than an air pistol." Twenty-three-year-old Alicia worried about the maniacs getting over the wall again, having barely escaped as her block of flats was overrun.

"I might ask for one of those as well, because 003½ really is a good teacher with that single shot pistol of his." According to a spy novel that had been found, assassins used pistols that fired two-two rifle bullets. Fifty-year-old Finn now had a James Bond style nickname. Alicia hesitated. "You know I've moved in with Abigail?"

"Yes, to help with her kids and give her some rest." Abigail had arrived worn down with stress and lack of food. Now breast feeding her new baby and dealing with her three-year-old son kept her exhausted. Alicia used her spare coupons to buy the best food available at the mart to help Abigail, since the marts didn't stock baby formula or a vast number of other items now deemed non-essential.

"That's why I need an air pistol to hunt rabbits, ducks, pigeons, and maybe geese." Abigail shrugged. "If I shoot them they'll go into the food stocks at the canteen, but I thought I might be able to make a case for a nursing mother getting the richer parts such as hearts and livers and that."

"Go for it, or actually come with me for an air pistol. We've got oodles of pellet ammunition but try not to waste too many." Harold sighed. "I don't know if we'll ever get any more." As they set off Harold tried to inject some caution. "You can't just go off hunting at the drop of a hat. Only go when there's a big party scavenging or checking the borders." Orchard Close claimed an area of abandoned buildings that stretched at least a mile in every direction.

"I know but I can walk in sight of them, yet far enough away to get a chance at any undisturbed birds or rabbits." Alicia frowned. "I thought all those armed groups coming through had stopped, Harold?"

"They did for a while but now there's a few more and these seem desperate. Be very careful not to get far from the scavengers. The groups we've seen are heavily armed but usually run because our scavenger parties outnumber them." Harold gave Alicia an air pistol and a tin of pellets then headed for the canteen because there were GOFS, Gods of Fire and Steel as one of the local gangs had called themselves, visiting. The armed groups were coming from GOFS territory to the west, so Harold wanted to ask questions.

* * *

He found the man he wanted in the canteen, enjoying a beer. "Hi there Cy." The GOFS fighters visited Orchard Close, their neighbours along one border, so they could buy home brew beer and rat-free burgers or stew. The gangsters tended to stay well behaved while they did both because of the draconic penalties for misbehaving, and their bosses weren't sympathetic if they didn't. The GOFS leaders called by sometimes to stock up on beer, and didn't want the supply, or their gun repairs, jeopardised by a randy idiot. The income helped Orchard Close to buy more essentials from the mart to avoid having to eat rat or cat themselves. "Still trying to get a date with Patty?"

The GOFS gang member didn't look amused. "Ha, very funny. It'll be easier to get a date with her crossbow. Does she sleep with it?"

"Cripes, how would I know? Why would I risk life and limb trying to find out?" Harold sat down next to him.

"We know we're in Orchard Close when someone says cripes. Or not quite because we sometimes use it for a joke." Cy grinned. "Practice so we don't become crossbow practice." Cy referred to the Orchard Close penalty scale for obscenity – a fine for a first offence, then caning, then spending time as a moving crossbow target for three time offenders. Physically molesting Orchard Close women could mean gelding or being tied to a lamp post for the crossbow practice, if the woman didn't simply stick a crossbow bolt in the offender herself. Drastic penalties, but needed since many visitors had no such restrictions on their behaviour when back home.

Harold frowned at him. "You should be practicing your shooting, considering the nasty sods you keep letting through into our territory."

"We try." Cy frowned as well and put his beer down. "There's a steady trickle of small groups coming now. We do shoot them if they get near any of our people, but otherwise we let them through because they just want to get away from the floods."

Harold frowned, puzzled. "There's a lot of them. How big are the floods?"

"They were our neighbours to the north. It's all underwater along our border now with at least two small gangs fighting to control any dry land that's still left out that way. We reckon they'll all have to leave eventually as the water rises. The mob the other side of the flooded bit are like your lot, sort of normal. They're taking families but not letting any nasty bastards join up which only leaves one option when the water gets too high. Gofannon reckons once the rain stops the water will find a stable level, hopefully without coming further south." The GOFS soldier sighed. "Some of our estates, the ones we protect, have been attacked and robbed."

"I thought you took coupons from those people to stop that?" The gangs charged anyone living in any habitable housing in their area protection money, paid in coupons or goods.

"We do, which is embarrassing. That's why you aren't seeing many of us coming for a beer. Gofannon has doubled the guards on each estate and we've got an emergency response squad poised to go at any time. There isn't the spare manpower to hunt down all those who come straight through." Cy shrugged. "Though the armed groups coming through also stop the Barbie Girls taking liberties in our territory which is good." He looked round. "Unfortunately that means they don't visit you which is a shame. The Barbies that like men are usually up for some cripes on an overnighter." He chortled. "Told you we use cripes."

Harold laughed. "A bit out of context but yeah, that works. The other bit explains why the Barbies stopped coming. I'd wondered if we upset them but my love life isn't on the radio." The Barbie Girls had the only local radio station powerful enough to punch through the government interference, pumping out a mixture of rock music and scurrilous gossip.

"No, they stick with describing Caddi and his alleged antics with various animals and kitchen implements." Cy smiled and picked up his beer to toast an imaginary broadcaster. "Someone there has a filthy imagination. Hopefully she'll visit here for a stopover once the flooding stops."

"First the rain has to stop." They both looked glumly at the rain outside.

*   *   *

Though the continuing rain wasn't the problem a fortnight later. Harold, Soldier Boy, the ruthless ex-soldier feared and hated by the surrounding gangs, pleaded with his big sister. "I don't want to go to a dance, Sharyn. Especially the Valentine's dance. It's too soon."

Sharyn stood braced with jaw jutting obstinately, one hand on her hip and the other proffering a tie with a big red cloth heart pinned to it. "No it isn't, and even if it is you're going. I will not come back to hear you ranting again."

"I don't rant."

"Not much. After the Guy Fawkes bonfire you were stomping up and down waving your arms about, blethering on about squirrels, abused women and soldiers."

"That squirrel business is er, codswallop."

"What about the rant at Christmas, about the government having a new plan to drown us all? Or at New Year, when I came home to a lecture about how there seemed to be fuel for lorries to cart soldiers about but refugees were traipsing through chest deep water because there was none for boats?" Sharyn waved the tie again. "Put it on. The girl club know you're off-limits and so will whoever you walk home."

"I'm not walking someone home."

"This might be brutal but Holly has been dead nearly six months. This part is definitely cheating and unfair because I know the answer. Do you think she's waiting for you or watching over you?"

Harold's reply was inaudible.

Sharyn cupped a hand to her ear in a theatrical flourish. "Pardon?"

The second "no" sounded just as sullen, but louder.

"No, because you are a dyed in the wool atheist which means she's dead, you're sad, but life goes on. No happy lies, you said, well no sad ones either. Now our enclave, the people who rely on you to keep them safe, need to see their mighty leader has recovered and is up to the job." Sharyn suddenly grinned. "I'll get Liz to come and beat on you?"

"No!" Harold sighed and reached for the tie. "I'm not dancing or going in the hat for the last dance draw."

"Yes you will because you're too much of a gentleman to say no when you're asked." Sharyn sniggered. "If you get bolshie I'll trade for the last dance with you, though I might throw up afterwards."

"Cripes no." Harold took the tie. "What sort of a theme is this?"

"Lurve, because it's Valentine's Day. They'll all be wearing hearts, especially the girl club. How big and how many, and what else in some cases, is keeping all the younger single men really intrigued." Sharyn inspected Harold's tie knot. "At least the Army taught you something. Here."

"I don't need my stick for a dance." Harold looked at her expression, shrugged and took the walking stick with the big brass boss on the top. "I can use it to beat off Doll or Suzie."

"A few of the new single female refugees have joined that competition. They've been warned off you for now, little brother. Come on, smile." Sharyn hooked an arm in his. "After all you started this tradition, all the dressing up and drawing partners to walk home."

"To cheer them all up for one New Year dance. It wasn't just me. Liz and Casper helped."

Sharyn laughed. "The perfect combination. A soldier, a gay giant and a woman who refers to herself as the blacksmith slut. No wonder it's still working over a year later." A knock on the door announced the arrival of Rob and Susan to babysit. Harold realised he'd never had a chance of refusing. They brought five year old Sukie, very excited about a sleepover.

"Cripes, Daisy will never sleep." Daisy, Harold's six-year old niece, might have been classed as hyper-active if anyone bothered with labels after the schools, hospitals and doctor's surgeries were either closed or attacked and destroyed by the mobs.

"Nor will we spend all evening up there reading stories and drawing or colouring once Daisy and Sukie start playing." Susan smirked. "Whoever walks Suzie home could get a lovely surprise tonight, providing it's the right man, because there's no babysitter to act as gooseberry."

Harold glanced at Sukie and kept quiet about what sort of surprise. "Another fix?" He frowned. "Has Suzie got her eye on someone?"

Susan patted Harold on the shoulder. "It's best if you men never know. Now shoo."

* * *

Harold hesitated at the door to the dance house. Sharyn pushed him in, then Harold stopped again. "Cripes, Doll's won, or lost. Was the competition to show their knickers or get closest to it without flashing?" Harold shook his head. "She's actually only wearing knickers."

"The competition isn't either of those. Doll is also wearing her best approximation to chaps without any leather, cowgirl boots, a Stetson and a love heart bra but you're right, none of the men will notice those. Anyway, how can you tell what's under those two hearts, or the top two?" Sharyn grinned.

"There'd better be knickers and a bra or Lenny will have to brush up on his heart attack treatments." Harold headed for the refreshments but a hand caught his arm.

"Hello Harold. May I have this dance please? You said I'd always be on your dance card."

"But. Oh, right, of course Celine." Harold smiled and propped the stick against the wall. He had once told Celine that any time she needed a safe dance for her version of rape therapy, he'd be available. Celine wore her long white gown as usual but had pinned little red hearts all over it. Harold carefully put a hand on her waist, just, before holding his other hand out for hers because Celine still had trouble being near men. She had decided that dancing would help to get past her nervousness because Celine refused to let one asshole ruin her life. "You haven't managed the little green dress yet."

"Oh no, but I'm getting there. Hand properly round my waist please Harold, and hand on shoulder like this." Her hand came up, hooking round onto Harold's shoulder. "A few more of these dances and I might have to branch out a bit." She glanced down. "It would be a shame to cut this. I'll have to look for a slightly shorter dress." Celine sniggered. "Though I could just take it off and go for the Doll look."

"Cripes yes, that's extreme even for Doll."

"Not really, that's how it's supposed to be. A singer called Christina Aguilera apparently wore real chaps with knickers like that, and another called what was it, Myles Cyrus? Unless she was the one with pink hair who sang in a top hat and corset, that might have been her." Celine laughed at Harold's expression. "Doll's Ma liked country which is why she's called Dolly, but her Grandma must have been a bit more raunchy in her day. We're finding more of that old music in among the CDs we've scavenged and Doll recognised some of the singers."

"Let's hope none of them look up Mylie Cyrus, which was her real name, for a costume. One of the squaddies had a video of her singing starkers which will wreck any competition and kill any bloke with a dodgy ticker." Harold looked round. "Sharyn said there were new contestants now that Sal's been gartered and Matti has apparently retired."

"There's a Bethany, a Fergie and a couple more possibles, and Gayle is coming out of her shell a bit. Then there's Veronica and Hazel?"

"What?"

"Gotcha. They're not quite sixteen yet and even then they'll take a while to work up to competition." Celine giggled. "I haven't really done that for a while." She smiled up at Harold as the music ended. "Thank you for the dance, Harold. You really are good at this therapy business, both sorts." Celine meant how Harold encouraged her to beat offending gangsters with garden canes.

"I aim to please."

The dance with Celine did settle Harold, and his succession of dancing partners were definitely better behaved than in the past. Then a voice he didn't recognise spoke up behind him. "I'm supposed to call you Harold in here, aren't I?"

Harold turned. "All the time except if I'm slapping scroats. Blimey O'Reilly, what's that? Well its Sal's red dress, or was, but what's the disguise?" He smiled. "Let's start with your real name, then get to that."

"I'm Fergie and we met when you gave me sanctuary, but I'd covered up because I still didn't quite believe I'd be all right here. I mean, for, er, cripes sake who really thought it was true, this place? An enclave who beat any gangster swearing in public and kill gropers?" The tall young woman with long dark brown hair put a hand on Harold's waist with the other on his shoulder and giggled. "This is weird as well, proper dancing. Don't put your hand round the back unless you… Oops, I've been told you won't mean it anyway."

"I also know that dress is backless." Harold smiled in genuine humour. "I once slow danced with a Jessica Rabbit wearing that."

Her eyes widened. "You did? Did she play pattycake?"

"Ask Bernie because I think she still does." Harold grinned. "Sal made a spectacular Jessica before she settled down with her Roger Rabbit." Dancing seemed to be like riding a bike, because Harold could still avoid tromping on feet even with a twirl. "What is that costume supposed to be?" Harold looked at the headband with a big heart on the front.

Fergie glanced down at the two big hearts on her chest. "Queen of tarts of course." She looked round. "Suzie has a baseball bat with a heart attached. She's wearing some fur collars as clothes and a little fur jacket someone found, because she's Queen of Clubs." Fergie finished her dance and hi-fived another young woman Harold didn't know. He'd been in some sort of competition after all. Umeko moved in with a shy smile. Harold knew this would be another very quiet, careful dance as she worked through her own experiences.

Just before midnight Harold drew his number for the last dance and waited to see who turned up. The usual flurry of trading started, a mix of people trying to pick a particular partner or avoid one. He expected Liz or Patty, or someone else the younger men classed as drawing a blank because they wouldn't get a doorstep kiss or cuddle. The woman waving her number at him surprised Harold. "Celine? Two dances? People will talk, especially with this being the last dance."

"You should be so lucky. I've decided I'm ready for a walk home with a man who might be dangerous in the right circumstances. A step up from the ancient, decrepit or gay." She giggled. "Oops, twice in a night. Walking me home will give Nigel a chance to walk Sharyn home without you lurking."

"Nigel and Sharyn?" Harold didn't think his sister had got over losing her soldier husband, Freddy.

"Not really but they do get on well, as in talking about lone parents raising kids. If they talk a bit longer then Berry and Seth get more time together. Not that they need it but Nigel still thinks she's thirteen, not seventeen." Harold twirled her and Celine smiled happily. "Careful, if you keep this up I might forget to be good."

"As long as I don't come over all rough soldier you're safe."

"I know, which is why I can say things like that to you." Her light green eyes twinkled briefly. "The time to worry is when my skirt hem starts to move up."

"You'd better do that gradually so I've got time to run."

"Ah, but when I'm finally wearing my little green dress the skirt won't slow me up so I'll catch you." The music stopped. Celine looked up at him for a moment, debating. "Arms right around my waist please Harold. I'm safe here in the middle of the dance floor and this is the last dance." She took a deep breath. "It's time."

Time for what became clear as Celine put her own arms round Harold's shoulders and came up on her toes to kiss him very quickly and gently on the lips. "Whew, my first last dance kiss since… Hey, that was all right! Sort of an anti-climax after all the build-up." A relieved smile lit up her face. "I've been working up the nerve to do that all night and I'm fine." Celine hooked her arm in Harold's. "Now you can really worry when you walk me home."

*   *   *

Harold still wore a little smile about walking Celine home when he opened his own front door. His smile widened at Sharyn's greeting. "I thought you drew Celine, little brother. Did you trade?"

"No, why?"

Sharyn frowned just a little bit. "Cherry Tree House isn't that far."

"And I've been a while. Celine wanted to stand and talk because she's feeling more confident, which she's really chuffed about. In any case, Casper is the house mother there now so I had to be good." Harold had definitely been good because in the dark Celine became more nervous, settling for just a peck on the cheek, though she insisted on standing in the dark and talking for a while. "Now you've cast aspersions on the spinsters of this parish, just how long did Nigel take over his nightcap because he only just came out of the road end?"

"Stop it." Two spots of colour appeared on Sharyn's cheeks. "We were talking about raising kids alone, since I'd promised Berry I'd delay him so he arrived home later."

"I'll believe you, thousands wouldn't. Now tell me what the hell Casper came as?"

"Cupid."

"Oh, I thought he'd come as a love-child because of the nappy thing. He's doing better these days as well, more like his daft self, though I'm surprised Amber didn't come to the dance." The brown and tan Doberman-Labrador cross bitch might be seven months old and nearly as big as her parents but Casper tended to treat her as about ten weeks old.

"She's with Thandia, being puppy-sat." Sharyn smiled. "You know, if the rain had eased off a bit this might have actually cheered me up."

"Rain is good. Scotland is still under snow." Harold frowned. "No doubt they'll get their floods when that lot melts." He turned to the study, his bedroom these days. "I'm not going to start ranting, I'm off to bed. Sleep tight."

"You too little bro."

Harold did sleep well, relatively. Some of the people he'd failed to protect came in dreams but there were also those he had helped, the Celines, Umekos, Fergies and Abigails. People who could be safe inside Orchard Close while the rest of the world went mad.

*   *   *

At least the dance meant that the shopping party the following day were in a good mood as they gathered at the gate. Though since a few people slept in late, or not at home, the party were delayed while people ran up with last minute requests. That led to few sharp replies because none of the shoppers wanted to wait any longer than necessary in the rain. Eventually the group trudged out of the gates and along the road to the bottom of the access road.

The delay didn't bother the soldiers, snug in their sandbagged shelter. "Shopping party, sarge." Harold waited until a bullhorn told him to come ahead, because the soldiers at the top of the access road weren't there to keep Orchard Close safe. The army posts all around the city were there to keep the inhabitants penned in. Harold smiled despite the wet. "Hi sarge. Are you sure we can't bring transport up here? A canoe maybe?" The Army sergeant in charge of the checkpoint rolled his eyes and held out a hand for Harold's ID. He scanned it while the soldiers ran a wand over Harold to check for weapons, then waved him through the sandbags.

"That wouldn't work up here, because we have drainage." Sarge looked along the gleaming expanse of wet tarmac roadway stretching each way. "You idiots are the only ones going shopping today."

"We daren't miss out because what we want might not be there next time. Our meat stocks are down which is why we're eating a lot of vegetable soup." Harold frowned and shrugged. "Not that spam is exactly meat, and neither are those dried strips."

"Hot vegetable soup is ideal in this wet weather. Not that I'd know." Sarge grinned because anything up to half a dozen women sometimes brought hot soup up to the soldiers on night duty. They came unofficially as a goodwill gesture, a gesture forbidden under the current fraternisation rules but definitely appreciated by the squaddies.

While they talked the rest of Harold's party came through, much quicker than usual because the soldiers wanted to get back under shelter. "See you soon, Sarge, because we won't be strolling in this weather." Harold put his head down against the blowing drizzle, setting a fast pace for the five mile trek to the mart.

* * *

The mart, a grim blocky building surrounded by mesh fences, armed guards and barbed wire, didn't look any more welcoming in the rain. Unfortunately the inhabitants of Orchard Close had nowhere else to shop. Harold and the other men with metal frames in their backpacks went into the toilets. They removed the frames, which unscrewed into iron bars for self-defence, and shared them out. No weapons were allowed along the bypass that the Army controlled, but most shoppers were escorted by gangsters so they didn't come through Army checkpoints. That meant they carried clubs, knives and machetes or similar weapons since those were allowed by law. The other permitted self-defence weapons, bows and crossbows, weren't allowed on the mart premises.

The rain seemed to have deterred most of the other shoppers or more probably their gangster protectors. Harold's group filled up packs with spam, dried meat sticks, and even some tubes of what the mart labelled meat paste. Those were the only three meat products on sale. The shoppers took all the cans of spam in case there were none next time. "Harold, since there's no rush, can we take some potatoes?" Now Harold knew why Curtis, Orchard Close's gardener, had come on this trip. For potatoes, not just as company for Emmy, his gartered wench or whatever wives were called without any form of official marriage. In Orchard Close, confetti and a garter had been adopted as a substitute.

"Why would picking up some wizened potatoes take time, Curtis?" Harold frowned. "I thought we still had plenty left in the cellar. Enough to thicken soup anyway."

"Ah, well, these aren't for soup." Curtis looked almost embarrassed. "I want to examine each one to pick out all the ones with the best eyes. Then back home Emmy can help me chit them."

"Not a problem since at least we're dry here. What is chit... on second thoughts your love life is your own affair." Harold grinned and ducked away from a half-hearted attempt to smack him on the back of the head.

"Hey, leave my main man and his loving out of this." Emmy, a six foot Jamaican with half her hair cropped short and the other half in long thin beaded plaits, smirked. "I can't help it if I drive all you bad boys wild."

"True, I'm only jealous. Come on then, let's go and find Curtis his evening entertainment." The whole group followed him. Nobody shopped alone in the mart since the mart guards wouldn't interfere if shoppers were mugged. "Did you bring enough coupons?" Coupons issued by the government had replaced all money.

"The Coven gave me extras out of the emergency funds." Emmy giggled. "I promised more potatoes for chips later in the year and they didn't want details either."

"If it means chips, I'll learn to chit." Matti and Doll, the two sisters, spoke as one.

"I'll help you with yours." Jeremy looked hopefully at Matti and she considered.

"Hmm. I'll have to get the sordid details about this chitting from Emmy first but maybe."

By the time Harold called a halt Curtis had carefully selected several stones weight of the decidedly second rate potatoes. "Enough Curtis, we've got to carry this lot."

"But each one will make several potato plants."

"I don't want to know the love life of potatoes either. Now come on, tear yourself away because I've been given coupons for clothing." Harold nudged Curtis. "Emmy might buy something to encourage you to chit?"

"Stop it." Harold ducked as Emmy swung again. "Who are you buying underwear for?"

"Just Daisy, Wills and a couple of the other kids. I suppose Doll and Matti will be looking further along the aisle. What about you, Patty? Are you buying something frilly to torment your fan club?"

Patty sneered. "My crossbow keeps their attention firmly on what matters, though I feel half-naked here without it."

"Really?" Jeremy inspected Matti. "Now I know why Patty keeps her raincoat firmly closed. Are you half-naked under yours?" The banter about what various of them might or might not be wearing under raincoats kept everyone amused until the clothes shopping had finished. They all headed for the checkouts where they were able to use one each today because no other shoppers were waiting. The shoppers went into the individual locked rooms, had their purchases scanned, fed their coupons into a slot, and were let out into the yard and the rain.

* * *

Patty at least still seemed to be in a good mood after the joking inside. She tried to cheer up the rest as the group came out of the compound gate and paused on the road to the bypass. "I'm singing in the rain, just getting soaking wet. I rub myself in spam, so I've not gone rusty yet."

Emmy giggled. "Stop it Patty. If I open my mouth to laugh I might drown."

"It's sing or cry, and if I cry the extra water will drown us all." Patty squinted upwards. "I'd say it must stop soon but I said that at least a fortnight ago." She laughed. "It'll wash some of the soot away after Liz's spring rites night."

Emmy nodded towards Alfie. "At least now Liz has had a fix it'll be safe for Alfie to get a bit sweaty at the Easter dance, even with all those muscles." Liz the smith liked muscly men, especially blacksmiths, but thought chasing Alfie would class as cradle-robbing despite his physique.

"Stop it you two and huddle. Not just to hide the packs while we stow the iron bars, but to stop the packs filling with water." Harold was only partly joking because there were some items that really shouldn't get wet. "We'll have to shuffle goods about because nobody wants to be carrying all Curtis's potatoes."

Curtis grinned. "If there's enough we can rip up the big car park to plant them."

"Don't start that. We need a clear field of fire across that tarmac." Harold rolled his eyes. "Gardeners!"

"Watch out buster. Don't you give my main man... look out!" Harold staggered forward as Emmy cannoned into him. They tumbled over the packs with Emmy on top.

He heard a cry of pain, then Alfie shouted, "There." Harold saw the young man running at full pelt towards one of the derelict houses the Mart owned, and movement at a window. Then Jeremy, Bernie and Patty obscured his view, running after Alfie. Harold struggled free, relieved to find Emmy unhurt. He set off towards the house with his three foot iron bar ready.

Even as he did Harold heard an anguished cry of "Curtis" behind him, but he couldn't stop to check. Not until whoever Alfie saw had been dealt with. Harold jumped through the house window, already cleared of any remaining glass by those in front, nearly falling over a man. The man, still getting up off the floor, reached for a machete. He wasn't one of Harold's people so Harold hit him across the head with the iron bar before glancing around. Jeremy slumped in a corner while nearby Patty wrestled with a gangster. Alfie had his man pinned against the back wall but the gangster's machete arm had almost wriggled free. Harold headed towards him.

"What the fuck...?" The new man appearing in the doorway at the back raised his crossbow. Harold threw his iron bar, hard, and ran in after it. A crossbow bolt went past someplace overhead as the man flinched before crying out when the bar struck and Harold bulled him back through the door. Harold grabbed the crossbow with one hand, a handful of jacket with the other, and kept driving forward across the hall into the next room. His opponent smashed into the far wall, giving Harold a chance to knee him good and hard in the solar plexus. Not the nuts because Harold remembered that if this was a Ferdinand, he might be wearing a box.

The man doubled over, his grip slackening enough for Harold to wrench the crossbow free. Since he'd lost the iron bar, Harold beat the man over the head with the captured weapon until he crumpled. Harold stomped on his head to make sure, then whirled at a cry of "Jeremy!" Even as he ran back towards the front room Harold registered that the cry had been rage, not pain or fear, and definitely feminine.

Harold scooped up his iron bar as he came through the door to see Doll and Matti helping Patty, beating on her opponent with their shorter iron bars.

Bernie, though bleeding, retreated slowly while still keeping his opponent occupied. Alfie's opponent had his machete free and now tried to hang onto Alfie as the youth tried to back away. Alfie pulled back hard, yanking the man off-balance as he swung but the bloke raised his machete again for a chop at Alfie's right arm, the one still being held.

Harold's bar came down on the man's upper arm and even through the thick jacket he heard a clear crack as the bone broke. Alfie yanked his own arm free when the man screamed and reeled away in pain. The youth's own iron bar came down twice, hard. "Thanks Harold." They both turned towards Bernie's opponent but the man staggered back, dropping with a set of flights sprouting from his chest. The crossbow Patty had picked off the floor must have been loaded. Beyond her Doll still beat on a recumbent figure while Matti knelt, tending to Jeremy.

"Enough Doll. He's had enough." Well past enough from Harold's quick glance. "What's the matter with Jeremy?"

Matti looked round, tears still trickling down her cheeks. "I don't know. Where were you?"

"Dealing with another in there but he's out cold." Doll nodded, picked up a machete and headed through to check. Harold turned to Bernie and Alfie. "How are you two, and what happened to Jeremy?"

"Jeremy came in first, because he runs like a bloody whippet." Alfie pointed at the one Harold hit on the way in. "That one there had another bolt loaded but had to bash Jeremy with the crossbow. Jeremy sort of ran him down anyway. I took a swipe at the next bloke to stop him chopping Jeremy, and he ducked." A white-faced Alfie held out his left hand. "I tried to punch him in the face but he turned his head. I punched that bloody helmet instead so I can't use my hand just now." Alfie shrugged. "Then he grabbed my wrist and since I kept going, we ended up against the wall."

"I saw. Bernie? Do you want someone to tighten that, or can you manage one-handed?"

Bernie looked up from his arm but kept winding the strip of cloth round it. "You can tie it off it a sec, please. It's a long cut right through my sleeve but not deep so I reckon I'm better off binding my shirt and jacket onto it to stop the bleeding until we get home." He grinned. "That practice worked. I nearly got his eye with a jab before he got out a knife as well."

Harold nodded, before heading across to check on Jeremy. Matti looked up, tears on her cheeks. "It's his nose, just his nose. I'm going to slap the hell out of him back home, just for frightening me." She turned back to Jeremy as

Doll came out of the back room, throwing a machete and knife onto the floor.

The machete Doll still carried dripped red. "He's cold now." She checked the other gangsters but they were cold as well, or cooling anyway. "You ruined that crossbow back there."

"We can't take them anyway." The rest looked at the weapons now scattered about and frowned, because weapons were valuable. "Now let's see who this lot are." Harold wanted to check on Curtis, and Emmy's state of mind, but first he had to try and identify the shooters.

Unfortunately nobody recognised the men, and their clothing bore none of the distinctive emblems gang members wore. The only weapons that might have been pointers were a Geek Freek crossbow and a GOFS-made machete. Although the construction of one and the design and steel in the other were easily recognisable, the other weapons were pre-crash meant for gardening or sports. Patty brandished the crossbow and the machete. "These could have been bought anywhere."

"The rest are rubbish, but we shouldn't leave them for some oik to find." Doll looked at the heap of weapons. "Except that broken crossbow. You'd better ruin it properly though." Harold beat it against the chimney breast, thoroughly twisting and bending the crosspiece,.

"Harold?" A pale-face June looked through the window. "Can you come please? Curtis is hurt, badly."

Harold climbed through and limped across the overgrown garden. He looked at the small group ahead, clustered around the packs and a prone figure. "How badly?"

"Very, we think." June, a small woman nearing forty and definitely not a fighter, sounded distraught. She took another few steps. "Maybe dying."

Harold missed a step because he didn't want to do that again, watch someone he knew die. "Maybe?"

"Emmy is on about the pair of them going up to the Army. She'd rather go to a camp with him if the Army can get a doctor."

Harold bit back his first comment, about what a sergeant once told him about the camps including not sending women in there. "Hey Emmy. What happened?"

"When I pushed, the bolt missed you but hit Curtis. Look. There's blood in his mouth." Emmy stayed on her knees but moved aside a little for Harold to see.

"Not a lot of blood. I've seen more." The crossbow bolt still pinned Curtis's bicep to his body since the bolt had carried on into the side of his chest. "It has to have missed his heart, and maybe just nicked his lung." Harold assumed Curtis would be dead or spitting blood if the bolt had struck his lung properly.

Emmy looked up, her cheeks wet. "But he'll die anyway Harold. Lenny and Patricia can't deal with this, can they? They're not doctors." She tried for a smile. "I'll take him to the Army."

Curtis had laid quiet but now he croaked, "No" and reached across with his other hand.

"I agree with Curtis." Harold softened his voice. "You can't go, Emmy, it's a really bad idea. Curtis might survive but even then you'll be separated while he's fixed. Then he might be sent someplace else, to a different camp. That's if they'll take you."

Emmy opened her mouth to protest but June spoke up. "Think about the baby." Emmy looked stricken.

"You're pregnant?" Harold stared. He was about to ask if Emmy was insane but got hold of himself.

Emmy nodded, managing a little smile through her tears. "There were all those puppies and kittens, and everything settled down, and I told you once. I wanted a nice steady bloke and rugrats, the whole bit."

Harold nodded. "I'll go up to ask the Army. Someone ask the others to bring out the weapons so we can sell them to the mart guards." With luck the guards would offer some cigarettes that Harold could trade elsewhere, as they had another time. Harold put a hand on Emmy's shoulder. "We can always sneak out and rescue him at some time if this mess doesn't get sorted. Piece of cake with your bad girl look and my scowl?" Emmy nodded, but she wasn't convinced. Nor was Harold as he limped up to the Army post, because they'd never find Curtis again even if the gardener survived.

"Can I speak to the sergeant please?"

The soldier with the detection wand scowled. "Why? Are you coming through or what?"

Harold kept his voice calm and polite. "No, we've got a badly wounded man. Please ask the sergeant."

The corporal currently scanning IDs frowned. "Why? One bloody animal more or less won't matter."

"He's our gardener but some scroat stuck a crossbow bolt in him. He'll die without real help. I was told once you'd get medical help if the wounded person was willing to work off the debt." Harold shrugged. "Curtis will be a lot more use on your farms than the arse who shot at him."

"Is he wounded as well?"

"Yes, fatally. Now what about Curtis?" Harold cursed silently, that had come out a bit sharp.

"A gardener? Hang on." The corporal went into a sandbagged shelter, and the sergeant came out.

"A gardener? Where from?"

Harold handed over his pass. "Orchard Close." The sergeant scanned it.

"Wait one and we might be able to help." He went back into the shelter, but came out in minutes. Long slow minutes to Harold, but not really that long to the rest of the world. "The ambulance is on the way if you get him up here."

"An ambulance?" An Army lorry had taken a wounded gangster, Razzle, away for treatment when he'd been injured. Harold hadn't seen a real ambulance since just after the crash.

"You don't want it?"

"Too bloody true I do. Can I run back down?"

"In this instance yes. Get him up here sharpish because it won't be long." Harold stared for a few seconds, turned, and started to run. The sergeant meant it, and Harold began to believe Curtis had a chance.

Halfway down he started to shout, "Yes, hurry. Get a door to carry him," and several different variations. By the time he panted and limped to a halt, Alfie, Patty and Doll were carrying a door from the nearest house. "We'll have to be very careful." Harold put a hand on Emmy's shoulder. "They're sending a real ambulance, Emmy, so he's got a real chance. Now give him a hug and a kiss to keep you going until he gets back, because every minute counts." Harold held her eyes. "Remember, Emmy, it's just until he gets back, not goodbye."

The sergeant had told the truth. Even as four of them carried the door through the gap in the sandbags, covered by wary soldiers with rifles, blue flashing lights came up the bypass. "Carry him over the central divide. You're allowed just this once." The rifles meant be very careful even this time. "Come straight back or the ambulance will leave without him." Emmy bent and kissed Curtis before the four of them came back to the sandbags. The sergeant took one look at Emmy's streaming eyes and let them stand there as the medics quickly loaded Curtis. The ambulance turned round and screamed off down the bypass. "That's it. Back down there or go home."

"Thanks sarge." Harold shepherded Emmy down the slope where the rest of them had sorted out the packs and stowed the iron bars.

June looked at the group and back up to the bypass. "They really took him? In that ambulance?"

Harold still had trouble believing that even if he'd just watched it happen. "Yes June. From the way the medics treated Curtis, they will try and save him."

"Thank all and any gods for small mercies." A few muttered amen to that.

"Are we really giving these weapons away?" Doll looked over the machetes and knives.

"Selling, with luck." Harold looked over the heap again and frowned. "Where's the baseball bat, the crossbow and the bolts?"

Doll looked shifty but Patty spoke up. "Well hidden in those houses. We even took the crossbow apart first. We also hid that good machete and the best two knives just in case we need serious backup sometime. If some scroat finds them fair enough, but if not weapons might come in handy one day." Harold nodded because Patty might be right.

The mart guard looked down from the tower as Harold came closer. "Near enough. What do you want?"

"Why didn't you shoot? He was stood in that window pointing a crossbow." Harold pointed.

"Not at me." The guard eyed the group around the packs. "What are you going to do with all those knives and machetes? We'll take them if you like?"

"Since you don't seem too worried about who gets hurt down here, you'll probably sell them to some other nasty little scroat." Harold should keep his mouth shut but this bloke seemed to be a real ass and right now Harold hadn't quite worked off his temper. "You could at least knock the damn houses down."

"Too expensive according to our bosses. Anyway, the scum are too smart to shoot at us, since there's a machine gun and an armoured car back there." The guard nodded towards the weapons. "You can't take weapons on the bypass so we'll come and get them anyway once you're gone."

"OK. Luck with that." Harold turned and stomped back to the group. "You heard the bastard. He's not the happy smiling type we've dealt with before so I'm leaving sod all. We can break the machetes, but what about the knives?"

Patty pointed at a manhole in the road. "Let them scrabble through shit if they're that keen." She picked up a machete. "I'll lever the lid off. Then you can explain how to break this."

"Easy. Stick it in a drain grating at the side of the road, then bend it back and forth. It'll snap eventually. You might even build a bit more muscle for that crossbow of yours." Harold picked up a machete. "For me, it'll work off some annoyance. Otherwise I might just climb that tower and feed him the damn thing."

"I've got some annoyance to work off."

"Me too."

"Can I share?"

*　　*　　*

The group walked back in silence. Harold had a lot to think about. Firstly that Mart guard had been downright belligerent. In the past some had sneered and made comments, but others had smiled and sometimes even joked. Lately that had changed. Shopping while men pointed guns wasn't restful on a good day, but Harold had always assumed they'd hesitate before shooting an unarmed woman. Now he'd started to wonder.

Worse than that, Harold had a real dilemma. Emmy thought she'd pushed him out of the way of the bolt, and might resent Harold being unhurt while Curtis could be dying. On the other hand Harold knew where he'd been standing, and the scroat hadn't aimed at him. If Emmy hadn't pushed, the crossbow bolt would have hit her.

On top of whether to tell her, Harold had to wonder who the hell wanted to kill Emmy, specifically? Most gangsters wouldn't count a woman as a fighter, and would try to capture rather than kill her. Einstein from the Geek Freeks, a neighbouring gang, would love to kill or capture Emmy but in that case there'd have been three or four crossbows in there, Geek ones. With that firepower the fight would have gone the other way. By the time the group were getting near home, Harold had made one decision. A higher proportion of men would go to the mart, or out scavenging. He wasn't losing another, and especially a woman.

The sergeant beckoned Harold as the group lined up to leave the bypass and go down the road home. "Did he make it?"

Harold stared at the sergeant. "Curtis? He was alive in the ambulance. How did you know?"

"We received a message asking me to confirm that Orchard Close had a decent gardener, someone who knew how to actually grow things. Considering the acres you lot have cultivated, I said yes." Sarge glanced at the rest of the party, filing through the sandbags to walk down the short stretch to Orchard Close. "She looks upset."

"He was her fella, and they're having a baby. Not smart but it mattered to them."

Sarge nodded, watching the rest file through. As the last went out of sight he sighed. "If you ever breath a word that I said this, I'll accidentally shoot you. We've been told to arrest gardeners on any pretext." He hesitated. "We've also been instructed to detain women who might be promiscuous or abused. That's the criteria for accepting female refugees, though we'll also accept anyone who appears to be badly psychologically damaged."

Harold stared, trying to make sense of that. He found a worrying reason for the gardeners, but, "Why the women?"

"You worked the gardeners part out? I've got my own suspicions as well, based on the lack of fresh greens in the NAAFI." Sarge stood for a few more moments, visibly wrestling with a problem. "My unofficial, never ever spoken suspicions about women have to do with the new comfort facilities for troops." Harold stared, because he still couldn't make sense of that, but Sarge continued. "The sort that squaddies in foreign parts go to on a Saturday night when there is no female company. There are murmurings those sort of facilities are opening near the barracks soon, because there's a distinct lack of young female company in the Army camps." Sarge gave a wry smile. "In my assessment your beer and chips girls don't come under that heading, but take care if a new squad takes over." He looked pointedly at the gap in the sandbags and jerked his head.

"On my way sarge. Thank you for not telling me." By the time Harold reached the gate to Orchard Close he'd decided, no women at all on mart runs. After a heated exchange with a succession of annoyed women and a tearful Emmy, the rest agreed with him. After really thinking it through Harold came up with a reason for someone to target Emmy. Harold, Alfie and Emmy could all shoot well with either of the two big rifles. If someone killed Harold the other two would go after whoever did it or their gang boss.

If Emmy had already been killed then Harold's deterrent had gone because the gangs, the Hot Rods especially, knew Alfie couldn't take over. They wouldn't consider a seventeen-year-old a serious threat, but the gangs all knew Emmy had enough standing to run Orchard Close. Harold became even more determined to keep Emmy safe, and not to train anyone else as an expert shooter and therefore potential target. The bastards had already killed Holly, another rifle trainee, and Orchard Close already had more shooters than big rifles.

Chapter 2:
Soggy Mudpuppies

Deep under rolling countryside, the UK cabal members had their own worries as they eyed the new man taking a seat at the polished table. He used Nate's seat, or it had been Nate's. The distinguished looking chairman gestured towards the innocuous looking middle-aged newcomer. "This is Maurice. Unfortunately a roaming gang of miscreants ambushed Nate's car. They were wiped out of course, but not before one of them reached him." Owen shrugged. "A salutary lesson about getting complacent. Maurice is replacing Nate, and will deal with information collection and dissemination in the future."

"Spying and propaganda." Vanna narrowed her eyes. "Which were you doing before, Maurice?"

"Information retrieval. Joshua in particular is, I believe, grateful."

"Very, and welcome Maurice." Joshua looked around them. "Maurice is responsible for the efficiency with which some successful gang leaders have been removed by an unseen sniper, one wearing Army uniform." Joshua smiled happily, nodding towards the tall Asian woman before sweeping his gaze across the rest of those present with a wry smile. "Despite my reservations, Vanna's civilian contractors are training up well while controlling the breakout attempts from York and Gloucester. We can probably clear the population from about a third of each city while they are flooded."

"Good, because the pork content of spam is down to a half now, so any reduction in demand is a plus. We really need the food from Argentina, especially Corned Beef or something similar to give the scum their fat intake. After all, the UK had to import over half our food before we acted. Despite the culling so far, we still can't support what's left." Ivy frowned. "How is the petrol situation? I'd heard somewhere that fuel spoiled over time."

"Not with additives, or not as quickly. Diesel for my lorries might be more of a problem because of the amount used in food distribution, though we should be getting fuel from the Falklands soon?" Gerard looked questioningly at Owen, the chairman.

"Keris tells me that is coming along slowly but surely. We've had compatibility issues while building the new refinery because the parts are coming from several different ruined ones. The crude oil is flowing from the underwater wells and that's being stored, though crude oil has never been a problem." Owen glanced over at Grace. "How is the recruitment coming along for the brothels? Ah, we'd better vote first." He looked around the table. "The motion is to create a system of brothels to service the Armed Forces, and the civilian contractors guarding the marts and work camps."

"Can we find enough prostitutes?" Henry looked up suddenly. "I'm not objecting, just looking at possible problems." He glanced towards Maurice, seated where the only serious objector to brothels used to sit before his fatal misadventure.

"The recruitment from the work camps has gone very well, with the incentives I am able to offer. Moving to anywhere but another camp is usually enough to get volunteers." Grace smiled. "Those rescued from the cities by the Army are generally compliant once my people explain the options. If not, a visit to a work camp and a look at their alternative bunkmates does the job."

"Good. Then are there any objections?" Owen looked around the table. A couple of people glanced towards Maurice but didn't object. "Good, we'll put the brothels on an official footing, then Grace can increase her recruitment drive." He glanced at his paperwork. "The next item is farms. How will the continuing rain affect food production, Henry?"

"All the crops will genuinely be late. Even the mechanised farming has been affected because the land is truly sodden. The teams of workers on the hand tilled areas might get started sooner, though that will be brutal work in the mud."

Ivy scowled. "Probably the first time in their lives the scum have earned their keep. That is providing they actually are growing food instead of ruining it? How is the gardener recruitment going Henry?"

"We have some but as Grace warned most of those in her work camps are city scum, not gardeners. The system is working though, with the scum quickly getting the idea and doing as their supervising gardener says. It'll become more useful as the growing season really gets under way. The Army have arrested a good few gardeners for one reason or another, but the soldiers could try harder? Perhaps be a little more proactive?" Henry glanced at Joshua. "The guard posts should have an idea of which enclaves have the best crops."

"I'll send a memo round them all, pointing that out, though we could do with the surveillance photographs. That or a list of enclaves with good crops?" Joshua glanced at Maurice who nodded acquiescence. He glanced back down at his papers and frowned. "The Army has also collected some very badly traumatised men and women. Are they what you wanted, Maurice?"

"Yes Joshua, we want to test some treatments. After all, your soldiers will be traumatised by some of what they find going into the cities and we'll want them cured, won't we?" Maurice smiled. "If we can fix these, we can fix your squaddies."

Joshua smiled and relaxed. "Ah, I did wonder. Excellent. There'll be more of all the target types from York and Gloucester when the captives from the flooded areas are processed." He nodded towards Vanna. "Vanna's people are dealing with that."

The discussion spread into details of numbers arrested and processed, then moved on to how the late arrival of new crops would impact food supplies. Grace would divert some of the work gangs currently unable to get onto flooded fields into scavenging. There were still many areas of depopulated housing, villages and small towns, that would contain food. Eventually the meeting had dealt with all the important topics and Owen rapped with his gavel.

"Before we adjourn, I have another person who you should all meet." Owen pressed a button on a control. A few moments later a slightly obese woman with short dark hair entered. "This is Irina, the woman who will be in overall charge of the brothels. She has considerable experience in women's prisons, and young offender's institutions. Please, treat this as a job interview. Ask any questions you wish." Owen sat back to let those with any qualms have their say. He took careful note of attitudes, in case any harboured the same convictions as the late Nate about utilising young women to amuse soldiers.

*　　*　　*

Almost two weeks after the cabal discussed possible employment for women from the cities, a woman who would definitely be trying to avoid that fate tapped on the door of Harold's study-bedroom. "Harold, Harold."

"Yes Sharyn." Harold stood up from the chair, one of two he'd brought into the converted study, and opened the door.

"No guns, no panic. We've got a refugee but she's running around on the exclusion zone. So far the soldiers haven't shot her." From in here Harold could hear the Army bullhorn, but not what sarge said.

"Hasn't anyone told her to come this way?"

"Yes, now come on." Harold went out of the back door, heading towards the group looking over the wall at the bottom of his garden.

Casper turned as Harold came up. "She's not tracking right Harold. She's frightened of us, of the soldiers, of the shadows under the bypass, everything. Sarge has told her to ask for sanctuary five times but it's not getting through."

"Cripes." Harold whispered because he'd just seen the refugee. A thin, painfully thin girl anything from a tall ten to a late developing teenager, dressed in a torn, dirty shift but barefooted. Even as he looked the girl stumbled over the rubble towards the bypass, then swerved and went towards the access road.

"Stop her Soldier Boy. Don't let her come up here." Sarge sounded desperate.

"He won't shoot her. Will he?" Casper stared up at the bypass. "Surely not."

"He's trying to avoid arresting her." Harold looked over the group. "Jeremy, you can run fastest I'm told. Get to the end of the access road and wave your arms, scare her away. Alfie, Casper, follow him."

"She won't come near enough to grab, Harold." Emmy looked up to the bypass. "We have to go and get her."

Harold cupped his hands. "Sarge, can we come on there to get her?" As he shouted the girl stopped and stared at Harold, then staggered towards the access again. She saw the men racing past and swerved towards an archway supporting the road.

"Clearly unarmed. Before she reaches the wire under there or I've got no options." Sarge sounded desperate as well.

"For Christ's sake!" Harold glanced at Emmy then away as her blouse came off. Even as Emmy climbed over the wall in her underwear, Sharyn and June were stripping.

He cupped his hands and shouted. "Clearly unarmed sarge. No photos." Stripping was the quickest way to prove they weren't armed, but Harold didn't want the three women decorating some squaddie's wall.

"No photos. Be quick." Harold could hear sarge shouting at his squaddies, hopefully to put any bloody camera phones away.

Even with three obviously harmless women coming for her the girl tried to get away. She veered away from the bypass, from the shadows underneath, stumbling off across the rubble until Sharyn caught her. She kept struggling until Emmy and June arrived as well, then went limp. Harold and the rest of the men studiously ignored the three women as they carried the girl to the wall where Matti, Liz and Patty were now waiting.

"OK little brother, you can look now."

"You should give me warning before streaking. Thank all and any gods this sergeant is a decent sort. Some of the ones we've had up there would have shot her out of hand, or arrested her for the camps." Harold looked towards the girl club where Liz carried the still figure inside. "How bad is she?"

"Starving for a start, she's skin and bone. We can probably sort that, but she's off in some nightmare, Harold. We can't do much but hope." Sharyn patted him on the back. "Patricia is on the way. We'll try and sort her out in there. She's bloody terrified of something. Leave it with the girl club."

"And the coven. You might need all thirteen." Harold waved his arms, beckoning Casper, Alfie and Jeremy back from the bottom of the access road. From the way the girl had run away when she saw the men, the girl club might be a really good place. Whatever her story, the girl had just been incredibly lucky.

Much later, after Daisy-story at bedtime, Sharyn gave Harold the first verdict. "Starving but no abuse. The cuts and bruises just look like living rough with no other clothes or shoes. Lenny came to look at her but the lass almost passed out so he didn't go near. She said Elise when we asked for her name, but that's all we're getting." Sharyn's little smile showed more sorrow than humour. "Everyone with a dog might be volunteering their furry friend, since she wants to be near Thandia in preference to any human. Though it might be Thandia's size that's comforting." The Mastiff would certainly be a reassuring guard.

* * *

By Easter Harold knew the girl's name and age but only that. Thirteen year old Elise wouldn't or couldn't say any more, though Liz confided that Thandia probably knew. The painfully thin girl spent hours murmuring to the big dog but shut up as soon as anyone came near.

Harold spent the Easter dance on guard duty because an Easter dance would be too bitter-sweet with memories of Holly. Rob and Susan still wanted to babysit Wills and Daisy so he couldn't stay at home. Practice they said but no rush to go for the real thing, a rugrat. After all with the current lack of medical facilities and Susan being in her thirties, babysitting might be as near as they got. Harold turned at a noise and stared. "Cripes, are you a guard now Sooty?"

"Not that dopey lump, he'd open the door and offer a paw. I told Finn to get to the dance because June and Janine are both there. He laughed when I told him its good for a man's ego when women fight over him which proves my point." Emmy put a crate containing six bottles of beer on the floor. "I'm not sitting on that this time."

"One of those nights, is it? I should break a window, and set fire to something." Harold and a wounded Emmy had once spent a night keeping watch after yobs had done both.

A shadow of Emmy's smile flitted across her face. "Yeah, just to set the mood. Though I'm not sure who'll be sogging on who this time."

"Mutually absorbent?" Harold moved another chair over near the firing slots and Emmy sat.

"Maybe. I sat at home with Sooty, and started thinking about Curtis, and that's not good." Emmy put a hand on Sooty's head as his tail thumped. "Then I thought who else might be sat thinking of someone absent." She picked up two beer bottles. "A name came to mind."

"I do a lot of thinking, and some of it with beer. Is beer all right?" Harold gestured towards Emmy's tummy.

"Don't you start! Anyone would think a woman has never been pregnant before." Emmy sighed. "I haven't. Now I'm thinking this was a stupid thing to do."

Harold's first reaction had been that Emmy must be crackers to get pregnant in the current situation, but he'd never tell her. "You'll be fine. Whoever is in there will have lots of friends, Uncle-this and Aunty-that and a Mummy-Casper." Harold flipped the infrared viewer down over his eye to carefully scan the open ground and the nearest ruins. "There could be a bloody army in those houses."

"The six big ones? Come on Harold, let it go. Those houses are barely damaged so it would be a terrible waste if we just pulled them down. They're not much over three hundred metres away and in a year or three we might need extra housing." Emmy looked out of the nearest loophole. "They're boarded up now which should stop any army getting inside." She laughed. "They're full of furniture, plywood and window frames we've taken out of storage here, so we can use these houses for people."

"True. Though now I think about it I'll get Finn to run electricity out there, a buried cable. We'll put a heater in each room so nothing goes mouldy, and a light. Then I'll drill some little holes in the ply over the windows. If the lights go out, or something moves behind the holes, we'll know my paranoia is right." Harold smiled. "Though I'm willing to be proved wrong? Better still, that'll keep the houses dry and aired until we do need them because Elizabeth is right about planning ahead."

"Cripes, listen to us talking about two or three years in advance. We never thought this would last six months." Emmy sniffed. "Though Curtis had plans for longer, for a real farm and orchard. Do you think he's all right, that he made it?"

"Yes. I said gardener and that sergeant bust a gut to get an ambulance. I told you all about the Army arresting women and why, but I worked out something else." Harold reached out to put a hand on Emmy's shoulder, then squeezed gently. "The rubbish on the TV is at least partly true. The government are having trouble growing food. They'll have taken Curtis to a proper surgery, and he'll get proper aftercare, because the bastards need him." Harold chuckled, more or less. "We'll ask every new squad of soldiers if they've seen him, because I'll bet you've a got at least one picture on a phone fit for public viewing. It'll be a hell of a shock for Curtis when you arrive to bust him out and his first job is to change a nappy."

"Better wait until he or she is toddling and can carry them. That's me reassured and all that, what about you? Last Easter, ending up with Holly gartered and all that." Emmy sighed. "I went through something close when I lost Davey, and now with Curtis." She actually giggled. "Cripes, Harold, we were all trying hard not to laugh. We think of you as, I don't know, an older Uncle even if you're my age, and then Holly turned you into shy sixteen."

"She never seemed old enough." Just like that Harold finally let go, talking about all the bottled-up emotion though not necessarily about Holly. About how he'd gone from seventeen to Army to the Middle East before coming back to this mess. Yes, he did feel very old sometimes, when everyone expected him to have the answers. He talked about thinking big sister Sharyn would have it all sorted out, but she'd gone to bits. About worrying over gangsters, all the girl club teasing and tempting, about not wanting the rugrat thing. Then Holly being there all of the time which somehow meant the worries weren't too bad, then she was gone. About protecting people by shooting and beating scroats. Eventually Harold ran down.

"That protection thing makes sort of sense and the rest explains why you sometimes seem too old for your face, as it were. We do appreciate your scowling face when the oiks act up. Once my bump is gone I'll definitely want some more of that machete training to help with that." Emmy chuckled. "That teasing from the girl club was partly relief at us all surviving, and partly just that, teasing. A few wouldn't have said no to a fling. I fibbed a bit, Harold. I wasn't tempted that Christmas, because you were hooked and landed and to be honest, so was I. Curtis said he took one look when we arrived, and fell in love." Emmy moved her chair closer.

"I know he did because he told me."

"I still remember Davey, but Curtis is different. One day you might have the same luck? Curtis was crackers about me, still is, and it's the real thing this time for me." Her voice wavered, then Emmy sobbed. "I hope you find a rugrat girl, and I really hope I can find Curtis again. Can I be soggy first?" Harold presented his shoulder and put an arm round her.

Harold walked Emmy to her house after the guard shift. He went home afterwards more settled, somehow. That absorbent shoulder thing really did have some benefits for both parties.

*   *   *

Emmy seemed to be more settled or maybe determined after her Easter soggy. Everyone soon realised her new mission. Emmy set into making sure every scrap of gardening knowledge in Orchard Close, much of it from Curtis, would end up producing more food. She wanted to improve on last year, which should mean plenty of salad during summer and thick veggie soup for winter. Harold wasn't the only one to get blisters or an aching back as she drove them to clear more bricks and undergrowth, then dig over the ground further and further away from the walls. As an added benefit, the bricks were barrowed the increasing distance to Orchard Close where Casper used them to thicken or raise the walls. Harold thought that even without mortar, some of them would now stop a car or van.

Even the abandoned roads outside the walls were stripped of tarmac and stone fill, used to create pathways through the fields. Once the ruins were demolished the house foundations were robbed out and they, and the roadways, were filled with soil deep enough to allow the gardeners to grow food. Some of the original footpaths were left in and the resulting network made life much easier for those carrying or wheeling loads outside the walls.

Once the rain finally eased off, the fine mild weather seemed to urge the crops to make up for lost time. In some places the underground drains had survived the Army bombardment so those parts dried out faster. When they did, crops were immediately planted as Emmy drove everyone remorselessly, because according to her every leaf would count. Harold produced his best scowl to insist that Emmy had the right idea, and back gardens inside Orchard Close became veg plots. After all, the damn rabbits couldn't get at the shoots in there. Soon Emmy had a system running to bring on the seedlings in safety before planting them outside the walls when the loss of a couple of leaves wasn't fatal. Though after a near-rebellion the lawns at the front stayed as grass so the residents could sit there in good weather.

*   *   *

Gayle the dental trainee became more confident after fixing the mess in

Wellington's mouth, even if the scarring made the Geek's smile hideous. She drilled and filled teeth and pulled one for senior members of the neighbouring gangs in return for coupons and some gardening tools, electrical spares for Finn, laughing gas and putty. Harold insisted the dental patients came to Orchard Close for the work and Gayle always wore a balaclava, because all the gangs were much too interested in identifying Orchard Close's dentist. Caddi and the Geeks also wanted to identify the smith and the radio repair man, though they all knew the knitter. Patty's scowl and crossbow stopped anyone considering actually kidnapping her.

Medical work, dentistry and knitting were dealt with when needed, not according to the rota system that governed other repair work. Orchard Close repaired weapons, radios, plumbing or electrics for the three nearest gangs on a strict rota basis. All three insisted on their turn, if only to stop the others getting extra work done.

The request for a meeting with a senior GOFS, Vulcan, came as a surprise since Orchard Close had just finished the GOFS work. Harold had another surprise when he reached the border a mile away, because Vulcan met him personally to explain that the meet would be deeper inside GOFS territory. The group would include two other gangs, Barbie Girls and Geek Freeks.

The escort vehicle pulled up outside a small bank, now fortified to provide protection for most of a housing estate that still had water and electricity. Vulcan opened the bank door, waving Harold forward. "Just you please, Soldier Boy. Your bodyguards can wait with the Barbie Girl and Geek Freek version if they play nice." He grinned because Casper being gay would annoy the hell out of the Geeks, and frustrate the Barbies since they couldn't tease or tempt him.

Vulcan ushered Harold into a room containing five others, all sat around a table. As a declaration of truce all the handguns were in the middle of the table with the clips removed, so Harold added his as Vulcan followed him in. He looked round the table, naming those he recognised. "Gofannon the GOFS of course, Hawkins and Wellington from the Geeks, Chandra the Barbie but who did you bring this time, Chandra?" The second Barbie Girl dressed like a man, a six foot tall heavily built man, an impression spoiled by the blond wig and her obvious bust.

"This is Ken and one of the original three Barbie Girls. She's here because Ken leads our fighters into any serious strife." Chandra waved a hand around the rest. "That's why Wellington is here for the Geeks and Vulcan for the GOFS, it's a council of war." She smiled. "As Soldier Boy you're a boss and general. A man who multi-tasks. Wow, I suppose there had to be one."

"Thanks Chandra, now if I can regain control of the meeting for a moment?" Despite the words Gofannon wore a tolerant smile because Barbies were always wild cards.

Harold frowned. "Council of war? Caddi?" Cadillac ran the Hot Rods, the large and ambitious gang bordering most of those present.

"I wish. Between us we could trim that bastard back a bit but you three bloody fools have a treaty." Ken scowled. "You do know he'll break it when he's ready?"

"Then you can come with us to trim him back down to size. All done?" Gofannon sounded a bit more impatient now. Ken shrugged and settled back in her chair. The GOFS leader turned to Harold. "We may have a bigger problem on our northern border, or the Geek's western border. The General is on the march."

"How much of a march?" Harold tried to work out how that meant a problem for him.

"The General is called that because he won contests playing computer war games pre-crash, the strategic type not the shoot 'em up ones. Since the crash he's built up a big gang well beyond the other side of the swamp, the flooded area, just the other side of the Pinkies, Pink Panthers. He will be directly across the swamp if he keeps marching and might not stop. The people coming through the water now are running from him because he's found allies." Gofannon frowned. "The Bloodsuckers are maniacs but he seems to have them under control as shock troops and he's picked up more fighters after taking over at least three other gangs."

Wellington spoke up. "Worse than the numbers, the MiB, Men in Black, have allied with him. They have plenty of automatic firearms, allegedly pillaged from the city centre before the Army and RAF came back to seal it."

Gofannon nodded towards Hawkins and Wellington. "They haven't got a swamp in the way and if the General comes through there we're all flanked."

"Though we have got a flooded railway line in a cutting along our west and northwest borders. We've rigged up a couple of good throwers to cover the gap." Wellington grinned, a hideous sight due to his badly scarred mouth. "At the moment we're putting in brick strongpoints as well so he might think the swamp is the easier option."

Gofannon picked it up again. "Either way, he'll have to take out two relatively soft targets first. Both are what we would call civvies, groups or enclaves like yours Soldier Boy, smallish groups that have no nasty criminal types in charge." He smiled faintly. "Thought these actually are comparatively soft targets since they haven't got a nasty soldier bastard either. Then he might come after us or the Geeks. If he takes one of us, either Orchard Close or the Barbies are outflanked, or both." Gofannon looked straight at Harold. "He won't be able to resist all those experts of yours."

Harold shook his head. "I can't send people across a swamp to fight."

"Nor us, since it'll work both ways as a defence line. I don't mind helping you stop this General at the edge of the flooding." Ken looked over at Wellington. "I'll even recommend we help you nasty shits since we don't want to be caught between the General and Caddi."

"Too true. Caddi would either attack from behind and snip off a few estates or make a deal to split the proceeds." Harold looked round. "Is that the idea? We all agree to help out whoever is attacked?"

"Yeah, then if Caddi does get ambitious we turn round after the General bounces and carve the Hot Rods a new one." Ken curled her lip. "It'll need doing eventually."

Gofannon ignored Ken's comment. "Will you all agree to a self-defence treaty? The four of us should agree to combine if the General attacks any of us." Gofannon looked round the table. "That includes ancillary support as well as line troops. We'll want your medics and best shooters, Soldier Boy, and your medicinal supplies and the doctor, Ken."

"The medics will work for cost, and you still supply whatever drugs are available?" Harold could live with that since his fighters would be fewer than the other gangs could supply.

"We'll sell medical supplies at fifty percent for battle wounds and give free advice, but doc can't leave Beth's. That's not negotiable." Chandra tensed but relaxed as the Geeks and GOFS nodded. Instead they all began to talk about practicalities, such as the passage of armed troops through each other's territories. Harold promised to spread his three best shooters to cover the three weakest spots, providing someone gave up a big rifle and ammunition for one of them.

Gofannon produced a real typewriter to type up four agreements, all with a carbon copy, then all seven signed and added their thumbprint. On the way back Harold wondered just how serious a threat this General might be. After all there were still two enclaves in the way. Perhaps Gofannon just wanted to pull the Barbies into some sort of agreement since they were definitely wild cards, and on his western border.

* * *

Only two nights later Caddi's next turn for repairs meant Harold driving home as night fell, again, which seemed to be the latest Caddi form of harassment. At least this time Harold knew there were doubled guards with night vision goggles watching on all three sides of Orchard Close, so he didn't worry about being late. He did worry about the bullet out of the night that hit his pickup! Harold looked towards the flash, blinking as the night lit up. The Hot Rod escort emptied their weapons in every direction. He jumped out of the cab. "Stop you morons! Bloody hell, now we're all night-blind. The scroat could be ten feet away!"

"Did you see him Harry?" Harold ignored the Harry because Caddi and Cooper now used it as a wind-up. "Where is he?"

"Halfway to the city centre with luck. If not you'd better hope he had his eyes open. Otherwise he's the only one who can see so he'll shoot you all before stripping our bodies." Harold inspected the hole in the back of the pickup. "Are you lot letting strangers take pot-shots at visitors, Cooper?"

"No chance. Caddi says that could cause really big problems. Though this is a problem. If it was daylight we'd get him but at night?" Cooper shrugged. "We'll have a look when it gets light. Good job he's a crap shot in the dark."

"Yeah right." Harold drove the rest of the way thinking hard. The Hot Rods knew if Harold had been killed on Hot Rod territory in daylight then Emmy and Alfie would come after Caddi's scalp with the rifles. Caddi would be held responsible for sheer carelessness at least. Harold had mentioned that, and that the other two gangs would be pissed off at losing gun repairs. Unfortunately Harold didn't think Caddi had forgiven him for killing Hot Rods or the sniping, and might not care about the gun repairs if he got payback. At night the gang boss might get away with claiming ignorance, and inability to stop whoever fired the shot. Harold decided he'd have to be more careful about travelling through Hot Rod territory at night.

* * *

Harold should have been more worried about bushwhackers near to home, because Emmy descended on him the following morning with a tray of chitted potatoes. Harold now knew chitting meant cutting potatoes so they had an eye each. She arrived with Seth in tow, definitely startling Harold because Seth's only interest in potatoes usually came after they'd been dug up, peeled, and deep fried as chips. Usually Seth preferred working in the brewery and chasing Berry, the brewer's daughter.

Emmy thrust the tray towards Harold. "These are ready to plant, they need planting, and the ground is too wet."

Harold looked from one to the other helplessly. "I can't help that. The rain wasn't my fault and neither is the land not drying up yet."

Emmy wasn't mollified. "Not being able to plant in the only dry land is your fault."

"Where?" Harold really tried to work out where because as far as he could see, the unplanted portion of the area used for farming seemed to consist of sloppy mud.

"Over there." Emmy pointed dramatically. "There's acres of well-drained land not being used at all."

"The car park? The big one where.. where the fuel tank is?" Where I nicked my motor from wasn't the best description. Harold sighed. "We can't. It'll take for ever to rip up all that tarmac and barrow it away."

"But we don't have to. Dig a trench in the tarmac and we can fill it with soil from the gardens belonging to the derelict housing at the far side. That'll be easy. The remaining tarmac means the surplus water will run away so the plants won't get waterlogged."

"Cripes Harold, we've got to do something. The potatoes are late in already. We'll run out of chips." Seth sounded desperate. "I'll come and wield a pickaxe or whatever." This really must be a crisis if Seth had volunteered to leave the brewery and Berry.

"I surrender, sort of. We'll try a bit first. If the plants are blanking out the field of fire we stop. Hey, put me down, you don't know where I've been." Emmy put Harold down after the bear hug and retrieved her potato babies from Seth.

"When?"

"Go and chit or whatever. I'm on it, right?"

*   *   *

An hour later Harold and Casper were hard at work with four others. They were checking floorboards or cutting firing slits in the plywood blocking the upstairs windows of a row of damaged terraced houses. The windows over-looked a wide stretch of tarmac that had once been used to park new cars prior to shipment, back when such things mattered. "We'll need extra guards in here if there's crops, because the guardhouse up at the corner won't be able to see along the rows."

"If we keep the rows end on to Orchard Close the same as the rest of the gardens, nobody will do much sneaking through them. The infrared should get them from the corner anyway since it'll only be potatoes which aren't very high." Casper elbowed Harold. "Now stop wittering."

"Yeah, all right. Paranoia parked up. In any case Emmy is right, we need the potatoes. Veronica found a bit about production in an encyclopaedia while looking for something else. I told her she'd accidentally find out all sorts like that." Harold looked at Casper's puzzled expression. "Oh yes, it said an acre could feed eight people if they got their meat elsewhere. Potatoes are one of the very best crops for food value." Harold gestured at the tarmac. "That's over four acres so in theory it will feed thirty two people."

"Cripes. Give me a pickaxe." Casper grinned. "I don't fancy running out of chips either."

By evening almost half of Orchard Close, pretty much everyone who could find tools, buckets or wheelbarrows, felt the same way. Trenches were quickly torn through the tarmac and the stones beneath and the spoil carted away towards the ruins. There the wheelbarrows, handcarts and buckets were filled with soil to be brought back and put in the holes. By nightfall the following day Emmy and her gardeners were bringing out the potential plates of chips, carefully planting them along the lines of raw earth.

A solid week of hacking, carting, blisters and aching backs, and the trenches had been dug. The rain had stopped, but the rest of the arable ground couldn't be worked yet so Emmy kept planting potatoes. As a bonus some of the tarmac and stone came around the side of Orchard Close to extend the network of paths through the mud. Even as the workers relaxed a bit Emmy warned them not to get complacent. Once the potato shoots poked above ground more earth would be needed to heap up around them, until finally each one grew out of a little mound. Every spade full would have to be carted in from a quarter mile away. By then nobody had the energy left to argue or complain.

*   *   *

Emmy soon had had plenty of other gardening jobs to keep them occupied. Harold trudged up the road to home after a day in the fields. At least now that the rain had stopped the sun began to dry the soil but mud still impeded every effort to work outside the walls. He opened the house door and leant against the frame to remove his wellies. "Take off your boots out there. Don't you dare trek mud in here."

"Yes Sharyn, I hear and obey." Harold smiled to himself as he scraped his boots then put them on a mesh over a water tub, using the hosepipe to get the mud off. "I'm even saving the mud so Emmy doesn't beat on me for stealing her garden." Harold sluiced the worst off his hands at the same time, then went inside to finish that in the washroom.

Sharyn inspected him as he came into the living room. "Good. As a reward, you can have rhubarb tonight."

"Without sugar."

"Without sugar. The sugar beet fields were flooded or some other rubbish while you were on your timeout last year."

Harold frowned. "That might be true." He sniggered. "Maybe the squirrels ate it all."

"Don't start with squirrels again. What are all the mudpuppies doing out there in that mess anyway, planting rice?" Sharyn waved in the general direction of the fields.

"Planting out baby this and baby that. The plants can either swim or breath water according to Emmy. She swears the sludge otherwise known as soil will be good for them." Harold shrugged. "I can believe that, because the weeds love it. Worse, we've got bramble seedlings starting up."

"Mmm, goody, blackberries."

"No. Bad, if they're in the gardens." Harold scowled. "Though Emmy won't let us throw them into the compost or they'll sprout there. Worse, we have to nurture the little swine and replant them half a mile away out in the ruins once she lets us straighten our aching backs from her muddy acres."

"Mmm, goody, blackberries."

"I give in." Harold stopped, looking at the carpet. "Ah, I thought you were quick off the mark about boots." A line of dark footprints led across the carpet towards the stairs, accompanied by a set of smaller ones but with twice as many feet.

"The school took the children to help with the seedlings, and Daisy brought one home." Sharyn sighed. "I caught her halfway up the stairs taking her prize to show Daddy, and ask if he wanted one in the love place." Sharyn sat down. "Is that healthy? She's got half a dozen drawings on her wall of dead people. They're all smiling and happy and surrounded by fairies and unicorns but even so?"

"She's also got drawings of Angel, Casper, pirate ships, and the Red Cross Elephant. There's an Orchard picture and even a couple of pictures from her colouring books that she liked." Harold shrugged. "At least she knows where Daddy is, unlike too many other kids."

"True. Oh, be careful going out the back. Emmy has claimed the conservatory as an extra greenhouse." Sharyn smirked. "I managed to get Daisy to put her plant in there after Daddy saw it, so it's not lonely. I didn't fancy Daisy loose in her bedroom with a watering can full of stinky water."

"Cripes no. Has Emmy claimed all the conservatories?" Sharyn nodded which didn't surprise Harold in retrospect. He hoped Emmy would eventually ease off her drive to plant and grow food because Curtis would have, before it became a real obsession. Though right now her drive kept dragging or driving the residents out into the mud where a polite request might not. Everyone knew why Emmy did it. Her baby bump reminded any who needed it, and so far nobody really resented her pushing. After all Orchard Close truly did need every bit of food that could be grown. The marts had less and less fresh food every time Harold went.

"Uncle-Harold, come and look! Aunty-Emmy has given me my very own greenhouse to look after. Can I have a stinky water tub in the back garden please? For my greenhouse." Harold looked over at Sharyn as a small hand tugged him towards the conservatory only to see a shrug and a smirk.

"I'm not sure about a tub of stinky water, not next to the house. You'll have to check with Mummy." Harold stopped in the doorway to the conservatory, staring at the rows of trays and plant pots full of greenery. "Cripes. I thought you had one plant?"

Daisy pointed at a bright red plant pot. "That one is my practice plant, then if I don't kill it I can have more. We need more shelves though, Aunty-Emmy said so. To Mummy but I heard her. Can you put up shelves please? Can I help?" Harold rolled his eyes and gave up any thought of resting his aching back.

"I'll need some tools and wood. I'd suppose we'd better include Wills or he'll complain." Inspiration struck. "He could be your helper in here. You can train him not to spill stinky water or trek mud inside." Hopefully training Wills to be careful would mean Daisy remembered to do the same. By the time they were called through for tea Harold really hoped those plants were hardy, considering the amount of inspection and 'care' they were receiving. Though none of them would ever be eaten by a bug or caterpillar with two very keen pairs of eyes watching over them. Both four-year-old Wills and Daisy seemed very happy to be included in the gardening and hopefully they'd work off some energy there.

*   *   *

A week after Daisy started her gardening apprenticeship, and well over a hundred miles northeast, the improvement in gardening conditions brought smiles to the faces around the table in the bunker. "Sunshine at last. I trust the farmers are out there making hay, or at least something to put in my marts for the scum to eat?" Ivy smiled sourly. "Yes I know some fresh food has arrived but not enough and we are still having to scrape the mouldering remains of last year out of storage."

"Not for long Ivy. As a plus I am assured that unless we get some really terrible weather everything will grow very well because of the extra moisture and milder temperatures. The increase in arrested gardeners is noted with gratitude, especially that influx from the marts. Arresting them for shoplifting was very effective, Ivy." Henry nodded his thanks to Grace as well. "Ask no questions and all that, Grace, but however you are motivating the gardeners seems to be working really well from the reports coming back. Very few are failing, though we still have a steady wastage of scum in their work gangs who can't understand the consequences." Henry sat back. "I really believe we have a chance of hitting the food production targets this year."

Owen, the chairman, nodded. "Just in case your increase in crops isn't big enough, we will make plans to close down another city. We considered the second largest, Birmingham, but Joshua wants something more manageable for the first trial of the civilian contractors. We are looking at these." The map came up on the screen with five cities highlighted. "These all originally held about half a million people, though now they only have twenty percent of that or probably a lot less left. Any comments?"

"Not Edinburgh. If the animals are pushed like that, some may break into the castle and free some very embarrassing prisoners. Even if they're killed instead of freed the Armed Forces may become restless. Having their commander-in-chief tucked away safe, recovering from wounds, stops any hotheads and gives us legitimacy." Faraz, the RAF liaison, shrugged. "Especially with the feral population of Edinburgh stopping any closer scrutiny."

"Not Bradford or Sheffield, not for a trial run. If this goes wrong there's half a dozen big population centres nearby and if their containment is breached we'll lose Lincolnshire at least." Henry glanced upwards. "Not only is Lincolnshire a breadbasket but that could be personally very embarrassing, possibly fatal." The rest glanced upwards briefly.

"There's one where we could allow a breakout when the weather is really bad, if you can wait until winter? They'll be heading into wilderness, but nicely contained so we can use artillery without destroying anything useful. As a bonus the buildings in the city should be in a better condition if there's no actual fighting around them." Joshua highlighted one location. "If we can ensure they go north?"

Owen chuckled. "An excellent solution that allows the terrain deal with survivors, especially bearing in mind Henry's point. Better yet, if they break out we won't be left with another London needing a permanent garrison. Are you sure the training of Grace's people is finished, Joshua?"

"They came along well enough for us to push on to a second stage. The civilian contractors are currently clearing out the unflooded areas of York which means the whole eastern area of England from Middlesbrough to south of The Wash will be cleared of scum. Apart from Hull, but that isn't big enough to be a problem so we can clear the place next year." Joshua grimaced. "Vanna's civilian contractors are processing the population from York without all the bother of feeding or accommodating them."

"I did point out that even if they weren't really soldiers, they would do the jobs your Army boys wouldn't." Vanna smirked. "We reopened one of the special facilities so the clean-up won't take long. Does this mean the Army can move further west, letting the tractors spread out?"

"Yes, their new line will run south from just above Leeds." Joshua highlighted a road running down the country, cutting off the eastern, less populated third of the country.

"Have you enough tanks?" Ivy ran her eyes over the map. "That's a long stretch of road to seal off, about two hundred miles."

Joshua shrugged. "Lighter armoured vehicles will carry out the actual patrolling. We couldn't pull the heavy armour from the Middle East or Ukraine before the balloon went up. Now we must optimise what we have. We are pulling more vehicles out of storage and training crews as fast as possible."

Ivy smiled happily. "We should be able to roll straight up the country once that's done, to finish the culling. We've already achieved one major objective by reducing power consumption to what can be produced by eco-generation."

"About time we achieved one of them at least."

Joshua ignored Boris's sullen comment. "We won't be able to use most of the vehicles for culling cities. They are light reconnaissance vehicles, only useful for protecting convoys or sweeping the approaches clear on a motorway because the vehicles must avoid close action." He looked around the table. "We weren't able to get our heavy fighting vehicles out of the Middle East or the Ukraine before the plan went into action, or we might have tipped someone off. At least let the army reactivate the rest of the mothballed heavy armour before pushing for more attacks. Many of the large population centres are concentrated." He outlined a group of cities. "I suggest we leave this central and north-western part of England until last."

"I have no problem with that. The current progress is excellent because the tractors can move into much more farmland." Henry looked at the map. "Wales or Cornwall would be my choice for the next area targets?"

Owen chuckled. "Steady down Henry. First we shut off supplies to a major population because new areas won't produce food this year even if you can use tractors. Demand must go down. Christmas, Joshua?"

"As long as I can use Vanna's people in the Army posts during the initial revolt, rather than lose more soldiers? If Vanna can sort out people she can spare, clean house a bit?" Vanna nodded. "Then we'll organise everything before Christmas. Will there be plenty of transport?" Joshua turned to Gerard.

"Yes but try to keep movement to a minimum because the Falklands refinery will be some time yet as explained. Ways around the problem have been found but fuel and food won't start arriving until late autumn. There simply isn't the spare fuel to ship large amounts before then." Gerard shrugged. "We are bringing one big cargo ship full of coffee beans over or there'll be riots. Ivy assures me the preparation will concentrate on quantity rather than quality but one load should be enough."

Ivy sighed. "Perhaps, but there are other imports in very short supply. What about tea? We are bagging up the dust from the warehouses at the moment. We've had to improvise which means at least half the leaf in there is not tea. Perhaps tea can be brought from South America, in the same convoy?"

"Good point Ivy, after all if the marts run out entirely we may have to deal with unplanned riots. Please consult where necessary to work out the minimum of both tea and coffee needed to supply the marts into the New Year. The emphasis should once again be on quantity not quality." Owen raised his cup. "For most of it. Will the meat products hold out over winter if we cut out another city?"

The red-haired woman shrugged. "We've got just about enough frozen pork left to give a hint of flavour. One less major city to feed will definitely help. We cram any sort of meat in the dried or paste products of course, but must have pork to provide the taste in spam." She grimaced. "I don't care about most of the consequences of not enough fat but vitamin deficiencies and widespread depression could cause massive rioting. We have to provide them with a balanced diet, because too many of the enclosed populations are reading up about dietary deficiencies."

"If there are further problems with supply, I really don't care what you put in their food to keep them quiet short-term. On second thoughts, don't put people in there. The packers might get upset if a relative turns up for mincing." Owen laughed but some seemed uncertain if he really was joking. "The navy can lay up a battleship to provide fuel for cargo ships to move coffee beans, tea, and probably beans for chocolate since we don't want half the population up in arms. Maurice, if you would start preparations for Joshua's clearance operation this winter? Let him know if someone might be a problem and the snipers will deal with him."

"Or her. There are some truly impressive women appearing as leaders. I can prepare, but might need a trigger, something for the final push." Maurice frowned. "Stopping tea, beer and coffee works for triggering mart attacks, but to get them out of the city might need more?"

"Give that some thought. Let us know if you need anything extra. Now Gerard, how is diesel going to actually restrict Joshua, or food distribution?" The meeting bent over their files.

As they left Owen delayed Maurice. "How are the traumatised coming along?"

"Promising. Give me six months, because this isn't a precise art, but then we should have a control method perfected." Maurice hurried to catch up with the Vanna, to discuss ways of improving the collection of information from the enclaves.

* * *

The current problem in one enclave wouldn't really concern the cabal. Emmy headed towards Harold's house with an expression that meant trouble. He briefly considered hiding but she'd already spotted him. "Don't blame me. Those shelves were fine for plants but not for children to climb." Daisy and Wills had chased each other up Harold's shelving in the conservatory, pulling about half of it off the wall. Allegedly they had been hunting a really hungry, nasty bug.

"That's not a problem. We've already put the plants back into pots and watered them in. I doubt we'll lose more than a handful. What I need right now is your glower." Emmy beamed. "But first I want your lawn."

"Lawns again? I thought we decided that the acreage out there could feed us all." Harold frowned and skipped the next bit, about what Curtis said. "Won't it?"

"Maybe, if everything grows properly. Curtis worried because if we lose some to a pest or a disease, the rest won't be enough. I've been thinking about that." Emmy brandished a broken roof slate. "Look, it's all worked out."

Harold looked at the chalk drawing on the slate, showing stick people moving little plants here and there following arrows. "I give in, I'm baffled. Though Daisy will love it." He ducked but too late to avoid a gentle clip on the head.

"The seedlings are reared in here, in conservatories and greenhouses, but then they need hardening outside. Not only that but we need the space in greenhouses to start more seeds. Outside the walls the poor seedlings will be subjected to an onslaught of rabbits and birds." Harold nodded since that cleared up what those little squiggly things were. "Inside Orchard Close we have no rabbits and the birds have to be careful because of cats. Better yet, we can keep a closer lookout for caterpillars and leaf miners, and a list of other disgusting little critturs in my gardening book."

Harold looked round with a sinking feeling of inevitability. "How many lawns? Most of the back gardens are already under veg."

"Not much over half the back gardens have been dug up yet, but even if they are all used it isn't enough. We need all the lawns at the front as well. This way we can plant oodles of everything then if some fail we've either got new seedlings coming through, or extra hardened plants. When the last ones go out into the fields a few more can mature in here as a final crop before winter. With the three cellars in here and those big houses with cellars outside the walls we can store the extra, especially since some veggies won't want freezing or preserving." Emmy stopped to wait while Harold caught up. Unfortunately that all sounded perfectly logical, which wouldn't matter to some.

"I'll ask."

"Glower and tell them."

"I'll ask."

"Wimp." Emmy smiled. "I'll cry?"

"I'll ask."

Harold asked, but just a selected few at first. "I don't care." Liz waved her hands round her forge. "I prefer soot and beating on iron." She frowned. "You'll need lots of backup, especially from the originals." Then she patted Harold on the shoulder and smirked. "The rest of the residents came through that gate under an agreement to do as you told them. Try Casper next because he's a pushover."

Casper agreed that as the Orchard Fairy he would stand behind Harold and loom, especially since the grass among the trees would be staying. "Though what about the dogs? You know, toilet walks. Rascal isn't up to walking as far as the other end of his garden let alone outside the walls."

"None of them wait to get to the ruins anyway. I have to carry a plastic seaside spade because Angel thinks anyplace outside the door is good enough." Harold paused. "Which is better than the alternative."

"Everyone carries a plastic spade when walking dogs, to bury the poop even out in the ruins. Especially after that bit in the books about an infection that gives kids an eye disease." Casper shrugged. "Offer the objectors one lawn for sunbathing or communing with nature, but not for dogs." He frowned. "I'm not sure Patty will go for it because veggies aren't her thing. She puts crumbs on the grass to attract pigeons so she can stick arrows in them."

Despite being a dedicated carnivore, Patty could see the benefits of spare veggies. Others came round when told that this was a 'Curtis said' issue, since Emmy didn't really rationalise too well over those. This wasn't the subject to oppose her over, because digging up lawns actually made sense, or it did to most. Harold finally decided he'd rounded up enough support from the originals, and called the rest together. Despite what Liz said, once he'd explained the residents didn't seem very obedient.

"But the kids need someplace to play."

"They can run around in the orchard."

"That'll also keep the birds off the blossom and young fruit."

"I thought the grass from the lawns made compost?"

"Dirty cabbage leaves or peelings from veggies work as well. We can collect more greenery from the ruins."

"But I want to sit on the grass sometimes."

"When?"

"Why?"

"Like a picnic, but not in a jungle out there where some scroat might shoot me?"

"I fancy that."

"Especially if we get some sun."

Harold finally got a word in. "If you can have one lawn, where will it be?"

"In the middle where we can reach it."

"At the back out of sight."

"Not for sunbathing. To eat. Outside the canteen?"

"Is that big enough?"

"The scroats might join us."

"But they'll be good, and we might civilise a couple."

"Some of us have civilised a couple already, so to speak."

"Slut."

Harold headed off that argument, about who spoke to gangsters and who wouldn't. "Right, enough. One lawn, a big one, across the front of the canteen. The rest get dug up to provide veggie kindergarten."

"I want to keep some grass at the back."

"I've spent hours on my lawn and just got it right."

"We could agree to differ? Anyone keeping a lawn gets less food if there's a shortage." Eyes centred on Cristopher, one of those fleeing trouble in the north the previous year, and he blushed. "Just saying."

"Sounds fair to me."

"I'm not going hungry for grass."

"Is that right, what he said?"

Harold shrugged. "Most of us have been hungry at one time or another. There were plenty of lawns about but they didn't help much?" He smiled. "If you all clear a big enough area of derelict housing out there I'll let you grow grass on a similar sized patch near the walls. Then you can play football or sunbathe if you like."

"Or both? I'll clear it all myself by hand if the girl club will play football in bathing suits."

"In your dreams Billy."

"In all his dreams."

"I'm up for that." Fergie grinned. "Get digging lads."

The meeting broke up in a lot of teasing about what the grass might be used for. "Did I get agreement?" Harold smiled. "I didn't have to glower."

"Not yet. Wait until it sinks in." Emmy smirked. "But you can glower the objectors into submission one at a time now."

Harold didn't have to go that far, but he had to lurk with a frown a few times while others pressed the point. Most gave in relatively gracefully when a team with forks and spades descended on their garden. Though Harold stamped on an attempt to make the football pitch right now because all the rest of the planting had to be done first. As the days lengthened the clearance volunteers would be able to get started, after their day in the fields.

The little plants in Harold's conservatory went into his garden, and more tiny green shoots filled the shelves. At least tending them all kept both Daisy and Wills partly occupied, especially when Sharyn surrendered and allowed stinky water tubs in the garden. As yet the concoction had a lid on while the mixture of old leaves and rainwater brewed. Harold began to relax, which turned out to be a mistake.

*   *   *

Alfie held up his hands in half-hearted self-defence. "Emmy said she was going to check something. It's Emmy. I'm not exactly going to say no?"

Harold scowled. "Nor me probably, but she shouldn't have gone on her own. Did she say where?"

"Patty went with her carrying that monster crossbow but I've no idea where they were going. They both had packs for some reason?"

Alfie looked relieved when Liz spoke up from behind Harold. "Don't worry, she's not gone gangster hunting. She's not even taken a rifle."

"Why not? If she's gone..." Harold stopped. "Not gangster hunting? Where have they gone?"

"Calm down. Emmy said she wanted that crossbow and aluminium bat from the mart attack, then if someone recognised either she'd take them into a dark corner to ask questions." Liz shrugged. "See, no problem."

"No problem? That's across Hot Rods territory! One report of Emmy's hair or Patty's crossbow and Caddi will hunt them down." Harold looked towards the south. "Now it's dark so I'll never find them."

"You charging about out there wouldn't help them hide, would it?" Liz sighed. "Are you going to trust them or do I have to beat on you, then get Sharyn and possibly Sooty."

"Sooty?"

"Well she couldn't take him with her so he'll be worried and need the relief?" Liz threw up her hands. "Cripes Harold, Emmy isn't going to run off and do something stupid with the baby and Sooty to worry about. They'll lay up tomorrow and come back in the dark. She needs this because Emmy can't beat up half a dozen scroats and execute one." Liz smirked. "They're too well-behaved these days after your little temper tantrum. Neither of you two wimps could have stopped Emmy or Patty anyway."

Harold thought of pointing out that Emmy was already doing something stupid, but that would be a waste of breath. "True. Back tomorrow night?" If they weren't, Harold would be gangster hunting rather than wait for Caddi to smirk before producing Patty's crossbow or Emmy's plaits.

"They promised. Now act as normal as you can remember how to. Go and growl at someone or draw an elephant for Daisy." Liz turned away. "I'm going to make a celebratory head for the new crossbow when it arrives, something intricate to keep me occupied. The hardened points for you are boring."

*   *   *

Though Harold didn't draw an elephant, not this time, because Daisy's ship had crashed at night. "The Red Cross Elephant can't find them Uncle-Harry. Who can rescue the cats now?" From the happy smile Daisy wasn't too worried, she just wanted something new. "There are no see-in-the-dark goggles in pirate cat-and-dog land."

Harold silently cursed whoever had shown Daisy the infrared headsets, or he might have got away with that. "How about the Red Cross Owl, or Bat? They've got night vision." The sound of stifled giggles from Sharyn wasn't helpful.

Daisy thought hard. "The cats need the Red Cross Bat. Maybe we can have a Red Cross Shark for the ones in the water?" Her big grin meant Daisy knew that wasn't a good idea.

"When did you learn about sharks?"

"At school. They've got big gnashy teeth like the pumpkin monster but bigger."

"That'll frighten the cats in the water. The Red Cross Bat can swoop down to scoop them up." Harold did his level best to draw a bat with crosses on his wings, because he really didn't fancy trying for a shark if Daisy had seen a picture of a real one.

"Brill. Georgina says Brill. Her Cindy Doll is called Brill now because she asked for sanctuary at the gate." Which meant the recent spat with Georgina must be over but the rest startled Harold. The kids were getting a really strange idea of how the world worked. Daisy set into drawing lots of smaller bats, then began to draw little anchors on each, with a bit of rope hanging down.

"What are those for?"

"The crossbows? Because these are Patty Bats. They are an escort so the scroats don't get the Red Cross Bat in the dark. They've all got their biggest needle loaded. See, there's the wool." Harold did his best to keep a straight face but behind him Sharyn gave up. With a strangled squeak she headed for the kitchen where she could descend into hysterical laughter in some sort of privacy.

Harold had to wait until all the cats were rescued, and he'd told a Daisy-story. He came downstairs to be met by a grinning face. "Patty Bats or Batty Pattys?" Harold had his own hysterics, smothered by a cushion so Daisy didn't come to investigate. That took care of his nerves for a while.

* * *

Harold sort of slept, then worried and weeded all day. He arrived at the guardhouse by the gate as dusk descended. "Did anyone hear anything?"

"No Harold, nor the fifty other times you asked on the phone. Hilda said she left the nearest guardhouse to the garden jacked into this one permanently to save time." Bernie pointed at the phone. "I'll let her know you're done now."

"You may as well do that on the way home. I'll finish your shift."

"Great, I can get home early. Shout if I'm needed." Bernie headed out of the door at speed. Harold settled the infrared headset and made his first sweep of the caravan park and buildings beyond, the first of many as the night dragged slowly by. Midnight came and went, and Harold started to really worry but there'd been no gunfire from the direction of the mart.

The two hot spots appearing and disappearing in the ruins to the south were an immense relief. Harold reached for the phone. "Hi Faith, they're coming in, or at least two people are being sneaky from the right direction. Let the others know please. Sorry about waking you."

"It's all right Harold. I've been worrying too much to go to bed." Harold went back to using the headset, searching left and right for pursuers. The couple looked right for size and eventually he could see them clearly. Not clearly enough for identification even as they walked up the access since both wore hooded jackets, but he was sure. Not just from Patty's crossbow and the size of Emmy, but what other two women would be wandering around in the night armed to the teeth and wearing short skirts?

"Cooee. The password is stick a scroat."

"The password is naughty girls." Emmy's head came up and Harold saw the white of teeth as she grinned. "No, that doesn't get anyone spanked. I suppose you expect us to open the gate so you don't have to walk round the back?" Harold couldn't be angry at the pair because he felt too happy about them being safe. Alfie and Jeremy were laughing and already heaving the gate open to let the pair in.

"We are the naughty girls is a song. Though now I think about it maybe it's cheeky girls? It's on one of those old CDs." Patty laughed as the pair came in waving their weapons. "We fixed that little problem, Harold. No more scroats in ambush."

"Stop shouting. I'll come down, no, I'm on watch." Hands lifted the headset from Harold's head and he turned to find Matti.

"Go on. I'll get the gory details later. Jeremy is on duty anyway so I may as well stay here." Matti and Jeremy were fast approaching confetti and garter time, ever since she'd nursed him after Jeremy's broken nose.

"Ta." Harold clattered down the stairs to where the pair were waiting with huge smiles. They'd brought the aluminium baseball bat, knives, the machete, and the crossbow.

"Wait up." Liz came down the road waving hello. "I want to know as well." Harold waited while a half dozen others arrived.

"Solved what scroat problem? You do know I almost had a heart attack worrying about you?" Emmy grabbed him in a bear hug. "Ouch. Remove some heavy metal first, please."

"Grouch. Just because we had all the fun." Emmy grinned. "What did the mart guard say about the houses, why they were still there?"

"Because it was too expensive to knock them down?" Emmy and Patty shook their heads so Harold thought again. "Oh, cripes. Because nobody ever shot at them from there. You didn't?" Harold looked at them. "You did." Both nodded. "You stupid… oh hell, you got away with it so I can't even be cross now."

"We were going to stick a crossbow bolt in the tower at dusk, as a hint, but guess who came on duty?" Patty beamed. "Laughing boy."

"How did you know it was him if it was getting dark?" Harold sniggered. "Because you're a Bat? A Patty Bat?" He straightened his face. "Did you kill him? How the hell did you get away?"

"He came on duty in daylight, late afternoon. How he feels depends on those vest things they wear. I used the pathetic heads that came with the other crossbow, since Liz's work is distinctive." Patty grinned and Liz smirked but Harold winced, the bolts with the crossbow were genuine pre-crash hunting heads. "I definitely hit the scroat." Patty preened. "I practice."

"Then we ran away very fast for two or three hundred yards. We nipped into a house, broke down the crossbows to put them in the packs, then went for a stroll." Harold opened his mouth and Emmy waggled her leg, pointing to her exposed knee. "Very obviously two women going for a stroll in the late afternoon, hand in hand."

"Hand in hand?" Harold looked at Liz, laughing like a loon and holding onto Alfie to keep upright. "Why?"

Liz managed to speak. "Two women, hand in hand. Possibly looking for privacy for the night?"

"Yup. A helicopter came over. Presumably the Army weren't impressed with what happened either. We hugged and waved." Emmy's grin hadn't wavered.

Neither had Patty's. "We walked a bit further away then went into a wrecked house before any Hot Rods came looking for the cause of the ruckus. We stayed there until well after dark with loaded crossbows and a bad attitude." Patty shrugged. "Nobody visited so we came home."

"Bet they knock those bloody houses down now, bastards." Emmy put out a hand. "Come on, girlfriend. I've got a Sooty boy waiting, and then I'm going to sleep for a whole day."

"That's not fair on Liz. A Sooty boy?" Patty took her hand. "People will talk."

Emmy laughed. "Some will talk about knocking down houses."

"Are you done now, or do you want to nip over to the Mansion and apple-pie Caddi's bed?" Harold tried to look stern. "I thought you got yourself straight at Easter or is my shoulder failing at last?"

Emmy grinned. "The shoulder worked great, but I needed just a little something more this time." Emmy and Patty skipped off down the street singing 'we are the naughty girls' leaving everyone else laughing. Harold realised a good bit of their behaviour had to be relief at getting away with it but he also had a big grin, as had most of Orchard Close over the next few days.

*   *   *

Caddi didn't have a grin three days later when he came to collect his repaired guns. "The Mart knocked down a quarter mile wide strip of my buildings as well as their houses. Now I can't get to the bloody mart without going through the neutral zone that the other gangs use. The houses lining that road have strays lurking, so I have to send bodyguards every time someone nips to the bloody shops in case they meet with an accident." He paused. "The mart guards reckoned somebody hit one of them with a crossbow bolt from a house full of very old bodies." The gang boss scowled at Patty. "Not one of your bolts, an ordinary hunting head though it blew through his vest. They aren't happy about that because their own tests reckoned a crossbow wouldn't penetrate from there."

Harold didn't think the mart had used a monster weapon like Patty's, a one-off trial version. The big weapon drove bolts into targets much further than any of the pre-crash crossbows they'd tried, or even the recent Geek versions. "You seem to have a lot of detail about the marts and guards? Just how friendly are you?" Harold's paranoia suddenly wondered if that might be why the mart guard didn't care about the scroat with a crossbow.

"Not friendly at all. The two young ladies who sell their favours to mart guards are very good friends of mine. They bring me every bit of information the idiots let slip." Caddi smirked. "They bring most of their earnings as well, but it's the information that's sometimes worth more. I've even got some news for you. I reckon you'd have lost your man anyway because the marts have been told to arrest any gardener for shoplifting, even if they aren't doing any."

"Cripes."

"At the very least. They're also after ladies of easy virtue, but my pair are safe because the guards don't want them taken." Caddi frowned. "I'm not sure why they're taking the crazies as well, but I've pushed a few that way because they're just a waste of space. Maybe they just get a bullet and turn into fertiliser."

"We could do with fertiliser, but not badly enough to put you and your escort under our veggies." Harold smiled at Caddi's sharp look. "Have you got any real fertiliser?"

"No, and there's none in the mart." The gang boss raised his beer bottle. "At least they keep the hops and barley coming, and their crap beer. Though some of my lot reckon it's a toss-up if ours or the mart beer is worse. The coffee is really rough now." Caddi smirked. "So I'm told. Luckily I have pre-crash stocks."

"The tea is rough as well, but drinkable." Harold raised his bottle. "Luckily, we have good beer."

"Smartarse. Yes I'll want a couple of crates and I've even brought bottles."

"Be careful they don't get broken on the way back, if someone takes a shot at you?"

"Cooper told you we'd look and we did. There was no sign of who it was or where they went. Maybe one of the others wanted me to get the blame?" Caddi shrugged. "You could stop over if it gets dark again?"

"So you could film me in my underwear?"

Caddi grinned and didn't quite look at Patty. "Not you. We keep hoping you'll bring a bodyguard." Patty ignored him, as did Harold as he settled down to persuade Caddi the additional charges for guns and two repaired radios were worth it. After Caddi left he passed on the news that he hadn't been able to trade for fertiliser which set Emmy worrying, though learning that laughing boy had died cheered her up.

Chapter 3:

Getting Medieval

Emmy kept on worrying about fertiliser, though Harold didn't realise how much until he found a small deputation waiting after the next mart trip, a week later. "Sorry, no fertiliser Emmy." Harold looked at the half dozen gardeners behind her and frowned. "What's with the hats?"

"We are the garden gnomes, gnomes are traditional in England." The young man smiled, adjusting the floppy cone-shaped hat so that Harold could read the lettering.

"Gnome, Gnome on the Range? Are you serious?" The big smiles said no, but as each one adjusted their hat Harold could see 'Give a Gnome an 'ome' and 'Omeless Gnome-lass' among a selection of similar gnome phrases. Harold turned to Emmy.

"Not my fault, I promise. I've come because if you've not brought fertiliser we'll need composting toilets. The gardeners need more compost to fertilise the plants and there's oodles, but it's all going down the drains. All we get is the odd bowl of mucky water when someone washes pots or peels spuds and chucks it on a garden, that sort of thing." Emmy managed her own version of a glower. "We need a proper supply for the big plots outside."

"But you've got all those plastic tubs we dragged in from various gardens out there. The ones full of stinky water because all those leaves are supposed to be good for plants. There's oodles of those." Harold stopped. "Who started the oodles?"

"Liz started the cripes. Maybe all and any gods are responsible, though Patty says it's an infection because all the new refugees catch the cripes really quickly. Now what about my fertiliser, or rather my toilets?"

"They'll stink. You can have the bathwater though it'll be a bitch to bucket it out and carry it downstairs." Harold grinned. "Though if you do it still wrapped in your towel there'll be volunteers."

"Behave. I can't help the effect I have on the bad boys." Emmy smiled. "You're wrong though, we don't have to bucket anything. We, me and Curtis, worked it all out." She brought out a drawing, on paper this time. "We'll need Rob to do magical piping things, and buckets for the downstairs sinks, but this will catch even shower water. Before you ask, as long as nobody gets bleach in the water the soap doesn't matter. The toilets won't stink."

"Even if that lot works, where do we keep it all?" Harold watched her big beaming smile and it didn't falter. "More big tubs from the gardens in the ruins?" Emmy nodded but Harold now looked puzzled, because that didn't add up. "I know I get a bit grubby, but I can't see there being enough muck in my shower water to provide a meal for a baby lettuce. So are you after something to fertilise the plants, or the water?"

"Yes. The plants need the dirtiest water possible, but more than that they need water. Curtis complained last year that we couldn't get the best results because the rain stopped over summer. Well, it didn't stop but there wasn't enough." She smiled happily, flourishing the paper. "We can throw leaves and peelings in the water or put them all on compost heaps but either way we need this, Harold. The difference between a small potato and a big potato is how much it drinks. Composting toilets will mean using less leaves and stinky water and grow even better everything."

Harold thought about it, but not for long. "You win but we won't find enough containers to store the rainwater and the bathwater as well. No to the toilets because they will stink. Probably yes to that drawing after a sanity check from Rob, or you'll cry until I give in."

"OK." Emmy turned and left, talking quickly and quietly to her gnomes. Harold looked at the drawing, briefly before taking it to an expert. Though as he walked to Rob's house Harold worried about why Emmy had given up on the toilets so easily.

* * *

Harold sat drinking weak tea without sugar while Rob looked at the drawings and notes, and scribbled on a slate with a piece of chalk. Paper cost coupons, whereas slate from a roof and the right bit of stone from a garden path did the same job for temporary scribblings. Daisy often drew on slate, or on the backs of labels taken from cans or food packets, though she still had some colouring books that weren't finished. Eventually Rob sat back with a sigh.

"We can do it, or most of it. This will cost some serious scavenging and a lot of work, but if we really need the waste water then we can capture it." He tapped the drawing. "This won't all work as drawn, but there's ways." He smiled. "If Emmy wasn't pregnant I'd wonder what they did for fun because this took a hell of a lot of dedicated working out."

"How much will we catch? Will there be enough tubs to capture enough?" Harold frowned. "Some of the metal containers out there have already rusted through."

"With a bit of judicious redirection we can get some of this water into the unused sewers outside the walls. I'll seal those off so they don't drain away any more, which makes them into an underground tank. The gardeners can bucket it back out of a manhole as required." Rob frowned. "Get me enough down-spouting and we can pipe everything from the perimeter houses out across the fields. We'll have to line some holes to hold it where the drains are knackered."

"There's garden ponds here and there in the ruins that still hold water. A good few will be those fibreglass things which we can dig up." Harold frowned. "We can use old baths as well though we'll have to sink them into the ground so they don't provide cover for scroats. How far can you get the waste water to run?"

"Starting from upstairs? As far as the fields go I reckon. We can use the whole sewer system under those six houses out there as a reservoir since we don't use the houses to live in." Rob looked at his slate. "I don't know where those drains run to. I'll have to find a good spot to break in and seal that main."

"Don't do that. I had a discussion a bit back about one day needing them for people to live in." Harold grinned. "There again, they can use composting toilets. It'll make Emmy happy and we won't smell them here."

"Whew, I hope not." Susan looked over Rob's shoulder. "That looks like one of those Monty Python things where the pipes grew and grew, or was it a kid's game? Mousetrap?" She cocked her head one way and then the other, peering at it. "Definitely a Heath Robinson contraption."

"Nope, a Curtis contraption which means Emmy will personally build it then cry if it doesn't work, unless I fix this so it does." Rob smiled. "Which means everyone else will cry as they stagger round the ruins removing plumbing of all sizes and types, with great care." He glanced at Harold. "I'll start a list if we are really going for it?"

Harold sighed in resignation. "I can't get fertiliser anywhere. This will allegedly deliver our dirty water to thirsty plants. It will stave off demands for composting toilets because Emmy can throw leaves and peelings in the water, if we've gathered enough. I think, because I'm not exactly Monty Don."

"The alternative is composting toilets? I'm sold on this idea." Susan kissed Rob. "So is he."

Harold looked at the drawing, then gave up trying to work it out. "Is there any way you can keep the rainwater separated, and clean. We still get water through our taps, but it just crossed my mind how much trouble we'd be in if that stopped during a dry spell."

Susan and Rob stared aghast, until Rob found his voice. "Cripes Harold, I really wish you hadn't shared that little gem." He hugged Susan. "Don't worry, love, now Mr. Doom and Gloom has mentioned it I'll fix it." He turned back to Harold. "I'll make sure the rainwater goes into lovely clean containers. The header tanks in the lofts will be ideal, but we'll need a lot."

"I'm not really happy I suddenly thought about the water being cut off, but I feel a bit better now." Harold walked home wondering about electricity, but decided he'd been paranoid enough over water. There'd never been a problem with either except a few surges in the electricity, and a couple of power cuts after storms.

*   *   *

Over the following two days everyone agreed that gathering plumbing supplies, plastic tubs and garden ponds beat the hell out of composting toilets in their houses. Harold had a shock when his workforce assembled because over eighty people gathered with determined faces and any tools they could come up with. The workforce included the teenage schoolchildren, because they were allegedly having a plumbing and scavenging lesson. Harold would have worried about the safety of Orchard Close but the guardhouses were manned with plenty of spare weaponry and ammunition and very little tolerance today.

"Anyone coming is a threat, right? I sent the spies home to tell Caddi we're shut for a week and bloody touchy about it. Messages have gone back to the Geeks, GOFS and Barbies with any of their people who were visiting over the last three days. Nobody else should be arriving."

"I've got it Harold. I'd come with you but the Coven won't let me." Emmy stroked her baby-bump. "I'm definitely short-tempered, and junior won't stop me shooting." She flashed a brilliant smile. "Thank you Harold. I promise oodles of good stuff on the tables in return?"

"You and your gnomes?" Harold nodded cheerio to the other guards up at the guardhouse windows and waved the crowd to follow him. The scavengers looked like an army crossing the cultivated area. What followed definitely resembled looting and pillaging.

The sheer volume of plastic guttering and piping coming off houses and the number of plastic tubs of all sizes being uncovered in gardens, sheds and lofts overwhelmed them in the end. The amount of baths, header tanks, boiler tanks, copper tube and fittings coming out of the houses didn't take up quite as much room but needed gentler treatment. Harold finally agreed to use precious diesel as well as the failing petrol vehicles to collect everything. Stacks of plastic and copper built up outside the main gates of Orchard Close, with more piles in the group of six houses

As the line of pillagers moved across the ruined and abandoned housing, they started to look more like locusts. The damaged or partly overgrown houses and garages looked bare without their guttering and exterior piping, as did gardens after machetes and feet flattened the new growth. A strange, almost party atmosphere developed in spite of those at the edges of the group being armed and watchful, and guards with binoculars watching from roofs or upstairs windows. Everyone brought sandwiches or snacks and bottles of water so they could have a sort of picnic at lunchtime. For the first time in at least two years and probably longer jokes and laughter rang out amid the desolation.

"I should get out more." Liz waved her machete. "I can use this as long as nothing bleeds." She stopped, staring at a tree stump or what had been one the last time anyone had really paid attention. "Cripes Harold, look how far this has grown. What sort of tree is it?"

"Pass." Harold looked round. "Did anyone find Rachel de Thame hiding in a house here? I need a tree identified."

"Trust you to look for a woman. What about Monty Don, you can find him by following the wheelchair tracks." Liz waved her machete at the clump of thin shoots that towered above her head. "I want to know because look how it's grown. What's the thinnest branch I can make decent charcoal with?"

Harold sniggered. "I never ever expected to ever say this." He raised his voice. "Help, I'm gnomeless. Can someone find me a gnome?"

The young woman with a floppy hat who turned up looked suspicious, probably because Liz and Harold were having to hold each other up. Harold took a deep breath and tried to wipe away the smile. "Hi, er, Gnome-lass?"

"Hah, hah. Tilly. Did you just want to take the piss?"

"No, Liz wants to know what this tree is? She has designs on it and probably any children if we find them." Harold pointed at the stump in question.

"That's a willow. There's a couple more over there. Is that it?"

"No because seriously, this is important. Liz is wondering about growing for charcoal." Harold saw Tilly's eyes sharpen with interest. "She wants to know which trees will grow quickest, especially if they'll make good charcoal. How long will it be before the new branches are big enough?"

"Willow is probably the fastest growing but I can't be certain, or how good it will be for charcoal. They like water so if we plant them in a marshy bit where the water pipes or drains are jiggered they'll grow faster." Tilly eyed up the tree in question. "There might be a way of pruning to make them grow better for what you want."

"Plant them? Curtis said seven years from seed for fruit trees so how long for willow?" Liz frowned. "I can't wait seven years for charcoal."

Tilly took three steps to slash off a shoot, then lopped off about three feet and drove it deep into an overgrown lawn. "Planted. That'll be the size of the original shoot in a year or two." She slashed again, making the remainder into two more lengths. "These will grow but might take longer or need protection from rabbits?"

Liz beamed. "How old is this stump? When did we lumberjack here, Harold?"

"A year ago? Less than eighteen months." Harold looked at the piece driven into the ground and then the shoots going up above his head. "Cripes, we could grow our own forest." He frowned. "We'll have to watch out for rustlers."

"First we ought to check the lumberjack sites." Liz looked around.

"We'll take note as we finish this job, a few days won't matter." Harold looked around. "Then Tilly gnome-lass gets all the info. After that we plant some trees, but we make damn sure they're where we can keep an eye on them."

"I'll ask the rest. Some of them really were garden gnomes in training before the crash, amateur gardeners or just interested." Tilly frowned. "I'll check with Emmy and then try the library. I'll bet there's something on types of trees used for coppicing." Tilly pointed at the stump. "That used to be done deliberately for eco-fuel which is how I know about willow."

"Sorted." Liz waved her machete. "Now I suppose we'd better get on with the piping or you'll be reporting us. Then Emmy will make us mulch as a penance."

Tilly looked at the two smiling faces. "Do you even know what mulching is?"

"No but it sounds disgusting." Tilly shook her head at the two of them and went back to work.

Five days later Rob reckoned he'd got more than enough pipe. The next two days were spent carrying everything inside the gates or stacking the plastic gutter and piping neatly among the six big empty houses. Meanwhile a team started on digging up garden ponds, though putting them back into the ground posed a real problem. A problem that needed a shopping trip to the Geeks.

* * *

Two days after the end of the great pipe hunt Harold sat in 'his' diesel pickup, with the petrol one parked just behind. "Remember, everyone be good. I haven't beaten on a Geek for ages so they've no gripe with us just now."

"Hah, they've got a permanent gripe on." Alfie leant forward. "Here they come." Three Geeks walked to the wrecked Burger King sat in the middle of the cleared area. Harold walked to meet them with Casper and Alfie as body-guards.

"Soldier Boy, what a pleasure." Darwin's curled lip didn't even pretend to mean it. "We've arranged another demonstration for you, since it seems Caddi wasn't over-paranoid about snipers. There's a gang leader north of the M6 with a fatal headache, one that arrived from over half a mile away." His eyes narrowed. "Have you been spreading the happiness?"

"Not at all." Though Harold did wonder who was, since Caddi had mentioned something like it a while back. "Sounds like an Army sniper." Or another rifle club man, or possibly a hunter though they weren't common in England.

"Exactly. We took down a few more buildings, but Wellington said an Army sniper might shoot further than that. He also said the bastard might shoot the crew on our trebuchet because they're out in the open so we came up with something else." Darwin looked at his watch and pointed. "Watch over there."

Harold did as asked. A couple of minutes later he heard a tremendous clang from the direction of the Geek HQ and a line of smoke curved down into sight, landing nearly five hundred yards from the compound. Moments later the missile exploded but with more smoke than flame and noise. Harold laughed. "Have you upgraded the thrower?"

"That's a steel catapult using springs from a duff Luton van to throw a pipe bomb. A demo as you put it, because I don't like dodging shrapnel either. It's really called an onager according to Galileo and Tell. It will also throw a lot of bombs but not as far." Darwin smirked. "Any bloody sniper will be blinded by a smokescreen or mincemeat if he's close enough and the crew are out of sight behind a thick brick wall."

"Only if Mr. Sniper is stupid enough to be where that's pointing or lets you see him, otherwise you'll just be using up ammo. Still, it should slow up an actual attack." Harold grinned. "Why isn't it the other side of your patch where you might get one of those?"

The Geek scowled. "Smartarse. Anyway, we haven't got a lot of strife just now, not northwards. The General tried to take the gangs that way but he's fucked because the mart and Army post are near them. He can't use that shitload of automatics near either. The three gangs around the mart have allied to stop him taking over with machetes." Darwin's face split in a smile as he waved towards the dissipating smoke. "If the General fancies coming across the railway cutting, the big crossbow and this thrower will sort the bastard out."

"Couldn't happen to a nicer bloke, especially if you blow up those Bloodsuckers." Harold smiled a little. "Well, fun though this is, I didn't come to talk about your new toys."

"Why are you here, especially with two trucks?"

"We want sand. Nice clean sand. Not the sort you sell us for mortar, just free of stones and rubbish. I know you've got a lot of the other sort in that builder's merchants place and can't really find a use for it, because you keep trying to flog it to me." Harold grinned. "Well now I'm buying some but it'll be cheap."

"You've found a use for it? What?"

"To put under a garden pond. We're landscaping."

"Hah, hah. How much do you want?" Darwin looked at the pickups. "Over a ton if both if those are here. What are you paying with?"

"The gun repairs you've got waiting? A few bobble hats or scarves?" Harold shrugged. "If that's not good enough I'll call on the GOFS or Caddi. Then I'll pay with their coupons."

"Smartarse. Have you got any rhubarb plants for sale?" Darwin scowled. "Some of ours aren't coming up this year. The only reason I can come up with is they've drowned or rotted in the wet. About this time of year some of us would kill for fresh fruit, even bloody rhubarb."

"It'll rot your teeth, though if you'll risk it I'm sure we can find some." Harold knew he could, because the scavenger sweep for pipes had found several rhubarb plants and a few fruit bushes that had been missed the first time round. Having garden gnomes along had been a bonus. "It'll cost though because the mothers back there will play hell. They want fruit for the kids."

"Your lot are all mothers. Hah, the rhubarb won't rot teeth now. We've all eased off on sugar since Einstein had a toothache." Darwin sneered. "He's too frightened to come for treatment so he used pot, tablets, coke and probably crack. Whatever it was fucked him up good." The Geek smirked but then his face sobered. "In the end Hawkins got us to hold him down while he used pliers. Fuck it, that was bad. I'll come to your dentist and risk not waking up if I get a bad tooth after that."

"How is he now?" Harold hoped for dying but didn't expect to be that lucky.

"He's trying to break fuck knows how many addictions and speaking with a lisp. Then it'll cost him a fucking fortune to replace the antibiotics because the bloody Barbies will skin us for them." Darwin grinned. "We gave him a nurse but it didn't work the same as with Wellington. He threw her back afterwards, maybe because he didn't get the same nurse. Wellington has threatened to geld Einstein or anyone else who touches his woman. He's gone all domestic."

"There's benefits. How much medicine have the Barbies got?" Harold smiled. "Apart from some very strong pot." He'd been curious since the mention of medicine and a doctor at the treaty meeting.

"They've got a real chemist shop and an honest-to-god doctor in that shopping centre. The doctor costs a bloody fortune, or rather the advice does because she don't do house visits." Darwin grinned. "Which is smart. But the medicine and advice from the Barbies is spot on, if the patient is worth the price they want." The Geek hesitated, with a little frown. "Will your doc look at someone, at a bad injury? We bought antibiotics but his arm is a mess. We aren't stupid enough to send Galileo to the Barbies because they won't give a hostage for medical. He wouldn't come back."

"How big a mess? Our doc isn't the real thing, just closer than some." Lenny had been a nearly qualified paramedic and Patricia a trainee nurse when both jobs became redundant inside the Army cordon.

"Closer than ours. When Galileo made that onager, something sprang free. It smashed the fuck out of his arm. He won't go to the Army and the camps, but the Barbie doc says it's probably gotta come off if he doesn't get real treatment from a hospital. We'll kill him if we do it but if we don't the Barbie doc reckons the antibiotics will eventually fail and infection will kill him." The Geek paused, then pushed on. "One of your lot lost an arm but she made it, didn't she?" Darwin looked at Harold's stony expression and held up his hands. "Hey, not guilty. None of us know if Einstein set that up, honest." A little smile flitted across his face. "That might be why he didn't want to meet your dentist or be half stoned where your women could ask questions. Well?"

"I'll charge you for a look and a diagnosis, at Orchard Close. We won't give a hostage either and the medical staff will wear balaclavas. If you want an operation it'll work the same as Wellington's tooth. If he gives the women any crap when he's not under anaesthetic I'll hand him over to Emmy. You supply what we ask, we do our best, but if he dies hard luck." Harold glanced towards the Geek compound. "Is this part of the trading for sand?"

"It is now because he'll definitely come to have it looked at. After that it's up to Galileo or maybe what Hawkins will pay." Darwin grinned. "Be more careful driving around in the dark. Your little shit-heap is getting to be really useful. We wouldn't want that fucked up, especially if Caddi got there first."

*   *   *

Harold thought about that on the way back. Darwin seemed genuine, because unlike many of the top Hot Rods the Geeks didn't bother with insincere. They made no secret of how they felt about individuals, but apparently their opinion of Orchard Close as a whole had softened. Maybe not exactly softened, but Darwin wasn't a fan of Orchard Close. If he thought the place might be useful that made some sort of treachery a bit less likely.

Harold also wondered where the General might push next now he'd failed to the north. Harold soon put that to the back of his mind because digging out ponds without damage and then making similarly shaped holes elsewhere turned out to be filthy, tiring work. Lining the holes with sand, so fibreglass garden ponds didn't crack as they filled with water, took enough concentration to clear his mind of anything else.

The following day a Geek car carrying Galileo turned up, along with a Geek soldier whose upper arm had been broken by a bullet. The Geeks escort brought pure morphine, available because Hawkins had confiscated all medicinal drugs after Wellington's treatment. He'd kept the vials and other sealed drugs stolen from either chemists or ambulances, to trade for any future treatment. Lenny had a look at the damage while Patricia and Gayle put on their balaclavas because Galileo paid for full inspection under anaesthetic. Hawkins and Galileo read the report, then asked questions, but eventually agreed to the operation.

Galileo lost most of the use of his left arm when two stainless steel plates were bolted round the bones to sort of hold the mess together. The result might eventually knit but wouldn't take much strain, though his hand actually worked. Galileo reckoned being alive had to be a plus. He talked a little under medication about how he might find a really nice nurse, one like Wellington's with luck. Gayle asked a couple of questions and Galileo wasn't spouting the usual Geek gross. Wellington's personal private nurse volunteered to stop on after the Geek general healed up. Now the Geek general really had threatened to geld anyone who touched her, or deliver them trussed up ready for Emmy to play with.

The soldier, Mathias, seemed bemused by Orchard Close once the residents relaxed after the visiting gangsters went home. Gayle used her dental anaesthetics to put him into la-la land while Patricia and Lenny pulled out bits of crap and splintered bone then lined the rest up properly. Patricia started joking she'd have to take embroidery lessons from Kerry to neaten her stitching. Mathias treated everyone with scrupulous courtesy and went back happy to keep his right arm, even if he would never get full use back again. Five days later, when he left, Galileo mentioned he'd promised to skin Mathias alive if the idiot upset anyone, especially the doctors.

*   *   *

One or two of the Geeks were learning that the Orchard Close residents would be civil if they stayed polite and left their gangster swagger at the gate, though the numbers of Geek visitors stayed low. The Hot Rods varied from behaving well up to an occasional one challenging Harold, who slapped them down hard with his stick. The GOFs seemed the best behaved, visited most, and really did like finding new uses for cripes. The occasional Barbies found the rules funny. They flirted outrageously with men or women or sometimes both, but without being obscene or breaking the touching rules.

The increasing social interactions led to a deputation intercepting Harold, though Patty, Emmy and Liz seemed torn between little smiles and worry. "Cripes. What did I do?"

"Nothing Harold." Liz looked at the other two. They looked back and indicated Harold with their heads. "Wimps." She turned back to Harold. "I know you don't mind someone indulging in a bit of sooty passion?"

"As long as they don't insist on telling me the sweaty details. Why?"

"How do you feel about prostitutes? Paid passion." Liz seemed genuinely interested, not winding him up so Harold thought about it.

He'd never been to a prostitute, but he knew some who had. He'd known at least one prostitute though he'd no idea if Marcie had been typical. "I've never thought about it much. I suppose it's all right if the woman really is voluntary, though there's no real need here, is there? You know, everyone gets fed and has a place to live?"

"There is and isn't a need, Harold." Liz rolled her eyes. "I'd keep quiet but you'd find out. We've already got two on the game, here in Orchard Close." She smiled as Harold frowned, obviously trying to work out who. "They aren't obvious about it. In fact both of them are careful not to advertise, as it were. I'll bet you've talked to both. If you came to dances you'd have danced with them without knowing."

"You won't tell me, will you?"

"If you insist. Both asked if you should get a freebie as your share because you're the boss?" Liz's smile started to shade towards grin.

"No!" Harold glared at the three sniggering women. "Stop it."

"All right, but they need an answer. Can they carry on, or more to the point maybe branch out? At the moment they're getting customers from the single blokes, especially those who get excited after the dances." Liz snorted. "I reckon they should put Doll and Suzie and maybe a couple of the new ones on commission for winding the lads up."

"You said you'd stop taking the mickey. What do you mean by branch out? Stick a red light up outside?" Harold didn't think that would go down well with some residents though he did think that, put like Liz did, two women who were really volunteers wasn't a no. Maybe.

"They want to take customers from among the visitors. Whoa, steady on, they're not stupid." Harold assumed his expression had showed alarm at least. The scroats didn't need encouraging. "You know my weakness. At least one of the other women and a bloke have been sweet-talked into livening up a stopover. I promise this pair will be dead careful over picking potential customers. Any scroat types won't get the option which probably means Geeks and most Hot Rods are out of luck." Liz narrowed her eyes. "The rules about caning or gelding apply to anyone pestering a woman regardless of her profession, don't they?"

"Yes they do." Harold thought hard about the rest. If he refused permission these women would probably carry on anyway. Apparently some others already were so the only difference was the payment. If he said yes there'd be no secrecy which had to be safer for the women. "No red light or standing under lamp posts in a really short skirt with a for rent sign." Harold tried to glower at the smirks but had no effect. "You know what I mean. If they've got a gangster customer they have to tell someone, someone who'll make sure they're OK before the man leaves. They can let the man know that upfront. If he tries to run off without paying, the fine will bankrupt and possibly cripple him." Harold scowled as a thought struck him. "Explain that he really won't like the result if he gets rough. If the bloke still agrees, then OK."

"I'll tell the women." Liz sniggered. "Maybe you should. They'll be really grateful?"

"Smith off. Then you can Gnome off and you can Bat off so I get some peace." The three turned to go, still laughing, though Patty hesitated until the others had moved out of hearing.

"Bat off? You said something about Bats after I stuck laughing boy. Come on, that smirk is having more fun than I am."

"Daisy has a new rescue creature when the ship crashes at night. The Red Cross Bat?" Harold giggled. "He has an escort in case the scroats ambush him in the dark, the Patty Bats with crossbows. They've all got their biggest needle loaded, with a bit of wool hanging down to prove it."

"You nasty little, little, soldier!"

"Hey, not me. Daisy came up with them. Ask Sharyn." Harold knew he wasn't helping his case by laughing, but couldn't help it.

"I will. If I hear a hint you've passed that on I'll get you. Even in the dark." Her lip twitched and she pointed at her eyes. "Patty-eyes." Then Patty set off determinedly towards Harold's house. He went the other way because weeding and slug-bashing might be a better idea than that discussion.

*   *   *

The next deputation looked a cross between embarrassed and wary, but Harold smiled because they were interrupting slug-bashing. "How can I help?"

"You're an atheist, aren't you?" Pat's John, called that to differentiate him from other Johns, looked uneasy. "You don't believe in any God." He hesitated but just before Harold answered, John blurted out, "But what if someone does?"

"Believe in a God? That's up to them." Harold shrugged. "I really don't mind as long as they don't insist on me agreeing."

"But what if they want a church, for prayers?" John's Pat, the first speaker's wife and called that so she wasn't mixed up with other Pats and Patty, took hold of her husband's hand. "What about Sundays? Or saying prayers for the dead?"

"Give me a minute, all right? Just to think it through." Harold did, frantically. "No church, because we can't spare a house. You can use a house occupied by believers if all the residents agree. No crosses on the roof or big signs outside, because I'm not having a dozen sects start up." Harold frowned, thinking hard. "If you want to work longer the other days so you can have a day off, I don't care if it's Wednesday or Sunday. I don't want any hassle from anyone if Moslems or Jews or someone else sets up their own version." He smiled sadly. "As for prayers over the dead, anyone can say what they feel is appropriate. Ask the original residents about Gabriela."

Pat frowned. "Can't we put some sort of a cross up? Maybe on the front?"

"Probably once I've had chance to talk this through with others, but I need time. You can probably put one in a window, just don't ram it down everyone's throat." Harold sighed. "I don't care if you kneel and pray or dance naked round a bonfire as long as you keep it private. Fair warning; I won't change rules based on religious convictions. Now let me go and talk to some other people."

Harold spoke to Sharyn who consulted the Coven, the group of women who dealt with teaching, collecting coupons, making sure everyone had food and clothing, and generally kept the place running. They spoke to the girl club and then assorted others all put in their six-pennorth before coming back with their opinion. Though as Liz pointed out, Harold seemed to have already set the same rules as for the girls on the game; no advertising the premises or blatantly enticing new customers. That did lighten the mood but eventually the rules actually were close to Harold's first attempt. The Coven took on the job of making sure everyone knew that Harold didn't care what anyone worshipped, but his Soldier Boy persona would be annoyed about intolerance.

Most residents were a British sort of religious, not actually interested in organised religion, while a surprising number had been put off believing in any deity by the recent disasters. Harold's all and any gods had sort of gained some adherents who thought that explained the current shambles, though they were a small minority. The Coven turned out to be a mix of religions already. A bit of house shuffling followed and occasionally prayers could be heard from certain houses, but otherwise life moved on.

*   *   *

As an atheist totally disinterested in anyone else's ideas on the subject, Harold turned his attention back to Emmy's demands for waste water with a definite feeling of relief. Almost a month after the first pipes were scavenged the first trials were up and running so Harold went to have a look. Rob pointed to the pipes running down the outside of a house wall, outside the boundary wall, and across the ground between the rows of crops. "See. With the pressure of the water coming from up there, it'll flow right out as far as we've got pipe for. We'll bury a pipe under the road and wall to bring water from the houses further inside Orchard Close."

"Did you manage to keep the clean water in separate containers?" Harold inspected the pipes, but couldn't see how.

Rob nodded as he answered. "The rainwater gutters run back inside through the walls and into the tanks, with an overflow out to join the waste water. There won't be a tremendous amount, just enough to keep body and soul together for a while. I'm more worried about storing enough water for Emmy." Frowning, he pointed towards the end of Orchard Close. "I thought of using the sewer outside the north end of Orchard Close as a reservoir but unfortunately there's a definite whiff from there. Not from our pipes, from the row of ruined terraces outside the wall. Those sewers must be choked up."

Harold frowned as well. "That's a pity. I hoped we could use the houses one day."

"I thought you were going to knock them down because they're too near the walls? I know there's a quarter mile of tarmac and potatoes the other side, but you said the houses were too close to the wall and provided cover for attackers." Rob glanced out at the only other buildings still standing in the fields, the six big houses. "The sewers under those are really useful to collect water for Emmy." He frowned. "You said we might need those houses as well. How many more people do you expect?"

"In time? I've no idea but Emmy talked about three years. There's fruit trees being grown from seed which is a seven year project. If this does go on for years, eventually we'll be full." Harold shrugged. "If we put people in the terraces, they could use the working toilets in the nearest houses? Or you could put up outhouses at the end of the garden plumbed into our sewers?"

"I could do that. It's a shame we won't be able to hang up the traditional squares of newspaper in there. If we cut little shapes out of the door, we could get Patty to knit some cobwebs and crochet spiders to make proper outhouses?" They both laughed. "In any case that's in the future, and I wanted to talk about now." Rob pointed to six men and women laying plastic pipes across the fields. "I've got plenty of apprentices and pipe, but we need more connections. Can you scavenge again through an area we didn't strip the first time, only this time will you concentrate on fittings, joints and bends of any sort?"

"Not a problem. I'll take half a dozen people out and get it sorted, but we'll all come to see you or your apprentice plumbers first. At least they aren't wearing funny hats and making pipe jokes." Harold pointed. "Emmy's lot have brought back real garden gnomes from overgrown gardens, allegedly as scarecrows."

"They've got another idea now. If you ever find any live fish the gnomes want to grow them in those garden ponds, though I'm not really keen on the idea of goldfish and chips." Rob brightened. "Though carp and chips?"

*　　*　　*

Harold had to leave the scavenging a couple of days to deal with a visit by Ogou, picking up a few guns that had been cleaned instead of waiting for the arranged meeting. Ogou brought a woman with toothache, and sat nattering with Harold while she went for treatment. The GOFS paid in coupons for what turned out to be a straightforward drill and fill according to the dentist. Gayle assured Harold they'd asked the woman if she wanted sanctuary. She seemed perfectly happy to go back so perhaps the GOFS were treating some of their women decently after all.

When he originally collected the weapons Harold had wondered if the guns came from further away, maybe the Barbies. The GOFS looked after their weapons better than the Geeks or Hot Rods, but three of the firearms Ogou brought were filthy and had been roughly treated. They turned out to be captures, guns from another small group of fighters running across the flooded ruins on the northern border to escape from the General. Once started, Ogou seemed happy to sit and gossip so Harold took the opportunity to catch up on the local news.

The Barbies had a spat with the Pinkies or Pink Panthers, the male gays, and were triumphantly flaunting the pink lingerie from the casualties. The Pink Panthers had asked for a truce because of pressure the other way from the General. According to Ogou, the Barbies were hoping to trade for underwear without bloodstains because the Pinkies had a Victoria's Secret lingerie store. Further north the MiB, Men in Black, had bounced when they raided the SIMs, a group of apparently ordinary types who had some very good explosives including a wicked short-range rocket. The SIMs now had some really good automatic firearms since the MiB left a few behind. The MiB had allied with the General after that setback.

A gay refugee had told the Pinkies about a gang who had heavyweight fighters in thick black armour wielding long swords and wearing Darth Vader style helmets. They also had light troops with fantastic face paintings and decorated bodies or maybe body stockings. Those used long thin swords like those at the Olympics, or were proper archers. The Pinkies were still undecided if that was all true or he'd had a bad trip. Rumours from the far west talked of rogue police officers with a shitload of automatics and an armoured vehicle. Another gang who used blowpipes and poisoned darts had taken over Dudley Castle. They had allegedly kept a cow alive and sold milk.

If the subject matter hadn't been real despite being surreal, the gossip would have been more restful. Worse, the lack of solid news from outside their own part of the city, or even beyond their local gangs, accentuated how isolated each enclave had become. The motorways running through the city formed a T, dividing the population into three, and the Army patrolled or garrisoned the motorways. Occasional rumours made it across the divides, but little real news.

*   *   *

Harold churned that over the following day as he collected half a dozen helpers though he stopped worrying long enough to concentrate on the instructions from Rob and his helpers. Rob stressed that if the joint wouldn't come free the scavengers should cut off the pipe and leave most of it behind. His apprentices would free up the connections when the salvage arrived back in

Orchard Close. When the group set off Harold still hadn't really got his mind on piping. He worried about the General getting automatic weapons, worried hard enough that it took a jab in the ribs from Doll to rouse him when the pickup reached the edge of the previous scavenge.

Harold continued to muse about the state of the city and the world while working, because pulling apart drainpipes to collect the joints wasn't rocket science. He'd just put another armful in the pickup when Doll yelled and gunfire erupted. Harold ran back between two buildings with his pistol and machete to find a tangled group.

Billy, Tim, Doll, Patty and Casper were fighting hand to hand though Casper fought one-handed, the other arm hanging loose and bleeding. Alfie sat on the ground beyond the rest, bleeding from a leg. That didn't stop the white-faced youth from throwing anything he could reach in an attempt to help. He ran out of bricks as Harold charged forward, but tried to crawl towards a dropped pistol. Harold hesitated for a moment, unsure where to go first because he hadn't a clear shot at anyone.

One man grabbed Billy from behind, trying to pin his machete arm so the man at the front could get in a strike. Doll and Patty held their own against larger men, dodging and stabbing, while Casper tried to fend off three of them with wide sweeps of his machete. Tim's opponent got a knife into Tim's arm but as he pulled it back Tim hit the weapon with his machete, sending it spinning away. That left him machete against machete, but bleeding and with another man moving in.

Harold came up behind an attacker heading for Alfie, chopping him down with barely a sound. He turned as Patty finally got a jab home on her opponent. As the man's eye and face erupted blood he screamed and his machete point dropped. Patty brought her machete across and the scream stopped when her blade hit his throat. She turned, raising the pistol in her free hand, because from her angle she had a clean shot, and one of Casper's opponent's spun away with two or three bullets in him. Another attacker turned to face her leaving Casper with just one to fight, though she daren't shoot this one for fear of hitting a friend.

Alfie called out when a wounded stranger sat up with a pistol so Harold shot him twice, then turned back to the rest. Tangled as the fighters were nobody had a clear shot although Patty and Doll both held pistols. At least none of the attacking fighters held a firearm though both Alfie and Casper appeared to be shot. Harold shouted, "Oy!" as he ran towards the second man closing on Tim. The fighter turned towards Harold before getting in striking range of

Tim, but alone because the rest were already in a fight for their lives.

Harold cursed to himself as they closed because he'd brought a machete but not his stick. Since he couldn't shoot with Tim in the line of fire, the pistol wasn't much good against a knife once the machetes locked. Within three passes the man managed to slash Harold's arm, then nearly stick him. Harold backed off a little. He still couldn't shoot without hitting a friend so Harold threw the gun. When the man ducked, Harold took the opportunity to hack at his knife wrist.

The knife fell. The man swung with his machete but Harold knew how to use a long blade, really use one. The gangster might be strong and quick but two blows later Harold deflected his blade and thrust. Harold's opponent dodged far enough to save his face but lost an ear as the machete ran along the side of his head. He backed away desperately, eyes wide in pain and shock. Harold followed quickly, forcing him backward until the man stumbled on the rubble or undergrowth underfoot. Harold hit him hard on the shoulder. As the man yelled and his machete dropped from his nerveless hand, Harold turned away.

He would be too late to save Billy. The man behind had finally pinned both arms and the one in front avoided a desperate kick and raised his machete. As he did, Doll finally turned her man far enough. She suddenly aimed her gun at his gut, pulled the trigger twice, and the bullets went off into empty ruins with most of his kidneys. Billy's attacker glanced at the sound, then leapt back and defended frantically instead of hacking Billy because Doll spun and slashed at him. The man left Billy to the other gangster holding the youth, because now he was in a fight for his life against the blonde.

Without the machete threatening him, Billy managed to wriggle an arm free and began to turn. His opponent ran, scooping up a baseball bat as he did. He might have made it despite a leg wound because those holding guns were otherwise occupied, but Alfie had finally crawled far enough. Alfie's accuracy wasn't great, probably because of the agony in his leg, but between them the fusillade of shots got the job done.

Meanwhile Harold came up behind Patty's opponent, who would have definitely liked to disengage since he only had a baseball bat but he daren't give her room to shoot. Even though he wasn't in range yet Harold shouted, "Boo!" The man started to turn and realised what a really bad idea it was, but too late because Patty's machete bit into his wrist and the bat fell. He turned to run sideways, straight into Harold's slash, while Patty raised her pistol and fired past Harold. He glanced back to see his erstwhile opponent, hunched over with the pain from his shoulder, flipping backwards as the bullets hit him.

Casper had been driving his remaining opponent back with a huge manic grin on his face and finally a blow smashed straight through the defence and the man dropped. Casper took another two steps and the attacker engrossed in fighting Doll never saw him before the big machete descended. Patty and Harold headed for a pale-faced Tim, backed up against the house wall desperately defending, and his opponent also made a break for it. Both Patty and Doll still had their handguns so the man didn't make four steps. Just like that the fighting finished.

Harold looked around, seeing the three other crumpled men further away for the first time, and then looked for his gun. Before he could find it, a grinning Doll grabbed his forearms and started pulling him round and round in some sort of manic dance. "It worked Harold, it worked! The training worked! It all works!" Patty had dropped her machete and stood taking in big gulps of air while Billy sat down suddenly as if he'd been hamstrung. Doll looked around then headed for Alfie, dropped to her knees, and wrapped her arms round him. By the time Doll pulled back the pain still showed on Alfie's sheet white face, but he also wore a stupid grin.

"Harold. I feel proper wobbly." Patty took another deep breath and produced a shaky smile. "But Doll is right. They concentrated on the men and that stabbing thing really shook them up." She took another big breath. "Come here. I need a hug and I'll fall over if I try to walk." She glanced over at Doll, now cutting away Alfie's jeans leg to tend to his wound, and took another deep breath. "Don't worry, if I tried the Doll snogging thing I'd pass out from shortage of breath."

"I'll risk it." Harold hugged but briefly. "Proper one later if you need it, but now there's my arm, Casper and Tim to patch up."

"Cripes yes." Patty looked round. "We're all alive?" She shook her head in disbelief, straightened, and started towards Tim.

Billy seemed content to sit and stare about in some sort of surprise so Harold left him to it and went to tend to Casper. First combat, real bloody hand to hand, affected people in different ways though both Doll and Patty seemed all right now they had something to do. "If you were skinnier this would have missed."

"If I'd been skinnier there wouldn't have been three after me. That could have been bad for someone else." Casper giggled. "Cripes, I'm a bit hyper. Worse, Liz will never let me live it down. I've been rescued by Batty Patty."

"Don't let her hear that, she'll blame me." As they talked Harold had been cutting the sleeve off a corpse's shirt before slitting it lengthways to make strips. He unwrapped the two disinfected pads everyone carried and put one on the wound. "This is gonna hurt."

"It already hurts."

Harold put the second pad on the exit hole and tightened the impromptu bandage around them. "Not yet." He pulled the knot tight.

"Aah, nasty soldier swine."

"Fairy. In the Army we didn't even bandage these, just stuck a plaster on and went back on duty." Harold showed his slashed arm. "See."

Casper looked round. "Too late for the macho bastard talking. Liz isn't here anyway so you may as well bandage that." Casper sighed. "These bastards came out of nowhere and didn't talk at all. Luckily they didn't have many guns. Three of them started shooting at me and Alfie, probably because we're biggest, but they were running so most of it went wide." He moved his arm, then winced. "Alfie got one before he went down, then I reckon Doll and Patty having hand-guns under their jackets shook the bastards up. I think they shot two or three before the bastards were in among us."

A voice broke in from behind Harold. "Sorry Harold. I couldn't get a clear shot because they were the other side of everyone, then we were all mixed up." Tim shrugged, then winced. "I'm a crap shot anyway. Toyah will play hell with me about getting wounded again. She said I should come to more machete practice."

"Your man seemed used to fighting with a knife and machete together so even without more practice you did well. The bloke I fought had a knife and machete and got me as well, just not as badly." As Patty tied off a pad and bandage around Harold's forearm he nodded towards Alfie. "Alfie will be really annoyed that he never got a chance to use his machete practice."

"Yeah, because it worked. My bloke had some trouble with the jab and dodge thing but after he got my arm, moving hurt like hell which slowed me up." A rough sling now held Tim's arm and another held Casper's.

"Harold? This lot are soaking wet." Billy had stood up and gone to search the bodies, or maybe to make sure they were dead. "From the waist down any-way. Where would they be that deep in water?"

Harold looked west, towards the GOFS. "They came across the floods to the north of the GOFS I reckon, but waded to avoid the GOFS sentries on the shallow bits." He looked around. "I'll get the pickup round to here somehow so we don't have to move Alfie much, then get you wounded heroes home."

"What about the bodies?" Billy turned slowly, taking a proper look. "Cripes, there's a lot." He limped across to check on the one Alfie had shot.

"What's up with your leg?"

"This one." Billy spat on the body. "He hit me twice with that bat while I fought the pair of them, then grabbed me when I knocked it out of his hand." He nodded to Doll. "I owe you."

"No, because if you weren't fighting those two, one of them might have gone for me. They really did concentrate on the men." She grinned. "They missed Harold altogether until he came charging in like the cavalry."

Harold shook his head. "Not really, if I hadn't been here you and Patty would have cleaned them up on your own." Harold really did feel happier about that, because Doll and especially Patty had proved they wouldn't freeze when it got close up and nasty.

By the time Harold found a way into the back gardens and reversed though the intervening fences, Alfie's leg had been splinted. Casper helped him upright, more or less lifting Alfie with one arm. With Billy helping, Alfie sat on the rear seat so Harold could pull him backwards into the cab, whereupon he passed out. Doll crammed herself into the back seat to hold his head and make sure Alfie didn't choke while the rest threw the captured firearms and handiest weapons into the back of the pickup. Casper, Tim and Billy rode with them while Patty sat in the shotgun seat with two handguns and a really bad attitude. The journey back brought no further trouble.

As the wounded were taken inside Orchard Close Harold asked for a score of people, fully armed, to go and strip the bodies then burn them. He wouldn't be with them because he had to talk to some GOFS. Patty insisted on coming to see the GOFS because she wanted to know why those scroats had got through, but she promised to behave. Harold reminded her that he'd do the talking. Seth insisted on coming as a second bodyguard, because he reckoned his sawn-off shotgun should slow any other groups up a bit. Harold drove to the border and sounded the horn repeatedly for a couple of minutes, while calling on his radio for a GOFS to come and meet him.

* * *

Eventually his radio crackled. "Coming." The man who appeared looked around carefully before coming completely out of cover. Harold explained he needed to talk to a top GOFS, soonest, and the man went back into the buildings. A couple of minutes later a dirt bike set off westwards, towards GOFS HQ. Harold sat and drank water while talking through the fight with Patty because she still seemed very edgy. By the time an SUV turned up Patty had calmed down a bit, though she still held the two handguns with her cranked crossbow across her knees.

Harold recognised the man getting out of the GOFS vehicle when it arrived. "That's Vulcan. He has a sense of humour, a real one I think and he's sort of civilised so there won't be trouble." Patty looked at her two pistols, obviously reluctant to let them go. "Keep the guns, but put them in the back of your belt under your jacket. As a surprise?" Patty grinned, relaxed, and moved them out of sight as Harold got out and went forward to meet the GOFS. Two guards climbed out of the GOFS vehicle as Vulcan started forward while behind him Harold heard the doors open and knew Patty and Seth were getting out. One of the GOFs guards took off his knitted hat to wave it then put it back on so Patty had been recognised, her or her crossbow.

"I see you forgot to polish the motor again." The GOFS found it funny that Harold drove the beat-up pickup rather than a shiny SUV.

"The car wash ran out of wax." Harold didn't smile. "Though your northern car wash is open for business. I thought you were guarding the edge of the swamp?"

"A bit deeper than a car wash with all the rain. Even the access roads across there were awash for a while." Vulcan frowned when he saw the bandage on Harold's arm and the blood spatter on him and Patty. "Did some get through?"

"A baker's dozen. They were wet right up to the waist." Harold explained.

"F.. Damn. That explains it. We had another group of houses raided, one we are supposed to be protecting though in this case the doubled guards fought the bastards off. We've got guards on all the shallow routes now, or I thought we had." He looked past Harold. "Are your lot all right?"

Harold gestured at his arm. "Yes thanks. We've got wounded but no dead."

Vulcan smiled. "Did Patty get to test a bolt?"

"Too close too fast, though she's versatile." Harold smiled. "Our women tend to be."

"Oh yes." Vulcan raised his voice. "Shall I let anyone know you need flowers, or kissing better?"

"Flowers would be nice." Patty laughed. "Flowers would be a complete novelty these days."

"I'll pass the word." Vulcan looked back at Harold and lowered his voice again. "Sorry. There's a fan club, the sort of people who want to hug a tiger." His smile faltered. "I don't suppose we'll see one of those again."

"I hope not because it won't be in a zoo."

"F.. Cripes. I hadn't thought of that." Vulcan grinned. "That damn word has invaded our place, though it's more as a joke. Why do you lot use it?"

"First as a joke because one of us used to say cripes, then to make a point that we don't use obscenities. The refugees who came afterwards really took it on, possibly to prove they belong. The latest ones seem to feel they've got to use cripes at least once a day and outnumber us, the originals." Harold shook his head. "It's odd really. We just wanted to make a point but now even blasphemy is a dying art."

"Be careful, that's how regional accents start. We'll need translators in a generation." Vulcan sighed. "I really hope it doesn't go on that long, but I don't like the current alternatives."

"London?"

"Especially London but the floods in York looked bad. Right then, enough maundering. We'll seal up our little leak." He grinned. "If only to stop you getting their weapons."

"Fair enough and thanks."

Harold missed out the bit about London when he told the rest, though he took the opportunity to tweak Patty about her fan club. Vulcan and the GOFS were as good as their word, and no more wet gangs came through, though Harold had another chance to tweak Patty when two GOFS turned up with bunches of flowers. Vulcan might have been winding one of them up because he asked if Patty wanted her wound kissed better.

Casper's bullet wound went through the meat while Tim's wound turned out to be a stab in and out rather than a slash or tear, though both would take time to heal. According to Lenny, Tim would be using his arm within weeks but might still have trouble with the wound for months afterwards. Casper would be one-armed for much longer, though hopefully he would heal completely. Harold's arm looked messy but hadn't gone deep enough for stitches, so as long as he kept it clean he'd heal.

Harold had wondered if Doll might be nursing Alfie, since that seemed to be a bit of a theme after a fight, but apparently there were several other applicants. Hazel had to be among them since nobody would mention names. Despite Hazel moving out into the girl club, everyone still treated Harold as a sort of father-figure and wouldn't tell him anything that might embarrass her.

Alfie's wound caused everyone serious concern because the bullet clipped the bone, driving splinters as well as dirt and cloth deep inside the hole. The bullet had spread or broken up, taking a chunk of calf muscle, but the tibia broke rather than shattered and Alfie's fibula stayed whole. Lenny could only advise a lot of exercise once the bone knitted, if it knitted. The medics tried to keep the hole clean, tried to stop inflection, and admitted they were out of their depth.

Harold's slashed arm irritated more than being a problem but being wounded worried Harold. He could use a long blade, thanks to Stones's warped sense of humour back in Kuwait, but if the other man had a knife that was a weakness. Harold preferred his stick in the other hand, because he'd trained like that, but everyone couldn't carry a stick like his as well as a machete. He thought hard about it because too many gangsters were knife fighters, and none of his people were.

*　*　*

While Harold went over his options, far to the northeast others were also worried about how gangsters fought. There were only four people in the bunker this time and two were definitely defensive, especially the Asian woman glaring at the man in Army uniform. "Don't blame it on my people."

"I'm not, Vanna, or at least not completely, though trained soldiers would have done better." Joshua scowled. "It doesn't help that we can't stiffen your people with regulars or armour."

"You do not want your pure-minded soldiers to find out what my people do for a living, especially those from the special facilities." Vanna pointed an accusing finger. "Some Army genius came up with the campaign plan."

"Enough you two, because I want a simple answer." The chairman, Owen, gave them both a long hard look. "It's nearly the end of June. Without blaming each other, why is there still fighting in York? Why isn't the city cleared so that Henry can move his tractors into the fields?"

"Because nobody has ever done this before, tried to depopulate a modern city without heavy armour, air support or utterly destroying the place. The Americans used over ten thousand men against about four thousand fighters, blew Fallujah to pieces, yet didn't clear everyone out or kill even half the insurgents. The Serbs and Syrians tried and failed with smaller populations than York, even though they wrecked the towns, and the Iraqis tried again with Fallujah but still without depopulating it." Joshua looked over at Maurice, the spymaster. "There are a lot of improvised explosives we didn't expect, including a type of mortar. Some of the short-ranged rockets are damned effective against anything unarmoured."

"I've got a source in each gang or enclave, not an inventory. I've given you the smarter leaders as they crop up, with the locations of armouries where possible, but these animals have been killing each other for a while so they've got better at it." Maurice shrugged. "I expected armour to be used, which would have just trampled any opposition."

"He makes a fair point, Joshua." Vanna pointed at the screen, now showing York from the air with tall plumes of smoke or vicious explosions marking the limit of the advance. "I expected my people to get either armour or close air support."

"We can't let the RAF look too closely at who we are fighting. Most air strikes in York include collateral among the women and children so we are only using standoff weapons. Faraz tells me you don't want those landing close to your people." Owen pursed his lips. "We need another solution because this doesn't bode well for this winter's operation."

"You could turn over some of your precious armour to my people." Vanna smiled, or maybe snarled. "They won't care who they run over."

"You want civilian contractors to have control of battle tanks? That takes training and discipline or they'll kill your people as well as the scum." Joshua shook his head. "I can't condone that."

"Do you have tank personnel in the Army jails, Joshua?" Owen smiled. "If you use people locked up for something unpleasant, then they needn't ever return to their units or jails which keeps Vanna's operations secret." His smile widened, "Penal battalions."

"I could put a couple of my people in with each crew in case they feel independent, or develop a conscience?" Vanna frowned, thinking it through. "We wouldn't need much, just enough armour to break through each place the scum make a stand. If necessary the tanks can go back to the Army without any crews."

"That might be better, though there won't be a battalion. We probably have enough Army prisoners to crew a few tanks and armoured troop carriers. I can let you have two training vehicles to get them all settled in." Joshua thought for a few moments then sighed. "All right, as long as the armour comes back to the Army. I really wouldn't be comfortable with civilians operating that sort of weaponry." His face cleared. "With an adjustment to the overall campaign plan we should get York cleaned up in plenty of time for Christmas."

"I'll tell the men. Home for Christmas." Vanna's sarcasm came through clearly.

"Hah, yes, the first World War, not a good precedent. At least this mess is a fair warning. We must have the next target city almost empty before trying to clear the buildings." Owen nodded to Maurice. "We are relying on you for something effective."

"We aim to please." Maurice frowned. "Though when we do clear another enclosure the troops may have a different dilemma, the significance of which has just come to our notice. Between Vanna's men and my sources we have calculated that up to one enclave in three simply cannot be classed as scum, animals or murderous maniacs. They are fairly law-abiding communities getting by and staving off any of the others who take an interest." He shrugged. "The proportion of peaceful citizens is much higher but most are under some gangster's thumb."

"My soldiers won't want to clear peaceful communities with prejudice, especially if there's women and children and we'll need regular Army for many of the larger population centres." Joshua frowned. "Can't we kill the top man so they fall apart or someone nastier takes over?"

"Honest citizens will just elect another leader. My embedded people can't steer a democratic group towards something fatal." Maurice clicked to change the picture. On this overhead view Orchard Close and seven other enclaves were highlighted. "This is typical. All of those are what your soldiers would consider honest upright people, the sort they should be rescuing."

"That's in just a third of the city. Are the rest truly the same or is there a higher percentage there?" Owen looked shocked because the original plan, based on statistics showing the rise in urban violence, assumed a feral population rather than one working calmly and peacefully to survive.

"Can't we use them? If we wipe out the others, these people might become useful citizens?" Joshua shrugged. "After all they are sort of peaceful now, even under this sort of pressure."

"No. The plan calls for all urban populations to be eradicated to allow the country to be self-sufficient in food." Owen frowned. "If we start considering each enclave separately, we will get mission creep and end up with the same old problem; too many people." He glared at Maurice. "How big a problem are they? How can we get rid of them?"

"The picture is about the same everywhere and if these enclaves weren't cut off from each other we'd have a real problem. If they ever combined, we'd need to come out of the shadows to break them. We can encourage their neighbours to do the job, but that is why we have a dilemma. These enclaves are not weak targets and have already fought off attacks just to survive this long." Maurice shrugged. "We must let some of the more violent leaders survive until they grow big enough to be able to take them out." He looked at Joshua. "Rather than shooting him or her."

"Will that work?" Vanna inspected the map. "Won't whoever it is prefer to go after another gang he can take over by killing the top people." She looked at Maurice, puzzled. "Why would one of them want a group of rebellious liberal types?"

Maurice grinned. "Because in some cases I can feed him or her the right bait, because I have the right person in the right place. After all, in the gangs we want to use, there's only one or at most four people to steer."

"But if one takes them all out, that'll be a big gang, as big as the Newcastle one." Joshua looked at Owen with real alarm. "We might need more than one bullet. The place will be pure chaos, especially if the rest try to break out."

"I have a candidate to take out three of these enclaves, then your snipers can have him. We can find someone else to deal with the others." Maurice pointed at Orchard Close. "The one right by the bypass is a real problem because they are very visible to the Army and also a tough nut. I'd have to make sure my candidate has enough men by then, so they can do the job with machetes and crossbows."

Owen looked at the screen, considering the problem carefully. He didn't like another wild card in the mix. These civilised enclaves had to go, then at worse an air strike would deal with the triumphant gang and their boss. "Do that Maurice, but not just here. Find lunatics to wipe out as many of these aberrations as possible, especially in the target city."

The meeting broke up. Maurice left with Joshua, in deep discussion about sniper targets. Owen glanced after them. "A small armoured force that isn't regular Army would be helpful."

Vanna smiled. "I can put men in there to learn how to operate the tanks. Eventually we won't need the original crews. I will need your backing to retain the armour although operational necessity should work for a while." She frowned, then shook her head regretfully. "We could do with our own air cover but I can't train a civilian thug to fly in three easy lessons."

"There are all the foreign aircrew complete with their warplanes, the ones who fled here from the continent when their airfields were overrun?" Owen smirked. "They have been kept isolated, and understand who their benefactors are." He nodded towards the other two. "Maurice is running out of diversions so you had better catch up." Vanna nodded and walked off quickly.

*　　*　　*

Harold had a smaller problem than the cabal, but it probably worried him more. The only solution he could come up with involved sending a message asking to see a Barbie with a wig, one of the top ones. When Chandra arrived she wore her usual blonde wig and the dress made of two silk curtains laced up her sides but looked puzzled rather than teasing. "This is unusual. Not just the invite but where's that lad with the big muscles and bright red face?"

"Hah, yes. His face is only red because your women insist that Alfie searches them, then wriggle about." Harold didn't smile. "I've been told your doctor is the real thing."

"Yes, but you've got someone pretty good as well. Doc says anyone who is amputating without losing the patient has the right idea. She'd love to know what the hell you put into Galileo's arm because it sure weren't what a doctor would do, but he's kept his arm." Chandra frowned, looking at Seth standing in the corner with the shotgun where Alfie usually stood. "S.. Cripes, it's that big lad, isn't it? How bad is he, because we have the same policy as you about hostages for medical and to be honest he wouldn't come back. We don't allow any outsiders inside Beth's, or rather they never come back out."

"Why the hell would you do that to Alfie?"

"Do what? We wouldn't hurt him, nor would we kill him. There's some who come here just to be searched by Alfie and they wouldn't allow that. We'd keep him, and a few women would want to make him very welcome." Her face set, with absolutely no humour. "He wouldn't be hurt but we will not allow anyone to give even a hint of what's inside Beth's."

"Will you sell information? We need advice and possibly some medicinal supplies." Harold held up a hand. "Yes, I know, it'll be expensive." A tiny smile tugged at his lips. "We can trade dental treatment?"

A ghost of a smile answered. "We heard and maybe we'd be interested, though Wellington's looks a bit rough?"

"Wellington's looked rough when it got here. Someone hit his lips hard enough to smash a tooth, then the Geeks thought dope would work." Harold did smile now. "Ask Wellington." He smiled wider. "Ask Einstein about the alternative."

"We made a fortune out of Einstein and thinking about how much that had to be hurting kept a lot of people smiling. Wellington won't talk to our lot, not socially." Chandra sniggered. "He's all loved up." Her face straightened. "We'll deal but it will cost you coupons, beer, maybe dental work and possibly knitting. The GOFS have been showing off their woollens, but we're after something a bit special so just how good is your knitting demon?"

"Very, I'm assured, but I'm a philistine. How good are you Patty?" Harold smirked. "Yes, she really is the knitter, as the GOFS could have told you because she doesn't hide. Do you fancy trying to kidnap her?"

Patty lifted her crossbow a little. "Feel free to try?"

"Mmm, I could be tempted but not for your knitting." Chandra smiled as Patty ignored the comment. "Can you knit lacy stuff? You know, thin stuff with lots of holes, little flowers, leaves and all that in it?" Chandra laughed. "I'm a philistine as well when it comes to actually knitting, but some of us know what we like."

"You mean lace stitch. I can do that. We've even got the right wool but it'll cost, seriously cost because it's a stone bitch if you want flowers and leaves as well. That sounds like bespoke. The more vanilla versions from a pattern will be cheaper?" Patty frowned but in thought, not annoyance. "If you want bright colours that'll cost more as well because the marts only have earth shades and that puce green."

"You've got bright colours?" Chandra smiled happily. "Can I look at patterns to pick out what we want? You know, a bit from each? What colours have you got?"

Harold interrupted. "Whoa, medicinal first."

"Done deal, as long as you agree the price which might not be as steep if Patty can knit what we want. Just tell me what you want to know, with pictures and your best stab at symptoms." Chandra stopped and a huge smile spread over her face. "Oh, your medic will give a proper description with big words, won't he? Doc will swoon or possibly wet herself with excitement. We'll have to chain her down." She laughed at the looks from everyone. "Not really. Would you want an angry doctor operating on you? It's just that she always complains about the descriptions."

"Will pictures on a phone help? We'll want the phone back."

"That's the only way unless you've got a printer that works. Though if you have you'll make more money printing porn. Who would have thought that the death of civilisation would also more or less wipe out pornography?" Chandra looked Patty over again. "Perhaps if you wore those weapons for a football match?" Chandra had to mean the weekly swimsuit football matches in the summer, which the occasional better behaved GOFS or Barbie was allowed to take part in. "Unless, maybe if you wore a bit more leather and less everything else? Soldier Boy could kit you out with a couple of pistols and that shotgun?" She patted her skin-tight dress and faked alarm. "Oh no, I forgot my phone so I wouldn't get any pictures. Disaster. What if someone Tweeted or Buzzed?"

Harold had to laugh, because the delivery had been perfect air-head celebrity. "Will it be safe to leave you two together in a room full of soft wool?"

"Unfortunately yes. Several of our lot came back broken-hearted after bouncing off Patty." Chandra grinned. "I'll just have to lust over sexy woollens. That's best done in private so your tender ears and eyes aren't corrupted."

Harold opened his mouth to ask how woollens could do that, then snapped it shut. Knitting with lots of holes and bits of flowers and leaves would probably make him blush at the very least. He headed for the hospital instead, spending some time talking to Alfie while Lenny and Patricia took photos of his leg from all angles. Harold winced when the dressings came off, but Alfie swore he barely felt it. Then the two medics typed in reams of doctor-speak until they thought they'd covered it.

The bone was more broken than smashed, so both Lenny and Patricia wanted to save Alfie's leg. Unfortunately neither were sure if the other damage meant the leg would remain useless, or if infection from the rest would stop the bone knitting. They worried about the leg and foot eventually mortifying, even if they had dug out all the crap. Both seemed quite upbeat about having a real doctor to ask about it, enough to cheer both Alfie and Harold.

Chandra left, still chortling about corrupting innocents, with half a dozen knitting patterns and some short lengths of wool to show the colours. According to Patty whoever wanted lace knitting also wanted to rock somebody's world. Then she laughed off various questions about wearing leather and if she wanted to borrow a few firearms for Chandra's next visit. Patty already wore firearms but not where the gangsters could see her. She'd liked the idea that if they met her in a serious fight, a pistol would be a fatal surprise. Harold encouraged the idea because that way she might not be targeted as Emmy had been.

*   *   *

Though the following day Harold seriously considered targeting a certain gang leader. Hitting him would be easy from the man's own house, the Mansion, where Harold had gone to collect more business. Caddi wanted Harold to wait while he dealt with something, which rang alarm bells for Harold. The last time that happened, Holly died. "I'm not driving home in the dark again so if you'll be gone long, I'll go home now."

"No need. You could stop over?" Caddi held up his hands with a patent insincere smile. "I'm not going to get creative am I? Even if that lad is limping and that bitch is carrying a pup, they can still shoot, yeah?"

"Oh yes, that doesn't need any movement at all." Harold waggled his index finger. "Well just a bit."

"Ha, right. Look, you can stay in the same house that Cooper, Chevy and the rest use, eat the same food, fuck the same women. Oh no, you don't do that bit, except I hear you do? You've got a brothel?"

"Not a brothel. A couple of women who might say yes for a payment because they want to. They can also say no so anyone asking had better listen."

Harold scowled. "Remind your lot."

"No need, there's enough carrying scars for that though one doesn't care because he's brain dead. You were a bit rough with him." A little hot spot of anger showed in Caddi's eyes. "That's a bit beyond a spanking."

"If he'd pulled a knife on you instead of me, you'd have killed him. He got a clip beside the head so its concussion and he might come right in time." Harold smiled. "Maybe the steady trickle of idiots should be warned that my stick isn't a precision instrument." Harold thought Caddi sent the little scroats now and then, hoping one would get lucky. He'd shoot one instead, but most gangsters were impressed that Harold didn't find a bloke with a knife a serious problem and just beat them up with a stick. That helped to keep the visitors respectful.

"Noted. Do I get my gun repairs cheaper now you've got the extra income from the whores?" Caddi's smile became a scowl. "Not only that but some of my idiots will prefer to trot over there to give your whores our coupons rather than have a freebie here."

Harold looked over the selection on the table, mentally marking a revolver as unrepairable as his way of fining the bastard and also helping keep himself calm. "I don't know why your men prefer that, or even what they get charged." Caddi started to smile. "Nor do I expect a freebie, nor do I pay. I believe in willing, not coerced as you well know. Now if we're done with my love life?"

"Are you staying? If you do I'll get them to kill the fatted calf, or at least roast a leg of pork since we've got one." Caddi sniggered. "That got you."

He had. Harold hadn't eaten roast pork in years, literally since the mere smell of roast pork had caused riots in Kuwait so the Army stopped serving it. "All right, I'll stop over, but only if you spend diesel to let Orchard Close know." He smiled. "You don't want them to come looking."

"Yeah, yeah, right. I'll get off then and do some real work. I'll be back, as Arnie once said." Harold sat drinking decent coffee, wondering if he had been set up again, until Caddi came back so they could finish their business.

To Harold's relief, the harassment barely warranted the name. On the way Chevy steered Harold to a house with 'Back o' Rackhams' above the door. A reasonable attempt at painting a naked woman decorated the door itself. When Harold refused, Chevy laughed and took him to the house used by Caddi's chosen.

E-Type and Roller were reasonably polite company, especially Roller who sometimes seemed to be well educated. The gangsters even insisted that Harold chose from four plates with pork on and helped himself to the veg so he knew they weren't putting poison or Spanish Fly in there. Harold really did have roast pork with apple sauce, roast potatoes, mash, carrots and peas, all beautifully cooked. He enjoyed every mouthful. All of the gangsters swore they had no idea how Caddi got hold of the pork. Eventually they all agreed someone had found a butcher's freezer someplace that still had frozen meat inside.

The bedroom had no lock, but Harold jammed a chair under the door before sleeping well enough but not too deeply. He set off early morning with a Hot Rod escort to guard the guns, arriving home in time to get breakfast. He checked with Patricia but there'd been no word from the Barbies. Harold spent the day keeping busy in his gun room rather than worrying. He checked again before going home even though Patricia had sworn to let him know if the Barbies replied.

*　*　*

The following afternoon Harold went to see Patricia because the information from the Barbies had been delivered. "Is it any good?" A huge smile from a Patricia waving drawings and what might be a page from a book showing the innards of a leg were an answer. "Does Alfie know?"

"Yes, Lenny told him. We can definitely save his leg, though he might limp afterwards." Harold turned towards Alfie's room. "But…" The 'but' followed Harold down the hall, unheeded.

"Hey, Patricia says your leg…." Harold stopped because it wasn't Alfie's leg being tended to. Veronica pulled her head away from Alfie's and two bright scarlet faces looked back at Harold. "Er, right. I'll get the rest from her."

Harold turned sharpish to leave, blushing a bit himself as he came back towards Patricia's grinning face. "Alfie is being nursed right now, I'll see him later. I thought…" He stopped there because for all he knew half a dozen young women might come by and nurse him, or only Veronica. Harold didn't want to know.

"Yes, we always seem to have a volunteer for that sort of nursing." Patricia sniggered. "Which does wonders for his morale." She sobered. "Actually that sort of nursing really has helped him while we've been waiting to find out, which left us free to concentrate on Tim and Casper. They're both clear; it'll just take time for them to heal properly. Tim gets plenty of that sort of nursing from Toyah, but can you look out for an auxiliary nurse for Casper? Amber isn't up to it." She glanced at Harold's arm. "You seem to have managed without nursing."

"I'm a rough soldier type. I've had my eye open for a possible nurse for Casper since we first got here. I even offered to take him on a raid to find a boyfriend." Harold frowned. "Since I've no idea of the percentages I'm not sure, but shouldn't there be at least one other gay bloke here?"

"I've no idea either. Maybe they all went to the Pinkies?" Patricia waved her sheaf of instructions, indicating a bag full of something that had come with them. "Now go away so I can gloat and plot with Lenny. Oh, we've got a Barbie come for dental. Not a top one, in fact she doesn't act like a fighter at all."

The woman might not be a fighter, but she came with four who definitely were and seemed genuinely concerned. Gayle reported that she'd asked the woman about staying in Orchard Close. The woman looked puzzled and asked why, then clammed up. The five left in an SUV, claiming they would go through the edge of Hot Rod territory because the GOFS would have heard the motor on the way here and be waiting. Harold puzzled over why violent maniacs would risk it for an apparent nobody's toothache, then gave up.

* * *

During the following weeks nobody had the chance to think hard about anything since everyone who could stagger found themselves pressganged into bringing in everything but sheaves. Emmy talked about planting wheat or maybe hops or barley next year if she could get seed and enough land could be cleared. Harold had thought Curtis nagged last year but he'd been a pushover. At least there were more people this year to reap, then dig, fertilise and plant yet more baby somethings. The paths built of dug up tarmac and stone were invaluable for wheelbarrows. As more ruins were demolished the workers left a grid of more footpaths.

All the houses burned by napalm during the initial bombardment were now fields, with even the foundations and roads dug out and replaced with soil. The demolition had moved into the swathe of the houses 'only' shelled, until eventually the cleared area stretched over a quarter of a mile from the walls. After some serious discussion Emmy agreed she couldn't farm any more land, this year. "Where, exactly, is Emmy going to garden up to?" Liz stood with her machete, looking left and right. "We've got to plant my trees soon so Harold's rifle can keep the scroats off them."

"Does a squirrel class as a scroat Harold, because even you will have fun trying to hit one of those at this distance." Casper squinted back at Orchard Close. "Can you hit a real scroat from there?"

"Yup. Foul-mouth was further away than this." Matti looked at the distant walls. "Not a lot further I don't think."

"Not a lot because we are well over five hundred yards out now." Harold looked left and right. "Emmy reckons this gives her enough land in this direction, providing I allow her to expand sideways." He pointed. "Though I've agreed she can push out further opposite those six houses once people live in them."

"Cripes, how much more farmland does she want?" Liz looked over the crops and the workers toiling among them. "Is she related to aristocracy, and claiming her own personal estate or country park?"

"Stop it. You'll be pleased enough when you get soup instead of gruel in the winter. We can plant a belt of trees right here." Harold looked accusingly at Liz. "In addition to the clumps that seem to be sprouting here and there? Where shoots have fallen into convenient lengths before impaling a bit of innocent ground, usually a marshy bit?"

"It's the squirrels planting Hazel trees, honest." Liz grinned. "We really are planting quite a bit of Hazel because we get nuts as well as charcoal that way, providing there's no plague of squirrels this year?" Everyone scowled because that one had really driven home the sheer contempt the authorities had for the TV audience. She looked each way again. "We'll need a lot of space to plant all the types because the gnomes have given me a list. Willow and Poplar grow quickly, Hazel trees give nuts but grow a little bit slower, while Hornbeam is best for charcoal but even slower. We'll put in Leylandii and a few other firs as well because we can use the timber for arrows, and they'll look pretty in winter. This will soon be the New New Forest, since the bastards won't let us at the old New Forest and all those lovely trees."

"Not a forest, a strip of trees. You've got to keep the undergrowth beneath them cut back so Genghis Khan or Caddi or the Geeks can't gather an army behind them. I'll also insist you trim off the lower branches on evergreens so they can't be used as cover. I hope you'll cut the trees down before a man can hide behind the trunk?"

"Yes Daddy. Can we plant them now, pretty-please or have you come up with another problem to delay me?" Liz grinned and the rest sniggered.

"Don't blame me. Incipient Momma back there is the one keeping us all too busy to cater for your arboreal leanings." Harold headed for the nearest tree stump sprouting shoots. "This one?"

"No, silly. Wrong sort. I've been learning since I haven't enough charcoal to get hot and sweaty. Come on." Liz looked at a sketch before heading off purposefully. "You lot could all do with a bit of exercise for your machete arms."

* * *

Four hours of slash and plant left a surprisingly long strip of sticks sticking out of the ground, even if they weren't exactly forest-like yet. "That has to be worse than practice." Jeremy looked round and shut up about machete practice because not all the tree planters were trainees. "I've got a blister. Can I get it kissed better?"

Matti eyed his hand. "After a good wash. Then you can kiss me better as well."

"Cripes, ease off you pair, innocents present." Doll sniggered. "It'll be your lips that are blistered, Matti, since you never shut up."

"Though there was that shoot that sprang back and whacked you?" Liz tried for an innocent smile. "You might want that kissed better after the lips." Matti blushed as Jeremy looked a question. "Oops, my lips are sealed."

Harold had been going to suggest a new machete exercise if he could get the right people on their own, but instead he left them bickering. He headed home to get cleaned up, only to find the lounge full. Maybe not quite full, but all three brewers, Berry, Seth, and Nigel, were there along with an increasingly rotund Emmy and half a Coven. "I didn't do it."

"Hush. We want you to try these." Sharyn pointed to the dining table where four tumblers held differently coloured pale liquids. "You'll be dry after all the tree planting."

"True. We all carry water but that is a bit bland. What are these?" Harold picked one up and sniffed. "That's alcoholic." He looked at the four. "I'll be squiffy if I drink them all."

"No you won't. Try one, just a mouthful."

Harold drank. "Not a lot of flavour. Sort of cider but not. Apple juice, well-watered?"

Sharyn gestured. "Try the rest." Harold did. "Do you prefer them to plain water, or the tea we've been getting lately?"

"They're all better than the tea, but we'll all get drunk. Water is good enough, though even more tasteless after it's been boiled." Harold curled a lip. "The tea really is bad, especially without sugar, while the coffee is rough and expensive but still has a kick. Come on, give, what is this about?"

"I had to look up something about arrows and bows because someone reckoned the new trees will make both in time, for if we run out of bullets eventually?" Faith waited for Harold to nod. He knew because he'd had the original conversation about how long this isolation might go on, so he could plant the right trees. "The bit about archers mentioned small beer, and I wondered what that could be apart from half a pint. Small beer was weak beer so the archers wouldn't get drunk, but also because the alcohol made it safer than drinking the water."

"That one?" Harold pointed at a glass.

"Yes, a rough try. Very little alcohol but enough to help keep tummy bugs at bay we reckon." Berry beamed. "We thought perhaps we could do better. You know we were messing about with homemade wine?"

"Yes, that failed because the stuff ended up a thousand percent proof and drunks with firearms and sharp things is bad." The girl club and Coven had also stamped on really strong drink because both men and women made silly mistakes that way, or got very depressed if they were already down. Beer and cider did the job but slower so somebody should notice, hopefully in time.

"We kept the wine and the gear to make more. Now we've watered the wine, really watered it. The same with some of the cider." Berry indicated the jugs on the table. "That'll keep people hydrated, it's even safer than straight boiled water, and it'll taste better than the alternatives. Even the kids can drink it."

"Yes they can." Sharyn headed off Harold's protest. "They did, in France before the crash."

Berry jumped in. "Our wine isn't from vines but if we use the spoiled and overripe fruit with just a bit of sugar, I reckon we can stop buying tea."

"The coupons we save can go into sugar to provide this stuff for everyone?" Nigel smiled. "If I can get a word in." He ducked a Berrying, pointing at Seth. "Hey, you've got him for that now."

"You've insisted we always boil drinking water because you don't trust the government to keep the water right." Faith shrugged. "Well if a bug or two gets past that, the alcohol will help."

"Will we have enough fruit bearing in mind all the blackberry and black-currant juice the Coven made last year for the kids?" Harold liked this idea if only because he begrudged paying the mart prices for the dust labelled tea.

"Oh yes because the brewers will use what's left after crushing for juice or seedless jam, which will give plenty of flavour. We'll get more fruit this year anyway because we'll get there before the birds." Patty beamed. "I told you all those net curtains would come in handy."

"You told us everything would be handy so you have to be right once." Seth ducked but too slowly then pointed to his head. "This hurts." Berry hesitated.

Nigel rolled his eyes. "Oh go on, kiss him better. I give up, though let me turn my back first. Just don't let me hear that connecting door squeak in the night." Seth now lived in one of the semi-detached houses containing the brewery, with Nigel and Berry in the other, and the houses really did have a door between them.

"Dad!" Berry started towards him as Nigel turned away, then grinned and turned to Seth. "He just said it's ok." The rest studiously ignored the short but intense celebration.

"Now that's been approved, will you have time to brew and wine-make?" Harold shrugged as Seth and Berry glared. "Just asking."

"We could have a night shift." Seth grinned at Berry.

"Yes, you and me." Nigel had turned back. "Then I can relax."

"Though first Harold is going to explain to folk that tea is now a luxury that has to be bought out of personal coupons, but this stuff is free instead." June smiled sweetly. "That will settle it because we all know the rules, do what Soldier Boy says." The meeting broke up in laughter.

Vaguely alcoholic liquids gradually replaced tea in most houses because tea really did taste appalling, and had become very expensive. The switch to a medieval type of drink sparked interest in the period and several people helped Veronica search the books in the library. Half a dozen suggestions were made, such as aspirin from willow bark, maggots for infected wounds if the antibiotics ran out, and wooden overshoes, clogs, to save wear and tear on footwear. Within a fortnight Harold saw a man pulling a crude single blade plough while another pushed. He asked, and in ground already used once for crops the contraption turned the soil faster than spades. The garden gnomes were soon encouraging others to take turns as a plough-horse.

*   *   *

Harold thought of a solution to one medieval-type problem, knife fighters. At the next machete practice he waved a thin length of wood with scrap of cloth bound around the end to make a handle. "This is to deal with knives when a gangster uses one with a machete."

"A walking stick like yours? That thing weighs a ton." Mattie had actually tried waving Harold's stick about, though she still didn't realise the weight came from it being steel.

"No, just a thin stick to knock the knife aside. Both Tim and I were injured by a man with a knife and machete because we only had a machete." Harold shrugged. "I'm not a knife fighter so I can't train you, but the scroats have used knives for years."

"The machetes will cut a stick to bits, Harold." Doll took the stick from him and swished it. "We may as well use a garden cane."

"Not if we use an iron bar, the same as at the mart?" Patty smirked. "It they try to chop that it'll give us a clean strike at the scroat, game over."

"Better yet, if you hit the knife hand or machete arm, or anywhere much, it will hurt, really hurt." Bernie grinned. "That scroat when Curtis was shot got me with a knife because I only had one weapon." He lost the smile suddenly. "I'm not sure I can manage two weapons. I'll get confused."

"Practice will sort that out." Harold smiled happily because yes, an iron bar would work and that's what he'd been going to suggest. Someone else coming up with it encouraged everyone to think for themselves. Better yet, Harold had actually trained with something similar so he could make them all much more dangerous. "Though we've got to keep them hidden so the other gangs don't do the same."

"We can put a bit of rag round one end as a handle and make a sleeve to shove the bar down behind the machete sheath. Then it'll be a nasty surprise." Patty frowned. "When you had your wobble after Holly, you prowled around at night with a machete and an iron bar. You can already fight like that, can't you Harold?"

"Yup. I actually had training." Big smiles broke out on the trainees. They had an expert.

"Come on then. I'll leave my knife in the sheath to blunt it then you can show me how this works." Doll laughed. "With that stick, not an iron bar." Everyone started taking knives and sheaths off their belts.

Everyone except Casper. "I can use a baseball bat and a machete. Then the asshole can choose between brained or beheaded. Who wants to spar?" Oddly enough, nobody after that statement, or not until Casper had a thin wooden stick instead of a baseball bat. The shambles as everyone tried to use both hands at once didn't exactly make anyone more dangerous, not yet, but it left them with big smiles as well as bruises.

* * *

Ten days later Queen gnome Emmy wore a big smile as she intercepted Harold, which made him wary. "Waddle with me Harold." Behind her three gnomes looked like children with their hands caught in the cookie jar, guilty but not terribly sorry.

"How far, and do we need a wheelbarrow for you? More to the point, how near is the midwife?"

"Stop it and start walking. Rob will be waiting and it'll take me a while to get to the far end, to the terrace houses outside the wall." Emmy set off.

"You can't climb over that wall. If I let you the girl club will practice arcane rites on me, or is that the Coven?" Harold had plenty of time to talk because Emmy definitely waddled now. "I'm not trying to deliver a baby in a field."

"Stop it I said. I'm not due for six weeks." Emmy rested her hands on her big bump. "I did wonder but Lenny and Patricia agree there's only one heart-beat."

"Could be synchronised? The three of them might come marching out in lockstep wearing gnome hats and wellies." Harold could see Rob ahead of him, being chivvied along by another gnome. "Just what have you been up to?"

"Remember composting toilets?"

"That was the stink? Rob thought the sewers were choked up. We were a bit miffed because it meant the houses couldn't have proper toilets." Harold beckoned Lenny over. "Are you doing anything essential?"

"I'm going to look at a couple of outpatient cuts and sprains. They can wait a few minutes. What do you want?"

"We might need medical advice about sanitation, plus if Emmy gets ex-cited you know what you're doing." Emmy's hand clipped him gently at the back of the head. "How hygienic are composting toilets?"

"That depends I suppose. If the temperature is high enough it should kill most things." Lenny thought. "The actual toilet itself could be a real problem, not least because it'll attract flies and they'll spread disease." He smiled. "This wasn't covered in paramedic training, but that applies to most of the last couple of years."

"We've sealed them up." Gnome Sweet Gnome put a hand over her mouth. "Sorry. Emmy told us to shut up."

"Surely its Gnemmy?" Harold had his head clipped again.

"Stop that, I've got enough trouble with these idiots." She glared at the speaker. "Especially Bethany." As they came nearer the end of the road Harold did try to smell something. There were plenty of things to smell but not the raw sewage one from the damaged houses over the wall ahead.

That puzzled Harold. "The smell has gone."

Emmy smirked. "The first version was a bit niffy, but we've improved since May. The mark six Orchard Close patented composting toilet does not pong." Emmy waved a hand at the gnomes. "Due to two months of dedicated research which included the gnomes going over the wall when they needed the loo."

"Even in the rain." Bethany made a zipping motion across her mouth.

Rob waited impatiently, also sniffing the air so Christopher, Gnome on the Range, had mentioned the toilet. Harold aimed his glower at the mother-to-be. "You stay here Emmy. I'm sure Sweet Gnome won't mind explaining." Bethany opened her mouth but shut it again, smiling happily.

"All right, but remember you asked for her. Bethany, please don't start talk-ing until you get there or you'll have to explain it all again." Emmy waved at the wall. "Scat."

"But he said I'm sweet. Can't we talk about that?"

"He read your hat. The first Gnome is covered up."

Bethany smirked. "I know."

"Scat."

Bethany climbed over the wall with the ease of long practice and when Harold followed he found a plank on two piles of bricks as a step. "The idea of the wall is to stop scroats climbing over and this sort of defeats the object."

"We leave the plank inside the wall at night, and take it to the loo with us. Anyway, there's guards in those houses. Oops." Bethany put a finger on her lips with a completely unrepentant smile before leading the way across the garden to a kitchen built on the back of one of the houses.

"I'd point out a toilet here isn't hygienic, but some of the older houses already have a bathroom extension off the kitchen." Harold followed her inside and Bethany pointed.

"This kitchen isn't used. In any case, we put the loo in that old pantry. Have a look. Ah, hang on." Bethany banged on the door and listened. "All clear." She opened the door and waved Harold in.

The wooden box against the back wall had a cover over the toilet seat, which hinged up. Harold lifted it and sniffed. He detected a faint whiff maybe, but barely and there were definitely no flies. Harold lowered the seat and looked at the two buckets on the floor. One held leaves and grass while the other held earth, with a plastic beach spade in the earth. "How does this work?"

"A lot better with a bidet thing to clean with, I reckon. This took great dedication, giving up my bidet straight after finding it." Bethany wriggled partway past. "This is not a loo for two." She pointed. "Sit and whatever, then leaves and grass, then earth to seal any pong. A lot of leaves and grass without a bidet and let me tell you that's gross. I've run home commando to my bidet more than once. Er. Right. Toilet. Did you get that?" The blush died stillborn, replaced by a cheeky smile. "Do you need a diagram?"

"I need some convincing that we can shoehorn one of these into every house. How is that lot shovelled out without choking some poor volunteer? Now that will be dedication." Harold started to turn and stopped. "We don't know each other well enough for me to turn without you backing up a bit?"

"But you already called me sweet?" Bethany wriggled back out. "There you are, my chastity is safe. Now come round the back so I can show you how we get it out. The compost?" Bethany grinned and started for the kitchen door.

Harold rolled his eyes. "Did you get that?" Lenny and Rob nodded.

"Yes, though we'll probably look one at a time." Lenny looked after Bethany. "Do you want a bodyguard?"

"No, she's just wound up about this."

"Just don't call her sweet again." Rob went into the toilet without waiting for a reply.

Harold went around the back to find Bethany pointing proudly to a pair of wooden handles jutting out of the wall. "Pull on those, unless someone is actually testing?"

"No, just looking." Harold pulled and the square of wood came out followed by the rest of a wooden box attached to the handles. He bent to look in the hole and saw the inside of another box with a hole in the top.

"That came out easily."

"It's on skids to slide downhill. Then we drag it up the ramp to the compost heap and tip it in. Chuck more muck or other compost on if it pongs and the job's done." Bethany pointed at the box. "The liner is a plastic storage box with the top missing but we can use other plastic or even old ceramic sinks, anything waterproof we can wash out and put back will do." She put her hands on her hips. "Well?"

"I'd say sweet but you'll take it personally. Actually I can't see a fault, not straight off, apart from the sheer physical labour to empty them all. You'll need a pair of wheels or something to help get them up onto the compost heap. How will it work upstairs?" Harold tried to think how. "You can't use a shaft or it'll get gunked up."

"A downstairs loo isn't the end of the world is it, especially if we can grow our own food? Emmy reckons we can only get away with a couple of years using the soil in the fields before it'll be exhausted. Then it will need fertilising properly." Bethany grinned. "With a better fertiliser than stinky water."

"Will the compost itself pong?"

"Not really, not once its ready. The heat cooks all that out of it." Bethany frowned. "Turning the compost over is bloody hard work but Emmy has a bad girl solution. We'll start shovelling and look pathetic. With luck some big strong idiot will help."

"She's actually training you lot? May all and any gods help the poor innocent males of this parish." Harold shook his head. "Worse still it'll work. If you set the thing up on the main street you might even sucker some of the visitors into helping." Bethany's grin grew to match Harold's, because the macho ethos of the young gangsters really would encourage them to show off for the women. Possibly even as far as shovelling what they might not realise was toilet waste.

"Well then you'd better put that back, or do you expect poor little old me to do it?" Harold shoved the box home again, laughing at the Bethany version of a poor fragile female.

"I can't see a problem in the house Harold." Lenny shrugged. "As long as the crap stays covered up in the compost heap it'll work, hygiene-wise. Especially if Rob puts in a bidet." Smiling at Bethany he continued, "In fact it's a brilliant system under the circumstances."

"Downstairs toilets only." Harold pointed at the removal handles and both of the other men nodded understanding. "Everyone will be motivated to avoid smells." Harold grinned at Rob. "Now you can take out all those bidets you put in upstairs and fit them downstairs."

Rob shook his head in despair. "It's a good job I collected some apprentices. How come most of the plumbing work these days comes from gardeners?" He smiled. "I thought the medieval gardener used a bush, not a bidet."

"Yeuk, no. I suppose I'd better shut up now if we're going back to the boss?" Bethany took a step and stopped. "Oh, er, sorry, you're the boss aren't you?"

"Rarely, you got it right." Harold stepped up on the plank and came face to face with Emmy. "Apparently you're the boss so I suppose we'd better give in gracefully."

"You know I'm irresistible." Emmy kissed him on the nose and stepped aside, while Bethany followed Harold over, giggling.

Though that wasn't quite the end of the battle. As each person or family conceded defeat Rob and his team moved in but Harold thought Christmas might be long gone before the last house converted. Rob became sneakier, sending teams of women apprentices round to deal with grouchy males, though sending young men to the reluctant women didn't always work as well. The girl club and Coven would gang up on the diehards eventually, using sweet reason and then Soldier Boy's name as a club.

Chapter 4:
Splish Splash Bunnies

While the composting toilets gradually spread through Orchard Close, the rest of life moved on. Especially with regard to the neighbours and their requests for various repairs, though soon nobody's repairs would save the petrol engines. Harold didn't think the canned petrol in the cellar would be useable much longer. All the other petrol, that not canned and stored just after Orchard Close had been established, had already been removed for use on pyres or in bombs. One pickup and the girl club armoured minibus still ran on petrol, just, but the rest had quit. "I'm not sure the pickup will make it back this time. I might need a tow."

"Don't worry Harold. If you aren't back by dark we'll send a search party, one with a bad attitude." Patty glared at the Hot Rods accompanying Charger.

"I won't be back tonight, though if I'm not home by dinner tomorrow go on alert. I should be all right, because this is just Caddi playing games again." Harold grimaced because Charger hadn't arrived as a hostage until mid-afternoon so Caddi had done it deliberately. "He'll treat me well enough and probably even spoil me a bit. Even so I'd have told him to stick it but we need that salvaged diesel van overhauled. Get Charger to look it over since he'll be here overnight."

"All right Harold. At least Charger is one of the better behaved lieutenants so there'll be no comments about providing overnight entertainment." Patty smirked. "I did consider nailing Chevy to a door for my own entertainment."

"Be good." Patty grinned, and shooed him towards the pickup.

* * *

The gate guards at The Mansion didn't search Harold, because Cooper took him into a nearby house. The Hot Rod quickly frisked Harold before putting the handgun and machete in a locker and giving Harold the key. "Caddi put in these lockers to stop someone switching ammo on his visitors again." Someone had replaced Harold's ammo with corroded rounds while he visited Caddi. The next Hot Rod visitors to Orchard Close found their ammo replaced by duds made up with badly damaged brass. "You should get a mechanic to look at that motor. It sounds a bit rough."

"No point, because the petrol is about useless." Harold shrugged. "At least we've saved some diesel up to now, though we've had to dump what came from old vehicles and a couple of central heating tanks. Some of that even had plant scum in it. The diesel we put in storage right at the start is still good."

"We lost all our fuel-injected cars first but Charger is a genius. He's put diesel engines in all our poser motors, which means performance is down but who the hell will notice?" Cooper waved a hand towards Caddi's house. "Are you here to sample our fish?"

"That's the only reason I came. Charger promised me fish and chips?" That intrigued Harold. Fresh fish had become a legend once the food in household freezers had been used up.

"The real thing. I'll see you later for my share." Cooper headed off elsewhere.

A dark-haired maid opened Caddi's front door as Harold came near, another different one. Each new one seemed to have a shorter skirt or tighter blouse. At least this one wasn't showing any visible signs of abuse, except in her tense pose and the way she kept her eyes lowered. Harold noticed a slight flinch when Caddi spoke from just behind her. "Come in, Soldier Boy. The maid will show you through." She did, scurrying from the front door as soon as she'd closed it to open the study door. "I considered a butler but I don't swing that way."

"That might be dangerous anyway, don't butlers clean and sharpen the knives?" Harold didn't wait for an answer, nodding to Caddi's bodyguard as he went past. "Hi Mack. You'll collect dust stood around like that."

"You crack me up, 'Arry." Mack laughed. "E lets me run about a bit when you've gone."

Caddi went through the usual charade with the maid. Harold asked for white coffee and two sugars because Caddi still had really good coffee. As the maid delivered the drinks the warlord smirked at Harold and then nodded towards her. "You never say what hair colour you prefer. Do you want her to put on a wig for your blow job?"

"No thanks, coffee is all I want." This maid actually looked up at that and Harold gave her a slight nod before remembering he shouldn't show interest. "Not interested." Caddi smiled, the little one that meant he thought he'd scored somehow, and she left.

Caddi swung into the dealing. The weapons weren't in bad condition and there weren't many. Harold asked and for a change Caddi wasn't disputing a border anywhere. The cleaning and repairs were because his men were practicing. Caddi complained about wasting ammunition because the men were bored, then sourly pointed out he'd better keep them occupied or they'd spend their coupons in the Orchard Close brothel.

Eventually the prices for the repairs and more beer were agreed, but then Caddi wanted tomatoes and lettuce. The Mansion lettuces were riddled with caterpillars and slugs, and the geese had got into the greenhouses and wrecked the tomatoes. Harold hoped Caddi didn't find out who'd arranged that. Whoever it was made a definite donation to Orchard Close because Caddi and his fighters didn't eat the crap from the marts, Caddi's description.

Eventually Caddi opened the study door and waved Harold out. "That was boring. You really aren't any fun on these visits." The amount of coupons, charcoal, garden produce or beer finally changing hands would depend on Charger's assessment of the diesel van, and as usual Harold came away feeling he'd been stitched.

Harold smiled, because Caddi always complained he couldn't get a rise. "Fun is for home. After all, you don't let yourself have fun in Orchard Close."

"True. If I'm spanked I expect the spankee to know her limits. Actually I don't much fancy that end of the abuse at all." Caddi sniggered. "Have you come up with any more punishments yet? I'm running out of ideas. You could practice on this one and she could tell me about it afterwards?"

"I doubt I could come up with anything suitable Caddi." Harold glanced at the dark-haired young women holding the front door open, with what he hoped was a reassuring look. Her eyes dropped so maybe it didn't work.

"Pity, since you're staying over you could have experimented. We did look for whoever took a shot at you in the dark, but it's very hard to spot someone sneaking about." Caddi barely bothered with trying to sound sorry.

"Especially when a bunch of morons let off a couple of hundred rounds in all directions and leave everyone night-blind." Harold smiled. "Though its true about people hiding. I'm sure I saw a light on that concrete tower block as I left last time." The tower block stood half a mile from The Mansion, at the edge of the cleared zone.

Caddi lost his smirk. "Too true you did. I've got people up there watching out for lost cyclists and stray snipers." Harold took note, if he had to shoot someone else here the bicycle escape route wouldn't work again.

Chevy waited outside to escort Harold to his meal and bed. "I know the way Chevy. No detours this time."

Chevy laughed. "Yeah, we know. Though it's a shame. You could see the red light we've put up over the door. We could sell you a couple of red bulbs for your whores?"

"But they're fussy and wouldn't want just any old toerag turning up." Once again this sort of tweaking had become almost a ritual, though the Hot Rod heading purposefully towards them with a hand on his machete wasn't. Harold checked but nobody else seemed interested. "I'm looking forward to finding out just what you call fish and chips. I'm likely to be really rough on anyone delaying me?"

Chevy didn't answer for a couple of moments and then he laughed again. "I can understand that." He probably thought the headshake to the advancing gangster wasn't noticeable but Harold had been looking for it. The man stopped, then headed off at an angle. Harold hoped that had been the extent of Caddi's new fun and games and he could now sleep in peace.

Just in case Chevy hadn't got the message, Harold hammered it home. "I get enough problems with stroppy gits visiting Orchard Close, so I'm likely to be short-tempered if I'm challenged someplace else. I'm not very precise when that happens." Caddi would understand the precise bit when Chevy passed that on.

"Yeah, yeah, yeah." Chevy waved towards the house door. "This should cheer you up."

True enough, any annoyance faded when Harold came into the dining room of the house used by Caddi's lieutenants. "I give in, did you find some fish fingers at the bottom of a freezer?" The smell already had Harold's mouth-watering.

"Oh no, better than that." E-Type, Cooper and Roller were already sat at the table. Roller waved towards a seat. "Come on, sit down. The cooks were told to have the meal ready when you arrived so it won't be long."

Harold looked at the salt, vinegar and ketchup alongside the thinly sliced fresh bread and frowned. "This is a bit elaborate for a windup?"

"Not a windup, I promise." Possibly not because all of them looked like kids with a big secret, bursting to say something but not wanting to spoil the surprise. E-Type seemed to be a breath away from giggling. "Beer, coffee, tea or wine?"

Harold opened his mouth to ask where Caddo had found wine, then saw the bottles. "Our beer?"

"Oh yes, Caddi serves it to visitors now just to wind them up about what he tells them is our home brew. He'd like to sell them some but doesn't want to make you even richer." Cooper smiled. "You could bring your brewer over to give ours some pointers?"

"Yeah, sure, then I'd be buying my beer from Caddi."

The men all burst out laughing. "Too true, Caddi would trade one of us for decent beer." Chevy shook his head. "If he ever suggests one of us as hostage against a visit by your brewer, I'm gonna hide." He sobered. "It's here."

Wherever the fish had come from this must be the first time this lot had been fed any, judging by their rapt attention as a young woman brought in a plate heaped with big battered lumps. Another young woman put a warm plate in front of each man but they were too engrossed in watching the fish arrive to even pat her ass. The food landed in the middle of the table and four pairs of eyes fastened on Harold. "Go on Harry, you get first choice." That was so Harold knew he wasn't being poisoned but he didn't care about the reason. He stabbed a battered portion with his fork and put it on his plate.

By the time Harold reached for chips from the steaming bowl just deposited on the table the rest had claimed their fish portion and were waiting again. Harold didn't delay them long because now he really did want to see what was inside. Salt, vinegar, and he cut the crispy batter open. Harold stopped, staring because the white flaky portion inside looked dead right, which should be impossible. "How?"

Chevy, E-type and Cooper were too busy chortling over Harold's reaction to answer. "Eat, because you won't want spraying with the answer and we'll all be chewing." Roller promptly filled his mouth with fish and a blissful expression crossed his face. Harold didn't wait any longer, quickly turning fish and chips into a few stray crumbs on his plate. There were plenty of chips to finish off with a butty, before he sat back with a sigh.

"Right, give. Has Caddi bought a trawler and air freight service or has he trained a seagull or cormorant?"

"The fish came from a gang over to the west, called the Bargees. Maybe they've got a trawler because the boss is called Skipper. Ten of them came through with a big refrigerated transit. They reckoned it started the journey full of this fish. Caddi is working on an agreement with the Ferdinands or Murphies and Trainspotters to get free passage for the next trip. Otherwise the van will never get this far, not now they know what's in it." E-Type grinned. "I told the driver he should have a proper van with fryers and sell fish and chips, wrapped in newspaper, and he reckoned we should open a pub with your beer."

Harold joined in the laughter because the few attempted pubs had been wrecked the first night as hordes of heavily armed customers descended on them. A van selling real fish and chips wouldn't survive five minutes. "If you opened a pub we could replace the dartboard with a crossbow target?" Roller grinned at Harold. "We'd have to give Patty a handicap or she'd clean us out."

"Can that Emmy use a crossbow as well? She must, because she can shoot." Cooper winced. "Christ, don't ever lend Caddi those pair for punishment practice." All four were completely relaxed, all the gangster swagger gone over a plate of fish and chips.

Harold found himself relaxing a bit as well, enough to enjoy the beer and backchat. "If we could find where those fish came from, Patty could shoot us some?" Harold mimed a crossbow firing downwards.

"Oh, we know where, because the cocky bastards told us. Nobody will try to nick them unless they've got a frogman's outfit. That or one of those spy or special forces things to breath underwater." Cooper looked Harold up and down. "Did you tuck one in your back pocket when you left, Harry?"

Harold patted his pockets. "Damn, it fell out. You still haven't said where the fish is from except in water, and I'd guessed that part?"

"Bloody canals. They've got a territory with canals on every side and some through the middle. Even the General wouldn't fancy getting across what bridges are left." Cooper shrugged. "Even then there's no way to raid for fresh fish." He held his hands out as if holding a fishing rod and put on a posh voice. "Just keep those heavily armed ruffians at bay lads, and keep the noise down or you'll frighten the fish away."

After the laughter died down Roller chipped in. "I reckon it's because of all that cleaning up that was done, the eco-thing before the crash where they cleared out the canals?" Everyone nodded because it had been a big exercise with lots of publicity. "Since then nobody has been throwing old bikes or fly-tipping waste in there so the water is finally clean enough. With the Crash the fish have been left alone to grow. I'll bet that lot have nets or something to stop the big ones getting out of their stretch."

The discussion about what to feed the fish, how much water you'd need, and if there was an abandoned cut near enough for a raid to catch some little ones rambled on for a while. Once that died away Cooper and Chevy started to revert to type, so Harold went to bed. He didn't want the evening spoiled. "Goodnight lads. It's been memorable."

"Do call again sir. Just leave the waitress a tip." E-Type stood up. "Allow me to escort you to sir's room."

"Better yet, leave the waitress. We'll need her again."

Harold ignored Cooper and went upstairs, escorted by E-Type, "So you don't get lost." E-Type showed Harold to the same room as the last time he stayed, then left. Harold closed the door and jammed the chair under the door handle instead of a lock or bolt. Then he whirled at a noise from the en-suite, stick coming up ready.

"I'm sorry." Her voice barely whispered. The bits of lacy something were probably meant to be sexy but not with an expression like that on her face, nor with the cane marks.

"Sorry. I thought you were one of that lot. An attack." Harold realised he still had his stick raised and lowered it. "Tell Caddi sorry, but no thanks." He turned to the door and removed the chair. Before he could open it, the young woman had hold of his arm.

"No, no, don't. Please? I'll be good, I promise."

"You don't need to be. This is Caddi's idea of a joke. I don't, won't do this sort of thing. Now off you go." Harold tried to open the door but now the girl crammed herself between him and the exit so he had to let go or get very personal.

She clung on tight. "He'll cane me really hard and put me in the house if I don't stay all night." A tear trickled down her cheek. "Mr Cadillac said you were interested, he could tell. You can do what you want. I'll be good, I promise."

With a shock Harold recognised Caddi's 'maid' from this evening, realising her cane marks must have been under her miniskirt. "I'm not interested, and he knows it. Tell him I said no thanks."

"No, please, let me stay tonight. I'll do anything if you let me stay."

Harold thought over what she said. "What do you expect to happen? No, not what you think will happen, but what he said you must do, exactly?" Harold thought about Caddi's sly tricks and twisted humour. The lass was insisting she wanted to stay, not have sex. The gang boss had to know that Harold would walk out rather than have sex with an unwilling woman, on camera or not. Though just in case, this room would definitely be wired up.

"I'm your bed warmer. He said you like spankings. I've to do whatever you want." She took a breath. "If I don't stay in bed with you all night I'll be punished for trying to get away. Then I'll be put in the house." The young woman clung closer. "I really will be good, even if you spank me really hard. I brought a cane?"

Harold stepped back, carefully removing her hands. "Go and get yourself cleaned up, then get in the bed." He kept his voice level. "Be careful because you're on film. Use a towel or something then pull the covers over you."

Her flat answer had an edge of bitterness. "Too late for that." She went across into the bathroom. Harold thought about Caddi's wording, and smiled.

When she came out he didn't ask her name, because that would also be interest and Caddi would use it. "Get in and get covered up." Harold went into the en-suite, washed and shaved. He'd be off early tomorrow before Caddi came up with some other type of harassment. When he came through, fully dressed, a pair of frightened brown eyes watched him cross the room.

Harold smiled before walking round the bed and lying on top of the other half of the quilt. "Same bed, all night. Now you stay under there, I stay on here, and the cameraman has a really boring night."

"But Mr Cadillac said…"

"This covers in the same bed all night. I'm sorry, but you've been caught up in a game between me and Mr Cadillac. Hopefully he'll be a good sport because you've done your part and he'll think this is funny." Harold really hoped so, for her sake. He turned away, taking a firm hold on his stick. This would be a long night because despite appearances he couldn't put it past Caddi to have offered her freedom if she killed Soldier Boy.

*   *   *

Harold didn't sleep much, so he didn't come downstairs in a brilliant mood the next morning despite the tiny shy smile when he left the bedroom. Early as it was, Chevy already sat at the table. "You're up early?"

"So are you, Chevy." Harold wondered if someone stayed on watch when he slept over.

"Caddi wants to talk to you before you leave."

"He'd better hurry."

"You'll have to wait for the escort." Harold held Chevy's eyes in a steady gaze until Chevy looked away. "All right, you don't but it won't be long. You could have coffee?" The offer wasn't gracious, but Harold needed coffee so he accepted. Sure enough by the time he'd finished, Chevy reported that the convoy had gathered and Caddi had arrived.

Harold barely stepped out of the door before Caddi started. "I thought you were interested? I certainly thought she was motivated enough."

Harold smiled. "She did exactly what you told her. But supposing she'd been threatened if we didn't have sex, now that could have been really embarrassing."

"Yes, especially if your lot saw the film." Caddi grinned. "After all those rules."

"Oh no, I meant having to apologise for permanently crippling Cooper or

Chevy." Harold kept his voice level and pleasant as he saw the anger in Caddi's eyes. "For stepping past good manners."

"Really?" Caddi kept the anger bottled; probably his curiosity helped. "How?" Behind him Mack tensed.

"You know I don't believe in forced sex and also my opinion of manners and limits if we are to continue doing business. You wouldn't push that or I'd stop doing business, then you'd not get your guns or electrics repaired. It would have been one of those two, Cooper or Chevy, who set it up judging by their laughter as I went to bed." Harold had spent most of the night thinking about how to deal with this. "I'd have to explain I didn't find that funny."

Caddi narrowed his eyes. "Permanently crippling sounds a bit extreme."

"Brutalising a lass for not being able to force me into sex would be excessive. Just crippling seems reasonable since they haven't threatened me directly, otherwise I could have just waited out there and shot them." Harold watched as Caddi kept his anger bottled under the threat of losing his gun repairs, or a rifle bullet out of nowhere killing a lieutenant. "Since we are playing a game, and I avoided your little trap, I'd assumed she'd be clear?"

"Oh yes, she can come back to my place once she's got her nightie off." Caddi watched to see if that had any effect. "It's a good thing none of my lot made that mistake. I'll warn them against it."

"Thanks, I wouldn't want to be impolite."

"Just hang on a few minutes while I check the convoy is ready." Caddi walked away a few steps then spoke quietly to Chevy, who looked startled then trotted off in a hurry to be someplace. Caddi spoke to another man who headed for the gates but came back in a few minutes. Harold looked around the compound while he waited but the place seemed deserted at this hour except for guards on the wall nearby and outside Caddi's house.

Caddi called and waved, so Harold walked over. "All ready. E-Type is going as escort since you didn't seem quite as peeved with him. Let's hope Charger has remembered his manners and comes back unscratched."

"I'm sure he will." Harold smiled as they headed towards the exit because Charger might be the most polite of the lot, though Harold wouldn't trust him as far as Daisy could throw the man. A loud voice interrupted.

"Fucking Pussy. I reckon she cut yer nuts off. A wench like that in the bed and you can't get it up?" Seven Hot Rods had come out of a house near the gates, heading straight for Harold. The speaker looked a lot like the man Chevy had called off the previous evening. "Soldier Boy? Soldier girl, unless you've taken up with that fucking queer."

Harold looked at Caddi. "I'm a bit annoyed this morning. Do you really want this?"

Caddi smirked. "Not permanently crippled, Soldier Boy. After all, he's only threatened you not the girl."

"Could be borderline, definitely concussive, and possibly fatal. I warned Chevy about how imprecise I can be when I'm annoyed." Harold meant that as he headed straight for the man, since the Hot Rod had a small No Cycling sign on his arm as a shield and wielded a machete. Harold would have to really stop him hard, even though the man only held one of the thinner, smaller machetes sold in hardware stores before the crash. All the gangsters thought Harold carried a wooden stick. He'd try to avoid blocking the machete if possible so Caddi didn't find out about the steel tube.

"Ooh, are you going to spank me?" The others laughed as the Hot Rod raised his machete and brought the shield round and forward. Harold didn't answer, just kept coming with his stick on his shoulder. The man expected to catch the blow, either a jab or swing, on the shield. Then he'd chop either Harold's arm or the stick. Harold started the blow as he took the next step, a wide looping swing out and round to hit the man at the side of the shoulder or head.

The man ducked a little and put up the shield, but Harold bent his legs and waist as he took the next step. He'd deliberately put plenty of power into the swing, enough so his opponent knew he hadn't feinted. The man knew Harold couldn't stop his swing, but crouching lowered the impact point, too fast for any reaction. A yell of pain heralded the steel tube striking against his hip bone and his leg gave a little. Harold straightened, taking another step as the man froze momentarily in shock and pain, then as the machete started coming over to chop he caught the man's wrist.

Harold stepped in close, pinning the shield between them, and grinned right into the startled face. Harold practiced long hours with the heavy steel stick, so his wrist muscles and grip were definitely over-developed. Now Harold closed his hand around the man's wrist-joint bones and flexed them. The Hot Rod's eyes flared with pain. "Let go or I'll crush it." Harold couldn't but knew that flexing the joint against itself and the thin layer of flesh around the bone caused excruciating pain. Stones had demonstrated once. The machete clattered to the ground.

"Enough, Soldier Boy." Harold stood very still, his other hand already raised to drive the brass boss of his stick down onto the Hot Rod's head.

"He wanted a spanking." Harold kept grinding the wrist bones, keeping the man close enough to pin his shield arm and in range to deliver a very bad headache at the very least.

"Don't worry, he'll wish he'd got spanked. Very bad manners like that deserve some sort of punishment." Caddi spoke without any real menace, but Harold saw the fear replacing pain in his opponent's eyes. He pushed the man backwards, stick at the ready, but the Hot Rod looked beyond him towards Caddi. Harold took a couple of steps back, glancing sideways. Caddi had his little smile back but rage flared behind his eyes. Behind him his bodyguard, Mack, had brought his baseball bat up to his shoulder, ready for trouble.

"I'll leave you to it." Harold knew whatever happened would be excessive because he'd already wound Caddi up, and now the gang boss had a victim. Harold felt momentarily sorry for the man, but then remembered the scroat would have killed him and been rewarded if the meeting had gone as planned.

"No, you should see. That's how it works at your place." Caddi smiled with his mouth, his good humour apparently restored. "I take notes." The gang boss looked over to the man now nursing his wrist, favouring his hip, and being supported by one of his friends. "Fifty yards range, keep running until I say." The man looked horrified and opened his mouth. "Since it's Soldier Boy, we'll let the women have a go."

Harold saw the man's relief and knew why. Caddi had copied the live crossbow target idea to give his men practice, but Hot Rod women wouldn't have any expertise. "Your women won't dare hit him."

"They'd better try fucking hard, or I'll put them out there." From Caddi's look he meant every word.

Harold ended up watching the most bizarre crossbow practice ever. Thirty women of varying ages dressed in everything from full cook's whites through to two scraps of nothing and aged from maybe sixteen to about fifty did their level best to stick crossbow bolts into a man limping as fast as he could. The women soon realised this wasn't a joke because the other Hot Rods were winding the crossbows for them, making bets, laughing at the bloke and giving advice. Harold kept his face straight as his companion of last night joined the practice, still in her 'nightie.'

Despite their inaccuracy, the sheer volume of bolts meant one of the women hit the target eventually. "That'll do. It's not moving target practice if he's laid on the floor squealing and bleeding." Caddi sounded much happier now. His men were laughing and joking like a bunch of schoolkids. The man had a crossbow bolt in his thigh opposite the hip Harold had hit, so he definitely couldn't run though he'd reverted to yelling rather than squealing.

Harold leant a bit closer to Caddi, speaking quietly. "Some might consider it unfair him having a machete and shield when I have to disarm. As unfair as our women wandering around dressed like some of these to get more victims for caning."

Caddi stayed silent for a few moments before answering. "A fair point. If they did I'd have no fit men in a week. These silly fuckers would have to come and check, then wouldn't be able to keep their stupid mouths shut or hands to themselves." Caddi raised his voice. "All right you bitches. Fun over, back to work." The women scattered back to the houses but a good few were still smiling.

"E-Type is ready, Soldier Boy." Chevy looked happy as well. He held up his hands showing his thick, muscled wrists. "I'm gonna try that because I reckon I'm stronger than you."

"There's a knack to it." Harold avoided any challenge about relative strength or he'd end up arm wrestling or some other stupid test. "Are we leaving today or not?" Caddi smiled as he accompanied Harold to the gate, where the car and four motorbikes parked behind the pickup made up his escort. All the way back Harold tried to decide if he'd stopped Caddi's worst excesses, or if he would be safer driving in the dark and risking a bullet. Caddi wouldn't risk a bullet in daylight because then he'd have to produce the gunman, especially if the man missed.

* * *

Nearly three weeks passed before Harold needed his stick again, but not for fighting this time. A grinning Liz tugged Harold into line. "Come on, hold your stick up to make this official. We were going to get Barry to hold his fireman's axe the other side but Jeremy is worried he'd let it drop. After all, Jeremy is here for his youngest grandchild." Harold held his stick up and outwards to complete the double line of smiling residents and tapped Casper's machete, being held out from the other side of the path. He smiled because Alfie sat in a wheelchair halfway down the other side of the line, holding a spear because a machete wouldn't reach from down there. At least part of the smile came from the faint blush when Alfie's nurse today, Hazel, saw that Harold had noticed.

Another part was that if she'd agreed to move out of the girl club and set up home with Jeremy, Matti really was over being kidnapped and dragged off into the night. Harold watched Jeremy knock on the door and heard Thandia's deep bark in response. The door opened and Harold nearly let his stick drop down. He hadn't expected Barry to answer the door. From the look on his face neither had Jeremy! "Yes, what do you want?" Barry had a superb deadpan face but Jeremy didn't seem to appreciate it.

"Um, er, Matti? Please?" Howls of laughter issued from inside the girl club and from those behind Harold who had been in on the joke. Everyone knew just how protective Barry tried to be where his granddaughters were concerned, even if the pair did their level best to avoid protection.

"At least you've got the decency to make an honest woman of the poor lass." More howls of laughter greeted that. "That is what you've come for?" Harold had no idea how Barry kept his face straight but he did.

"Yes? Please?" Jeremy tried to see past Barry but the broad ex-fireman more or less filled the doorway.

Then Barry looked back over his shoulder. "You can untie Matti and let her come out, because he really does want her." Barry put his hand on Jeremy's shoulder, shaking his head gently. "You're a brave man." Then he staggered, before moving sideways for Matti to squeeze past.

"Move over gramps, you're off the hook. I don't need a bodyguard now."

"Not quite off the hook, one to go yet." A smiling Barry moved outside as Doll, his other grandchild, followed along with the rest of those in the girl club including Elise and Thandia. For once Elise looked happy, actually throwing her confetti first even if she immediately reverted to holding onto the Mastiff. Sort of confetti, because long hours went into cutting coloured bits of plastic into tiny pieces. Every bit possible would be reclaimed and washed for reuse. Jeremy and Matti ran down the path under the arch of machetes, baseball bats and garden canes as more confetti showered down, before jumping over the twig broom at the end.

The pair went down the street hand in hand carrying Matti's clothes in bags and the crowd streamed off towards the dance house for the start of the monthly party. The couple would be back for the dancing but their names wouldn't go into the hat at the end. Three of those throwing confetti looked a bit baffled through their smiles. They were new refugees, who had just gone through their own official welcome at the gates since all these new rituals took place on dance day. Harold kept a wary eye out these days for that cauldron, especially since Sharyn had given in and accepted a black kitten called Grimalkin.

"Are you coming to the dance, wimp?"

Harold smiled. "No Liz, I'm on guard duty."

"Every dance night, apparently. Some of those new lasses are getting really curious about what it will take to get your name in that hat." Liz nudged. "Don't give me that look, they're just grateful." She raised her eyebrows. "Ooh, I wonder how grateful?"

Harold laughed. "I'll never know, because I don't accept grateful."

"That's another thing intriguing one or two, just what would you be interested in. Bethany is crowing that you called her sweet, at least twice." Liz raised an enquiring eyebrow.

"That's because of her hat. She keeps the first Gnome covered so it reads Sweet Gnome."

"Only since you called her that." Liz laughed at Harold's expression. "Oh Gods, you are so easy to wind up over women. They all know you're off the dance card but are wondering about in between dances." Liz nudged him again. "I'd tell them to break down and cry on you but its more fun watching them plot. I'll know if any of them succeed because you'll come into my forge to cry when they've done with you."

Harold smiled. "They could just let me be? The men don't bother you."

"Because they know they aren't sooty enough." She sobered. "Some of the new women are just having a lark, and a few can't understand why a gang boss hasn't got a woman. One or two actually want to be the gang boss's woman for the prestige or whatever, which isn't helped by the visitors asking who she is." Liz sighed. "It's this stupid world. I'd say pick one who'll just hang on your arm but that's not going to happen again is it?" Her face brightened. "Why do I care? I'm heartless, feckless and fancy free and it's dance night."

"You'll be more interested at Harvest Festival."

"There's going to be one this year?" Harold laughed and Liz scowled. "Ooh, you rotten soldier you. I'll just have to hope someone visits, though I'm getting worried." She frowned. "Wayland has stopped over four times now. For a sooty butterfly this is getting a bit like a relationship but he's the only smith who is allowed to leave his gang and go visiting. What's the Hot Rod smith like?"

"He's no more muscly than me but more to the point Caddi keeps him chained to the forge, more or less. I'll ask if the Ferdinands or the Murphies have a metal-beater." Harold nudged her this time. "One who's allowed out now and then, for sleepovers." Liz rolled her eyes in simulated ecstasy before heading off to get dressed for dancing.

Harold stood guard on dance nights, at either the gate or the corner guardhouse the other end of Orchard Close. He also looked after Amber while Casper went dancing. The young Doberman cross had been spoiled as she grew up, so she'd never become a ferocious guard dog like her sire. Sooty or Amber would bark hello at either friend or foe, though that worked for guard duty on dance night since only foe would be outside the walls. Tonight Emmy wasn't on duty with Sooty because Lenny and Patricia agreed the bun had probably cooked long enough. The slightest excitement might trigger the birth.

Matthew and Beth stood guard in number six, 'their' guardhouse halfway down the wall, because they claimed they had no need to dance in public. They'd moved into the front rooms of number eight, the next house along the wall, and now wanted a pup if more were bred. The dogs had better ears and eyes than the human guards, especially at night. Malt the Staffy cross often stood night guard with them for a while because he barked at approaching strangers. Better yet, he seemed to mean it, but wouldn't stay all night as he preferred to sleep in the brewery.

Tonight, in between scanning the old caravan park with the charred rubble at the far end, Harold worried about accommodation. Two of the last three refugees had moved into occupied houses, while one of the girl club moved out to make room for the other. There were still spare rooms in many houses but very few held whole families or even people who had been friends before the crash. Orchard Close had room for more refugees, but Harold worried that too much crowding would breed friction.

After Jon and the other traitors the girl club and Coven tried to defuse small disputes, but that would only work if the tension didn't rise too far. Harold thought it through, but the only solution was to find additional accommodation now, before crowding caused trouble. By dawn Harold decided the best way would be to get Finn and Rob to take a proper look at those terraced houses just outside the walls, to see what they'd need to make the whole row habitable.

* * *

Though with Rob still working on Emmy's water capture, Harold decided to leave it a couple of days. "Harold, Harold." Harold grinned and straightened from the weeding. It had been ages since Hazel had come running up yelling like that. She stopped, smiling back at him, trying not to hop from one foot to the other as she used to. After all, at sixteen Hazel had left her home with Harold and become an adult, sort of. "There's GOFS and Barbies, two of each and they want you."

"Ask someone to put them in number three please Hazel, while I get spruced up."

"No need. Vulcan says there's no need for all the, er, cow poop, because this isn't that sort of a meeting." Hazel blushed, just a little. "Chandra asked if I'd taken over searching from Alfie."

"Chandra would, but she's only joking. Though you could have brought Alfie down to the gate in his wheelchair?" Harold moved on sharpish as Hazel started to blush properly. "Is she wearing the silk curtains?"

That stopped the blush because Hazel giggled. "Yes, but with a pair of jeans under them and a jacket over the top. I know she was joking because they aren't coming in anyway, to save some time." Harold sped up from a walk to a trot, because that sounded urgent.

The gate had been left partly open, with Chandra, Ken, Vulcan and Ogou waiting just outside. Harold had barely put a foot through the gate when Vulcan spoke up. "Both gangs, GOFS and Barbies, are taking six top people to sort out a non-shooting problem. Bring the five people you need to make some serious decisions about extra refugees, your committee or however you work things out, and we'll lead you to the problem."

"Refugees?"

Vulcan grimaced. "The General has just taken the enclave across the water from us. Those who could escape have come through the flood and need help. These people aren't the fighters. They're in deep er, whatever and need a roof and a future. Will you help?"

"Yes, give me time to gather someone up."

Emmy came out of the guardhouse and Chandra pointed to her belly. "Good luck. Free advice from doc if you need it but you pay for medicine." She grinned. "Yeah, I'm a sucker. We'll wait in the cars until you get sorted." The Barbie turned, heading for her SUV while waving off the thanks.

Harold spun on his heel, and went back through the gate. At least contacting everyone didn't take long with the telephone. Within five minutes Casper, Billy, Patty, Sharyn and Lenny had arrived at the gate. Shortly afterwards Liz, Sal, June, and Seth turned up and more were coming down the road so word of a problem had spread. Though Harold only needed five, including a medic because if these people were running, they might be in a bad way. "Lenny, you are coming to meet the GOFS and Barbies."

"I'm a pacifist, Harold."

"Yes Lenny and if trouble starts, duck. You'll be behind the armour plate in the minibus with someone willing to do all the shooting necessary. Patty and Casper to be exact." Harold held up a hand. "Yes Casper, you're one-handed but you'll have that nasty sawn-off of Seth's." Seth opened his coat enough to show the weapon before passing over a box of shells.

"No, take Seth because he'll reload faster." Casper passed the ammunition back. "You're already taking two non-combatants."

"Yeah ok, but Sharyn will carry a pistol as if she can shoot. Lenny, I will want you to assess the health of some people but quietly." Harold looked round. "I said bring firearms, Patty."

Patty turned, pointing at the back of her jacket. "I brought three." She waved her crossbow. "If I need them."

"I brought the two-two rifle and four pistols between you and me?" Billy smiled at Harold. "I'll pass them across in the pickup."

"You need a big rifle Harold." Liz indicated her coat. "I carried it for Sharyn."

"Not this time. The big rifles are better left here in case Caddi gets ambitious while we're preoccupied." Harold turned. "Casper, walk down with us please. Put your shotgun in the pickup for Billy without the Army seeing."

The minibus coughed and spluttered into view with Louise behind the wheel. "This might not make it back."

"I've got a towrope in the pickup and that's diesel." Harold nodded towards the SUVs waiting down the road. "Let's not keep them waiting." Everyone loaded up and followed the GOFS and Barbies.

*   *   *

On the way to wherever these people were, Harold stressed to Billy that this should be a peaceful meeting, to deal with refugees. The young man's job would be to guard the vehicles, with a shotgun, but he should only shoot if others did. As they travelled further Harold realised where the convoy would end up. Sure enough, the vehicle ahead turned up a long road parallel to the edge of the flooding to the north of the GOFS. A crowd of vehicles and people ahead turned out to be more Barbies, more GOFS, and a lot of people who didn't belong to anyone local. Over half of them seemed to be wet anywhere from ankle height up to some waists.

Gofannon waved Harold and his group over. "We've asked and these people would rather not go to the Geeks, so Hawkins hasn't been invited. Anyone left behind won't have much option now, it'll be whoever they can get to." He raised a hand and pointed. "If you look through between the houses you'll see that the road is blocked now. Here, use these." Harold used the binoculars. A mile away two vehicles with about a score of armed people blocked the road, one of the only three dry routes left through the flood.

"What about the other two roads?"

"Blocked or will be soon." Ken gestured at the refugees. "Some of these came in motors but most walked or came through the water because they couldn't get to the roads." Even as she spoke another six partially wet people came through the houses further along the road and trudged forward to join those waving in the crowd.

"Why are they running? Is the General that bad?"

"Probably because he's using the Bloodsuckers as shock troops and they are barbaric bastards. Most of these can't stay because their homes will be uninhabitable. The shooting you can hear is their fighters, dying to give these folk a chance to get away." Ken sighed. "They've smashed holes to let the canal water into their drains to stop the toilets working, wrecked the electric junction boxes, and those plumes of smoke are their food stores. Scorched earth, or flooded anyway." She indicated the crowd. "They're not fighters, but damn they are good haters."

"Are they all that's left?"

"Yeah, they weren't much bigger than your lot, but had good neighbours one side and the water as protection this side. Then the Generals, Bloods and MiB teamed up to roll over their neighbours. This lot took in refugees from the conquest, a conquest because every hint of free will or speech ended up dead in a hole. These people tried to beef up their fortifications but too little, too late." Ken looked out across the water. "That General will take some stopping now, though our moat is a bit wider than most."

Harold looked at the refugees. "How many so far?"

"A hundred and fourteen but they tell us more might be coming." Ken jerked her head. "Come on. Now you've seen the problem we have to talk because none of us can take all of them."

By the time Harold joined the GOFS and Barbies he'd brought the rest of his people up to date. Lenny had already pointed out that the refugees looked fit and well fed. Providing they had shelter, warmth and food Lenny thought they should be fine. Harold looked them over, adding more clothes, bedding, and electrical goods such as kettles and heaters to the list of what was needed. Some of the people only carried packs, though the six vehicles were piled high with bundles and packages.

* * *

"Mercy or mercenary?" Harold looked around the group of gangster leaders. "Are you going to trade for profit out of this, or are we going to chip in together to fix those people up?" He held up a hand to stop the immediate protest. "I know you'll take some coupons for protection, but are you gonna charge them for every seed or spade they need to feed themselves, or every electric kettle, or blanket?"

A Barbie that Harold hadn't met before answered him. She acted like one of their elite, but didn't need a wig over her mop of golden curls. "Fat chance anyway because they're broke, but no. The thing is, we can't because we haven't enough of everything, even using the new goods still in Beth's. The first problem is shelter because apart from odd houses here and there, there's no empties with both water and electric. We've got suitable groups of decent houses, ones with mainly intact roofs and windows, but they're missing either water or electric."

The GOFS boss nodded. "We've got houses like that, weatherproof and with electricity or running water but not both. We even know where the break is in one water main but the government team reckoned it's too badly damaged and sealed the pipe. To be honest, we can't fix them up with heaters, beds or kettles either, because we don't have that number of spares. Wayland can make pans, spades, forks, anything in iron, but it'll take time." Gofannon wry look took in all Harold's group. "We laughed at your people out there clearing those houses to make fields and how you were always out scavenging all that crap. Now I'll bet you've got plenty of spare electrical kit, beds, seeds, spades and that sort of shit."

"Not plenty, but a decent amount. You've got more than you think, in all those houses that are without electric or water but not derelict. Electrical goods will be damp and probably need some TLC but we've got a man for that. We'll trade repairs and seed for some goodies from either of you." Harold grinned. "The dearer you make what we want, the less you'll get in return so mercy or mercenary?"

The GOFS and Barbies eyed each other, muttering among themselves until Chandra threw up her hands in mock despair. "Everyone knows I'm a sucker anyway. I've got no fucking reputation to lose. I vote for mercy, all right?" She pointed at the refugees. "For fuck's sake look at them." Chandra shrugged at the Orchard Close group. "You'll have to plug up your ears today because it's a bit beyond cripes."

Patty nodded slowly. "Yeah, quite a bit beyond. In any case, we're off our patch." She shrugged as well. "We're not prudes, we just need the rules to keep the visitors in line."

"It works as well." Vulcan turned to Harold. "How many can you take? I reckon we can find housing for fifty plus in a nice neat defensible block providing your bloke can sort out that water main. I've no doubt he can, but I mean at a price we can afford." He looked at the refugees. "There'll be more trickling in so we'd rather you two took most of these."

"I'll have to talk to the rest." Harold hooked a thumb at his group. "We'll have to squeeze up as well as repairing some houses. If anyone's got cement we'll trade for that?" He scowled. "That or I'll be trying to get some out of the Geeks and they'll sting me."

A medium height, middle-aged woman wearing a blonde wig and a smart suit with a knee-length skirt, a mile away from the usual Barbie shocking, held out her hand. Harold shook and she gestured to a tall black woman with a blonde wig. "I'm Malibu and that's Christie, with Ken the three original Barbie Girls. We've got something to help you with the cement. We'll pay some of the electrician's or plumber's bill with soft toilet rolls and wet wipes." Malibu's smile widened to a grin. "The Geeks might all be arses, but I'll bet the managers care enough about theirs to trade cement for soft wipes." The whole group laughed and agreed, then split into their gangs to talk about practicalities.

Harold's main question had to be how many Orchard Close could fit into the existing accommodation or the nearest damaged houses. The next problem would be how to find enough food for them. The refugees would supply coupons to buy food from the marts, but that might not be enough to feed them over winter. The other big problem would be how well these folk accepted Orchard Close rules. Since they came from a working enclave instead of being scattered refugees, the new influx of people wouldn't just blend in.

Before any of them were accepted, they had to agree to obey Orchard Close rules regardless of their previous arrangement. That included paying into the Coven, working in the fields or anywhere else needing extra labour, and sharing the food. If the refugees agreed, the influx could be temporarily housed by cramming everyone into the occupied houses. Most of the refugees could then move into the terrace block as soon as they were fixed, though the work would now be a priority.

Sharyn and Patty were in the Coven and had a rough idea of the food situation. With the good harvest coming in and a bit of belt tightening, both thought Orchard Close might accommodate forty refugees though they hoped for less. Over the coming winter the extra labour could clear and break new ground to raise more food next year.

* * *

When the gangs reassembled the Barbies were willing to take fifty plus in a small cul-de-sac without electricity. They would pay for the Orchard Close electrician, Finn, to find and fix the break. If he couldn't, the Barbies would supply the labour to dig a trench to the nearest electricity supply. They would scavenge cable if Finn gave them an idea of what he'd need, and pay him to connect the new supply. The Barbies laughed when asked how they would pay, asking Harold if he wanted to come round Beth's with a shopping trolley. Though once they sobered, Malibu promised there were a variety of goodies in there, and they'd supply a list.

The GOFs could take up to sixty, but not all of them now. Even the first ones needed the Orchard Close plumber, Rob, as soon as possible to connect running water. Until then the new people would stink a bit since they'd be carting every drop from the nearest working taps. Gofannon revealed he still had bolts of cloth to help pay for repairs, and boxes of thread for sewing or embroidery. Wayland promised he had the metal to make up garden tools, but they'd be rough because he'd use brute hammer power instead of charcoal or coke where possible. He'd also provide machetes, or pretty much anything that could be made out of a lump of scrap iron or steel.

"What about a shaped leading edge for a wooden plough blade?" Harold had just remembered how much those with hand ploughs complained the metal edges weren't right to turn the earth properly.

Wayland laughed. "Ploughs? Why not, I'm sure we can find a picture someplace to work from. Do you want me to shoe the horses?" A ripple of laughter greeted that; any horse had long since become steak or stew.

"We'll hammer out the nuts and bolts, or ploughs, later. For now we agree we can take these people?" Everyone nodded and Gofannon stepped out from the group, waving at the anxiously waiting refugees to get their attention. "We can find homes, but you'll have to obey the rules for each gang." Gofannon indicated left, then right. "We are the GOFS, those are the Barbie Girls, and those are Orchard Close or Soldier Boy's mob." A ripple ran through the refugees.

"Which one is Sanctuary?"

"Some people call us that but sorry, we can't take you all. We're one small enclave, with no extra housing nearby." Harold shrugged. "We've knocked the nearest down and a good bit of the rest of our patch is derelict."

"Here, look at this, it's Orchard Close. Pass it along and use Bluetooth to copy the picture but I want the phone back." Ogou held out a phone for a man to collect. He passed it along the refugees, with some copying the picture to their phones or in a couple of cases to tablets. Harold held out a hand for the phone when it came back. Ogou had taken a long shot of Orchard Close, with a wide swathe of crops and the gardeners working busily among them.

"Emmy would love to see this." She would because nobody from Orchard Close had thought to take one.

"Copy it." Ogou scowled at the other GOFS. "I took that because I've been trying to persuade these idiots we should do the same." He took the phone back then passed it over to Malibu.

"Bloody hell. Our lot always rabbit on about the gardens after they've visited but I've never realised how big they are. How many acres is that, Soldier Boy?" She copied the picture onto her phone and passed Ogou's phone back. "How many does that feed, with veggies since I didn't see a goat or cow?"

"We reckon there's well over twenty, maybe thirty acres. There'll be more once we've finished demolition and dug up the caravan park, the one near the gate. Emmy reckons that once we've got it all working properly, it'll feed well over two hundred if we get flour from the mart. Rabbits and spam provide the fat and meat." Harold smiled. "She's not satisfied with that. Emmy really fancies growing wheat or hops and barley."

"Fucking cripes. You'll get tourists." Malibu laughed. "You can set up weekend retreats where us executives can get back to nature." She sobered and looked at the picture again. "I'll want to talk sometime about what it takes to organise that sort of acreage, because that's got to be more complicated than dig and plant." Her eyes narrowed. "For starters you don't rely on the mart for seeds, do you?"

"Not completely." Harold smiled. "Though we'll not charge too much."

"I'll bet our refugees will want some at any price. I don't think they stopped to dig up much before running." Malibu turned back to the refugees, raising her voice. "Right, who wants to join the Barbies? We can take about fifty but it could be rough until you dig a bloody great trench for Soldier Boy to fix up electric. Then you'll have to build a wall around the houses for defence, and find furniture or gear from any house that has some."

An anonymous voice spoke up. "What about the men, our men? We've heard rumours." A ripple of agreement ran through the crowd.

Malibu scowled at Chandra, but without much heat. "Our reputation is fucked now anyway, so I may as well own up. The men and women out in the estates, where you'll be, are safe enough. The guards we supply might try to tempt a few of either into Beth's, our headquarters, but it will be temptation not kidnap. Though you stay clear of Beth's unless you're invited because we really are mean bitches." She shrugged. "Pay your shares, don't give us any shit and that's it. If any of your women fancy getting payback from the General, we'll fix them up with weapons."

Gofannon smiled at her sour tone. "We feel more or less the same way as long as you pay up. Some of our men might try to tempt your women but no kidnap or rape. We hope some men want to be fighters because that greedy bastard will come this way sooner or later. You pay for protection and we supply guards full-time to stop any roaming assholes. Building a wall around the houses and finding any furniture from nearby housing will be up to you. You'll carry water by hand until a plumber sorts some type of supply but the houses are sound." He waved a hand to include the other two gangs. "Between us we'll fix you up with basics, and a way of growing some food, but it'll be tight this winter."

"Do you charge for electric?" Another anonymous voice spoke up but once again a mutter of support went through the crowd.

"No, none of us do. The Geeks will if you go there. If we pass you through Caddi won't, but he'll sort through your young people for women and fighters and won't ask." Gofannon mock-bowed Harold forward. "This I've gotta hear, because none of us are sure what his lot do."

Harold stepped forward, smiling quietly because he'd never tried to put it in words before. "I suppose it's a sort of commune, but no free love. Everyone will pay into a fund and work part of their time in the fields, which provides them with basic food. No rent, electricity is free, but anyone wanting coffee or other luxuries buys them out of their own coupons. We've got a medic, a dentist, and people who'll fix your kettle or maybe a TV, knit a jumper, or make a shirt or skirt. Anyone with a skill provides that instead of working those rolling acres. They can trade with other gangs and will keep most of their profit. If you are willing to help with self-defence, I will train you." His smile widened. "The committee, usually called the Coven, deals with collection of coupons and distributing food. This is Sharyn, my sister and head witch."

A few smiles showed in the crowd, then a voice spoke up. "You and your sister run the place?"

Harold laughed. "Not really. Patty here is part of the Coven. As you can see, she doesn't take to being bossed about."

Patty waved her crossbow, letting the laughter die out before speaking. "Maybe not, but if there's a dispute and Soldier Boy lays down the law, then I salute like a good little soldier. He doesn't do it often, but you've got to understand that part." She shrugged. "If you don't, I'll be right behind him with this to make it stick." Patty raised her crossbow again.

Gofannon raised his hands to get attention again. "Soldier Boy will take thirty five, the Barbies fifty, and we'll pick up the rest and any more that trickle in. Now decide." He turned his back. Among the refugees discussions sprang up and groups began to coalesce.

* * *

"We did wonder just how Orchard Close were organised. That wouldn't work for us." Wayland smiled. "Can you imagine the soup kitchen chugging round each estate on a winter's morning?"

"True. We're all within one set of walls, though that is going to be a problem in time." Harold shrugged. "I didn't expect to grow like this, not as quickly." A shout interrupted them, from a man upstairs in one of the houses looking over the floods. Gofannon beckoned to Harold and Ken, so they went to look. A pickup truck had reversed out from the far side of the water, stopping halfway, about half a mile away. Four men drove in stakes either side of the roadway, before stringing police tape between them. Two 'No Entry' signs, the old council workmen variety, were placed on the road to drive the message home.

Gofannon pointed to a group of four refugees who broke clear of the nearest flooded houses further along the road. "Here's some more." They were wading through deep water, stumbling now and then over unseen obstacles while the smaller of them had water up to her chest. The men by the pickup had climbed back in but it stayed as the small group finally reached the shallows. GOFS watchers from the houses came out to help the refugees get clear of the water. A shot rang out, from the General's pickup. The refugee bringing up the rear threw up his hands and fell face down in the shallow water.

"You nasty fuckers. Did you bring a fucking rifle, Soldier Boy?" Ken shook her fist as the pickup drove away. "What the fuck was that for?"

"A warning. That's the boundary and they've got a decent shooter with a good rifle." Harold glared at the pickup. "I said this wasn't a rifle type trip which is a pity."

"He's laid in the back and only his head shows." Gofannon's lowered his binoculars and his eyes sharpened. "You can nail him from here?"

"It won't be the first time, though I had an Army rifle last time. That poser thing of mine will do the job." Harold indicated the dead man, definitely dead even though he'd been turned over and pulled out of the water. "If someone pulls that sort of stunt again, you send word. 'Bang bang' on the radios and I'll burn diesel and tyres."

"I'll buy your ammo and fill your tank. Waiting until that poor sod thought he'd made it was just plain fucking nasty." Ken spat in the direction of the now retreating pickup. "Now let's sort out these poor fuckers." She turned on her heel and stomped back to the main group.

There were no fighters or firearms and few machetes or homemade spears among the refugees. They'd brought over two hundred rounds of ammunition, two reloading kits, some brass, primers and propellant so the General didn't get them. The firearms were being used by the men and women dying the other side of the water to give their families a breathing space. After a quick discussion, every refugee's name and where they went would be recorded by the

GOFS. If any of the fighters survived to make it across the flooded stretch, they could re-join any friends or family.

Harold stopped the pickup by Caddi's spies on the first trip home. He pointed out that the really pissed off refugees coming behind him might kill any arse they found alone. The two men took the hint, leaving with a message that Orchard Close would be closed for business for three days. Eventually thirty seven people including six children chose Orchard Close instead of the GOFS or Barbies. All the Orchard Close diesel vehicles were needed to ferry them and the bedding and household goods the refugees had brought in packs and cars. The shooting died away across the water as more columns of smoke rose into the sky. The last of the stores and strongpoints were being torched to stop the conquerors getting them.

* * *

Harold made three trips in his pickup, taking the Blaser rifle just in case, but the General and his allies were busy consolidating. Hopefully, according to the last refugees Harold picked up, the General and all his allies were beating their heads bloody in frustration because with luck even the weapons would go up in the last fires.

Then the rest of what the man said registered. "You want pens? What for, chickens?" Harold stared at the square shapes under sacking and two rolls of netting.

"No, rabbits." The man gestured to the side. "I'm George and this is Mary-am. We brought Flopsy and Mopsy. Rabbit Bob over there brought his three because the car is his. He's got Rocket Man the buck, and two does called Pinky and Snow."

"Why? I mean why bring rabbits not the names."

"Rocket Man is a prize buck. We bred rabbits for meat." George sighed. "We had an agreement that ours, the first ones, wouldn't go into the pot. We killed all the others and everyone ate as much as possible, then flushed what we couldn't carry so those bastards didn't get any."

"But why? There's rabbits everywhere." Harold found he really had scratched his head.

"Not like these." Maryam flipped the cover off a cage. "These are New Zealand Whites. We can grow a hundred and eighty pounds of prime rabbit meat every year from this pair, and that fur is pure luxury inside your winter mitts." She smirked. "No chasing, and depending on when they're harvested these are a fry-up, roast or stew."

"What about food? Do they need something special?" Harold remembered someone suggesting keeping rabbits but they'd meant catching wild ones. These big white meaty beasts were a whole new ball game.

"Rabbit pellets would help, but if not we can find enough forage among the abandoned housing. That's not as good so it will slow breeding but not too much." Maryam glanced anxiously at her husband and then at a nearby man who must be Rabbit Bob. "Can we keep them?"

"Yes, if the Coven agree but that sounds good to me. I might even get you some rabbit food, pellets was it?" All three nodded eagerly. "Come on then, load up." Harold looked at the estate car. "On second thoughts if that's diesel, just bring it." The whoop from Rabbit Bob answered that.

*   *   *

Liz, Emmy and Sharyn were waiting when Harold came back with the rabbit express. "We've got most of them in the dance house or the canteen while we work out where the hell to put them." Emmy almost wrung her hands. "I didn't cater for all this lot when I said we'd grown enough. Cripes Harold, how do we feed them?"

"From your rolling acres helped by their lovely coupons buying lots of mart rubbish?" Harold pointed out of the gates at the estate car. "Wait until you meet Rocket Man and Rabbit Bob. He wants to grow giant bunnies for the pot, though we might not want to advertise that to avoid rustlers in the night." Harold looked up the street. "More important, can we cram all these people in someplace tonight?"

"Yes, but temporarily. We'll need those terrace houses Harold, and right now." Liz grinned. "Though I'll give these people their due, they're keen to set into whatever work is needed." Her grin faded. "When the final list is sorted out, of who will cram in where and who will move house, your glower will get serious overtime. Not to impress the new ones, but from those who have got used to a four bedroom house with two or three residents."

"What about the two who possibly need their own house?"

"Our two ladies of the night? Not a problem because there are two bed-roomed houses. We'll make sure they get one of those. As I said, we'll explain the options while you glower." Liz smirked. "With Patty and her crossbow as backup I hear."

"In case someone cries and he goes soft on them." Emmy patted her bump. "Since I can't look threatening just now."

Harold spoke to some and glared at others as directed. Although some refugees overnighted on the floor of the dance house, the second night those still without beds slept on settees in houses. In many cases the new residents just moved in because Orchard Close had a policy of putting furniture in un-used bedrooms and keeping every room aired and dry. Several days of scrambling about and cripesing in the six storage houses produced enough extra furniture to give everyone a bed and mattress, though some still slept clothed or in sleeping bags while quilts were made. The extra beds now crammed into bedrooms and sometimes lounges or studies would eventually furnish the terraces, though first there'd be some serious repairing and scavenging.

*   *   *

Meanwhile, extra people weren't the problem the other side of the swamp, in the conquered enclave. "Well that was a waste of time and fucking manpower." The man in pseudo-Army uniform with a lot of extra braid and a peaked hat scowled. "These miserable bastards more or less wrecked the whole fucking enclave. We ended up with fuck all." He glared at one of his advisors. "This is your fault. Rhys, you said these two enclaves would be easy with plenty of fucking and loot for the Bloods."

"I didn't expect them to do this. On the bright side you didn't have too many losses once the Bloods got over the wall. The first enclave supplied entertainment as well as civvies and a few fresh fighters." The older man shrugged. "You've ended up just one gang away from Orchard Close. That's a really rich prize, better than these two combined." Smiling, Rhys finished with, "They can't flood that place and there's a shitload of tradespeople."

"Easy wasn't painless. They killed some and wounded a lot of my men before we closed in. Now the Bloods will want to work their annoyance off on someone. I can't go round this water, and going through can't be rushed. I can't push to the northeast because the fucking Army are too close. I need a quick and easy for the Bloods, one with some rape and pillage at the end." The General turned as a man behind him cleared his throat. "What is it Branson?"

"You owe us an enclave in return for the automatic weapons. If you want a fight that will supply some women for the Bloods, we've got one for you though I'll want the women back as workers. We'll be keeping the enclave so the Bloods can't have the loot." Branson smiled despite the sour look, because nobody would start on the MiB boss or his lieutenants since all three carried automatic rifles. "It's one that needs lunatics with machetes, because it's too near the Army for our weapons. A good practice for this Orchard Close?"

"Let me see the details, because we'll have to wait for the minor injuries at least to recover. When we've dealt with your problem we'll have to wait another three months for the serious injuries to heal up properly. I'll get a few people to look at ways round or over this water." The General glared across the water towards the GOFS. "Though there's still a few arseholes hiding in this bloody mess. I want the fuckers dead." He climbed into his Humvee and roared off, much to everyone else's relief. The remaining fighters and commanders shrugged and got on with flushing out any surviving defenders. They'd captured the bloody enclave, and not too many died, so that seemed good enough for the men up on the sharp end.

* * *

Even as the General's men rooted out the few hidden fighters or they escaped, a few miles away other gangs worked to make all the escapees comfortable. In the ruins that belonged to Orchard Close and had already been searched once, a small party clustered around Patty. "Floorboards? Are you serious?" Bernie stared while the gang of scavengers tried not to laugh at his outrage. "Cripes Patty, I was joking before about taking up the floors. Are we building huts for them to live in or what?"

"I told you before. Everything is useful, it just takes time to work out what for." Patty shrugged. "Those moving into the terraces might like the holes in the floorboards filled up but more importantly Rocket Man and his ladies like a proper floor, not a bit of rough concrete."

"This is for the perishing rabbits?" Bernie paused. "There's only five of them altogether."

"But they have already had their own welcoming dance, straight after arriving. Apparently we've got about a month before the hoppity-hop of tiny bunny feet. Well technically just under two months before they hoppity hop away from mummy, by which time she will be looking at a nest for the next batch. Breed like rabbits? Does that ring bells?" Patty tapped Bernie on the head. "Ding dong?"

Bernie smiled. "How soon can we eat them? Because I reckon we can actually get a joint off those beasties, slices of real meat."

"Fry-up at ninety days but some bunnies will become mummies, so we need floorboards for more runs and hutches. They're going to live in high-rises inside garages. We need oodles of Vinyl, laminate, or wood, preferably not rotten, and lino will do nicely to stop top bunny leaking onto bottom bunny." Patty pointed dramatically. "Go forth and be fruitful, your orchard needs you."

A competition quickly developed between those gathering bunny food and those trying to build up compost heaps but Harold called a truce. The two parties agreed that the bunny food came first because that turned into food faster, and anyway any left over each day went into compost. Any surplus greenery weeded, trimmed or otherwise available, went into compost as well as rabbit droppings and the soil in the runs when that needed changing.

Within a week Emmy had consulted with her gnomes and they began to supervise the bunny farmers. Emmy approved of a spare reservoir of protein. Overgrown lawns outside derelict houses became hay, to be carefully dried and stacked in nearby empty garages. Scrawny self-seeded root veggies from the ruins, peelings, veggie tops, borage, leaves, and shoots all went to bunny for snacks pre-compost. Liz gave up her tempering experiments, this time to make brackets for bunny-runs. She also turned some of the old style machete blades into a type of scythe.

Useful skills appeared among the refugees. Charlie, an electrical engineer, seemed very happy buried inside recalcitrant appliances from washing machines to vacuum cleaners. A real carpenter with his hand tools took over Sandy's old workshop. Three good hand knitters, none of them quite Patty, swore that with all the lovely wool and patterns to work with they would improve. Extra gnomes with their own expertise and experience joined Emmy's gang while enthusiastic amateurs volunteered to collect calories or dig new ground.

*　　*　　*

While the Orchard Close scavengers worked to make the new residents comfortable, their plumber and electrician spent their time fixing up houses for the GOFS and Barbie share of the refugees. Chandra stayed in Orchard Close as a hostage while Finn connected the mains electricity supply to a group of houses for the Barbies. Harold made a request just before she left, which definitely threw the usually unflappable Barbie off-balance for a moment. "Why would you want them?"

"Does it matter? I know you have a pet shop in Beth's. Now I want a pickup full of rabbit pellets in part payment for the electrical work." Harold smiled. "The stuff is no good to you so it's a cheap way to pay us."

"It might be less cheap if I knew why you needed it." Her suspicious look moved from Harold to Patty and then Casper without finding any hint of an answer. "Are you trying to capture and breed rabbits?"

"Not a chance. Any rabbit we catch goes into burger or the pot. Do you want to trade or not?" Harold shrugged. "I'll take soft loo rolls?"

"No you won't, or not many, but since you are all immune to my wiles I'll have to consider rabbit food. Though not everyone here is immune." Chandra smirked. "One of us will find out sooner or later."

"By which time you will have already let us have the bunny food. Maybe we have a new recipe for stew or curry?" Harold laughed at Chandra's mock scowl. "Though I will still want some other seriously desirable goodies from

Beth's, since Finn reported there were a lot of smaller problems in those houses. They've been stood empty a long time."

"I know, I know. I don't mind the trading for pet food, it's not knowing what the, um, cripes it's worth that bugs me." Chandra frowned again. "I'll have to talk to the others, and see how much we've actually got. We've been more interested in eating the rabbits than if we can feed them." She smiled rue-fully. "This is really mean, bringing it up just before I leave so I can't investigate now."

"But think what fun you'll have investigating another time?" Harold laughed as Chandra pouted and carefully smoothed out her tight dress.

"Oh, not just me." She sighed dramatically. "I know the answer will be yes, but not the value."

"Good enough. Just weight up what anyone else will offer."

Shortly afterwards Harold, Patty and Casper watched the Barbie convoy head off, Barbie Radio hammering out at full volume. Patty smirked. "A few people will have a lot of fun resisting the questioning." She sobered. "I'll just have a little chat first, to point out that they'll have a lot more fun if they keep their big mouths shut about yummy bunnies. Better yet, if they keep quiet they won't have me popping round for a visit." She patted her crossbow.

Harold frowned. "You, me, the Coven and the girl club."

"The Barbies will find out eventually, Harold." Casper grinned. "Then they'll try and kidnap a bunny."

"Before that, we have hutches to fix, for both bunnies and the new refu-gees."

To fix up the latter, bricks were gathered and stacked to connect the ter-race houses into the wall surrounding Orchard Close. As soon as the new walls grew high enough willing hands tore a hole in the original barrier, utilising the bricks to raise and thicken the new addition. Fixing the plumbing and elec-trics had to wait until Rob and Finn, with their apprentices, had finished their work on the new GOFS and Barbie estates. Though an electric cable across the gardens for blow heaters to get rid of the damp sparked a flurry of other work.

Despite boarded front windows and a lack of furnishings or bathroom facilities some hardy souls moved in just to get some space. Willing hands wielded brooms and then paintbrushes, carried in the furniture, or raised a row of four composting outhouses. The windows at the rear sported curtains, and radio music and even laughter rang out while the block still echoed with the sound of hammers. Elsewhere other new arrivals set to with a will, farming, ripping down more ruins, or tearing long trenches in the old caravan park tarmac. Food might be a bit short this winter, but the latest arrivals were making sure it would only be one winter. Under it all ran a deep, brutal truth. This had to work, because now they had nowhere else to run.

Chapter 5:

Spreading the Happiness

In the bunker deep beneath the countryside, the mood seemed more relaxed for this meeting. Owen looked at the screen which showed lines of prisoners in orange suits digging up potatoes. "How is the harvest going this year, Henry?"

"Very well. We'll do better next year with the extra farmland." Henry nodded to Grace. "The extra gardeners from York will help, though not in Yorkshire of course or they'll be tempted to run off home."

"Can I take it that the new arrangement worked, Joshua, Vanna?" They glanced at each other and Joshua spoke up.

"Much better. Vanna's people broke the resistance with armour, prompting a serious attempt to break out. We were waiting with regular Army units. The soldiers showed no reluctance when faced with just another mob trying to overrun the guard posts." Joshua smiled happily. "Vanna's people kept sweeping them forward onto the guns, then mopped up as the survivors ran."

"My people, those seconded to Joshua, are now working back through York making sure they didn't miss anyone. With some judicious repairs to water and electricity we can move people, our people, into some of the better housing to develop the area." Vanna grimaced. "Civil servants. We can even reopen marts for them since this time those weren't specifically targeted."

"We should bring in factory workers, good little drones to process food that is produced in the newly liberated area around York." Ivy smiled. "There is a bonus even before Henry's tractors get busy. A quick survey shows a lot of sheep on the Yorkshire Moors and the Scottish Borders, and even some feral cattle and horses. We'll get them rounded up and York will make an excellent centre for processing them."

"Will there be enough to keep the cities fed?" Owen shrugged. "There is a hiccup with the Argentinian supplies. Buenos Aires and Montevideo haven't been starving fast enough because they have access to open ocean, an ocean teeming with fish. The Argentine Navy stopped the fishing and both cities went crazy." He sighed. "Cutting off the fishing from both at the same time turned out to be stupid, not efficient. Several thousand of the scum broke out of Buenos Aires and spread out across the countryside, which unfortunately contains a lot of food. The escapees won't starve so they must be hunted down, which will disrupt food production."

"I hadn't intended using the sheep and cattle for the cities. I intended giving our drones some real meat for a change, but only the older animals because Henry doesn't want us to clear all the livestock. He wants to leave enough sheep running about to provide a yearly supply until we can begin formal sheep farming again." Ivy's brow wrinkled in thought. "I can arrange for the pork content of spam to go down again but the scum are already noticing a difference. Perhaps I can use the older mutton to raise the meat content." She suddenly smiled. "We can put in other meat. Henry, can you arrange for all vermin caught on the farms to be frozen and forwarded for processing?"

"All of it, not just the rabbits?" Henry grimaced. "There's a good percentage of rodents?"

"Meat is meat as long as we cook it to kill any bugs, and the less civilised scum already eat rat-burgers." Ivy turned to Owen. "Though we can't do this for ever or there'll be no pork content at all."

"Can't we give the cities some of the fish? There's plenty coming in now the retained population have trained up as fishermen. With the foreign fishing boats we rounded up at the beginning as potential spies and terrorists, we have some sizeable fleets out now." Victor, the navy man, smiled happily. "We've revived the British fishing industry, and the Naval vessels protecting the fleets are still snapping up extra boats operating out of small ports on the continent."

"Not a chance. That fish is providing the oils, fats and protein for the Armed Forces, Vanna's people and our civilians." Grace sneered. "If we start to give fish to the scum either in the camps or the cities they'll expect us to continue. Feed them rat with no pork if necessary."

"No need, there's a delay but it shouldn't be a long one." Owen looked around the table. "Any other real problems? I mean ones that need addressing here."

"Alliances. Even the maniacs are making treaties with each other, to allow them to trade or defend a particular area. Worse, some alliances include the very enclaves we want them to turn on." Maurice frowned. "My people can only hint, suggest and very occasionally mislead. They have to be careful because these savages are paranoid, and I've already lost people who were caught making contact."

"Just how do they make contact?" Joshua frowned. "We monitor the few working radio frequencies and there's no hint."

Owen answered. "Need to know, Joshua, operational security." Joshua nodded understanding.

"How solid are the alliances?" Grace smiled. "Just how hard would it be to break them?"

Maurice frowned. "It will take more than hints or suggestions, because the alliances make sense. They'll fail now and then, though probably just until one or the other gang gives up a street or whatever. Then they'll be established again because who wants to lose access to the local dentist, doctor or pot grower?"

"But there is still rivalry between the rank and file, even between the leaders." Grace still smiled, her tone dismissive. "In the work camps we have found that putting large numbers from rival gangs together sparks violence. That's even with the threat of execution hanging over them. I can't see these alliances standing up under any sort of strain, so we shouldn't worry too much."

"I can encourage that. If their fighters have to combine for some reason, then there'll be an opportunity once the reason had been dealt with." Maurice started to smile. "A hint of betrayal, or a single shot at the wrong person or group, could cause a bloodbath. Excellent. I'll give that some thought."

Owen leant forward. "The other arrangements, emptying a city and stamping out some of these little democracies, they are all on track?" He shrugged. "We don't want you getting side-tracked with interesting projects. Nate tended to do that, and came up with some very unhelpful results."

"I understand and yes, I will prioritise." The meeting moved on to the reports on how each phase had progressed. Boris the diplomat seemed interested in the numbers of peaceful enclaves, and suggested taking some of those people to establish farms. He wasn't totally satisfied by Owen's objections to mission creep, pointing out that the population of Europe had been culled well beyond the expected levels so a few extra survivors in the UK, productive citizens, shouldn't matter. In the end he accepted that the local situation meant everyone in the cities should to be processed. The discussion about Europe brought up the rise of some centres of organisation on the continent. The cabal authorised limited air strikes to break up strong groups, and more later to destroy accumulated food and fuel stocks.

This time Maurice and Vanna hung back but left without speaking to Owen, which allowed them to speak privately. "How hard is Joshua looking for your system of contacts?"

"So far he's just curious, though not in the right directions." Maurice smiled. "There's no risk to your nest egg yet, Vanna."

"Our nest egg. It's a hell of a big nest already and growing fast. After all, you need a method of collecting information and there's no law saying we can't make a profit out of supplying one?" Vanna sniggered. "There's no law at all out there among the ruins."

"Just the law of supply and demand. If Joshua or anyone else gets close we might need something creative. I'm working on one possibility, but maybe you could look among your people for another? Especially now you've got those bloody great cannons." Maurice grinned. "A training accident?"

"A tank shell to close an inconvenient mouth? That's overkill but definitely kill, which is the point. I will have to wait until we have totally replaced or thoroughly suborned the Army crew members. My people must be trained before we can do that though we're already crewing some of the lighter armoured fighting vehicles." Vanna wiped the smile from her face and walked a little faster to catch the rest.

* * *

Meanwhile, in accordance with his local treaty and trade agreement, Harold sat in a ruined Burger King near the Geek Freek compound. "No point in asking for a burger and fries since I can't smell hot grease, which is a pity because I've got to sit and wait until Hawkins comes out to trade."

Darwin glared. "Why the fuck would he? You're getting ideas above your station."

"Billy?" Billy threw a package to Harold. As usual the Geek Freek and Orchard Close bodyguards sat at tables each side of the ruined fast food outlet, while the two actually trading sat at the same table in the middle. Harold unwrapped the nine-pack of soft toilet rolls. "Still sealed. I might have more and you can't set a price, can you? Or you can't set one I'll accept."

"Fucking hell, where did you find them. You jammy bastard." Darwin looked closer. "You didn't find them, there's no dust on that. Christ, did you raid the Barbies?"

"Raid? Tut, tut Darwin. I've been shopping at Beth's."

Harold watched as Darwin absorbed that, rejected it, looked at the toilet rolls and reconsidered, then realised it was impossible. "Smartarse. What the fuck did the Barbies want bad enough to part with these?"

"My body, but only rented of course. Now are you going to get Hawkins or shall I trade them elsewhere?"

"No, sod it, hang on." Darwin didn't even leave, just used his radio though he took care not to broadcast what had been offered. "Someone get Hawkins out here to trade, because Soldier Boy has something worth his time."

"No extra guards, or you might get tempted."

Darwin hesitated, looking at Seth's sawn-off before thumbing the button. "No extra guards or he'll leave." Darwin tittered. "Or maybe shoot these two."

Harold refused to talk any more until Hawkins arrived. He went through the same back and forth, after which Hawkins looked at the size of Billy's and Seth's packs. "The new refugees brought them?" He frowned. "The ones we've had swam across the flooded railway line so they couldn't bring much. A couple of them reckoned the GOFS would get more gear." He looked hard at Harold. "How come you got some refugees from the GOFS? You don't buy people."

"No but we take refugees. I told the truth about how I got these because the Barbies wanted something badly enough, though I didn't do the trolley dash round Beth's." Harold grinned. "Home deliveries are safer."

Both the Geek managers fell about laughing. "Oh, too true. Now what do you want? You can't have the other chink because Wellington won't let her go. Even weirder, I don't think she'd leave."

"I'll let Umeko know." Umeko would be happy to know that her friend had moved out of the bedding store, the Geek brothel. Better yet she had apparently found some sort of safety. "Now just how much cement can I have for one of these nine-packs?"

"How many have you got?" Hawkins thought for a moment. "Can you get more?"

"We'll set a price for one pack, which might be the only one so bid hard. Your ass will thank you?" Harold grinned. "Your ass will also want to spin these out since the Barbies might not be as generous again."

"Too true. We've managed to trade one, I repeat one, toilet roll out of the bitches that occasionally come here. Fuck, you got to meet their top bitches didn't you?" Hawkins looked Harold over. "No visible scars? Are they all dykes?"

"I know how to treat a real lady." Harold smirked. "Now come on, trade."

Harold sang along happily to Barbie Radio on the way back home with a ton of cement split between the back of his pickup and Rabbit Bob's estate car. He would be back for a ton of sand to make mortar. Casper could seal the end walls of the row of terrace houses as well as bricking in the lower windows and doors facing away from Orchard Close. Malibu had been dead right as Hawkins, and Darwin, valued soft loo rolls and wet wipes well above building materials. From the jealous looks, the Geek bodyguards wouldn't be getting near the luxuries.

Harold had still paid some coupons but expected to get those back with interest. Once again something had blown in the local supply and cut off several Geek houses. It happened often enough for Harold to suspect the tenants were finding ways to get round the meters so they didn't have to pay for electricity. Finn would no doubt fix the supply and reconnect the score of houses, but he never told the gangsters what caused any problems.

Willing hands loaded the sacks of cement into barrows to carry them to the other end of Orchard Close. By the time Harold came back with the sand, the window and door frames had been taken out, and cleaned bricks stacked ready. Those already living in the row of houses were relieved at having something better than ply as protection against an attack. After some serious consultation one front door remained, faced with steel and barred on the inside. That would simplify the passage of farmers and bringing in crops. There'd be more of that next year since Emmy had already starting making noises about demolition north of the tarmac. Umeko sang happily as she worked, cheered by the news about her friend Thien.

The additional willing hands really made a difference in the gardens, or fields as they had become. Some of the extra people gathered hay for rabbits and foliage for compost deeper into the derelict housing, which led to someone rediscovering the bees. Last year the honey hunt had been abandoned after Holly's death, but the bees had survived the winter and the rain. According to the books in the library, a beekeeper collected his harvest in August.

*　*　*

Despite the warm, sunny August day Harold frowned. "Can we use honey in the pipe bombs, since sugar is hard to get?"

"I don't know. Possibly?" Barry chuckled, unusually for him when bombs were mentioned. "You're a braver man than me if you take honey off the girl club."

"Whatever we get won't all be fit to eat. Some will get too dirty or have squished bees in it I'm sure. Well?" Harold finished checking that the four layers of net curtains covering Barry's wide hat hung well clear of his skin at the back as well as across his face.

"Haven't we got enough bombs?" Barry turned. "Let me check your netting now."

"For one attack, I hope. I still get the collywobbles over how fast all the firearms ammo and the arrows went when the rioters came." Harold turned for Barry to check the back. "With the sugar shortage we won't be able to build more bombs very quickly."

"Maybe we can, without either sugar or honey. There'll be ways I'm sure when I think carefully about what burns fast and all that. I just didn't up to now." Barry sighed. "I'm still not really comfortable making things burn or bang."

"Sorry, but Caddi or Hawkins will just commandeer everyone else's sugar in their patch if they needs some pipe bombs." Harold frowned, unseen under the netting. "I can't or won't work like that."

Barry shrugged. "If it becomes urgent ask for sugar. Tell everyone why, and I'll bet you get donations. There's also all that old petrol. A bit of bang in a container of that will be quite effective." The next part came out sad but determined. "In the meantime I'll think about it on an evening."

"If you can with Violet squalling."

"She doesn't." Barry sounded defensive. "Anyway I can't hear properly in that granny flat. Grandad flat now."

"Alicia is sure you'll hear if she yells help, though these days she'll probably shoot the scroat herself. She might still call for help, to shift the body." Harold sniggered. "There was a book on you and Alicia at one bit but that's died off."

"Cripes no, I'm old enough to be her grandad." Barry laughed. "I had to be useful someplace once Doll went into the girl club and Finn moved into Cherry Tree House. I moved into the flat because Abigail likes having a baby-sitter handy."

"Odd that, Finn moving straight after June and Janine did. Though that could be tricky because they're sharing a flat." Harold pointed. "Here come the bee bashers." Another dozen people dressed in thick clothes and gloves with cuffs carefully tied to seal them were coming across the open stretch of gardens. They also wore headgear with wide brims and lots of net curtaining.

Twenty minutes later they were all very, very pleased they'd been paranoid about sealing up. "I thought smoke calmed them!" Jeremy stood almost in the deliberately smoky fire just upwind of the bees' nest, shaking to get rid of his buzzing passengers.

"Maybe this is calm, or maybe these bees have got a bit more African Killer in them than most?" Barry wafted smoke towards the pile of bricks and a seething mass of very angry stinging insects, taking his turn with the piece of plywood.

"Just remember to replace the bricks afterwards. We want to come back next year." Harold kept wanting to brush the bees off his netting but Bernie already made that mistake, pushing the net too close to his face. He'd gone to find Patricia after suffering at least four stings.

"You can come back if you want but not me. Cripes Harold, what happens if they follow us to reclaim their honey?" Patty also raised a hand to brush at the bees but remembered not to.

"They won't because they'll be guarding and mending the hive. Come on, the sooner we get this done the better. Careful! Bloody Hell!" Despite the buzzing cloud those actually removing bricks paused for a moment as the first comb came into view.

"Ooh, yummy. Carefully now, try to get whole pieces. Use the ladles and spatulas." Patty had forgotten all about brushing bees.

"Somebody pass me a dish, a big one." June carefully lifted a brick with a section of comb attached. "Scrape that for me please,"

"Remember, we leave them plenty for winter. Don't take it all."

"Yes daddy. Honey daddy. Is that like a sugar daddy?" Liz looked at Harold. "That's not fair, I daren't stick my tongue out at you."

"Cripes, don't do that. Ooh, somebody pass me one of the roasting dishes because there's a big bit here." Patty jumped back. "Ow! One of them got through. Somebody scoop that while I get smoked and check to see if they've chewed a hole someplace."

Despite the occasional sting where a really determined bee found a way inside, a happy crew finally put the bricks more or less back in place against the stump of a wall. They had to light the emergency smoke fire halfway back to finally drive off the last of the bees. The honey didn't provide much when split among everyone, but did spark determined plans to capture bees. Harold vetoed housing bees inside the walls next year, but some began to build hives in the fields. Then everyone turned to beating back an invasion of wasps looking to share the fruit in the infant orchard, followed by a surge in ant numbers.

The news about honey encouraged the neighbouring gangs to look for bees. Several wild nests were raided, but everyone became more careful after one of the GOFS died from stings. Nobody could be certain if he'd been susceptible, or if the cross-breeding of bees had made the stings more potent. Despite some spirited discussions between gangs, at both boss level and between rank and file, nobody had a beekeeper or anyone crazy enough to capture a complete swarm. Surprisingly even the Hot Rods seemed interested in honey, possibly because the marts had just cut the ration of sugar again. Not exactly a ration; they put less on the shelf and let the customers fight for it.

* * *

Harold visited The Mansion in late August. The maid had changed again because, according to Caddi, "Spanky" had a different job now. Harold didn't ask what but hoped it wasn't the brothel. Once again the weapons repairs showed that Caddi wasn't indulging in much more than minor skirmishing. His geese had escaped again, this time rampaging through the peas. Harold hoped whoever arranged the mishaps kept being careful. Caddi grumbled then bought fresh peas from Harold, enough for himself and his lieutenants.

The Hot Rod boss complained about Harold nobbling job lots of refugees without sharing, but Harold ignored that. This time Harold traded for charcoal since Caddi claimed to have raided his neighbours to cut down some of their trees. However he'd done it, Caddi had plenty of clean charcoal for sale. This time Harold drove back in the dark, refusing to stop over because of how impolite the Hot Rods had been last time. He changed the route after setting off so the escort had to follow a long roundabout route back to Orchard Close. Nobody shot at him this time.

* * *

Work slowed on almost everything in Orchard Close for just over five hours the next day, until a loud aggrieved squalling noise meant everyone smiled and relaxed. Harold in particular smiled happily since if Emmy's bun had arrived a day earlier he'd have been at The Mansion. "Hey there big Momma. Was he or she wearing wellies?"

"No she wasn't, cheeky." Emmy smiled proudly. "Come on Tammy, give him the bad girl smile." Emmy looked up with a grin. "Maybe not yet, but beware."

"Too true. Does this mean you're out of action so we can all relax? Can I lounge around having a beer or throw my potato peelings where I like?"

"Not likely. My gnomes will make a note of anyone wasting a single leaf of possible compost, or failing to harvest one single extra calorie. Then when we're up and about, me and Tammy will gang up on the culprits." Emmy sniggered. "She's a bit late leaving her comfy tummy-home. Maybe the rabbits finally gave her the idea?"

"Cripes yes, they're multiplying while we watch. Well not actually watch, but nobody dares blink or they'll have doubled in size. Still, I've got to admit that George and Maryam are right about the size. Those big beefy bunnies will be a lot easier to catch when the wild ones are being bashful. I've had to agree the originals are safe from becoming pie fillings." Harold laughed. "We've already had to ban any of the kids from having one as a pet or the place will be full of rabbits we aren't allowed to eat."

"Cripes yes. Hear that Tammy? Nasty Uncle Harold won't allow you to have a bunny. It's not my fault, so beat on him."

"Already?" Harold laughed again before leaving as instructed to let Patricia do nurse things.

The hallway outside held all the original girl club, while beyond them the queue of later members stretched out of sight. "Come on, how much does she weigh?" Sal smiled happily. "Going by Emmy's belly I'll bet she's a real porker."

"What colour are her eyes?"

"Has she got much hair?"

"Cripes, give me a chance. I don't know. Tammy's eyes are shut, her head's wrapped up and I didn't ask about weight. I asked how Emmy is?"

Liz rolled her eyes. "Typical bloke. We know Emmy's all right because we asked the midwife. Soldier off then so we can get to the good stuff."

Alicia waved flowers and so did three others. "Did you take flowers?" Harold opened his mouth to point out that was Dad's job but shut up and took his abuse manfully. He took further abuse from the latest members of the girl club, the gnomes, and what seemed like half the residents when he couldn't tell them the same vital information.

Harold admitted ignorance to the same questions even more times as he headed to the far end of Orchard Close to help with building hutches. Four more garages were being fitted with rabbit hutches since the refugee bunnies were already doing what bunnies do best to fill them. Rabbit Bob claimed that the first kits should arrive in about a week. Harold thought there'd be nearly as much interest in them as in Tammy. Not as food, this generation of new bunnies would get refugee status to build up the production line.

* * *

Though before the bunnies arrived, all the new people were formally given sanctuary at the gate. Another four refugees had arrived since the big influx, fighters who had survived the final minutes. Now they were re-united with their families before volunteering to join the Orchard Close defence. All of them brought their weapons, but none had a single round of ammunition left. The long line of forty-one men, women and children filing in the gate one at a time underlined the scale of the disaster that had driven them here. The massive party that followed seemed a little wilder than most as many re-banished their own ghosts.

One additional person finally asked for sanctuary, though Elise had already been inside Orchard Close for five months. Despite her arriving in such a terrible state, the girl club and Thandia finally worked some magic on Elise. The skinny waif still wouldn't say how she ended up outside the walls or where she came from, but at the beginning of September Elise became an official refugee. She still needed the Mastiff, Thandia, to stand with her when she stood at the gate to ask for sanctuary, and Elise disappeared back into the girl club rather than join the party.

The youngster still wouldn't play computer games with the others, refusing to even go to school. Elise volunteered to be Trev's apprentice so she could learn how to fix radios and earn her place in Orchard Close. After a few days Trev admitted that she learned fast and would be a big help. Though since Elise insisted on taking the mastiff to work with her, Trev also complained about a crowded workshop.

*   *   *

A week later Harold had to ban scroats again for a one-off welcoming, for someone who allegedly refused to wait until October dance night for her welcome. "What the hell are they doing that for?" The girl club minibus came up the access road with a smiling June behind the wheel but no engine noise. Harold wondered why, though the eight men pushing from behind might be a hint.

Sharyn nudged him. "Shush. Do your job."

A grinning Emmy, carrying a wrapped bundle and followed by Sooty, climbed out of the minibus and walked up to Harold. "We have a new applicant to join Orchard Close. Will you give her sanctuary, Soldier Boy?"

Harold shook his head, matching Emmy's grin. "Welcome to Orchard Close, Tammy. Though I'm a bit dubious about letting in your mother or that hairy lump."

"Catch." Emmy carefully deposited her daughter before kissing Harold on the end of his nose. "You know you can't resist."

Harold chuckled. "Sad but true. Sucker and wimp, guilty as charged. Come in then." He turned as Emmy moved up to walk alongside. "Did you charm or bully those idiots to push the minibus?"

"Some of both though we made it a bit easier for them. We emptied the fuel tank."

"Seriously? You've taken it off the road?"

Emmy sighed. "Yes, the engine ran rougher and rougher. We parked the durn thing up after using it for Elise." She sniggered. "But Tammy insisted on arriving in style. After all, she's got the signature hair already." Emmy reached over to uncover Tammy's head, showing the little yellow ribbon on a tuft of her sparse black hair.

"Cripes yes. The youngest boys had better start running now." Harold frowned. "The minibus really is retired? I thought the girl club, or some of them and ex-members, would want to keep that going."

"We will, if you OK it. If not Liz will beat on you or I'll turn Sooty and Tammy loose in your study."

"I surrender. What's the plan now there's no petrol engines working?" Harold had stopped using the petrol pickup before it broke down someplace. The remaining petrol wouldn't even fire up the motors in cars that hadn't been used. Searchers had found another diesel van that ran, more or less. The next time Caddi wanted guns repaired Harold would have that and Rabbit Bob's car serviced.

"We'll take out the engine, gear box, and all the bits that make it drive. If we stick a towbar on the front you can tow us into battle with your diesel pickup, a sort of armoured battle-trailer." Emmy smiled happily. "The paint job will frighten the scroats all on its own."

"You're leaving the armour in?"

"Too true, that's why it took eight of them to push me up the street." Emmy stopped. "Right, now you'd better give Tammy back before she learns any bad habits."

"Or before she works her charm and we run off together." Harold followed Emmy into the house where a crowd waited to celebrate.

Better still, Harold found himself celebrating, and not just Tammy's ceremony. At least here, inside Orchard Close, the living conditions seemed to be improving. Food would be tight, but the new refugees were throwing themselves into clearing, digging, repairing and scavenging with real enthusiasm. With their coupons, and the rabbits, the Coven assured him they would have enough food over winter. Better yet, a combination of his glower and threats of violence seemed to be keeping at least this one enclave a civilised place to live.

* * *

Unfortunately Orchard Close stood alone, as the only civilised enclave among the surrounding gangs. It grated that Harold had to pretend indifference to any excesses he saw in other gang territories, but nothing he could do would help. Luckily Harold only saw the really raw side at The Mansion since the GOFS and Geeks preferred to deal at a trading site outside their headquarters. Finn and Rob tried to avoid visiting any gang headquarters, though they didn't mind dealing with problems in the housing claimed by the gangs and rented to the other survivors.

Gofannon had claimed the women were safe on the estates and Harold started to wonder just how bad the GOFS really were. Unfortunately he had no way of checking what really happened in The Castle, the GOFS headquarters. According to Rob and Finn the conditions on the estates ruled by the GOFS, small areas of viable housing, were relatively benign as long as the residents paid their tithes. Only relative to the Geeks and Hot Rods, because those outside The Castle were definitely second class citizens. Caddi treated his tenants as serfs while in addition to the abuse, the Geeks even charged their tenants for the free electricity.

More electrical and plumbing work trickled in from the Barbies, and surprisingly the Barbies had told the truth about how their refugees would be treated. Apart from taking rent and providing a few guards, the Barbies left their estates to get on with their own lives. That gave Harold food for thought. The supposedly crazy Barbies were better landlords than at least two of the other gangs.

Shopping took his mind off the neighbours because the conditions at the marts deteriorated with more fights as the amount and quality of the food decreased. The mart guards seemed to be less friendly every visit and many were now downright hostile. Harold had expected to only need a small group, three men, for shopping at the mart this winter to top up on underwear, salt, soap, children's clothes, contraceptive pills, spices, spam and chew sticks.

Unfortunately the food reserves wouldn't be enough for the new influx, so now Harold needed veg and fruit as well. He took up to a score of shoppers each time, all men and most of them armed with iron bars once the packs were dismantled. After a few trips Harold found it harder to find people who would ignore the taunts from marts and gangs. In addition the shoppers daren't mention any expertise, especially in gardening, or the soldiers might arrest them.

A pattern emerged each time the soldiers in the guard post changed. The newcomers were suspicious and tense, which gradually eased towards the end of their term on this guard post. Once they relaxed enough, a mixed party would cautiously offer chips or soup, and Harold would show the phone picture and ask about Curtis. So far none could remember seeing Curtis anywhere, though since Harold never told Emmy it didn't upset her.

* * *

Though it wasn't soldiers who brought a smile to Harold's face as he walked up the street early one mid-September morning. "Bringing in the sheaves, bringing in the sheaves."

"What sheaves, or has the sooty butterfly been scorching her wings again?" Harold laughed as Liz turned, startled.

"Oh cripes, you weren't supposed... I didn't think..." Liz went from apologetic to indignant. "What are you doing up at this time?"

"I'm always up early when we've got overnight visitors. Though considering the visitor is Wayland, a sweaty, sooty smith with big muscles, I should have known he wouldn't be wandering. You did mention Harvest Festival." Harold paused. "Even if we didn't have one?"

Liz smirked. "You didn't, but that doesn't mean there wasn't one." She hesitated, and, unusually for Liz, looked a bit guilty. "I'm sorry though, you know, reminding you?"

"Don't be an idiot." Harold put an arm round her. "This is safe now you've had a sweaty fix. I wouldn't, couldn't begrudge you or anyone else their fun, jollies, or moonlit romantic moment of madness." Harold shook his head. "It would be mean considering what you lot put up with from me and Holly."

"What other behaviour could I expect from a simpering wimp? Now you can walk me home safe in the knowledge that I will spurn your feeble advances." Liz put out an arm for Harold to hook his into, and they set off up the street. "Bringing in the sheaves..."

Later Harold still had a little smile when Wayland left, but not as big a smile as the GOFS smith had. Wayland carried six novels, a mix including one cowboy novel and a bodice-ripper, exchanged for textbooks because the GOFS really did have some spare schoolbooks. Part of Harold's smile came from the reaction of Hilda and Faith since only one maths book had the answers in it. The teachers would have work the rest out themselves before using them to teach.

He lost the smile five minutes later when the radio crackled. "Bang, bang!" Harold drove like a loon. As soon as he hit GOFS territory he began to say, "Meet me with a motorbike" into his radio. When he came near the flooded area an SUV waved the pickup to follow and set off parallel to the water, two streets back. As soon as Harold saw a small knot of people and vehicles ahead, he warned Billy. "Just watch my back and keep your head down. The bastard can shoot."

"I've got it Harold." Billy jumped out of the pickup with the sawn-off to watch Harold's back, just in case the GOFS took a fancy to the Blaser rifle.

Harold ran across to Gofannon. "He's back?"

"Yeah, and this time he's staying. I've got Vulcan kicking arses to keep everyone's heads down because about half my bloody fighters and some Barbies have come to watch. They're hoping you kill him." The General's sniper had been back twice, to kill refugees in the water. The last time a GOFS soldier fired at the pickup even if the man had a vanishingly small chance of hitting anything with a pistol at half a mile. The sniper shot the GOFS but the pickup had driven away before Harold arrived.

Harold and Billy followed the GOFS boss to an upstairs bedroom overlooking the flood. Gofannon signed for Harold to keep to the side of the room and pointed. A body floated on the water about four hundred yards from the shore, clearly dead which puzzled Harold. "Why is the pickup waiting if he shot the refugee?"

"He hasn't shot them all. There's another four at least who ducked back into that house beyond the body." Gofannon curled a lip in a sneer. "I've no doubt the General will bring up more people when it's dark to flush the poor sods out. Then they'll light them up with headlamps so the sniper can shoot them."

Harold couldn't see the pickup without moving across to the window, which might be a bad idea judging by Gofannon's caution. "Is he shooting from the same sort of distance?"

"Yeah, exactly the same as the other two times even if he came up different roads. The pickup reverses to the boundary, the sniper shoots the refugees, then they drive off. If you kill the bastard the General won't dare send another shooter even if he's got one." Gofannon turned and beckoned. "I'll take you into the other room so you can see him without getting shot." The other room had a window that had been boarded except for a six inch diamond shape cut in the ply. "We've found that if someone keeps well back, they can't be seen through that little hole."

Harold shut the door and moved across the room slowly to look through the hole from well back. The rangefinder on his binoculars said eight hundred and seventy yards to the tailgate of the pick-up. Harold checked the back window of the cab, covered with a sheet of ply. "I'll need him to come up to make a shot, so he'll need a target."

Gofannon stared. "Fucking hell, he'll kill anyone who shows."

"Even if I miss, and I don't intend to, he'll be ducking and thanking any God he believes in. I'll say when." Harold smiled. "You didn't ask why I wanted a motorbike."

"Why did you want a fucking motorbike? And hard luck because we haven't got one." Gofannon still seemed upset about the idea of tempting the sniper to show himself.

"Crap."

"Gotcha. We've brought an electric quad." Gofannon laughed, his good humour restored. "We've got two, dead handy now the petrol is all fucked up. Why did you want it?"

"Put two men on it, the driver and someone to hop off and collect that rifle if he drops it because then they'll have to leave it behind. If someone gets out of that vehicle to pick anything up I'll shoot him and you can strip his body as a bonus, but I want the rifle if possible. As my wages." Harold took a look through the sights. The bit of height gave him an angle and he'd get a slightly bigger target, but not much. Harold had good look at the vehicle, and the sides had definitely been built up and probably with thicker steel plate than the original. "But first I want a decoy to get him to show. What will it take?"

Gofannon sighed. "Some might think it worth the risk if you kill that fucker. It's a deal on the rifle. Can I open this door?"

"Just a minute." Harold moved aside. "Just in case he can see in when its open and has checked these rooms out. The change of light when you open the door means he'll check again if he notices. I would."

Gofannon frowned. "I must remember not to piss you off anytime or learn to be sneakier. Can I open this door now?"

"Yeah. Arrange for someone to shoot at him and give him some sort of a target when you say, and for the quad to get out there with a fire up his ass when I say."

The GOFS leader hesitated. "All right but you'd better not miss. My blokes are still sore about one of them being killed."

Billy spoke straight after the door closed. "I've got your back, Harold."

"I know, but don't point that sawn-off at Gofannon because he'll be really annoyed. Don't worry I won't miss." Harold chuckled. "I really have done this before." Better still Harold had got well and truly angry at this bastard. He had absolutely no qualms about shooting the sniper without any warning, before the man could shoot again. There was water instead of sand, with the target slightly downhill instead of uphill, but oddly enough the wind riffling the water seemed about the same strength as the one that had riffled those papers in Kuwait. Back where Harold first killed a man, three short years ago.

Gofannon came back in. "Cy said OK but only if Patty lets him buy her a beer and sits with him to drink it next time he's over. Just that. He'll settle for

Bethany or Fergie but wants to brag about Patty sitting with him." The GOFS boss grinned. "With a picture if possible?"

Harold knew just how Patty felt about the bloke who shot refugees. "Deal, she'll even pose with her crossbow." Harold gave it three or four minutes for any spotter to finish checking. "I'll just shuffle some furniture." Harold used a bedside table and a chair to make a rest, with his coat padded up on the top. He placed the rifle and braced himself, then let his head drift into that quiet place and adjusted the sights, aiming at the rear of the pickup. "Tell Cy."

Harold didn't hear Gofannon's, "Start shooting Cy" except as some faint whisper, though he heard Cy begin to shoot. A black bump showed over the tailgate of the pick-up as the sniper looked for whoever had started shooting, but he'd be too late. Harold moved the sights across a little because the sniper didn't come up dead centre, and squeezed. The rifle barrel in the pickup jerked up and disappeared as did the man's head so Harold worked the bolt and moved the sights to the passenger door. As a man came out Harold retargeted and shot at the back window of the pickup truck the other side.

He worked the bolt and moved his sights back across to the man who had pulled himself up the side of the pickup to look into the back of the vehicle. The gangster jerked his head towards the cab, then towards Harold, then the 308 bullet picked him off the side of the truck and left him sprawled across the road. "Go, go, go!" Harold worked the bolt. He checked the tailgate for any sign of the shooter before holding his sights on the man in the road to check for movement. Gofannon yelled into his radio, sending the quad driver on his way. "Wait until they are nearly there, then tell them to bring the pickup truck as well. The General's men will hear the radio and realise the driver's dead, but by then it'll be too late."

"What!" Gofannon blocked Harold's view as he looked out. "I thought you'd missed the first shot."

"No, I shot the driver second, then him in the road. Remember, I get the rifle and ammo." Harold laughed. "Now get out of the way so I can take a pot at anyone who comes to object."

"Too fucking true. You sweet bastard." Gofannon moved aside but then looked back out, blocking the view again. "I have to see to tell them at the right time." He paused, then thumbed the button and spoke. "Heff, take the fucking pickup. Smartarse shot the driver. Either strip the one in the road or toss his body and weapons in the back." The GOFS boss moved aside. "Vulcan will laugh like a drain. He's the one who reckoned we should send that fucking rifle on instead of buying it because none of us could use it properly. He said we weren't likely to really piss you off, and you'd probably shoot some arse that needed it one day."

"You really did send those blokes to us? I thought they'd been to one of your estates. Tell Vulcan thanks, and he's off my target list." Harold patted the rifle. "This thing certainly backed Caddi off."

"Oh yes, we've been pissing ourselves laughing about all the demolition round The Mansion and the Geeks." Gofannon headed for the door. "Now I'm going down there to wave the refugees home and give the General the finger."

Harold settled in and waited. A car did start out from the far side of the floods, then common sense prevailed because by then the pickup had started reversing. The pickup brushed aside the tape and stop signs as it reversed all the way to the end of the water, to be met by a crowd of cheering, waving GOFS and Barbies. The cheering reached a new high when the five refugees waded ashore, towing the body of their comrade, then reached a crescendo when Harold came downstairs.

Harold answered the questions and smiled at the compliments, but his attention stayed on the pickup. The vehicle had been properly customised for this job, with the sides plated in what looked like half inch steel. In addition sheets of steel hung down the sides, front and back of the wheels. Steel plates covered the driver's door and the bonnet though not the windscreen and the rear and side windows were only covered in ply with viewing slots. Harold presumed the driver ducked while the sniper shot whoever attacked them.

"Oy, Heff, why didn't you turn round?" Gofannon laughed. "Or can't you manage a three point turn."

"I can, but the dirty bastard painted the inside of the windscreen with his brains and the wipers are on the outside." Heff opened the driver's door. "Though I don't think it was his idea." He climbed out and tried to look at his back. "I'm covered in shit, or piss and blood at least. Hang on." He took off his weapons and boots then ran over to sit in the water. "That's better. Has anyone got a bucket?"

One of the refugees actually went over to splash water on his jacket, then helped peel it off when that wasn't working. Another came over to Harold, holding out his hand. "Roy. We owe you when you need it."

"Harold, or Soldier Boy to most people. It was a real pleasure." This man carried a machete, knives, two pistols and a shotgun. The other four were well armed and had taken even more weapons from the body of their comrade. All of them were bandaged and sported bruises and small cuts. "Are you the last?"

"I reckon. That's twice I've had to run from the General." The man sighed.

"Next time I might not." He looked at the Blaser, then back to where the pickup had been. "I might not have to."

"It's only one rifle, though where I live we can't run anyway. Get sorted out, relax, and we'll talk later because just now I want to trade." Harold raised a hand. "Gofannon. Can we trade for this pickup?" Harold pulled himself up to look over into the back. "Well used, needs a good scrub down or jet wash."

Several men laughed and one climbed in to drop the tailgate so others could pull the body out. Gofannon looked the vehicle over. "Maybe, but you've got the rifle and ammo as pay, remember." Too true he had, and now Harold had set his mind at rest about that. He'd been worried about hitting the sights but fortune had smiled and his shot had torn through the other side of the sniper's face and head. Gofannon looked in the cab, grimacing at the smell, mess, and the body still crumpled in the passenger footwell. "I'll want coupons or maybe some more plumbing work. Your man got the water running by going around that break with several smaller pipes, he told me. Unfortunately there's leaks showing up now there's a water supply, where pipes must have frozen in the winter."

Gofannon liked to make a good trade, but without the constant barrage of aggravation Caddi used as a bargaining tactic and Harold thought he'd got a fair deal. He left first, in his pickup, to suggest Caddi's spies had a half day off because a small gang of trigger-happy fighters were looking for refuge. That also meant the spies didn't see Harold's new purchase arriving.

A laughing Heff, short for Hephaestus because he also thought it sounded like a disease, drove the roughly wiped down armoured pickup to Orchard Close since his clothes were already gunked up. Someone had to bring the vehicle because Billy couldn't drive. In common with several residents, he'd been too young to learn before his world came apart. After the deal, Harold told Gofannon why he wanted the pickup, to tow the minibus, though he'd armour plate the windows on the vehicle first.

Roy and his men didn't belong with any of the refugee families. They'd already been refugees, driven back by the General's first conquest, so they'd offered their guns to help stop the second. The seven men were angry enough to make a last stand, but tough enough that six survived the last crazy minutes as the defences broke. They cut themselves a path out of the chaos then hid because their guns were out of ammo. Today the six men ran out of food, so they made a break for the GOFS. The sniper had arrived before they made it. When Harold shot the sniper Roy and his remaining four friends had been preparing the flooded house to sell their lives as dearly as possible using only machetes and knives.

Harold had five more men, all seasoned fighters, because according to Roy they all owed Soldier Boy a life. Though if possible Roy and his men wanted to fight the General when he came. They were willing to try stopping him at the water instead of living in Orchard Close, if Harold agreed. After seeing the picture of Orchard Close the five of them wanted the option of falling back there if they survived a breakthrough. Roy reckoned if the General took the walls after crossing that open ground it would ruin the bastard. If the attackers bounced, Roy wanted to piss on their graves.

Gofannon laughed at that part. He thought that if the GOFS line broke there would be more fighters heading to Orchard Close with the same idea. In the interim he'd feed Roy and his men since they were on loan. Harold thought about that comment, about extra fighters. These might make a real difference because the attackers would have to come in without showing firearms, and all five were hardened veterans.

The girl club was really chuffed with their new tow truck, promising to decorate the armour once Liz had finished covering the windows. Better yet, some of the new refugees were happy to scrub the pick-up clean once they knew who left the blood on and in it. Rob rolled his eyes and pointed out he'd better do the plumbing to pay for the vehicle or his missus and the girl club would nag him to death.

Patty laughed about Cy and agreed to him getting his 'date' complete with her crossbow. She reckoned if she'd been there to see the nasty bastard in the truck die, Cy might have got a kiss in the heat of the moment. Harold parked the armour up for now with a tarpaulin over the top. With the extra weight the truck must drink diesel by the bucket-full, so Harold carried on using his usual vehicle for trips to the neighbours.

*   *   *

Caddi's turn to trade for skills came round again and this time Harold stayed over at The Mansion. He thought Caddi might have put out a screen of riflemen, and wanted to keep some uncertainty in his travel plans. The cooks produced a blistering curry, with fried rice. When Harold joked that the meat under the curry could be anything, Roller assured him only rabbit went in there. Caddi had put a camera in the kitchen, a very obvious one, and then a second one the staff knew nothing about. Harold hoped the cooks didn't try anything, because they really could cook so under Caddi's incentive scheme they were safe from abuse.

Harold didn't care about how much the cameraman laughed as he checked under the bed and in the en-suite. He checked the wardrobes but they were still locked. Harold considered smashing the locks, but there'd been no hint of deception in the conversation downstairs or his goodnights. He slept fitfully, woke early, and left without any hassle. Caddi would no doubt be working on some sort of harassment, but not women in the bedroom it seemed.

*   *   *

A week after Harold shot the sniper, Roy and his four men turned up to officially become part of Orchard Close. They'd been asking around, because all five stood in front of the gate while Roy asked, very formally, for sanctuary. Harold collected his stick to do the job properly but didn't send the Hot Rod spies home. A report of five heavily armed men joining Orchard Close could only make Caddi more cautious. The residents threw an impromptu dance, not much of a dance by Orchard Close standards but definitely more than Roy expected.

"This place is surreal. You do know there's bloody chaos out there?" Roy wore a bemused smile as various women insisted that each of his men put down their weapons for at least one dance.

"They know, and some of those women are perfectly capable of looking after themselves if hell comes to breakfast. It already did once." Harold nodded towards the dancers. "This is their way of giving all that chaos the finger. Brace yourself. You'd better give me the shotgun and possibly your weapons belt?" Harold pointed as Bethany headed towards them with a big smile. "If you're lucky a weapons belt will interfere with the dancing."

Roy looked at the close dancing a couple of his men were involved in and realised why. "She might be coming for you."

"I'm off the menu. Relax Roy, just for tonight you are safe." Harold took the man's weapons, turning to grin at Bethany. "Hi there Sweet Gnome, be gentle with him. He hasn't been around real people for a little while."

She giggled. "But you know the rules?" Roy nodded. "Come on then, because you have to dance at least once. Then you can go back and discuss all the serious stuff with grumpy. Hey, that's a real gnome g-name."

After five dances with different partners, Roy relaxed enough to talk seriously. Gofannon had agreed that Roy's squad were more than welcome to stand guard five days on, two days off. Now he'd seen Orchard Close, Roy wanted to spend all the rest days here but worried that he'd be eating supplies without earning them. Harold assured him that watching that strip of water counted as work but warned that if something in the fields needed digging or picking, Emmy's gnomes would recruit whomever they wanted.

By the time they went back on duty, all five men had spent time digging up potatoes, and seemed to enjoy themselves. Before they left, Harold had a chat to Roy about shooting and found that all five were self-trained in the hardest school of all. "Can you use a rifle as well? Accurately?"

"I've used one when there's been the chance, but not regularly." Roy smiled slightly. "I'm hoping you come quickly if the arses start across that water. If you can stop the lead vehicle so the rest have to come on foot?" His smile looked both hungry and eager.

"Would you feel insulted if I offered advice, about shooting a rifle?" Harold approached the subject carefully, so as not to bruise Roy's ego.

"After what you did? Have you got a spare rifle?" Roy glanced towards his men. "I don't know which of us would be best, but a rifle on the spot would be really handy?"

"I've got three big rifles and three shooters, but need them right here in case Caddi gets ambitious. Talk to Gofannon when you get back." Harold had thought about the GOFS passing on the Blaser rifle. They deserved some sort of payback. "If he'll loan you a decent rifle, I'll do my best to make one of you a decent marksman." Harold glanced down at Roy's weapons. "Your firearms were an agreeable surprise because you look after them, so the rifle won't need much maintaining."

"Yeah, we cleaned and oiled but we couldn't fix some things. Stu is dead chuffed you sorted that safety because he worried it would jam at the wrong time." Roy headed for the GOFS vehicle waving a hand in farewell. At least a dozen Orchard Close residents came to the gate to see them off.

Harold had a similar conversation about shooting with the four fighter refugees but they had never used rifles. Instead they were interested in this machete training, and happy to swap tips about pistol shooting. All four wanted to be here on the walls defending their families if the General came for them. At least Harold knew these four wouldn't freeze and might even be a bit too sharp. After their recent experience they might shoot someone who didn't shout a password quickly enough after dusk, so Harold tried to keep the newcomers on days for now.

*   *   *

All those weapons, and how well some could use them, were the reason only four people met around the large table in the bunker this time. Vanna and Joshua, representing the two types of armed land forces looked curiously at the other two. As Maurice took his seat Owen started the informal meeting. "You asked me to arrange this meeting, Maurice. What exactly is the problem?"

"The rule requiring the Army to shoot at anyone carrying any sort of firearm." Maurice activated the screen on the wall to show an overhead view of Orchard Close. "This place is typical of the problem though not the only one. It's near the Army, near enough for the soldiers to see that these are not animals or scum but ordinary people getting by. In this case there are two nearby gangs, one growing fast, which may be capable of capturing the enclave." Maurice highlighted the areas of crops. "These people have firearms of course and a few decent shooters. With this field of fire they might be capable of breaking an attack which would otherwise run right over them."

"What exactly do you want, Maurice? We can't allow the scum to threaten the Army posts just because of one problem enclave." Joshua pointed at the screen. "That place is barely outside the exclusion zone so any firearms at all in there are dangerous."

"Well, that's partly true since that depends on both the firearms and the shooter. In this case the local gang boss is ex-Army so any firearms face the other way. Even if that wasn't the case, just how dangerous would firearms be? I agree we don't want rifles aimed at the Army, but what are the chances of some nutter actually harming a soldier from three hundred yards if he's using a handgun?" Maurice spread his hands and raised his hands, palm uppermost, in a question.

"Virtually nil." Vanna frowned. "But those fields are wider than the exclusion zone so hand weapons won't help any attackers either."

"They'll mix rifles in with the handguns, but won't turn them on the Army since that'll mean artillery or napalm." Maurice smiled. "A couple of hundred nutters blazing away as they close should interfere with the resistance. Once they reach the walls it's all over."

"You want us to tell this Army post to allow handguns? Won't that show our interest?" Owen frowned. "That's a bit pointed, especially if the Army are friendly. Something might slip, a warning."

"We can send Vanna's people to relieve the Army just before the attack?" Joshua looked at the picture. "I'd rather put someone disposable there since the scum might not stop at the enclave."

Maurice altered the screen to show views of six cities, each with a spot highlighted. "These are the worst six, but we have similar problems elsewhere so the rules need relaxing across the board. That also disguises the specific reasons?"

"We need a feasible reason to do something like that." Owen scowled. "Not one of Nate's starving squirrel reasons. He got too clever for his own good with those excuses. Now nobody believes a word on the TV."

"I have a good reason for you, Owen, one that is at least partly true. Announce that the criminals and revolutionaries are preying on the honest citizens with illegal weapons." Vanna smirked. "Because we worry about the innocent we will allow handguns as personal protection for everyone."

Joshua spoke up quickly. "Though with a proviso that pointing them at the Army will mean severe repercussions."

All four considered that for long moments, then Owen nodded slowly. "That works, Vanna. Will that be sufficient, Maurice?"

"Perfect, thank you. Better still, the Army can take note of just how many firearms the enclaves nearby actually have once they are on show."

Joshua nodded as well, but wasn't quite finished. "How are the trauma victims coming along, Maurice? Especially since watching a few hundred innocents being killed and not being allowed to help might have a bad effect on some of my younger soldiers."

"There is enough progress to deal with light trauma such as that. We'll need more time and a few more experimental subjects to really get the job done." Maurice glanced at Vanna. "Vanna's people did find York a good source as the place fell apart."

Joshua frowned. "Are we still clearing another city this winter? After all York is a bonus plus Henry claims to have brought in a good harvest this year?"

"Yes Joshua, because that will help with the protein situation. We can test both Maurice's capabilities and the feasibility of clearing an already almost empty city. Your comments about clearing populated cities worry me." Owen clicked the map to show the target. "After what you said about using terrain, we will follow your idea but only once the conditions are right. We'll start starving the place after the first snow, then Maurice will trigger the breakout after there is a heavy covering." Owen looked around the table. "Everyone keep on with your preparations, to ensure this runs as smoothly as possible."

"Now I'd better get back before someone wonders about unscheduled meetings." Vanna smiled and stood. "Wouldn't want anyone thinking they weren't in the loop."

* * *

Meanwhile, back in Orchard Close, Harold greeted Roy's squad on their second rest break. After a short discussion he took them out into the derelict housing with the single shot hunting rifle Gofannon supplied. A few test shots showed that Roy had the best eye, in Harold's opinion. Harold didn't wait. He started the training immediately. The first job was to break bad habits, especially a tendency to shoot too quickly. To make Roy's job a little easier, Harold improved the accuracy of Gofannon's rifle. Roy promised he wouldn't mention either the rifle work, or exactly what Harold told his new trainee shooter.

Harold had sworn he wouldn't train more shooters after someone targeted Emmy. Now, if someone tried targeting Roy, the new man might solve the problem by killing the bastard. To help that Harold made up properly loaded ammunition to supplement the usual gangster version supplied by Gofannon. Roy would save the ten extra rounds for long range shooting or an emergency. The extra four rounds for each shotgun were the same; the tightly packed and smoothed buckshot might work better but shouldn't be used until they were a fatal surprise.

After Roy left, Harold used the case hardening that Liz had been developing for him to make up more of his version of an armour piercing round. Liz had hardened small lengths of steel rod to create a core for an otherwise lead bullet. Experimentation showed that another armoured pickup wouldn't be a real problem since the new rounds would go through the plate, or else the steel rod did. Two-two versions blew holes in the skulls that Harold found here and there, so he made up a few of each calibre he had a rifle for. Only a few because lining up the rods in a small jig to ensure they sat dead central was slow fiddly work, and closer in the lead rounds worked fine. Harold made up ten to fit Gofannon's rifle, for Roy to keep as another ace when the General finally made a move.

*   *   *

The General didn't wait long. When the urgent call came Harold took a score of men and woman armed to the teeth, and raced for the houses along the waterside. Cy, a GOFS fighter, waved them down and directed them into one of the houses guarding the end of a road crossing the water. There they sat and waited, bored because nothing happened. Vulcan turned up after an hour to find Harold and his party getting impatient. "I hope you brought flowers this time Vulcan, because you've disturbed Patty's beauty sleep. Not only that but there's another score on standby in Orchard Close for if they're needed."

"I'm assured that flowers will make no difference to her temper, nor is anything likely to affect her beauty." The GOFS general grinned at Patty. "Though most of our men are more fascinated by the amount of sharp steel she carries and especially those crossbow bolts." Vulcan's face sobered. "This wasn't a false alarm. The General tried a fast one, and I'm half expecting an assault across the water or down the roads."

"What sort of a fast one?" Harold frowned. "I haven't seen Roy or his men.

Are they all right?"

"They're probably having a celebration. I'd ask a couple of the women if they wanted to nip over to see them but those five aren't interested in the pros. You lot have corrupted them already." Vulcan held up his hands against Patty's glare. "All right, I'll give before you burst. The General sent boats across to put men ashore between the roads."

Patty looked alarmed. "How many?"

"Not enough. We watch between the roads ever since your little visit by the waders, and our night sights picked out the heads of a few of the passengers. There were half a dozen, low to the water but coming closer so the spotter sent runners to collect shooters. By the time we had the first of the reception committee organised, the spotter could see the boats, really low in the water." Vulcan laughed. "Roy and his men ran that bloody fast to get in on it I'm surprised they could shoot, ran because I wouldn't let anyone use radios or motors." The GOFS warchief smirked. "Though the message spread fast enough once the runner got to the nearest field telephone."

"You stopped them?" Patty relaxed, and seemed disappointed.

"Yes, but I'm still not sure we won't face either more boats or an assault down the roads." Vulcan looked serious for a moment. "What is it with your lot? He's not had that rifle five minutes but I saw that Roy dropping the bastards one after the other once the lights went on. They weren't easy shots but he kept banging away steady and deliberate like he was on a shooting range, and I don't reckon he missed one."

"Roy had plenty of experience before arriving here, and maybe he hates them enough to make sure?" Harold smiled quietly, because Roy had remembered to slow up and aim properly. He thought the experienced fighter would have used the longer ranged rounds with the extra propellant, just to make sure. "How near did you let them get?"

"We let the first boat get to within twenty feet of the bank, until the first men started to get out to wade. Point blank range for shotguns, pistols and crossbows when the lights came on. Better yet, we can salvage the weapons in the shallow water." Vulcan laughed. "Roy ignored them because someone started shooting from further back, covering fire from about four hundred yards. We lit them up as well and then the shits were too busy rowing like cripes to get away from that cripesing rifle." Vulcan grinned at Patty's little smile when he used cripes. "We'll try diving later to see if they dropped any rifles in the water."

Harold passed the news around after Vulcan left. As dawn finally broke through the low cloud, a crowd of men and vehicles could be seen a mile away across the water. Soon afterwards they broke up and left, so Harold's party went home.

* * *

Across the water, nobody celebrated. "I'd shoot the fucking idiot that came up with the idea, but the GOFS already did it." The General scowled as he trained his binoculars along the road leading to the other side of the floods. "Worse still there are too many fighters in those houses, waiting for us. The reports say the same about the other roads. I thought the GOFS only had about a hundred fighters, tops?"

The older man, Rhys, flinched. "They haven't many more, I promise. They must have called in Orchard Close or the Barbies."

"The Barbies? Shit, maybe we're lucky we didn't capture the end of a road and charge across. Hand to hand at night against those bitches would probably frighten even the Bloods." The General looked through his binoculars again. "Those boats weren't low enough or they've got forward scouts out. Scratch an amphibious assault, because any lower and they'd sink anyway. That only leaves the three roads and trying to force a crossing along them would be too expensive. I'll think again."

"You could stick an armoured truck in front. Send it across with everyone hiding behind it, because those new ones really are bulletproof." Branson waved his automatic rifle. "This will deal with even the Barbies close up."

"But those men over there know what they're doing. They'd move out to the sides a bit and shoot the shit out of the column following the truck. Then they'd fry the truck with Molotovs because it would be unprotected." The General frowned. "I have an alternative, but not while there's any sort of current in the railway cutting. Now I'll definitely have to wait for as many men as possible to be fit, and even then I prefer to launch the attack when their guard is down. If I can get over that water, I've flanked them all." He turned. "Patton, is that Caddi bloke interested?"

Another man, in a pseudo-Army uniform but with less braid, saluted. "He wants a lot even to do nothing. He's got a real hard-on for Orchard Close, or for a couple of women who pissed him off and the boss there. I reckon that Soldier Boy, the boss, is the shooter who nailed our man." Patton shrugged. "He's a half-mile man I'm told."

"That's moved him up my shit-list, because the smartarse planned that. The quad started rolling straight after the shooting so he owes me a truck and a rifle." The General headed for his vehicle. "We'll look into the neighbours, maybe see if those Pink Panthers will roll over. I'm not keen on queers but if they'll join up we can flank the Barbies. In the meantime I'll want someone to round up a shitload of civvies who are handy with a hammer and saw. Rhys, find out when those arses are likely to be off-guard, when they have their annual orgy or whatever."

"Who, the GOFS?"

"The GOFS, the Barbies, that Orchard Close and the Geek Freeks. We want an edge the next time even if it's only hangovers." He sighed. "I suppose we'll have to wait while our civvies finish getting their veggies in or they'll give us grief about shortages over the winter. Worse still, they won't be able to afford their rent."

* * *

Emmy agreed with the General's civvies about avoiding shortages in winter, and in Orchard Close her gnomes drove everyone to get in the veggies as fast as they ripened. October was the time to get in the last beans, tomatoes, and a half dozen other veggies coming to the end of their season. Beetroots, marrows and pumpkins were harvested, while to Liz's total disgust the first Brussel's sprouts were ready. Perishables were eaten, while any veggies that could be frozen, dried or bagged up were stored. The crops came in plump and delicious, because the dry spell over summer hadn't affected their growth.

Emmy had taken full advantage of Rob's new plumbing, putting teams of residents on bucketing waste water out of the reservoirs to sprinkle on dry plants. Now the increased rain had already started to top up the reserves again. With all the new residents as additional labour, the gnomes insisted that plenty of winter greens went in, along with broad beans and onions for next year.

For several weeks all the gangs were more interested in gardening than fighting, or in collecting a share of the produce their tenants grew even if the fighters didn't actually get their hands grubby.

* * *

The general feeling of peace and relaxation persisted when Harold went on his next visit to Caddi. Teams of peasants, as Caddi's fighters had started calling the tenants, were still harvesting on the open stretch around The Mansion when he drove up. E-Type seemed almost jovial as he locked up Harold's weapons except for the stick and escorted him to Caddi's house. Before he could knock a smiling maid with long light brown hair opened the door, though Caddi stood just behind her as usual. "This way sir." She indicated the study with a wider smile.

"Thank you." Harold answered automatically and mentally cursed for giving Caddi ammunition but the maid looked happy and gave a little bob. That startled Harold since Caddi's maids tended to be very subservient. Though this one didn't have cane marks showing on her legs below her very mini skirt so maybe Caddi had finally given that up. She closed the front door, then opened the study door.

"Tea, coffee, beer?" Caddi looked at the maid with an eyebrow raised instead of offering her as an option as he usually did.

"Coffee, white, two sugars please." The maid smiled again before heading further into the house, while Caddi ushered Harold inside his study.

Mack already stood in one corner of the room with his aluminium baseball bat, where he would be behind Harold's seat. Caddi grinned. "Two sugars Harry? Expensive habit that."

"Not really, I only have sugar here because I need keeping sweet. Hi Mack, do you live there now?"

Mack grinned. "Not all the time. Caddi lets me go 'ome now and then so I can eat."

"Too fucking true. I'm not feeding Mack as well as paying your prices, Harry. Can I sell you a cheap motor to even up?" Caddi laughed. "I can even sell you some petrol for it?"

Harold's laughed just as insincerely as Caddi. He sat down, bracing himself for the usual mixture of thinly disguised insults, windups and intense bargaining over every tiny item. That included the purchase of eight scarves with Hot Rods and a red piston rod knitted into them, probably because the Geek Freeks had been bragging about their versions with a simplified crossbow. After several attempts the gangs had given up on trying to get Patty or her knitting trainees to include any crudity or obscene logos.

The maid delivered coffee. Harold thanked her and she smiled again. Harold refused Caddi's offer of 'anything else' and thought for a moment she pouted, just briefly, before leaving. Caddi grinned. "She likes you. You'd better check under the bed tonight." He laughed because Harold always did, and everywhere else someone might hide.

"I might fancy a night drive." If Harold caught a hint of some sort of setup, that's what he'd do.

"You might fancy roast beef more. Only the very best for you, Harry." Caddi chuckled. "Cooper and the rest like you staying over, because they know I have to feed you properly."

"Why do you do that?" The Hot Rod lieutenants all swore Caddi brought out the best food when Harold stayed over.

"So I can sell you some, though I couldn't get the whole cow. I'll send you home with a spoonful of beef gravy on a Yorkshire pudding if you aren't interested?" Caddi grinned now because he knew he'd got Harold intrigued. Though the sale part had to be bullshit because unlike most gang bosses, Harold wouldn't buy just for himself.

"No unwilling women in the bed, or under it? Or paid ones?"

"I promise. Now stop pissing about and let's get down to real business." The weapons came out and the haggling started. The extra at the end this time turned out to be a surge blowing the electrics on one of Caddi's estates. Finn would be needed since the damage had affected the supplies, not just the electrical equipment attached to the mains at the time. Eventually the usual dealing finished with Caddi claiming to have been stitched while Harold felt sure he had been. "I'll trade for some of those new people, Harry. Your lot are a bit crowded now and could do with the space." Caddi smirked. "Unless you all like doubling up. In that case a few of my lads would like to come over and double up."

"We've got enough room for anyone who needs refuge. You don't want them anyway because the price for fixing up more housing for a group would cost you more than they're worth." Harold smirked back at him. "You know that because of what you'll be paying Finn." The occasional surges in the electricity didn't catch many people out now but did sometimes damage the supplies, giving Finn a steady income. More people were fixing fuses or smaller problems, but nobody messed with the supplies after a Geek fried because he thought he'd figured it out. Finn charged double because the man allegedly made the problem worse.

"How come the GOFS and those fucking bitches thought theirs were worth the cost? I've got more coupons to spare than either." Caddi scowled as he always did when Barbie Girls were involved.

"No coupons involved because we just shared around some assets. We needed this, they needed that, you'd be surprised what the Barbies will give up if you've got what they want." Including enough rabbit pellets from the pet shop to fill the back of a pickup truck, though that wasn't public knowledge. Caddi wouldn't find out many trading details because he wouldn't talk to Barbies, and the GOFS liked winding the Hot Rods up. Caddi might not even know about the rabbits yet.

Nor would he get to see the armoured vehicle, parked up around the back of Orchard Close with a tarpaulin over it the same as the old petrol vehicles. Since Harold now had a man capable of maintaining his vehicles, Caddi wouldn't even get the job of servicing the truck. One of the new refugees had volunteered, warning he couldn't fix serious problems. Maybe not, but William could strip out all the surplus parts of the minibus, leaving it as a working trailer. Liz had already made plans for plating over windows and protecting the wheels, using hard steel plate from the GOFS.

"We all know what those dykes will give up. Just remember to give your blokes, and women, a medical after they leave." Harold waited, but Caddi finished the complaints and final round of needling without mentioning a rifle or the armoured truck so his spy system must be running slow. That meant as long as Harold didn't let the spies at the traffic island see them, he'd got an ace. Sooner or later a GOFS soldier would brag, but even then finding he didn't know everything should help to keep Caddi cautious.

*   *   *

The maid opened the front door to let Harold out with a bright smile and another little semi-curtsy. "Goodnight sir."

"Goodnight and thank you." Harold really did wonder what had happened to Caddi's usual staffing policy.

Behind him Caddi sniggered which meant this had to be some sort of windup, then the gang boss raised his voice. "E-Type, feed Soldier Boy will you, and find him a comfy bed."

"Come on, you know the way." E-Type headed towards the house where Caddi's lieutenants slept. Harold did know the way since this was where he usually slept. This time E-Type neither detoured to the brothel or arranged a meeting with some scroat looking for trouble.

"What's for supper then?" He'd find out soon but Harold really had started to wonder.

"We've got roast beef, Yorkshire pudding and the trimmings. Visit again and stay over as soon as possible, because Caddi has put on a special again." E-Type waved towards two men and an older woman unloading scrap iron from a wheelbarrow, stacking the scrap next to the forge. "That lot get burger and hope there's enough rabbit in the rat to flavour it. Though cat tastes pretty good."

"I've never tried cat, unless that's chef's surprise tonight? We prefer our cats to catch rats and mice." Cat might taste fine but there were too many pets in Orchard Close for anyone there to feel comfortable about finding out.

"Our cats do the same, but the peasants catch wild ones along with rabbits and rats and waste not, want not. Cat tastes better than bloody rat I'm told, though I don't think I've eaten rat yet, or fox or dog." E-Type laughed. "The cooks don't pull a fast one on us, because we make them cook our meals with the heads on. Though with tonight's meal that would be a problem."

"How do you stop them poisoning you?" Harold really did wonder, because that cook the first time he visited had known she might end up in the brothel if Caddi found a better cook or felt vindictive. Not an unpaid brothel now, not since Orchard Close had women who charged for sex and some Hot Rods visited. Caddi had decided if the bastards had enough coupons to pay Soldier Boy's whores his men could pay at home as well, even if the women weren't volunteers. Harold wouldn't have wanted someone under that sort of threat cooking his food, even with a camera watching.

"Cameras can't catch everything so we've taken precautions. We've found a real chef for Caddi. He lives in the Mansion compound where we can reach his family so he's really motivated. Mack eats at home so even if the chef risks his missus and kids while a group of us are eating there, he won't get us all. If Caddi ever offers you a meal, accept, because that chef of his is pure genius." E-Type led the way into the dining room. "We have several cooks here, and not all of us eat here every night. They understand how bad it would be for all of them if we get a stomach ache."

The three gangsters continued to insist that they'd be having roast beef until Harold really did start to wonder. The wonderful smell wafting in certainly seemed to back them up. Eventually, as promised, a young woman deposited a plate with a damn great joint on the table. Harold chose three slices and his own Yorkshires, roast potatoes, veg and gravy. When he cautiously cut the meat and took a mouthful, still expecting a windup, the flavour went moo to his taste buds. As Harold looked up the three at the table chortled and slapped each other on the back, delighted at the response. "All right, you got me. Beef?"

"Maybe. That gang over to the west, the Bargees, trade with someone else for this. They brought some with the fish in that refrigerated van. There's a shitload of treaties and guarantees to let that van drive about." Chevy shrugged. "There's a trade route starting up because although nobody is sure if this goes moo or neighs, every boss wants some on his table."

Harold took another bite and his taste buds celebrated. "This might be horse? Not that I'm complaining."

"You'd better not or you can pass it over." E-Type grinned. "We daren't ask but one of our lads reckons he ate horse in France before the crash and couldn't tell the difference. Now eat your meat or I'm helping myself." Harold ate.

He finished his beer afterwards while everyone chatted but tonight wasn't totally relaxed because Chevy seemed to have a bit of a chip on his shoulder. Eventually Harold stood up. "Lovely ta. I'll get my beauty sleep now. Then

I can get off bright and early." If Chevy did much more winding up, careful winding up unlike Caddi's, Harold would smack him. That would cause trouble with Chevy being a senior Hot Rod.

"No sleepwalking, but if you do it's only the next house." Chevy grinned. "The one with a red light outside and a sign saying Back o' Rackhams."

"Not me, I stay tucked up in my own bed all night. Must be because my conscience is clear."

"There must be some reason." Chevy and Cooper both fell about laughing. E-Type showed him to the same room. Harold jammed a chair under the door handle, then relaxed a bit. A quick check under the bed and in the en-suite probably made whoever watched on the hidden cameras laugh, but Harold didn't care. He also tried the wardrobes but they were still locked.

Despite the chair at the door, Harold kept his stick close by while he used the en-suite. He even pulled the quilt right back before getting into bed in case Caddi had done something gross. He kept the stick gripped in one hand, and turned out the light, then Harold laid awake for a while thinking about that meat and fish wagon. Eventually he dozed and then slept.

* * *

Harold didn't know what woke him, but something had. He tightened his grip on the stick and tensed, listening, because someone had got into the room. Though the someone wasn't very stealthy because they were breathing quite heavily. Harold's hand had crept up to the top of the quilt so he could turn on the light when whoever it was giggled! Definitely a woman Harold's shocked brain told him, but before he could react a tug on the quilt preceded someone sliding underneath.

Harold went for the light and pulled the switch, then his hand had to dive underneath the quilt again to intercept hers. "Whoa, stop that." He looked at the happy smiling face now in bed with him, recognising Caddi's maid. "You don't have to do that, no matter what he said."

The pout caught Harold completely unprepared, and left him feeling confused. "But I want to." Her other hand moved so Harold let go of his stick to intercept her, which earned him another pout. "Mr Cadillac said you liked me, so I asked."

"Asked what?" Harold glanced round the room but nobody else had come in and the chair still jammed the door shut. An open wardrobe door, one that had been locked, explained how Caddi had got the woman in here. But why, because Caddi knew Harold would react violently to a woman under any sort of coercion.

"If I could come in here and, well, I can show you instead of talking." She giggled. "It'll be more fun that way." The way the young woman tried to wriggle closer didn't leave much doubt about what she meant.

"That's a game between me and Caddi." Harold paused. "You really asked?"

"Oh yes. Mr Cadillac told me about you, that Soldier Boy is the most dangerous man he knows." She stopped to lick her lips, and shivered. "He said you've killed more men than anyone else round here, so many that nobody could keep count. I like dangerous men." Her wide eyes and her thigh coming over and up Harold's drove home the emphasis on like. "Too many to count? That is so hot."

"Sorry, but no thanks." Harold got out of the bed, sharpish because holding her wrists wasn't even slowing this one up. Even as he snatched his stick and stood the young woman threw the quilt back.

"See, no marks. Nobody has to cane me if the man is bad enough because I'll do anything, anything you want." She ran a hand down her belly and thigh. "Even if you want to get rough, maybe spank me a bit, I might like that?"

Harold would have applauded Caddi's latest ploy if he hadn't been frantically looking for a way out that didn't involve getting near her. The cameraman would be wetting himself laughing. The gods alone knew what the hell had happened to this woman in the past, but she definitely wasn't being coerced. Harold didn't think she'd been drugged either. She really had volunteered and Caddi had finally found a way past Harold's payment and coercion rules. Unless. "Did someone pay you?"

"No! I don't do that." Her magnificent pout seemed totally genuine. "I don't do this for coupons. I only do this with men I really, really like." She arched her back. "Don't you like me?" The young woman licked her lips slowly and reached for the bow holding her very brief, silky top together. "Do you want to see the rest?"

"What's your name?"

She stopped, then laughed. "My name? Wow, nobody ever asked my name first." She tried to look coquettish, peeking up while ducking her head but considering how she'd dressed and posed that didn't really work. "I'm Virginia, but not for a while. Now will you come back and let me get into your pants?"

"No Virginia, because Mr Cadillac has been very mean. He didn't tell you I don't do this on film. You do know there are cameras?" Harold looked round, sticking his tongue out at the invisible cameras.

Virginia giggled. "I don't mind cameras. They're in a lot of places round here, especially bedrooms. Maybe you'd forget them if you get back in here?"

Harold shook his head and earned another pout but the next smile looked cheeky, teasing rather than her initial intense insistence. Virginia sighed, a long one that involved sticking her chest out as far as possible. Her face brightened and her eyes opened wide as if shocked. "What if you find me someplace private, with no cameras?"

Harold tried not to laugh because that had definitely been teasing. "We'll see." The answer would still be no with anyone Caddi supplied. Private wouldn't happen anyway because Caddi would want whatever happened on video.

"We could pull the quilt right over?" Harold didn't quite heave a sigh of relief but came close because Virginia had definitely switched to having fun over his refusal. "We could snuggle up really, really close so nothing showed?" Harold had to laugh now because her emphasis on really close had been accompanied by hugging herself and wriggling. A joking and teasing Virginia turned out to be an appealing Virginia. Harold had to get her out of here sharpish before she realised.

"Sorry but Mr Cadillac will tell you, I have real rules about being on camera and coercion." Harold smiled. "He seems to have found an answer to the coercion, but I doubt he'll ever take the cameras out. This really is a game between us. This time he has won and will be laughing at me."

Virginia preened just a little. "But you only said no because of the cameras. Maybe if I move on, I'll find you where there aren't any cameras?" Virginia looked around the room. "In private." This sigh wasn't faked at all. "Oh God. Dangerous, strict and in private. That is just so goddamn sexy and now I've got to go to my bed all alone." The young woman glanced at the wardrobe and giggled. "I don't think there's cameras in there?"

"Scat. I'll no doubt see you again, but in clothes. Believe me, Mr Cadillac himself is as dangerous a man as you will ever meet." Harold went to the door and took the chair from under the handle.

Virginia finally got out of his bed, though she paused for a moment. "I'm all hot and bothered now. You could help me shower to cool off?" Harold opened the door, sweeping a hand to show her out, and Virginia sauntered over. "A gentleman as well? You'd better watch out if you go into any private places." She came up on her toes and kissed him very quickly. "Ooh, I won't sleep now." Virginia finally left, though she did pause in the corridor to wiggle her ass and glance back over her shoulder with a grin. Harold shook his head and smiled at her then closed the door before jamming the chair back under the door handle.

Harold's smile died because if Virginia ever tried to move on elsewhere, or said no to anyone Caddi handed her to, Harold didn't think that cheeky smile would survive the aftermath. In that mood Harold used the brass boss on his stick to smash the locks on each wardrobe door, including the open one, before getting back into bed. He slept, but not well, because he kept thinking about what a nasty sod like Caddi might do to Virginia's smile one day.

In the morning nobody mentioned Virginia, though Cooper wore a little smile as he organised the escort for Harold and the weapons.

*　*　*

This time when he arrived back Harold didn't have time to worry about much apart from scraping mud off his boots and hands. The last of the radishes and the first of the swedes, carrots, cauliflowers and cabbages were ready. The gnomes had already started on planting for spring, marshalling as many volunteers as possible every morning before splitting them into work gangs. Harold joined them as often as possible to encourage the rest, since in between picking, collecting and planting there were all those acres to dig over and fertilise. All the heaps of compost out along the edges of the fields were eventually barrowed away and dug in.

If anyone looked to be unemployed the late pears and apples needed picking and not just in Orchard Close. Most of the really mature fruit trees were out among the derelict buildings and ruins so fruit picking expeditions had to be organised with guards. Everyone had a ration of fresh before the rest disappeared into the canteen kitchen along with boxes of empty jars. The Coven really must have a cauldron, Harold decided, judging by the amount of fruit turning into jam. Anything suitable such as blackcurrants produced fruit juice first, and any pulp would eventually become watered wine, Berry assured him.

Some preserves turned up in the marts so Harold brought a selection back to be tried out. Sharyn stared. "Jam in plastic bags?"

"An economy measure because glass jars are expensive to produce according to the blurb above the shelves." Harold looked at the sealed plastic bag of raspberry jam. "That'll be messy once its opened, and worse still not reusable."

"That'll mean more scavenging. We'll need every container that'll hold one of those." Sharyn rummaged in the cupboard, producing a plastic jug. "See?" She stood the bag up in the jug. "Cut off the top, then we can use the jam without spilling."

"It'll go mouldy if its left open." Harold frowned. "The Coven claimed everything with a lid for pickles or jam, even some topless jars because they're using elastic bands or string to hold the plastic seal on."

"Leave it with us. For starters the empty bags can be used to seal containers without tops." Sharyn rubbed her hands together and produced a convincing witch's cackle. "Don't count how many come to the meeting or it'll worry you."

"Eek, thirteen? I'm off. At least the cauldron is being used for jam making."

Harold managed a solid hour of machete practice with the trainees before Liz called from outside. "I come in peace."

"Come in."

"Is it safe for mice?" Liz came in, mock-flinching from Patty with her machete and iron bar, then stopped. "Why don't you put a hilt on that bar instead of that bit of rag?"

"We don't want them to be obvious." Patty slid the bar into the sleeve behind her machete sheath. "See? Though when I jab something my hand does slip down it a bit."

Liz held out a hand and Patty handed over the bar. The smith inspected it for a couple of minutes. "I reckon a small round collar welded here, sort of like a wide washer, will do the job? Not a big one, just enough to stop your hand slipping forward. Then I suppose you gross lot will sharpen the end of the rod." She mock-shuddered. "Perverting artwork seems to be a regular habit."

"Well that's your spare time sorted out, now why did you actually come to interrupt us?" Harold smiled at Liz's scowl.

"I've got an addition for the scavenge list."

"Cripes, what else can there be in those houses? The wallpaper and plaster?" Bernie stared. "We actually took the floorboards last time."

"Flower vases, coffee pots that don't work, jugs that are cracked, the holders for bog brushes, anything like that. We'll use boiling water to sterilise whatever you find but the food won't touch them anyway." Liz grinned. "As a bonus everyone can search the gardens as well wherever there used to be a washing line, because we need the pegs that held the washing. Even the spring middles if the plastic is knackered." Liz looked at Harold. "Tell them about the jam."

"I did."

"We need the vases and holders to put the opened bags in, and the pegs to reseal them. Wade reckons he can make wooden pegs. I'm sure I can produce artwork to do the same but it'll be slow." Liz frowned. "We'd try to manage without, but the Coven want us to use mart jam while there is some. The lack of sugar isn't helping with our jam making and the mart stuff seems to have more in it, the bastards." She grinned and pushed with her hands. "So off you go, shoo."

"I don't think we'll find many pegs. The gardens are going to be just a little bit overgrown, Liz."

Harold smiled. "Don't worry Matti. Clearing the bits we inspect will be an excellent chance to practice without hurting each other." He swished a wooden machete sideways.

Matti glared at Patty. "At least if we get it wrong we won't get a broken rib." She rubbed her lower ribs. "This will take some serious kissing better." Matti noticed the smiling faces looking at where she was rubbing. Unusually she blushed, though not as much as Jeremy, but then Matti shrugged. "Oh well, it's official anyway." She turned and wrapped her arms around Jeremy. "You can start now?"

A scarlet Jeremy nodded, speechless, and then he couldn't speak anyway while Matti collected her first instalment of healing. The practice broke up in a round of teasing and everyone headed home to collect water and coats if they were scavenging. Harold walked with Patty and Liz. "Even a thick bloke like me has noticed there's been no real broken hearts lately. Matti stopped winding other men up a long time ago but she didn't really melt Jeremy's brain either, not until they were a couple." They both looked at him and raised an eyebrow. "Cripes, don't do that. Caddi does it when he's asking a question without speaking."

"There's lots of heartbreak, but not serious, not after the arseholes took Matti." Liz smirked. "We sneak up on the men now. Well not me because as a callous slut I tell them straight out its just sex."

"Sneak up on them? That was sneaking?"

"Not now Matti has landed the sucker. All the new women refugees have a little chat with me because I have no morals and can't be embarrassed. If they want a bit of casual fun that's fine but no leading men on, not seriously, unless it is serious and she's sure." Liz winked and chuckled. "Then lots of leading on but don't tell him he's already pulled, and no two-timing or stealing someone else's target. If one of us gets serious, the rest back off until she lands him or bounces."

Harold looked from Liz to Patty and both of them were dead serious. "Cripes, that works?"

"It had better." Patty really wasn't joking now. "There'll be no more Lemmys, Jons, Liams and Willtoos, and no breaking up someone's family. The professionals know they're not to accept a married or gartered bloke. We're too small a community for any of that nonsense to stay secret and we rely on each other too much to start any feuds. The animals out there only need one tiny chance, Harold."

"Too true." Liz scowled. "Any arse who gets a bit too frisky after a no will be sent home without a last dance until he learns manners, and all the women will know why. He'll even get a no if he offers to pay." She grinned. "Though if the girl wants him to get frisky and he's nice about it?"

"I might be ready for some frisky now if I can catch the right one at a weak moment." Patty laughed at the looks. "Maybe? If the moonlight is right? Cripes, that sounds as if I'm after a werewolf."

Harold laughed at her. "I'll warn Sooty. How come I'm suddenly in on this grand conspiracy?"

"Because you noticed, and because if someone really needs backing down it'll be your job. You're off the serious hunting list at the moment, though if you ever go back on you'll never know until it's too late anyway." Liz grinned and nudged him. "Until then you just keep up the grim bit and keep an eye open for werewolves, lumberjacks and blacksmiths."

*　　*　　*

Werewolves, lumberjacks and blacksmiths seemed less important when the evening news came on the TV. Though if they'd got silver for bullets the news meant dealing with werewolves might be easier. The first pictures on the TV showed a group of men shooting unarmed men and women, then taking their packs and stripping the bodies.

"Despite the laws against bearing firearms, the criminals and revolutionaries are using such weapons to terrorise the law-abiding citizens."

"This isn't going to be good. What have they come up with now?"

"Shush Harold, there's no squirrels." Harold subsided because Sharyn did have a point. He'd been a bit paranoid about news items since those squirrels.

"To help the law-abiding citizens, the ban on handguns has been lifted. All hand weapons, either air pistols or firearms, can now be carried openly without attracting any reaction from the Army. This permission does not extend to long-range weapons that can threaten the Army posts, and anyone pointing a handgun at Army personnel will be shot. The allowed hand weapons will not be permitted inside marts."

Onscreen an Army post opened fire on a group of people carrying rifles. The group scattered into nearby houses, which were subjected to a brief artillery bombardment. The view switched to a small group carrying handguns, and the soldier watching from behind sandbags waved to them.

Sharyn giggled. "Subtle as usual."

"Bloody worrying. I've always planned on the assumption that any attackers wouldn't be able to fire at us, or that the Army would shoot at them if they did." Harold looked sombre as Sharyn glanced over. "What do you think would have happened in the first attack if the Army hadn't fired on those with handguns?"

Sharyn paled, but rallied. "But any attacker has to come further this time, across those fields. You can shoot lots of them before they get close."

"Not now. Any attacker will be firing as they come so there'll be a storm of incoming. We'll be ducking some of the time instead of shooting." Harold frowned. "This will encourage any attacker to come at night when they can hide rifles among the pistols. Worse, we can't pick out those with rifles because we haven't any night scopes. The glare from all the other muzzle blasts will probably mean the Army can't either."

"What can we do?"

"I'll think about it, with Finn and Barry for starters because lights out there or remote detonated bombs spring to mind. Then I'll ask a few more and we'll work something out." Harold blew out a long breath. "Enough for tonight. The rest of the news is just the usual about how many nasty people have been locked up, innocents rescued, and how lucky we are. I'm going to walk the boundary while I have a think." Harold held up his hands as Sharyn opened her mouth. "Just once to let this settle, then I'll go to bed like a good little Soldier Boy."

One thing became clear before Harold came home to bed, Orchard Close should still keep handguns hidden as much as possible. Then if the ruling ever reverted the people here wouldn't be in the habit of flaunting firearms. Curing a habit like that might be fatal this close to the Army, and even glowering might not remind people in time.

* * *

Two days later Harold glowered at the banging on his door, then had to smile when he opened it to find a grinning Bethany. "Come quickly, and bring your stick. Official Soldier Boy things but not shooting things." She looked past him, giggling. "Ooh, your secret den. Cripes, there's stuff laid everywhere. Do you want some help finding it?" She giggled again. "Your stick I mean?" Harold looked at her hat, reading Sweet Gnome again, and just shook his head. A few minutes later an unusually reticent Bethany led Harold to where Daisy and a gnome were arguing furiously.

"Uncle-Harold, this one is mine." Daisy pointed proudly at a pumpkin.

"Maybe, but remember everyone helped to grow pumpkins this year. You might not get first pick." Christopher, Gnome on the Range, looked up. "Cripes, Harold, explain will you?"

"Daisy understands don't you Daisy?" Harold grinned at her. "That pout won't work on me, nor will hands on hips or stamping a foot. Your mum has been doing those to me for years."

"I'll cry?" Daisy's tone seemed more hopeful than convinced.

"I've been cried on as well."

Daisy scowled. "You don't care because you're a nasty soldier, er, person."

Harold laughed. "Whoever said that is right as well. Why did you get first pick last year?"

"Because I grew one." The muttered, sullen answer turned into a big smile. "I don't want to choose. I want mine. That one." She pointed.

"Last time you chose which one you wanted. This year whoever gets to choose first does the same." Harold looked at the pumpkin. This year's attempt definitely outclassed and out-massed last year's attempt.

"How do we decide who goes first?" Daisy looked up as appealingly as possible. "You could just say the first person you think of?"

"Angel and Amber don't want one." Harold laughed at the magnificent pout. "All the numbers go into a hat."

Daisy opened her eyes wide. "Ooh, Doll's last dance hat." She turned and ran up the street. "Joey, Joey, we've got to pick out numbers for the pumpkin dance."

"Maybe we could do that at the dance, pick a number then choose the bloke we want?" Bethany's attempt at innocent didn't work any better than Daisy's.

"I thought that's what the women did anyway." Christopher smirked at Bethany's attempt at looking offended.

*   *   *

A half-hour later all the children wanting a pumpkin had been rounded up. A line formed but although Daisy picked a number first, she drew seven rather than the magical number one and retired to sulk on the sidelines. The ninth attempt, by Millie, a five-year old who came with those running from the General, produced number one. After the cheering finished the rest drew as well.

"Come on Millie, pick your pumpkin." Millie looked down, scuffing her toe a little before showing number seven.

Daisy smiled brightly, waving number one. "I traded, just like at the dances."

Harold glared at the adults present. "Who let that little gem slip?" Nobody apparently. He turned back to Daisy. "What did you trade?"

"Two walks with Angel and Millie can play with Grim four times." Everyone called Sharyn's black cat Grim, because she'd refused to say Grimalkin.

"Not a fair deal, and you've had practice." Harold beckoned to Millie, trying to look as non-threatening as possible since she already looked nervous. "Why did you trade? Don't you want the biggest?"

"I don't mind because they're all big, and I didn't have one at all last year. Mom said we must be grateful we've got a roof." The last came out as a whisper.

Harold sighed because this had seemed so simple to start with, and now he'd opened a can of worms. "Who is your mum?" A woman came forward, smiling nervously. "We'll just go over here a minute for a chat. I want to explain something." After explaining that this really was like their last place, and Soldier Boy might sound like a gang boss but didn't get privileges, Millie still insisted she didn't mind which pumpkin. Harold still wasn't happy, but more about the return the lass had got than the actual trading. Any of the children could come on a walk with Amber or Angel any time they wanted, and Grim didn't mind who played with him so Daisy really had stitched Millie. Inspiration struck. "Do you like colouring books, Millie? Have you got any?"

"Not now. They were all filled up. Then I lost my crayons when we moved. I liked drawing as well but slates aren't the same."

"This is when you learn to trade, or a first lesson." Harold straightened up, raising his voice. "Since Millie hasn't been taught to trade and Daisy has, by Patty, Millie needs an assistant." Harold smiled at Daisy. "Me."

Daisy scowled, then smiled. "I want Patty, please?"

After a spirited discussion Patty conceded defeat, claiming that someone must have been training Harold to negotiate but she'd done her best. After some sulking a grumpy Daisy finally agreed the new trade. Millie gained one colouring book, only half finished, three A4 sheets of plain, unused paper, two unused pencils and eight assorted crayons only half used up. In return Daisy had first pick of the pumpkins. Harold knew roughly how many books and crayons Daisy still had from his scavenging in the early days, which didn't help the youngster in her negotiations. By then several pairs of young heads were in spirited discussions and other tickets were changing hands.

As Daisy went for her prize and a delighted Millie took her seventh place in line, Patty elbowed Harold in the ribs. "You've just ruined my reputation."

"Not really, the next sucker will be lulled into a false sense of security." Harold nudged back. "Anyway, you took it easy on me."

"Of course. Though only because I fell for your boyish charm and innocence." She looked at Daisy. "That madam needed slowing up."

"Yup, because I think she's using being my niece to get preferential treatment." Harold nodded towards Millie. "With the new residents."

"Really?" Patty chuckled. "I'll pass that little gem to the teachers, Coven and girl club." Harold winced slightly. He winced several times over the next few days as Daisy stormed in because she hadn't got her way over one thing or another, and then the storm seemed to subside. Sharyn did confide that yes, some of the new refugees did expect to take second bite at any cherries. Though now the problem had been highlighted, fixing it didn't take long and included two of them joining the Coven.

Most of the possible reasons for friction disappeared anyway as the residents spread out a bit. All but three rooms in the terrace houses finally had electricity and running water, and a full set of heaters and furniture. The last residents moved over to take possession of habitable rooms, and heaters worked at drying the repaired walls of the remainder. There would still be some shuffling about, people moving back and forth, because sometimes folk just didn't get along. Until then the new and old residents celebrated being warm and dry, even if more cramped than before the General made his move.

Everyone turned to Halloween, with enthusiasm as the original residents explained girl club trick and treat, though some of the newer ones asked about a preteen version. This year Harold did answer the door to trick or treat, but the more traditional version being herded by mothers. He even proffered a dish of dried fruit slices dusted in a bit of chocolate powder or finely ground sugar, tiny coloured buns with a bit of jam inside, and pine sap drops that allegedly tasted like boiled sweets. The sounds of laughter as the Orchard Close girl club version of trick and treat spread the happiness later didn't sting too badly this year.

*   *   *

The bonfire five nights later certainly seemed more like Guy Fawkes this year. All the younger residents and quite a few of the adults oohed and aahed at the fireworks. These fireworks hissed rather than banged, but burned with pretty colours. Some spat out small sparks, while others dripped coloured fire from the piles of bricks supporting them. Despite being asked time and again, Harold refused to say where they came from. Barry remained bashful about his pyrotechnic leanings, as he called his chemical experiments, though he closely supervised the safety precautions.

Harold had warned the Army, receiving assurances nobody would get trigger-happy with the children present. This sergeant and his squaddies had been manning the post long enough to soften their attitudes a little. As a thank you several men and some of the girl club took them soup and beer though before putting on their costumes or, as a few residents pointed out, taking off their clothes. Not strictly true in many cases but the original Orchard Close or girl club tradition still persisted, the one about teasing the lads at Halloween and Guy Fawkes.

Harold didn't dance because a Wills-Womble and a Firework Fairy took a lot more wrangling this year, especially with more youngsters racing about. That seemed even worse because hissing fireworks didn't bother dogs so Amber, Angel, Mischief and Sooty joined in. Mischief seemed to be trying to live up to her name, stealing at least two of Elizabeth's attempts at hot dogs. Veronica, allegedly in charge of the fluffy Staffy cross, blamed Rascal's example rather than any fault in her training. Angel, Amber and Sooty all managed to beg their share. Eventually Harold carried a Wills-Womble back home. By the time he had been tucked up, Firework Fairy had gone to sleep still in her costume.

Harold intended turning up the volume on the TV again this year to drown out the party. He hoped there'd be no bloody squirrels on the news. There really were more about this year and the little gits had to be chased off the Hazel bushes and young trees. Squirrels were smarter than the birds and wriggled under the nets to get the nuts, while the mesh tubes to stop rabbits killing young trees were no barrier to the little grey acrobats. Sharyn interrupted his musing. "You are coming to the Guy Fawkes dance this year."

"I am not cavorting around a bonfire." After Valentine Sharyn had backed off about dances, but now Harold realised she'd just been biding her time.

"It's in the dance house because the rain is heavier now." Sharyn put her hands on her hips. "I'll send for another dozen women and the cauldron if you act up. I only got a pass for one year and so did you. This year you're coming to the dance for the same reason I had to, the state you get into left on your own. You looked bloody awful last Guy Fawkes and were in a hell of a state about squirrels." Sharyn held out a yellow homemade bow tie. "Now put on your bee costume."

A dark suit with the bow tie and yellow strips above the pockets and on the lapels classed as a bee costume, so Harold could hardly object. He retired to the study to get changed with not completely good grace. His acceptance lasted right up until he came inside the dance house. "Oh cripes, I'd forgotten Hazel." Harold stopped at the door while a startled Hazel in a yellow and black striped bee skirt stared back and blushed bright red. Not because of the skirt, probably, but because of slow dancing with Billy.

Billy looked like a rabbit in headlights and a lone rabbit because Hazel went through the double doors into the dining room and the other dancers at speed. "Um. Harold. I didn't. Haven't." Billy shuffled his feet and looked about twelve instead of nineteen.

Harold suddenly saw the funny side and laughed, really laughed. He'd not done that for too long. "Cripes Billy, she's a lass at a dance. I'd be more upset if none of you danced with her." Harold shrugged. "Even more upset if it was because of me. I promise not to look at numbers or follow to see who walks her home. Now will someone please tell Hazel the same?"

"I'll will, if someone hasn't already done it. Veronica has the same trouble because of Isiah and Kerry." Liz sniggered. "Especially when Alfie pulled her number out of the hat. Hazel was…" Liz stopped. "Through there needing me." She headed off.

"Well that's killed the party." Harold sighed, because everyone had stopped dancing to watch and listen.

"Not really." Harold turned to find a smiling Celine, in a black dress with yellow ribbon wound round it. Not a little black dress, but a lot nearer than her white evening gown had been. She looked down. "I'm getting there. As your therapy has a lot to do with it, and I know you are a good dancer and safe, you are on my dance card tonight."

Harold put his hand around her shoulder, and the other just around her waist. "I've always got room on my card for you, Celine."

"Oh no, I've made progress. One hand right round waist onto my back, buster, and properly round my shoulder. I've been saving my first proper dance for you." Her green eyes twinkled. "Not a huggy one yet, but if you're good I might get to that one day."

"One huggy dance, booked for when required." Harold found he could dance without stepping on feet despite his lack of practice over summer. He soon had plenty of practice as a steady stream of women came for a welcome back dance, and slowly Harold relaxed. Nobody wanted a huggy hands dance, but they didn't treat him like china either. Sweet Bethany insisted on a slow dance. She persuaded Harold to ask about her costume, and then insisted he called her Sweet Bee. Fergie had definitely joined the mystery competition with a bright yellow bikini under not enough net curtain.

Hazel made a point of taking her dance partners into the other room, as did Alfie funnily enough. "He's still wary about you seeing him kiss Hazel, and with that bad leg he can only slow dance so if she dances with him?" Doll sniggered. "Alfie kept jumping at shadows for weeks, or hopping anyway." Harold had gone to check on the guards one evening and come across Alfie and Hazel in a clinch. Both had avoided him for a while afterwards.

"Hazel kissed him the first time." Doll's eyes opened wide. "Don't you dare mention it since I'm supposed to have forgotten." Doll pouted. "Never mind Alfie and Hazel, what's your costume? Cow-bee? Bee-girl?"

"Ah, that's for the men to wonder about. You're too much of a gentleman to find out there's a sting in my tail." Doll waggled her bottom a little bit. "In a manner of speaking. But who gets stung is what really keeps them guessing."

"I'd pity them but they're all volunteers."

"True, but I've got to be more careful now because Matti is too distracted for a stopwatch and gramps is babysitting, allegedly." Doll kissed him on the cheek. "Welcome back Harold."

"I've been back a bit."

"No, Soldier Boy came back. Though now Harold has started dancing again, the draw at the end is going to be confusing. We'll be trying to get rid of your number instead of trading for it." She laughed. "Now you can worry the other way, who you'll be absolutely safe with."

Harold didn't worry, because there would be a conspiracy afoot. Sure enough he ended up walking Patty home, in the opposite direction to the girl club and Hazel's walk home. "Is it hand kiss or shake hands?" Harold knew the young men didn't reckon much to drawing Patty, so expected one or the other.

"Hmm." Patty made a great show of inspecting the sky. "Nope, the moonlight is wrong, and you aren't hairy enough. You can kiss me here, on my cheek. A lucky escape since I've never actually had a toy-boy."

"Whew. Though since I've already been one you might have been pleasantly surprised."

"You have?" Patty looked suspicious. "Do you mean an aged relative who insisted on a kiss for sweeties at Christmas, or were you targeted by some cougar when you were…? Hang on, you went into the Army at some tender age and off to the desert." Her eyes widened. "Were you kidnapped by a harem?"

"No such luck and not a completely tender age. The Army won't take infants and the uniform made even a pimply youth fair game." Harold chuckled. "There is a certain amount of training before we get thrown into the front line."

"Training?" Patty's grin had come back.

"Oh yes, and toy-boys get some of that as well." Harold sighed. "Though you're a bit young for me. There's only three or four years between us."

"Spurned, because I'm too young?" Patty sighed, then tittered. "Watch out if Celine finds out you aren't averse to an older woman because she reckons you're the right mix of dangerous, protective and gentle. She's looking for an older version for when the cure finally takes, but if I drop a hint?"

"If you do, then Batty Patty might become someone's new nickname."

Harold chuckled. "You need a gang name anyway with your rep."

"Don't you dare! After that I've lost any hint of interest. You can take me to the door and kiss my youthful cheek."

"Tarnation, failed again. I suppose I'd better take the long way home or Hazel will scowl at me." Harold laughed. "She's already nervous about me seeing who she dances with, let alone who walks her home."

"No need tonight, because Veronica wouldn't trade. Ah, forget that?"

"Forgotten. Goodnight Patty."

Harold walked home musing on the way life seemed to have finally quietened down a little. The crops had been harvested without any dramas, Caddi's last attempt to annoy him had been fairly harmless, and the new refugees seemed to be fitting in without too much friction. The GOFs and Barbies were downright sociable, the Geeks weren't winding anyone up, and even the General's attack had barely disturbed life in the enclaves. Harold really hoped it lasted at least until the New Year.

Chapter 6:

Orchard Close
Armoured Corps

The general sense of well-being after Guy Fawkes lasted all of nine days. A two-tone horn blaring out heralded Cooper arriving a lot faster than usual and without his guards on a quad. Harold ran to the gate to find out why without getting his stick first. Cooper jumped out of his motor, shouting as he ran up the access road. "Get Soldier Boy! We want fighters, lots of fighters." He paused as he saw Harold. "How many fighters can you bring, and especially those f.. rifles and shooters, serious shooters. There's a problem and Caddi is asking for help."

"From me? Who has he upset?" Harold couldn't work out who would attack Caddi and why the Hot Rods thought he'd help them.

"No you.. er, idiot. There's GOFS and Geeks coming as well, and everyone is to bring rifles. Bring anything else that shoots, or do you fancy managing without the mart this winter?" Cooper couldn't stand still, twitching with tension and the need to do something, anything, to release it.

Harold stared for a moment. The mart? "Crap no. Which... person is attacking the mart? The Ferdinands?"

"No, we've got every gang who uses our mart coming to stop an attack by a big mob from the south. They'll run right over the mart guards, and then the bastard government will blow up the mart and starve us all like London. For f... blimey's sake just get your people there and we'll all get the details." Cooper stopped twitching with an obvious effort. "Better not take a woman into the boss meeting, because not everyone will obey rules and might not take her seriously." Cooper spoke carefully and very seriously for once. "We know your Emmy and Patty are dangerous but others won't, OK? We don't need a fight kicking off among ourselves." He glanced over his shoulder. "The Geeks and GOFS will come through your traffic island, right?"

"It's a neutral road. I'll come in with them." Harold wanted to see if the rest really were in on this, or if Caddi had come up with a way to pull the rifles and fighters out of Orchard Close. "Scat. I'll be along with shooters and guns."

"I'm gone. Come mob-handed. I mean it." Cooper spun on his heel and ran back to his car, which his driver had already turned round. The modified Mini Cooper roared off up the road with the air horns blaring. Harold had already run into the guardhouse and picked up the phone.

"Faith, Hilda?"

"No, Veronica. I'm training."

"Listen carefully, Veronica. We are not under attack but I want everyone willing to shoot with a gun or crossbow to come to the gate, quickly. Bring every weapon and as much ammunition as they can because we need them. If you can't do that, ask Faith or Hilda to do it. Quick as you can."

"All right Harold. I'll ask Hilda. Anything else?"

"Put me through to Sharyn please, then get to it. Thanks." The connection made the familiar clicking and although it seemed ages, Sharyn didn't take long to pick up. "We need sandwiches or cold food of some sort and lots to drink at the gates as soon as possible please." Harold gave her a quick rundown. "We won't go until I see GOFS and Geeks but I want to be ready."

"Hellfire Harold, save the mart. I'll talk to the Coven while you go and do your thing." Harold made another call, to Patty asking her to rouse the girl club and bring her crossbow and a lot of bolts, and then ran for home. By the time he'd put on his long coat and slung the Blaser and two-two rifle under it, then filled the pockets and a carrier bag with ammunition and two handguns, Casper rang to ask where he was.

A small crowd had already gathered as Harold ran down the street to the gate. "Is this for real?" Emmy wore a long coat with a long shape hidden beneath it. She saw his eyes. "The sniper's rifle and I've brought all my ammo."

"I've brought my shotgun." Casper had no smile at all today. "How bad is it?"

Harold filled them all in, then started to sort out who would come. Meanwhile Patty went for the armoured pickup, with Billy to help hook the minibus battle trailer onto the back. The vehicle wasn't a pickup even if the name stuck because under the steel William discovered the engine, chassis and suspension from a small lorry, which explained why it could carry all that armour. Casper went to bring one of the diesel vans, a long transit, in case those two weren't enough. "I'm leaving two little rifles just in case, with the sawn-off and a single barrelled shotgun. All the single shot pistols stay, and some small calibre revolvers but I'm taking all the semis, and all the clips."

"I'm coming." Emmy looked ready for objections because she knew how Harold felt about protecting women, especially mothers. "You said shooters Harold." Harold nodded, because Emmy could shoot better than any of the others at long ranges.

"If I can stay in a vehicle then I'll come, Harold." Alfie tapped his coat. "I can't run about but I've brought the 303. There's not much ammo so I'll take a two-two rifle for when it's gone."

"I can use a two-two rifle Harold." Finn shrugged. "That's the same round and the same sights as my assassin pistol. I can use a nine mill though, closer in."

"I'm in." Doll opened her coat to show three pistols and her machete and she also carried a Geek crossbow with a full quiver.

As the offers rolled in Harold had to turn people down, since he couldn't leave Orchard Close unprotected. "Thanks Seth, but Orchard Close needs a few people who won't freeze if they're attacked. I know you'll use that sawn-off if needed, so you stay. Put all the dogs on the walls as sentries and I'll leave you two of the infra-reds. Don't take chances. Shoot first and ask the survivors what they wanted."

"Cripes Harold." Seth squared his shoulders. "Nobody will get in."

Billy ran up the road towards the traffic island with his machete and two handguns, and a radio to let Harold know when anyone else arrived. Meanwhile Harold turned down Bernie, but took his rucksack full of pipe bombs. Toyah seemed relieved when Tim had to stay. Tim accepted the explanation, that Harold knew Tim would definitely shoot to protect Orchard Close and Toyah. Where possible Harold tried to take single people but he couldn't stick to that if the volunteers were serious fighters. He took three of the four fighter refugees from the General, but left the married one. Jeremy and Matti, and Matthew and Bess, both came as couples since all four were veterans.

The rifles and shotguns went into the battle trailer and the pickup cab, and even more ammo arrived as non-combatants brought the reserves from the armoury or guardhouses. Saving the mart had to be worth taking some chances. Liz turned up with a huge bundle of crossbow bolts and then the food began to arrive along with containers and bottles of small beer and boiled water. One non-combatant brought a big pack, Lenny the ex-paramedic. "You need me."

"You aren't a fighter, Lenny."

"No, but this sounds like a battle. If someone is hit I'll be the difference between limping and dead, and tending them won't take a shooter off the line." Even as Harold hesitated Lenny opened his pack. "None of you can use half of this. I've even got morphine for if it's really bad."

"Fair enough." Harold didn't want to listen to any of his people screaming as they died.

The medic frowned. "Are you fighting from the armoured vehicles?"

"If we can, Lenny."

"Even if you aren't, take couple of camp beds in the transit. Put them someplace in shelter for me to treat wounded off the ground." Lenny bent to look under the trailer. "Wouldn't want something coming under and ruining my work."

"Done. Put them in the van and we'll park it behind the others. Get it organised." Harold turned to making sure the twenty-eight other men and women understood a few simple radio signals. They'd have to be simple with every gang using the same few channels. "Put a pushbike in the van in case we need a quick messenger."

"Harold?" He turned to find Isiah and Kerry. "This is the original test version field telephone. Clip on this car battery and the cable will reach from the cab to the trailer. It'll give you private coms." Isiah handed over the two small boxes with handsets and a coil of cable, while Kerry offered a car battery. "The battery is always topped up and charged in case of power surges and cuts."

"Harold, Billy is calling. He's flagged down a convoy of Geeks and GOFS and they're waiting." Emmy grinned. "He's told Caddi's spies to get aboard or you'll accidentally shoot them."

"Hang on, move over." Harold turned at the voice then got out of the way as Liz and four helpers came through with a sheet of steel on three wheelbarrows. "Prop this up and shoot from behind it." Willing hands slid the steel into the transit van and several lengths of timber followed. The helpers put more quivers of crossbow bolts inside after the steel.

"Enough. Everyone who is coming load up, and the rest shut the gates and keep inside until we come back. No gardening, nothing outside the walls." Within minutes the armoured truck groaned into motion with the minibus obediently following. Harold smiled to himself, with acceleration like this it certainly wouldn't be the usual gang poser vehicle. As he reached the traffic island Harold relaxed because if Caddi had pulled some sort of a stunt, this lot weren't going to be happy. Nine Geek Freek and five GOFS vehicles were waiting.

Five men struggled out of what were very crowded GOFS vehicles and four climbed into the back of the pickup. Roy opened the cab door. "Move up Billy, make room for an old man." At thirty-one Roy did look old among the fighters.

"How come you aren't fighting with the GOFS?" Harold smiled. "Not that I'm complaining, nor about you having Gofannon's rifle."

"Gofannon reckons I'm better than any of his with the er, bloody thing so I'd best keep it if this is serious." Roy grinned. "I told him we fight with our people when they need us and he said OK. The rest of them in the cars will be pleased we've got out. It's a bit cosy in there with all the heavy metal."

"Why only five GOFS cars?" Billy peered through the slit in the steel plate over the windscreen. "Are they worried about the General?"

"A bit but there's a car and big van gone the other way, to the Barbies. There'll be something like fifty GOFS in the end." Roy laughed. "The GOFS are all chortling about Caddi's reaction when they turn up with Barbies. The GOFS cars will warn the Hot Rod sentries so they can hide."

"Will the Barbies come?"

"Do fish swim, is the Pope Catholic? It's a fight and anyway they use the same mart so they'll want to save it." Roy rapped a knuckle on the plate covering his side window and peered through the loophole. "Cosy. Will this be enough?"

"That depends on too many things to list." Harold grinned. "Though anyone shooting the usual underpowered soft lead reloads from a pistol is going to be bloody frustrated. Billy, give Roy some cotton wool and a headband." Billy did, and explained about just how loud a gun going off in here might be.

Meanwhile the convoy headed out of Orchard Close territory, and a Hot Rods vehicle pulled out of a side turning ahead. A hand from the window beckoned them to follow, and the radio crackled. "We're meeting the other side of The Mansion, because there's others coming. Watch out because some of them will be bloody edgy." The voice laughed. "Especially the Ferdinands with both Caddi and Soldier Boy there. Did you bring your spanker?"

Harold didn't answer. When Roy looked a question he pointed to his stick, propped up against the dashboard. Billy explained spanking Ferdinands at the mart while Harold concentrated on driving. Not only did the slits in the plate restrict his vision but the difficulty in slowing meant he had to be very careful not to trample the car in front. The original truck brakes had to stop both truck and trailer, difficult because the steel plate alone weighed well over two tons without the original vehicles and the people aboard.

* * *

Harold almost changed his mind when he saw the number of vehicles and blocks of different gangsters waiting, but gritted his teeth. By the time he'd got the vehicle parked nearby all the fighters were looking, and a group headed by Caddi were on the way. They all stopped about twenty feet away, waiting for Harold. "Fucking hell, Soldier Boy, is this your tank?" Caddi laughed, probably a genuine one. "Choose wisely? What sort of logo is that?"

Harold climbed out to general merriment from the rest, except the Ferdinands led by an overweight man wearing an American footballer's helmet, shoulder pads and tight pants with knee and elbow protectors. Harold turned to shut the door before stepping aside so they could all see the paint job. "Seems clear to me." The girl club really had decorated the steel plate. On the cab door they'd painted a big circle with lines in it to denote the view through telescopic sights. In the sights they'd painted a tilted cross on a mound, with a bullet hole through the top part of the upright. On the crosspiece they'd lettered 'PEACE' in red.

On the rear half of the plate protecting the truck bed the artist painted a big red heart with a ribbon across carrying one word, 'PEACE.' The picture had been surrounded by cupid bow lips, balloons, streamers and shooting stars. The CHOOSE WISELY in big black letters on white between the two pictures seemed a clear enough message, the girl club thought.

"I can live with that, but 'We Come in Peace' and all the ribbons and hearts doesn't quite work." A tall teenager with a shamrock logo pointed at the trailer.

Cooper almost choked laughing but got it out. "It says 'We Shoot to Kill' on the back." The group laughed again.

"Come on Soldier Boy. Bring two bodyguards the same as the rest." Caddi nodded towards Casper. "He seems to be back in action. Who else?" The gang boss seemed to be in a tremendous mood considering the urgent summons and warnings of a serious fight.

"Take Roy, since I might get wound up among that lot." Billy shrugged. "He'll be more use than me in serious strife anyway."

"Roy?"

"A pleasure and an honour. Are there any rules?"

"No loaded crossbows and don't point weapons at people. If it kicks off kill the bastards, all of them." Harold grinned. "That's my rules anyway."

Casper spoke from just behind Harold. "I'm good with that." The three of them followed the rest to a cleared patch of ground. As he walked Harold looked at the numbers that had gathered. The five waiting blocks each held forty to fifty fighters, and the Geeks had brought the same. The GOFS brought less but Harold knew they weren't all here yet. Harold had thirty-five with Roy's squad but would be outnumbered by any one gang if trouble started.

* * *

The introductions were cut short while everyone stared and most started swearing at the nine vehicles full of Barbies following the rest of the GOFS. Caddi reverted to words first. "You are fucking crazy."

Gofannon laughed at Caddi. "No, the Barbies are crazy and you said a serious fight. Don't worry, we'll put them the other side of the armoured brigade to your lads and anyone else of a nervous disposition." Gofannon narrowed his eyes. "I wouldn't want any incidents to upset my allies before the General comes calling."

"Some allies." But Caddi only muttered as Christie and Ken came over with a woman Harold recognised from the puppy-buying.

"How's Splash?"

"Fantastic thanks, but this isn't the place for walkies." She grinned. "At least I can cripes here if I want."

"If Soldier Boy's girlfriends are done?" The tall solidly built man in his mid-twenties, Paddy, sported a big green shamrock on his leather jacket to show he belonged to the Murphies. He looked over the Barbies before pointing to people in turn. "Baggies, Ferdinands, Trainspotters. You know us and the rest."

"That urgent? Right, where's the fight and where do you want us?" Ken looked round as if she expected to see a horde charging right now. Considering the big GOFS-made sword held with the blade resting on her shoulder, maybe she did. "We've brought fifty, so worth about a hundred of you lot."

The meeting really started, with the Baggies supplying the information. They had been fighting off small groups of last year's refugees, the ones who fled south, for about a month. The floods last year hadn't ever properly cleared down south, and were already rising with the recent rain. In desperation all the groups down there, which had never formed proper gangs, combined to either conquer a drier territory or break out. One of them had run to the Baggies, trading a safe place in the gang for him and his family in return for information.

The middle-aged man brought into the middle of the group looked terrified, which seemed sensible. "Why are they going for the mart?" Harold still couldn't see the logic for that.

The man cringed away. "The area near the marts down south is flooded so there's only a narrow approach. Everyone down south decided this is the best place to break out. Maybe not the first place, but the first one with a mart and a clear approach."

"Why do they want a mart? An Army post without one would be easier to overrun because here the mart guards and armoured car will get involved." Ken might look like a maniac and Barbies had a reputation as lunatics, but she was using her brain right now.

The man cringed the other way, away from Ken. "Those organising it want the supplies in case there's nothing to eat out there."

"But the marts will shut and starve us like London." The Ferdinand, Bull of course, scowled.

A small youth with bright red dreadlocks, a Trainspotter according to his anorak, shrugged. "Why should they care if they've left the city anyway? What he says makes sense to me." He glanced at Caddi. "You said urgent, so when does this happen?"

A Baggie called Boing wearing a black and white striped scarf pointed south. "We've pulled everyone and everything out of the way because there's gotta be six or seven hundred at the very least. A mob that size will just trample us. We've sent a messenger to show them where there's a clear run. We reckon it'll take anything from a couple of hours to four or five because they're mostly on foot." He grinned. "There can't be anyone or anything left down south, because this lot have brought everything, and I do mean everything. Grandads, women, kids, and probably any kitchen sinks they can carry."

"Women?" Hawkins smirked.

"Keep your bloody donnies off them until the fighting's done, or I'll hand you to Emmy from Soldier Boy's lot. First we kill the fucking fighters, right?" Ken glared and Hawkins held up his hands, placating her.

"Yeah, right, first we kill the fuckers with weapons. Just sayin', when we sort out the take, right?"

"First we sort out how to win, or sorting out the take isn't going to happen, is it? Not only that we'll have no food so you won't exactly want any extra people, will you?" Several of the other's smiled since Harold didn't hide his sarcasm.

Though Hawkins didn't get a chance to react. "True, now shut it you randy bastard." Bull nodded towards Harold's vehicles. "You're a bit light on fighters, Soldier Boy, because we've all brought about fifty I reckon."

Harold just smiled. Sure enough Caddi spoke up. "First, we've no idea who is in there. Second, his lot will be killing them while you're still undoing your flies and finding your weapon."

"He shot a bloke through the head and then the two with him, at half a mile, too fast for them to drive away." Gofannon smirked. "Handy. It's where he got that truck and backed off that fucking General."

"Bullshit."

"I stood and watched them fall, through binoculars. Three shots, bang, bang, bang, all stone dead and two through the head." Bull opened his mouth, thought twice about calling Gofannon a liar, then looked very thoughtfully at the truck.

Though Boing still wasn't happy. "That's one shooter."

"He's got more." Ken looked at the minibus.

"We might even find out how many?" Caddi looked thoughtful now. "And how many rifles."

"We need another big rifle Caddi, to use all my shooters. How far can your bloke be certain of killing them with your old 303?" Harold wanted Caddi's ammo, not the actual gun.

"That hasn't got a scope, as you bloody well know." Caddi frowned. "Though you didn't need a scope to shoot at eyes that first time, did you? What sort of range will we be fighting these fuckers at?"

"Here." Another Baggie, Throstle, produced a page from a road map, and the leaders from each gang crowded closer to look as he explained.

"They'll come in through all these houses and down the neutral road. That'll all be close-range shit." Franco the Trainspotter grimaced. "That'll be bloody with those numbers."

"Don't fight them there. Let them come out of the buildings onto the cleared area near the mart, then hit them from behind. If the Baggies and Ferdinands move into the houses they've just come through? Or whichever gangs want to cut off any retreat?" Harold used his finger to indicate a curve on the map. "The rest of us stay here, keeping out of sight behind the derelict housing. Once the mob hits the mart, we move out and start killing from the other side of the strip the mart demolished. They've got to run right across that open space to get to us."

Wellington, the Geek general, clapped his hands. "Thank fuck for another brain among this lot. I keep saying that head on in buildings is a bad idea. The Army and mart guards will be at the other side and they'll use machine guns. If these aren't a proper gang, just a mob, they'll come apart."

"They'll be surrounded." Bull closed his hand as if crushing something, then frowned. "How far is that, from the mart to the first houses to the north and west?"

"About five hundred yards, but it varies." Caddi frowned. "The fucking mart knocked it all down because some smartarse stuck a crossbow bolt in one of their blokes." He glanced at Harold. "Is Patty along?" He grinned. "Is she a shooter?"

"Patty is along but maybe just for anyone getting a bit closer." Harold pointed at the map again. "I've got people who'll pick out and kill anyone pointing a rifle at that range. If you have they should concentrate on just that. The rest of your rifles just have to hit the main mass." Internally Harold winced because there'd be women and kids in there, but there were women and kids in Orchard Close who would starve if the mart shut. "Once they find we're killing their riflemen they've got to come over that open ground to get to grips, or to hit us with handguns."

"Told you." Caddi looked quite smug as he spoke to the gangs on his southern and western borders. "He's a soldier. His lot might not have numbers but they survived one of those mob breakouts during the crash." Caddi shrugged. "We only brought about fifty each because none of us would strip our places bare. Soldier Boy hasn't got a big army to start with." He glanced at the trailer. "Luckily or the bastard might have cleaned us all up."

The rest were more or less ignoring Caddi now, looking at the map and thinking or discussing with their own gang members. "I'll buy it. Better than trying to stop them getting to the mart." Franco, the redheaded Trainspotter, frowned. "We've got shooters who can do that, pick a target over five hundred yards away."

"As long as just attacking the mart doesn't get them closed down?" Christie had a point, and they all thought that over a few moments.

"If we try fighting in those houses, enough bastards might get through to attack the mart anyway." Throstle nodded slowly. "This way is good enough, once we sort out who goes where."

"Can you send someone to the mart, tell them we're on the way?" Harold smiled. "We'll arrive just too late to stop the first ones attacking. With luck the RAF will get there first. At the very least the mart will have all their posts manned with rifles or buckshot."

"Good point. I'll send the whores." Caddi whistled and waved, until a man ran across for instructions before heading for The Mansion at speed in a car.

"We'll go nearest to the bypass and the Army so we can flash our knickers at them." Christie smirked. "They'll be less likely to shoot at us poor females."

"We'd better put the armour next to protect us from you." Caddi sneered. "Then the GOFS I suppose or Soldier Boy might nick their girlfriends."

"We might be more interested in Soldier Boy's girls?" The rest of the bosses compared forces and gangs dropped into place along the impromptu battle line. The Trainspotters and Baggies volunteered to fight in the ruined housing, though the Trainspotter shooters would stay clear, to shoot at long range. Harold thought that made sense, going by what he'd seen of the Ferdinand's lack of hand-to-hand expertise.

"We'll take the bit next to the houses, then if it looks like the mob are breaking out again we'll get them from the side. Flank them yeah?" The Murphy looked at Harold with a grin.

Harold smiled back. "We'll make soldiers of you yet. Now we'd better get moving in case they arrive early. Unless someone else wants to start the ball rolling, we'll take the first shots to nail some of those with rifles before they take cover. Nobody get impatient because we want them all out of the neutral road housing first." After some discussion the rest agreed. Harold would fire the first shots then everyone would open up.

*   *   *

Harold waited until arriving at 'his' sector before briefing everyone. He held up the 303 rifle from Caddi and three boxes of rounds before throwing a box to Alfie. "Have fun, and keep the empty brass." He threw two full clips. "Save those for closer up."

"Who gets the extra rifles, Alfie's two-two and that big one?" Doll's little smile definitely volunteered her.

"Finn gets the 303 because he can shoot a pistol with the same sights. Just aim at belt buckle height, Finn, and I'll show you how to adjust the sights for when the range drops. Harold smiled at Doll. "You've used Finn's pistol, so you get a rifle."

"I had a go as well, when I moved in with Finn and Barry for a while." Billy shrugged. "If anyone is any better I'll step down?"

Harold looked at Roy, who shrugged as well. "You saw us all shoot a rifle. If he's used to those sights let him have a go. These blokes will be more useful with shotguns, handguns and machetes." Roy hooked a thumb at his four men.

"Fair enough." Harold spoke to the men directly. "The best shotgun ammo when they get in range, under a hundred yards, then use up the rest. At fifty yards everyone start shooting as fast as you can with handguns while keeping the muzzle down." Harold went through how they'd set up. "Just remember Bess, aimed shots if they break." Bess blushed and promised to remember.

A couple of tries showed what angle between the truck and trailer left a gap that could be covered by the steel sheet. "There'll only be crossbows, shotguns and pistols behind here. Keep down so you don't attract attention until they get into range, and save your pistols for if they get to fifty yards. We want anyone in that mob with rifles shooting at the thicker steel on the vehicles." Harold smiled. "Hopefully we'll have shot those people by the time they're in shotgun range."

"You'd better." Casper gestured at his arm. "That's only just healed up. We'd better have the bombs because we haven't got a roof in the way when throwing." Since the mob hadn't arrived they all practiced parking up and getting the steel into place. Those unused to their rifle practiced loading and sighting.

"Emmy?" Harold waved her away from the rest. "I don't want you in the vehicles."

Emmy scowled. "Don't go all protective now. I'm here to fight, Harold. I'm the best shot apart from you, and I've practiced with this rifle."

"Yes, which is why I want you up high. You get in the roof of one of the forward houses, that one just behind and to the left of where we will set up. The mob will shoot at the vehicles so you'll get a nice clean view without being under fire, and the extra twenty yards will make no difference to you or that rifle." Harold pointed at the group of people. "Take half a dozen with you to rip up timber joists or anything else that'll stop a bullet and make a low wall in the loft. Lie down behind the cover and knock out a couple of tiles. Send the helpers back as soon as the first warning comes."

Emmy narrowed her eyes suspiciously. "Why do you want me up there?"

Harold handed her a headset. "With this on you can shoot while talking to let me know what's happening. I want to know if the bastards have broken out someplace, or the Army have arrived, or we're being flanked." Harold sighed. "If the mart has been breached, because then we may as well save ammo and go home."

Emmy wasn't convinced. "Anyone will do as a spotter Harold. I'm a shooter."

"A shooter with a superb view and in the perfect position to use that very good rifle where it's needed. If Caddi or Hawkins start shooting at us by mistake, make it a fatal mistake. We might not even realise down here in the sound and the fury." Harold hadn't many reasons left, not ones he could say.

"I'm a spotter, to watch out for treachery, and in a good place for sniping without incoming, yes?" Emmy smiled, a little one.

"That's it."

"And you worry about me and Tammy." Emmy's smile widened.

Harold gave up and grinned. "Yes, and about explaining to Curtis if I lose you, and I'm a sucker for your sparkling personality and bad-girl look. If this all goes wrong, use that pushbike to get home. Tell everyone to dig in. Now will you stop arguing?"

"You really are a soft sod sometimes, Harold." Emmy kissed him on the end of the nose. "All right, since you asked so nicely." She set off towards the rest, calling for people to help her, and Harold heaved a sigh of relief. He really didn't want Tammy left all alone, especially since she still relied on Mummy's milk bar because the marts didn't have the powdered sort.

Harold soon had a distraction because Ken came over to talk. She saw the two camp beds in the transit. "Neat. If we've got someone hit bad and you've got a spare bed?"

"Bring her over and we'll try. We might have to blind her if she sees our medic?" Harold smiled because he didn't mean that but the Barbies were notoriously protective about their real doctor.

"If he saves her life she might stay to say thank you, repeatedly. We'll be generous over replacing medication, if it's needed." The Barbie warchief nodded towards the armoured vehicles. "You look to have about thirty which is a bit light on numbers if it comes to a ruck. We're near the Army and I don't reckon the mob will come straight at us. If you get into hand-to-hand watch where you shoot." She grinned. "We'll flank them, just like real soldiers."

Harold laughed at her version of Paddy's Irish accent. "I'll warn everyone not to shoot dangerous blondes, though someone will be watching out for Caddi or Hawkins getting creative."

Ken looked over towards where the other gangs were hidden by the housing. "Yeah, especially Caddi. He's got greedy eyes when he looks at your truck, and when all those shooters are mentioned."

"He should worry about them getting tempted while he's in view." Harold smirked. "I thought he'd burst something when he handed over the rifle and ammo."

"Have you really got that many shooters?"

"Not that good, but I needed more 303 ammo." Ken left still shaking her head and laughing.

*   *   *

"Tweet, tweet." Everyone near enough to hear a radio stopped what they were doing and looked south because that had been Throstle, the Baggie's lieutenant.

Harold raised his voice. "They're here. Get everything loaded up for the move." A flurry of action settled into a nervous wait for the signal to say the mob were through the derelict housing. The whole horde had to move far enough into the open for the Baggies and Trainspotters to close the back door. Long minutes dragged by before the 'Wagtail' confirmed the rear were moving through the last houses. Gunfire sounded from the south, beyond this last row of housing, so Harold started the engine.

"BG. Contact. Contact. Contact. Last ones clear of housing. Army machine gun shooting. Some of mob shooting back. Mart firing, mob charging the wire." BG for Bad Girl meant Emmy. Harold dropped the truck into gear and set off round the corner onto a short stretch of road they'd just cleared of bricks. Beyond the houses he turned into a road junction, turning the wheel again sharply at the last moment before stopping. That left the truck and trailer forming a shallow "v" pointing at the distant mob.

People poured out of the transit as it pulled in alongside the trailer, protected from the south. The sheet of metal, lifted by many willing hands, sealed the gap between trailer and truck. Stakes were pounded to jam them into a road drain or rubble, before leaning the steel at an angle to help shed incoming bullets. The fighters ran back to the van for their weapons, then got set behind the steel. On the pickup Harold helped to pull a tarpaulin across the back so the Army couldn't see the rifles, then sat on a cushion and opened the flap over the centre loophole. Billy opened the next one along, while Roy stayed in the cab to use the loophole there.

Patty lifted the field telephone receiver. "The bus is ready, Harold."

Emmy called on the radio. "BG. The first of the mob are nearly at the mart fence. The other gangs are coming out and setting up."

"Tell the bus to shoot when I do, Patty." Harold gave those in the bus a moment to get set, then settled himself. He picked out a man shooting a rifle towards the bypass. It did cross his mind that he'd never know for sure who he hit this time, with so many others shooting. Then Harold's first shot went downrange, the man staggered and went down, and the rest of the Orchard Close rifles opened up.

Harold fired at a figure laid behind bodies and saw dust spurt nearby but the rifle flipped up, falling to the side. Then Harold targeted a man shooting from behind an impromptu breastwork half a dozen bricks high. He saw a brick spit out dust and spin out of the loose stack. Either the ricochet or the bullet going through the brick threw the man back. That finally gave Harold a proper read on the wind so he could shoot with more confidence. Harold emptied the clip, four rounds, before reverting to single shot load and fire.

"BG. They've hit the fence but holding for now." She paused and fired. "Mart fence guards not shooting so dead." Another shot. "Some climbing the fence, some going for the Army." Emmy fired. "Bombs going off near the armoured car."

Harold began to worry because although people looked this way and some fell, the mass of people were ignoring the rifles. More of those in his sights began to drop, stagger or duck away. More of the crowd started to look and point towards Orchard Close. The other rifles must have held off momentarily, but although more bullets tore into the mass of people they weren't enough.

"BG. You've got their attention. Only GOFS and Barbies shooting properly." More and more of the mob turned towards him, but Harold ignored them to look for the ones taking cover or kneeling to shoot back. The crowd pointed or fired, beginning to bulge his way, but now Harold worried there weren't enough rifles to sting the mob into an attack. They had to be lured away from the mart.

"BG. The rest of the bastards have started shooting now." A ripple went through the mass, with more people staggering or falling. Harold cursed the other gangsters for holding fire because they'd nearly screwed it all up. More faces turned his way, more arms pointed, and finally the mob surged towards him. Harold had no idea how much of the mob had started his way. He concentrated on searching for anyone carrying a rifle or shotgun so he could kill them.

"BG. Here they come, a lot of them just at you." Harold could hear the strain in Emmy's voice.

Stu, one of Roy's men using the rangefinder and the field telephone to keep everyone on target, called, "'Four hundred fifty." Rounds spanged off the steel, but so far nothing had penetrated. "Four hundred." Harold loaded and fired in a steady rhythm now because nobody in the crowd stopped to take cover or aim.

"BG. Cripes Harold, there's a lot. Though now the rest can't decide." Emmy paused to fire. "Some are going for the Army, some for the mart, and the rest are sort of stopped."

"Three hundred fifty." A few of the attackers stopped to aim. Harold shot any he saw then went back to looking for dangerous weapons.

"BG. A big bunch are running back towards the houses." Emmy fired. "Another lot are going towards Caddi or near him." Harold heard relief this time, because the mob had split their fire and broken up though there still seemed to be a lot coming at him.

"Three hundred." Light flooded into the rear corner of the truck. Harold glanced over to see Patty on one knee raising her crossbow to loft a shaft towards the attackers. Harold found a target with a shotgun, crushing any pity as he killed her because more rounds were striking the steel now. He had women to protect right here.

"BG. Bombs from the houses, but not enough to stop them." Emmy fired. "Shoot fast Harold, there's still a lot." She kept firing and speaking in short sentences. "Shooting from houses. Not enough to stop them."

"Two hundred fifty." A wild-eyed man with a double barrelled shotgun threw up his arms and fell before Harold fired. He looked for another target and killed him, then another.

"BG. Mob in mart yard. Attacking doors." She paused. "Triple cripes, the armoured car is on fire." Emmy started firing again. "Armoured car retreating."

"Two hundred." Again Harold fired, but now he couldn't see any rifles and had trouble finding shotguns. The scope restricted the view now so Harold took the time to unfasten it. "One hundred fifty" was in a different voice but he had no time to look. Harold didn't take the time to make clean kills now, just put the targets down. This time a crossbow bolt stole one of his victims.

"BG. Big fight in housing." Emmy fired and spoke, again and again. "Paddy's attacking from flank. Mart guards have grenades. Machine guns on mart roof."

"One hundred." Hands pulled the tarpaulin back and with a deep roar a shotgun fired inside the rear of the truck, then another two. The mob running towards Harold flinched as more shotguns joined in, some emptying a second barrel.

"BG. Mob hitting Ferdinands." Emmy's voice rose to a shout. "Yeah, Go Barbies, go GOFS! Flank attack!" The shotguns began to add a heavier beat to the rifle fire as they were reloaded and fired as fast as possible.

"Fifty." The gunfire nearby paused, just for a moment as Harold pulled out two nine mill pistols. Then every handgun that could be brought to bear opened up, a cacophony of sound and fury that almost drowned out the sound of rounds still hitting the steel plating. The advancing mob stalled for a moment as the front ranks fell. The rest milled and surged as the pistols hammered away, relentless. More and more fell or staggered back, until at last the rest started to break. The survivors split, pressing to the sides. With huge relief Harold saw how few were left standing.

There were still enough to run over the Orchard Close party, except the erstwhile attackers weren't trying to. The survivors tried to get between the vehicles and either the Barbies or the GOFS but didn't go wide enough. The Orchard Close handguns stopped their frantic tattoo as the shooters remembered their instructions; once the mass breaks, slow up to mark your target. Or most of them did. With a small part of his mind Harold bet that the one still shooting as fast as possible would be Bess.

"BG. Watch left flank." She fired. "Army and RAF arrived."

Feet ran alongside the pickup, at the back, before shotguns and pistols sounded from near the cab. The defenders behind the steel plate in the centre must have moved to the flanks. Smoking trails in the air turned into vicious explosions among the attempt to bypass the vehicles. Figures fell or staggered, and more explosions blossomed among them. Finally the attempt broke, some running away while others turned towards Harold again. Beyond them machetes rose and fell. "Cease fire, cease fire. Friendlies mixed in. Take them hand to hand or single aimed shots." Patty scooped up the field telephone, passing Harold's message to the battle bus.

"BG. They're breaking Harold. At the houses and here. The mart is safe."

The ending became anticlimactic, with the last of the attackers charging in to get to grips since they had no missile weapons left. Barely a score ran in close enough to be dangerous. They went down in a quick flurry as Roy's squad, Harold, Patty, Billy and the defenders from behind the steel plate met them. GOFS and Barbie swords and machetes rose and fell among the rest, now trying to escape. Exhausted, demoralised and now outnumbered, the end came quickly. Harold finally had a chance to look around.

Some Barbies, those not finishing wounded in front of Harold, were already thirty or more yards out from their position, hunting down anyone running away. Harold hoped they stopped before getting too close to the mart guns. Even as he thought that, Harold saw Ken's distinctive figure waving and presumably shouting though it might be a while before Harold could hear properly. Other blonde-haired figures among the women fighters also started waving. The Barbies resorted to shooting at the fleeing figures.

To the right the GOFS had also charged forward, their big swords and machetes rising and falling as they finished the last few off. Some were shooting at the nearest of the fleeing attackers, while others worked back up the line of casualties making sure of the wounded. Halfway around the arc a tight knot of struggling figures showed where part of the mob had made full contact with the Ferdinands. Further away figures retreated from the housing on the neutral road, showing that the Baggies and Trainspotters had stopped any escape.

Smoke rose from near the mart marking where helicopters had joined the fight. At least those stayed near the mart; Harold had worried the RAF would take the opportunity to wipe out the gangs as well. A hand smacked him in the back, staggering him. Another hand tugged at Harold's head. He realised he still wore the headband and earpiece around his plugged ears. Moments later the cotton wool came away in time to hear Casper saying "Typical dumb soldier."

The door on the pickup opened and Roy looked out. He looked a little shell-shocked, then stuck his little finger through a hole in the plate covering the window and waggled it. A big smile split his face. "That put ten years on me." Roy looked over those who'd jumped out of the pickup and his face sobered. "Where's Stu?"

"Crap, boost me Casper." Harold turned to the pickup, barely registering the battered state of the paintwork before Casper heaved. Harold tumbled into the pickup then cursed, very quietly. Stu lay curled up against the far side, clutching his gut, with blood leaking between his fingers.

His eyes opened. "Wanted the General." Then Stu screwed up his eyes in pain and moaned gently.

"Medic! Lenny!" Harold dropped the back of the pickup, looking over to the transit but Matti, standing at the rear, held up her hand.

"A minute, Harold. It's Dolly. She's hit bad." Harold looked down and winced because Phillip had a crossbow bolt in his chest. Someone had covered his face with a jacket. Nathan, one of the refugees from the General, gently nursed a hand swathed in blood-soaked cloth. Roy came round to the back and looked in the truck.

"How bad?"

Harold shook his head, because he didn't know but the wound looked to be in a really bad place, just above belt buckle height. "We could try the Army?"

"No, he wouldn't want that. We decided." Roy looked up at Harold. "If that's how it is, can he go with your people near the bypass?"

"Our people Roy, that's the deal."

"Let me see." Lenny stripped a pair of red-spattered gloves from his hands as he came over. "Pull me up please." Harold did and waited until Lenny finished a quick inspection. The medic looked back, shaking his head. He showed two hypodermics, one half full and one full. "It'll be a long or short wait and longer will be worse."

Roy looked at the little needles. "Are you sure?"

"Even with the Army medics. I doubt he'd even get to a hospital."

"Give me a sec." Roy boosted himself into the truck to kneel by Stu, speaking quietly for a few moments while Harold and Lenny turned away. Harold busied himself tucking the rifles and shotguns out of sight in case the RAF were nosy. "Doc? Lenny?"

"Yes?"

"Quick and easy please." Harold left. Lenny followed him out of the truck moments later.

"How many more and how bad are they?" Harold didn't like the look of those gloves Lenny had pulled off.

"Phillip is dead. Finn's arm has a bullet through it, the same one as his last wound. Doll has a bullet in her chest. Jeremy has either twisted or broken his ankle. Nathan's hand is bleeding but I haven't had chance to check properly. Louie has lost a piece of his ear. The rest are scrapes, cuts and bruises. Doll is lungshot, but maybe a real doctor can do something I can't." Lenny shook his head. "I'm a paramedic, Harold, and not even qualified. I can stop her lung collapsing for now but that's it." He spoke to Nathan, who rose and followed the medic to the transit.

Emmy came running up, her rifle only partly hidden, and went into the van. "Soldier Boy." Harold turned to find a very sombre looking Christie. "How good is your medic? We've got three who might not make it to doc."

"Bring them and we'll try." Christie moved aside to reveal three figures being carried on doors. Two were thrashing about but one lay very still. Lenny waved them towards the van.

Harold stopped Christie from joining them. "We need your doc, or a real doc of some sort." Harold looked towards the bypass, where soldiers were moving down towards the mart, shooting as they came.

"You know the rules." Christie paused. "Who is it?"

"Doll, the blonde usually wearing a Stetson. Hang on, let me talk to her sister." Harold raised his voice. "Matti?"

Matti came over, her face pale and drawn. "She won't go to the Army, Harold. Some of us decided, after what you said. Anything but that." Matti turned to Christie. "What about your doc?"

"She won't be able to come back, Doll that is." Christie put a hand up to rub her head and paused. She took her blonde wig off and scrubbed at her tight curls, looking at the transit and thinking hard. "How badly will Doll want to get home?" She grimaced. "She's a fighter so we'll not be able to stop her easily, will we?"

"Matti is her sister, and her grandad is back there." Harold shrugged. "She won't stay willingly, though to be honest she might not make it anyway."

"F... Damn, damn, damn." Christie looked at the van again then took a deep breath. "We'll put her in an empty storeroom. She stays there, with a bag on her head if the door opens. One attempt to look out the door and she stays at Beth's, right?" Christie looked at her wig. "This means I'm one of those in charge. The deal will stand even if I get shit about it. I'll call it fair exchange if your man gets even one of ours back to doc alive. Can they travel in there, in the van?"

"As long as you don't keep Lenny or the van or the rest of our wounded. I will be truly pissed off."

Christie shrugged. "Fair enough, but your people wear a blindfolds when we get near to Beth's, and your medic answers doc's questions before he leaves."

A big smile split Harold's face. "Deal. Matti, ask Lenny if he can work on the move."

Matti ran to the van and moments later the answer came back. "Five minutes, tops, then yes as quick as possible."

Christie nodded. "I'll send an escort car and another driver for the transit. She'll blindfold your bloke when they get nearer." She put her wig back on and her teeth flashed white in her dark face. "I'll pass the glad word about the deal so nobody gets out of hand. The escort vehicle will be full of our wounded anyway." Christie turned and began to jog back to the rest of the Barbies.

"Harold." Casper touched his shoulder. "The GOFS have two that are pretty bad. Can Lenny plug them up or something?"

"Bring them in with a top GOFS because there might be a little problem." Harold had a talk with Vulcan. The GOFS warchief left to talk to the Barbies, to try and arrange for his wounded to stay in the van until it arrived back to Orchard Close. Vulcan didn't think the blindfold healing option would be on offer. The transit van would be crowded since Doll, Finn, Nathan, Jeremy and Matti, with Matthew as the driver, would be going with Lenny, two GOFS and the three Barbies. Louie reckoned he didn't need an ambulance for his ear.

* * *

The radio call interrupted the arrangements. "Soldier Boy? If you've finished the orgy with those fucking lunatics, we need a quick word." Caddi didn't seem happy to have survived. "And bring my fucking rifle."

"In a bit, Caddi. Calm down, or you'll need a trip to the Barbie doctor for your blood pressure." Harold wasn't taking the usual crap, not over the open radio channel. The Barbies were certainly listening because Ken waved. She climbed into a car heading his way, slowing for Vulcan to catch a lift by standing on the bumper.

Vulcan gave a thumbs up as he jumped off the car. "My pair will be allowed to stay in the van if they wear blindfolds. Right now Gofannon will be going to see what's twisting Caddi's knickers so I'd best turn up as well. Bring your bodyguards, Soldier Boy." Vulcan clapped him on the back. "Celebrate, the mart is still standing and so are we, or most of us."

Ken claimed a lift in Harold's truck with her one bodyguard. She'd come in the car carrying Barbie wounded so it could set straight off for Beth's. Vulcan also claimed a lift in the armoured truck, allegedly so Ken didn't get all the bragging rights over riding a tank. Harold remembered Caddi's greedy eyes, so he left the trailer hooked up. Emmy came out of the transit van, taking her rifle into the trailer, so with those in the truck bed he had ten bodyguards even if they weren't visible. Though after the transit left Harold would have to cram in twenty-five people and two bodies to get everyone home. Vulcan offered to organise a lift home for any of Harold's people who needed one after they'd looted the nearby bodies.

Gofannon waved them over as Harold pulled up, while behind him Caddi scowled as Ken hopped out of the back. "Do you have anyone badly injured, badly enough to go to the Army? There's a car going to ask, with a couple of Ferdinands, a Hot Rod, and two Murphies who need help fast."

"No thanks, ours are dead or will make it." Harold crossed his fingers.

"Ours as well, thanks." Ken smiled at Caddi, but not sweetly. "What else needs sorting out?" She looked over towards the soldiers and helicopters, still hunting down scattered figures or herding a few towards captivity. "I'd rather get far, far away before they start getting more ambitious."

"Loot?" Bull waved a hand at the spread of bodies. "Weapons, ammo, shoes, boots, clothing, maybe even coupons. There's a fortune there."

"Whoever bled to kill them, strips them." Ken looked towards the mart. "We're not going too far out there until we see what the Army think is their new exclusion zone."

"But all the best bloody firearms are further in near the mart, the rifles for starters. There'll only be pistols and maybe shotguns closer in." Caddi scowled. "Fuck it, I want my ammo back at least."

Harold grinned at him. "I'll trade some of whatever loot I get for propellant. Powder?"

"Can't you..?" Bull shut up as Caddi shook his head. "All right, maybe. Depends what we get here." Everything including underwear looking at how the nearby Ferdinands were stripping corpses.

"What the fuck!" The half dozen shots and the clanging of lead on steel brought everyone's heads round.

"Hold fire!" Harold shouted because four rifle barrels showed from the bus loopholes, another rifle along with two shotguns poked out of the truck, and Patty popped up with a scowl and her crossbow aimed. He looked where they were aiming, at a group of Ferdinands. Harold turned to Bull. "I want whoever that was."

"How do you know it's one of mine?" The defence had to be automatic, since Bull looked as shocked as anyone. The Ferdinand looked at all the rifles. "I didn't organise that because I'm not fucking suicidal." He turned to his men. "Lower those guns you fucking idiots. It's armoured." Half a dozen Ferdinands who had raised their weapons lowered them.

Harold thumbed the radio. "Emmy? Anybody hurt?"

"No Harold. One round came through a loophole but we're fine. Just tell the Ferdinands that we know who we want, and we'd just as soon shoot through the front row." Everyone with radios heard her, and a ripple of movement left one man standing on his own with a pistol in his hand. "Do we just shoot him now, Harold?" Three men behind the target scattered to the sides, quickly, while he looked around desperately.

"I'd rather ask the twat why he did that." Bull looked bloody furious.

"Yeah, that could be interesting." Caddi raised his voice. "Disarm that little shit so we can have a chat."

The man paled even further, looked at the Ferdinands moving towards him and shouted "No!" He put the gun barrel in his mouth and pulled the trigger.

"Fuck. Messy." Franco, the Trainspotter with the dreadlocks spat. "He didn't want to talk to you Caddi." The small group beat the subject to death for a few minutes, but concluded the bloke just didn't want to suffer whatever Bull had in mind, or Caddi, or possibly Emmy. The last part came from Wellington, raising a laugh from all those who knew about her.

As Harold headed towards the trailer to collect Caddi's rifle, Wellington intercepted him. "If a woman arrived with permission to run, what would you do?"

"Be suspicious. How would I know she'd got permission?" Harold frowned. "I'd have to think it was a setup from your lot." He felt a hand push something into his pocket, hidden from the rest by Wellington's body.

"Proof. She'll bring the same." The Geek warchief raised his voice. "We'll trade repairs on your crossbows or new crossbows for repaired firearms or decent machetes."

"I'll be in touch." Harold delivered the rifle and empty clips to Caddi, ignoring the abuse for not saving all the brass. On the way back to his truck Harold put a hand in his pocket. Wellington had passed him an envelope. Harold left it for later.

"Hang on, I'll get a lift back. It'll give me a chance to sweet-talk Patty."

Ken paused before climbing into the back to inspect the side of the pickup. "Do you need more paint to touch that up? We've got plenty at Beth's." Harold looked at the vehicles properly and they'd both need paint, because hundreds of rounds had hit though most either splattered or scraped off strips. A bit of paint seemed a good price to pay, because every other gang he could see had more dead and wounded than Orchard Close.

* * *

Everyone considered one warning shot to be downright tolerant of the Army. The Army rifles aiming towards the man who'd gone too near were explanation enough. The scavengers or looters took note, staying a very generous three hundred and fifty yards from any mart or Army personnel while they stripped their own section of corpses. When Harold arrived back, the bus and truck passengers joined the rest to scavenge. They couldn't collect all the crossbow bolts because Patty started shooting at nearly three hundred yards, lofting her shafts into the crowd. Casper reckoned he'd nearly wet himself when her crossbow first twanged just above his head.

Harold's people collected what firearms and ammunition they could see, checking pockets, as well as picking up all the decent machetes, knives, hatchets, empty brass, crossbows and bolts. Few of those from Orchard Close had the stomach for stripping clothes from bodies beyond taking warm coats and good footwear. Less than an hour later Harold's people just wanted to go home, so Harold told the GOFS and Barbies they could have anything else.

Everyone seemed subdued on the trip back, possibly due to the news from the mart as well as their personal reactions to the fight. The car with white flags had been allowed to approach. The Army took the wounded including another eight with the usual proviso, they wouldn't be back. The second part of the meeting worried everyone more.

A representative from TesdaMart had thanked them all for their help and promised to ask the government to keep the mart open. Unfortunately, that would be down to the Army and the government because the building had been damaged and both guards and soldiers killed. Nobody trusted the government's benevolence.

* * *

Once he had parked up, Harold walked home to wash. He drew pictures and read with Daisy, then when she went upstairs to play with her horses Sharyn wanted to know what happened. Harold didn't know, except what Emmy told him. He spent most of the time explaining that all he could see of the fight had been framed by the loophole, up to the very end. The armour had worked really well, but that did cut down on any appreciation of the wider picture. Harold assumed Casper and the others behind the steel plate in the centre had a better idea. He told Sharyn to ask Emmy for the real story.

The mood in Orchard Close lifted a little at dusk when the transit van arrived back with a worried but hopeful Matti. Doll had survived the trip, as had two of the Barbies and one GOFS. Surprisingly Cy, the badly injured GOFS, had been accepted for treatment on the same no-peeking proviso as Doll. According to Malibu, the boss Barbie, two lives for the two seriously injured Barbies who made it to Beth's alive counted as a fair trade. Two lives if the GOFS survived since he hadn't roused yet and had a bad gut wound. If Cy made it home he'd be a legend, doubly so since his 'date' with Patty.

After reading Wills-story and Daisy-story, Harold still couldn't settle. He called into the hospital again to check on the wounded. Finn would keep his arm but with a second wound he'd never get full use back. Finn seemed remarkably cheerful about that, pointing out he could still 003½ with one hand, or maybe only 002 if it slowed reloading. Nathan might never grip properly with his right hand because a machete had hacked into the back, but reckoned that wasn't a problem. Learning to use his left hand would keep him too busy to mope, and might get him some girl club sympathy. Harold thought the medication might be helping Nathan and Finn to cope. Louie claimed that losing half an ear counted as a win if a bullet or crossbow bolt came that close, but still might get him some hero credit at the next dance.

Jeremy had gone home, allegedly for a beating because his sprained ankle had worried Matti so she needed the stress relief. Lenny seemed down about losing two casualties, four with the Barbie and GOFS in the van, but he eventually admitted he couldn't have saved either even with a fully equipped ambulance. At least there had been few hand combat or minor wounds this time. The numerous grazes or cuts from either spattered lead or people banging against armour only needed cleaning and an antiseptic pad on them overnight.

Harold walked the walls, speaking to the guards, but still felt restless. On the way he studiously ignored Hazel and Alfie going into the guardhouse with their arms around each other. He went to load brass because they'd used an awful lot. The loose brass in the trailer had been scooped up with a shovel when they got back. At least the loot included a good few replacement pistol rounds, though not as many as Orchard Close had expended. The looted ammunition, probably underpowered, could be taken apart later and he'd make them back up properly.

Harold would reload his own brass first, because the captured empties would probably need annealing and resizing which would cost some of the precious propane. That at least made Harold smile a little. He was seeing more weapons for repair with rounds either split, jammed or exploded inside the chamber. Nobody else knew the brass deteriorated, or about his special rounds, or so Harold thought. Liz would be using up some charcoal to harden steel rods, because all the special rounds were gone. They'd been used first to ensure penetration and maximum damage to anyone they hit at long range.

Sharyn had promised to ring Harold if the news mentioned the mart, but the phone stayed silent while he worked. After making up some rounds, Harold started cleaning Orchard Close firearms. Eventually he yawned, realised he'd worked well past midnight, and decided to sleep at the gun room house.

Harold went through to the little bedroom set up for him and put on his electric blanket, then headed for the shower. His mind still ran over the day, wondering if he should have parked at a more acute angle. Harold stood under the water jet debating if a better angle might have saved Doll and Stu when the light went out! He cursed, wondering if there'd been another power cut, then jumped when two hands ran up his back and down his arms.

"Shhh, the shower fairy is here, or maybe elf. The fairy is sleeping with his dog."

"Patty?"

"No fair. I'm supposed to be the one with Batty vision." Patty sounded a little breathless, her hands slipping round to soap Harold's chest. His back suddenly had a personal Patty-sponge, very personal because she had undressed first.

She'd completely thrown Harold since Patty hadn't seemed that bothered about men yet, certainly not ready for shared showers. Though she'd mentioned moonlight and Harold had wondered briefly, that night he'd walked her home? "Fancy a toy-boy after all?"

"Mmm, sort of." Patty giggled. "I want to celebrate being alive, but not a party sort of celebration." Her hands kept soaping, or maybe just wet stroking. She sighed, hugging tightly for a moment. "I'm also a bit sad. Stu and Phillip and Doll, and then all those poor sods who only wanted someplace to live." Patty giggled again, very un-Patty-like. "Something, maybe the sheer shock of surviving, made me feel lonely. I fancied some loving, the really personal sort of loving and remembered being told several times that you keep secrets. Then I thought I'd find out if you'd done your usual after some strife, stayed over here. You seem to be feeling lonely as well now. Perhaps you should turn round?"

Since by then Harold had reached behind to soap some of Patty, he could hardly deny that. Some breathless mutual soaping later Harold chuckled as Patty turned the water off. "Do Batty eyes need a light or do I have to get dried in the dark?"

"Not quite. No lights, but it's not you you're drying and I'm not drying me. Is that bed warm?"

"The electric blanket is on."

Patty sighed. "Thank all and any Gods. I worried that you might be all hardy soldier and spurn such comforts. Though as long as the chill is off the sheets, I reckon we can warm up properly now."

*　*　*

Harold's surprise shower certainly stopped him worrying about how he'd parked the truck, and banished his usual paranoia about what else he might have done differently. In the morning Patty reckoned she'd sorted her loneliness for a while, then she smiled and threatened Harold with a hunting Patty-Bat in the night if he opened his big mouth. A still bemused Harold promised not to howl at her window during full moons.

The drizzle throughout morning seemed right somehow, because nobody felt triumphant despite winning. During the day everyone made an attempt at chores, but the sight of two pyres being raised meant nobody could really concentrate. An hour before dusk Harold came down from the bypass where the sergeant had reluctantly agreed that two women could spread the ashes. Sarge had only agreed because of the line of little markers already in the exclusion zone, or possibly because of Harold's comment about the dead preferring scroats bleeding on them to pissing on their graves. That comment seemed to work quite well.

Harold looked up at the light rain with dark, low cloud scudding across the sky, then back down to address the mourners. "Phillip and Stu came here, to our walls, asking for sanctuary. We welcomed them. Yesterday they left the safety of these walls to put themselves in harm's way. Not to defend Orchard Close itself but to prevent others from stopping the food that our children will need this winter. They didn't ask for anything in return, but at some time this winter please remember what they paid to ensure your warm bowl of soup or your fresh bap."

Pat's John and John's Pat, to differentiate them from other Pats and Johns, came forward to speak about their son Phillip. About how proud they'd been when he spurned the gangs, when he chose to stay home to do the decent thing to protect his parents and friends. With a small group from their church they prayed briefly for his soul, then for Stu and for Doll's recovery. Others from their group of refugees or from the rest of Orchard Close spoke a few words about Phillip. His No Place Like Gnome hat went on the pyre with a tear from Tilly.

Roy spoke up for Stu, about his life before the General smashed their world, and about Stu's determination to dance on the General's grave. About how nine friends became seven, then five and now four but the four still hoped to watch the bastard's army die under these walls. He thanked everyone for welcoming them, before bidding his friend goodbye, as did the other three in his little group. Then they stood stunned as others came forward to speak up, among them a couple of gnomes Stu had helped with the gardening, some of the refugees from the General, and several of the extended girl club.

Harold bid Stu, and then Phillip, fare thee well, turning to face the mourners as the flames took hold. Nearly a hundred and fifty had gathered out here on the gardens or along the wall above them, a proper send-off. "Atoms reborn into grass." Harold didn't know if the girl club or the Coven had arranged everything, but everyone who'd been to defend the mart joined in the next line.

"Fire and passion stilled at last." Then more and more joined in each line until just as once before, even the children's voices finished the farewell.

"Clouds, of happy what might be's
Scattered showers of grief and tears
Fading memories, not quite true,
One day, my friend, this will be you."

Harold stayed out all night with the pyres, as did Roy, his three friends, and all of those who'd gone to the fight except Doll, Nathan and Finn. This time Orchard Close had no damage to repair, no visible evidence of the fight, so they stood vigil. Phillip's parents were joined by their church group and others who knew the dead men until over sixty people watched the stacks finally collapse. Finn and Nathan came to stand for a while until Lenny and Patricia insisted they went back in, though Louie and Jeremy stayed. Through the night others brought hot drinks for the watchers or stood with them for a while.

Soon after dawn, willing hands offered help with pulling out the charred timbers. Stu's four comrades and Phillip's parents collected the ashes, then carried them to the boundary. Phillip's mum spread his ashes on the no-go zone, while Patty stepped up to claim the honours for Stu because the Army insisted on a woman.

The rest of the day passed quietly again because of the funerals, the weather, and most probably because nobody knew if the gamble had kept the mart open. Harold apologised for him and Casper missing Daisy-story while watching the pyre. He helped Daisy to draw a love place picture for Stu and for Phillip with his gnome hat. They finished by drawing one with lots of fairies and unicorns watching over Doll in a hospital bed.

Harold spent most of the rest of the day reloading what ammunition he had propellant for, because Orchard Close had nearly used up the lot. He cleaned more Orchard Close weapons, and stripped a few of the captured ones so they could soak. As usual, he found the work calming and in this instance the guards on the wall really did need the ammunition. He had time to assess what they'd gained, and he now had enough pistols to give every shooter two each and had doubled the shotguns up to fourteen. The looted ammunition would need reloading because it would be underpowered, but it would do in an emergency.

Harold had promised a free clean for Caddi's rifle at some time. He didn't mind because Orchard Close gained thirty extra empties for the 303, and eleven extra unused rounds. He'd given Caddi nearly forty empties back, claiming the rest were in the rubble. As he worked, Harold wondered how he could prise more propellant out of the surrounding gangs, because they always seemed to have plenty. Eventually Harold went home to eat.

*　　*　　*

"You can stay home this evening." Sharyn's hands went onto her hips and Harold smiled just a little. "After Casper has finished Daisy-story you can park yourself on the settee and watch the news. I am not gnawing my knuckles all on my own again tonight."

"After I walk the walls, sis, I'll come home like a good boy." Harold threw on a warm jacket because winter had definitely arrived. The mid-November chill made sure he didn't waste any time tonight and the guards would be pleased of the warm guardhouses. The guards didn't actually stand on the walls, just wrapped up to walk them at irregular intervals or watched from firing slits.

"Back already?"

"Make your mind up where you want me. I thought we could have a cup of coffee first because it's freezing out there." Harold headed into the kitchen. "Stay there, I'll spoil you."

"Make three cups since Casper doesn't fancy gnawing his knuckles alone either." Sharyn chuckled. "I asked him and no, he didn't see much either." Her voice sobered. "Emmy doesn't want to talk."

"There were a lot of women and kids in that mob, and a lot of guns just firing into the crowd. Cripes Sharyn, the coffee is low."

"We all donated some last night for the pyre-watchers. I hope you've got spare coupons for more?" Sharyn sighed. "I have to sacrifice mine for drinking chocolate." Then she laughed because although most went into Daisy's breakfast cereal milk, Sharyn managed a drink once a week.

A bang on the door heralded Emmy with Sooty, and Tammy in a carrycot. "I sat and watched on my own last night." That didn't need any more explanation. Harold went to make another coffee. By the time he'd done that, Casper had come downstairs and Sharyn had turned on the TV for the news. At least they didn't have to wait long, as they all realised when the talking head spoke.

"The animals and scum cannot understand simple facts. If they attack one mart in a city all the marts will close. Even if they succeed in capturing the mart, the RAF will ensure the attackers do not gain from their murderous and criminal actions." A picture of the horde came on the screen as they began to stream out of the housing. "Despite this, over a thousand of the maniacs have attacked the very people who feed them, too many for the normal defences to stop. The mart guards are valiantly defending the store, desperate to save the food that keeps the innocent citizens alive."

"Desperate to keep themselves alive. That is our mart isn't it Harold?" Sharyn frowned. "I've not been for ages. It looks different."

"The paint has faded, and that wide strip is where the houses were knocked down after the naughty girls visited." Harold smiled at Emmy. "Caddi hated that, but yesterday the open space came in dead handy." He eyed the screen. "The Baggies underestimated by a good bit, but a thousand seems high."

Sharyn frowned. "Where are you?" Onscreen the horde still pouring out of the derelict buildings had begun shooting at the mart.

"Wait." Casper pointed then sounded a bit uncertain. "Cripes Harold that could be a thousand, it's a hell of a lot."

Onscreen a flickering line of light reached out from the Army post to tear into one flank of the mob. Some turned, shooting back while the main body closed on the fence around the mart. The guards in the towers nearest the gates and some of those on the roof died. As the first attackers closed in on the mesh fence the picture shifted, showing groups of people coming out of the derelict housing along the edge of the rubble.

Casper laughed. "That's our street cred gone." The TV showed a clear view of the armoured vehicles, zooming in on the painting without any commentary. The view went back to the mob now pulling at the fence or climbing it. Pipe bombs started exploding in the mart yard, but the view kept returning to the Orchard Close vehicles. In between were shots of other gangs moving out of cover to take up their positions.

"Others are now arriving but the authorities were not sure if they were more attackers, or had come to scavenge after the mart had been looted. The appearance of an armoured vehicle alarmed the Army, because the helicopters had not yet arrived."

"More crap because Caddi sent a messenger to tell them."

Sharyn waved a hand to shut Harold up. "Never mind that Harold. How did they get these pictures if there were no helicopters at the start?"

The three others stared at Sharyn for a moment until Harold bit back a real Army curse. "Drones. The bastards have got at least one drone up." He looked at the screen. "More than one. Here we go."

The picture showed puffs of smoke jetting from the armoured vehicles. Men began to fall on the side of the mob away from the mart, while a few others scattered or dived for cover. Meanwhile a section of mesh fence went down. The leaders surged through, many of them falling as the mart's armoured car went from bursts to continuous fire. The camera view pulled back showing occasional shots from elsewhere around the arc of gangsters, though Harold's group, the Barbies and the GOFS contributed almost all the rifle fire.

"These local law-abiding citizens have rushed to help and are attempting to protect the mart. Despite being heavily outnumbered, the brave local citizens have opened fire. Between them and the Army, they are giving the mart guards time to bring up reinforcements and heavier weapons."

"They don't need that. We warned them." Casper put up a hand to Sharyn in apology. He mimed zipping his mouth shut.

More of the attackers turned towards the Orchard Close vehicles, pointing or shooting, until a large section started forward. As the mob bulged outwards a shudder ran through the whole mass, while all around the perimeter spurts of smoke showed that more rifles had joined in. Even then they looked totally ineffectual against the sheer numbers attacking the mart.

Onscreen the attackers running towards the Army post or still trying to tear a bigger hole in the fencing paused. Meanwhile the gangsters' rifles kept firing until finally more of the mob turned to face them. In those few moments as the crowd eddied, uncertain, the attack stalled. The drone cameras panned around the arc of rifles, lingering on the armour and lettering again.

"More of the local citizens have arrived, throwing themselves into the fray to help the mart guards and the Army. Maybe they will be enough, because the criminals and revolutionaries have been caught by surprise. The Royal Air Force and Army are already on the way if the situation can be contained long enough."

"They're winding it up for the rest of the viewers." Casper curled a lip in disgust. "We're a bloody game show."

Sharyn tittered. "Yeah but guess who's getting all the phone votes? Orchard Close!" She punched a hand up in the air.

The section of the mob bulging towards the Orchard Close vehicles surged out across the rubble. Firearms along the front ranks jetted smoke towards the tiny truck and bus, overwhelming in comparison to the number firing back. Another section of the mob tried to break northwest, away from the battle bus towards the city and The Mansion. Even more turned and ran, retreating the way they had arrived. Those recoiled as the previously empty derelict buildings spat fire and smoke.

"The valiant citizens have relieved the pressure on the mart, but the animals are still trying to kill the brave guards and soldiers. At least the forces of law and order now have a fighting chance. The RAF will be here soon, if the guards and Army can survive just a little longer. These brave citizens are buying that time with their lives."

The camera zoomed to show local gangsters, aka brave citizens, falling as the mob fired at them. The sheer volume of fire meant some of the pistol rounds found targets, as Harold knew by the noise of them hitting the armour. Casper sniggered. "Cripes, there'll be a memorial to Caddi at this rate."

"As long as that creep Einstein isn't killed and they put up a statue." Sharyn mimed putting her fingers down her throat. "I might be tempted into graffiti at least."

"I might have been tempted to shoot him if I'd seen Einstein." From Emmy's tone of voice it would have been a stone certainty.

"Only Wellington and Hawkins were there, and both survived. Ah, remind me about Wellington later." Harold shook his head at the look, pointing at the screen. "Watch now, that later. Cripes, comparing the mob to our lot, the gangs, there might have been over a thousand."

The cameras zoomed in here and there as all the forces clashed, showing pipe bombs exploding as those retreating closed on the buildings now held by the Baggies and Trainspotters. The mob had few bombs left to throw in return but sheer numbers took the retreating mass into contact. Machetes flashed in the early afternoon sun.

"These brave men are preventing the criminals and murderers from escaping justice. The Army are almost here and will apprehend any that are still trapped."

Onscreen the Murphies ran forward, shooting and then hacking into the side of those trying to force a way through the housing. Paddy really had launched his flank attack. The scene cut to a pair of Army lorries loaded with squaddies speeding along the bypass. The next shot of the mart showed the mob in the yard, either shooting up at the guards or trying to break in the mart doors. The burning armoured car retreated, breaking out through the fence onto the exclusion zone,.

"The armoured car has withdrawn to prevent the scum capturing or destroying it, but continues to fight valiantly. Assistance and heavier weaponry has reached the mart guards at last."

Men ran across the mart roof to join the guards still firing into the mass. Explosions tore into the crowd in the yard. The reinforced guards on the roof threw more small objects and again explosions rippled across the space. Some of the reinforcements had automatics, but not Army rifles, the shorter versions previously issued to the police.

Harold glanced at Emmy. "You said grenades and machine guns. Why the hell didn't they use them before?"

"The script, Harold." Sharyn sneered. "Wouldn't want to defeat them too easily, that's not good TV. Worse still, whoever delayed them knew mart guards and squaddies would die."

The crowd in the mart yard retreated, targeted by the guards on the mart roof and more grenades. The crew of the armoured car extinguished the flames on their vehicle, but their weapon wouldn't be needed now. On the bypass the two lorries spilled squaddies who quickly formed up and moved down the access roads, firing as they came. A short clip showed a part of the mob hitting the Ferdinands, with Caddi and the Geeks firing into the side of the mass before moving in with machetes.

"Here the mob are killing the brave citizens as they try to escape, but others are throwing themselves into the fray, plugging the gap to save their friends and allies."

All four of them laughed briefly at Caddi or the Geeks being anyone's friend. The TV screen returned to the Orchard Close vehicles as their section of mob came nearer, with a close-up of Patty launching a crossbow bolt before frantically rewinding. The editor timed the commentary to perfection.

"Despite their brave attempt and the support of their neighbours, there are too many attackers for these brave men and women to stop. Let us hope their sacrifice will not be in vain, that they have saved the mart so their children will not starve this winter."

Moments later Harold knew the exact distance to the attackers - fifty yards.

The sheer volume of smoke from the two vehicles and the protected gap between as everyone opened up with handguns surprised him. An uncharitable part of his mind wondered if there'd been a bit of CGI added to enhance the effect. The shudder that went through the attackers, and the way they fell or flinched away to split around the vehicles, didn't need CGI. Nor did the flank attacks by the GOFS and Barbies, launched as the mob hesitated.

"This is the difference between mindless animals and scum, bent on death and destruction, and the brave citizens. They have drawn the killers into a trap and are now driving them back towards the Army and justice."

Harold broke out laughing along with the rest. "Oh crap, that is priceless." He took a breath. "The GOFS and Barbies are chasing them to kill as many as possible so they can loot the bodies later."

Though the next part, the killing of any wounded, wasn't shown on the cameras. Those now concentrated on the RAF swooping in to destroy any attempt by the remnants of the mob to rally. The Army moved across the front of the mart and, aided by the mart guards, shot anyone showing any sign of resistance. Here and there small groups of women and children were herded up onto the bypass where they sat in long lines with their hands on their heads, but no men were captured. The cameras zoomed in among the housing where Baggie and Trainspotter dead mixed with the corpses, then switched to views of dead attackers mixed with what Harold knew were dead Murphies, Ferdinands, Hot Rods, Geeks and GOFS. Several views showed dead Barbies, all clearly female but without blonde wigs.

"No large views now Harold. They wouldn't want to show the brave citizens nicking underwear from a corpse." Emmy's bitter tones matched the mood of the others. The bastards had left their own people to die to make a better show for TV.

"Nor are they showing any clear gang logos or someone had been busy erasing them." Sharyn shook her head. "Now we know just why the news is always late. To the rest of the city a heroic sacrifice by ordinary citizens just saved the mart in the nick of time. No nasty gangsters involved."

"Those dead gangsters did save the mart even if the script has been tweaked." Harold scowled. "Unfortunately the cameras also showed the General our armoured column."

Onscreen the car approached the mart with white flags flying and an Army officer met the deputation. The wounded gangsters were being carried to the bypass where real ambulances turned up to take them away. More wounded were taken up there as more ambulances arrived. Close-ups showed more dead locals, then zoomed down on the battle bus and truck. Phillip stared up with sightless eyes before someone covered him, and Stu curled up in the back of the truck as Lenny leaned over him before shaking his head. Bess helped Finn across to the van while he cradled his arm, and Nathan huddled over his hand. Emmy ran over, anguish clear on her face, while Jeremy limped to the transit, held up by Casper. The drone camera zoomed on Doll being carried from the bus to the van with red splashed over her front and kept zooming until her face, screwed up in pain, filled the screen.

"That's out of synch, wrong way round."

"Script Harold, shush."

A man in a suit came from the mart, talking to those in the gangster cars with white flags. The scene switched to a side view of the truck and bus showing the bullet scars that had pitted and scored the paintwork.

"TesdaMart have recognised the sacrifice of these brave citizens and asked the government to let the marts stay open. Despite the deaths of soldiers and mart guards, and the damage to the mart, how could your government refuse? Thanks to these brave people, bloody but unbowed, battered but not broken, the marts will all stay open."

The view went back to Doll for long moments, though at least not the close-up of her face. The scene and commentary cut away to shoplifters being arrested elsewhere. The four of them stared at each other, until Sharyn smiled. "I should be very, very angry with the nasty, cold, calculating bastards, but I'm too happy. The mart stays open Harold."

"Listen." Casper held up his hand. Outside someone, then several some-ones, cheered. "A lot of people are happy." Harold turned off the TV and the cheers and laughter were louder, with some voices calling for a party.

Emmy looked at the carrycot, and an oblivious Tammy. "I'll never feel right about shooting at women, but now I know it was worth it."

Harold stood up. "Ask Betty to babysit, then come to the party and celebrate living. I'll bet the Hot Rods and all the other gangs are having a party as well."

Harold got it right, as the GOFS arriving at lunchtime the following day to collect Roy and his men confirmed. The drivers were all wearing dark glasses and wincing at loud noises. In contrast the Orchard Close party didn't involve as much alcohol, but Roy's group were a bit bleary-eyed from lack of sleep for two nights. Despite their own lack of sleep, a crowd of residents turned out to smile, wave and call out good wishes as the reduced group went back on duty.

* * *

Not everyone felt as happy about the whole affair. "I thought you were supposed to be keeping an eye on things. Sort of spymaster? Remind me why I bother to feed you Rhys?" The General looked decidedly unhappy while the older man, Rhys, looked wary. "I could have rolled over the lot while they were busy at the mart." The General turned to look at the other uniformed man. "I thought you were supposed to be in contact with this Cadillac?"

Patton, the other uniformed man, shrugged. "I suppose his priorities tended more towards surviving?" He frowned thoughtfully. "I doubt we could have organised everyone fast enough, certainly not the Bloods. It's a pity the Pinkies don't want to join up because they were near enough to the Barbies to have launched an attack."

"Not yet, they're too frightened of the bitches." The General smiled, very unpleasantly. "Once they are more frightened of me we'll use the pansies as shock troops alongside the Bloods. Well Rhys, what's your excuse?"

"Short notice. None of them knew until the day, and they were all back by evening. The GOFS and Geeks left men to watch the frontiers anyway so a quick strike would have bounced." Rhys smiled. "I have found out when they will be relaxed?"

"About time you earned your keep. When?" His smile belied the General's words.

"Christmas. Orchard Close like parties, and it's rubbed off on the rest. They all shut down over Christmas."

The General scowled. "The Bloods and most of the other idiots do the same. They'll not agree to missing their Christmas stockings, or what's in them." He curled his lip in a sneer. "Well actually they ignore the stocking and just go for the women and the booze."

"But they'll be sober again soon after, and done with the women. Orchard Close, that armour and the shooters will be partying from Christmas to New Year, and the other gangs shut down for the same period. Half of them will be pissed or nursing hangovers for the whole week." Rhys held out both hands, palms up. "Your Christmas present."

"Can you do that, Patton? Get the Bloods sober and ready to fight by Boxing Day?"

The uniformed subordinate thought about it for a few moments. "Maybe, but it will probably take another day or two. Have the civvies done building the kit for the attack?"

"Yes, we can move everything forward once I give a date. A lot depends on the weather. If we don't have any rain, the water in that railway cutting will be barely moving." The General smacked a fist into the other palm. "Once we're across I'll be having a word with that Soldier bastard about stealing my vehicle and equipment."

"Though he did give it a nice paint job." Patton smiled. "What about Caddi? Do you want him in?"

"I'll think about it. After all, he seemed very pally with the other gangs on the TV, didn't he?" The General frowned. "If the reinforcements on the GOFS front go home at Christmas we don't need the greedy bastard. Get out there, ear to the ground, and get me some real information Rhys. Then we can have a very special New Year party."

*   *   *

As the mart attack played out on the screen in the bunker the atmosphere definitely didn't promise a party. "The mart wasn't destroyed. It didn't come close." Maurice sounded decidedly defensive.

"There were deaths and the result looked very close. Those are burn marks on the outside walls and part of the wire has been torn down. That armoured car caught fire. It came very close to destruction." The woman responsible for food supplies, Ivy, pointed at the screen now showing the aftermath as the bodies were cleared. "TesdaMart are not impressed. They pay well for these concessions on the understanding we won't allow any to be overrun without warning. The senior manager visiting the facility didn't appreciate the excitement."

"Over half the Army personnel in the guard post were killed." Joshua, the Army man, looked and sounded downright belligerent. "A few more lucky or accurate bullets and that mob would have captured a machine gun."

"The helicopters were very close, waiting for orders, and the grenades could have been handed to the mart guards sooner if required. I heard about what this group planned and tried for several birds with one stone." Maurice shrugged. "I remembered something Grace said in here, about putting several gangs together."

Owen, the chairman, frowned. "You set that mob onto a mart just to get a few scum to kill each other? That seems past risky, Maurice."

"No, no, I wouldn't do that. The animals came up with this plan. Then there were several ways to deal with them. The RAF could have destroyed the lot on the march, but they weren't actually doing anything wrong then and the RAF aren't keen on burning women and children." Maurice glanced at the man in RAF uniform. "There have been incidents of constructively misunderstood orders to avoid just that."

"True." The RAF man lapsed back into silence.

Maurice spread his hands. "This way we've emptied the far south of the city and wiped out everyone who lived there. The other possibility failed." Maurice clicked a control and the screen played out the Ferdinand shooting at the bus, then killing himself to avoid questioning. "That man should have sparked a bloodbath. The idiot fired at armour plate instead of some gang boss and those inside didn't feel threatened enough to retaliate. I can only assume he thought the occupants had really itchy trigger fingers."

"That man is yours?" Owen looked at the body on the screen. "Was?"

"Unfortunately yes. Now I have to get someone else into the gang, though we did get a propaganda bonus. The editing team nearly wet themselves over those armoured vehicles and the blonde woman. We'll be showing these highlights nationally." He chuckled. "But not these." The screen showed several Barbie girls blowing kisses or pulling down their jeans to waggle their knickers at the soldiers, who were cheering and waving.

"We want that blonde woman if she survives." Vanna grinned. "If she comes to a mart, arrest her for anything at all. Either Grace or my people will motivate her and she'll be a terrific mouthpiece for the loyal citizens."

"I'll let the Army know." Joshua made a note. "She might turn up for medical attention because that looked bad."

"Tell them we want her for hospital treatment, or to give her a medal or some such rubbish." Vanna waved towards the soldiers onscreen. "After all, the Army will love her."

Owen grinned and looked around the rest. "We could actually give her a medal?"

"Oh yes, better still. What about the other cities? Is there any danger of an unplanned attack on marts there?" Vanna frowned. "That would be an unpleasant surprise."

"Doubtful after they all see this film. Though this will make closing other marts simpler when we do organise another attack. In the future it'll even be their own fault when the locals fail to protect the guards and Army. Though it is a pity that particular city is too big or we could have sealed the place anyway." Maurice smirked. "The footage of the local scum that wasn't broadcast is amusing and they were definitely thinned out as a bonus."

"No we couldn't have shut that mart, because that really was a senior manager and TesdaMart were very insistent. They want to encourage the locals to protect the marts." Ivy scowled. "We can't afford to really upset them, not at that level."

"Personally I think leaving it open is a better lesson for all the enclosures.

As long as that armoured thing won't threaten the Army?" Grace frowned. "What if it attacks a mart?"

Joshua waved away her concerns. "Jacketed bullets from an Army rifle or an armoured car should turn it into a colander but if they don't a cannon shell will. I'm not worried about that, and I'm really pleased by the number of rifles we captured. I am worried about the amount of ammunition the scum seem to have. Most of the ammunition we collected from the bodies had been reloaded by amateurs, but I would have expected any propellant to be already used up."

Vanna glanced at Owen, who looked at Maurice. The spymaster smiled and pointed. "You saw the amount of smoke, Joshua. It is obvious that someone is making propellant but not to the same standards. All the materials must be available in a city, so it only takes one bright spark." He shrugged at Joshua's unhappy expression. "I'll do my best to find out who it is."

Ivy, the woman responsible for supplying the marts, had been waiting for her chance. "Good. Now can we get onto another concern that seems to be sourced in your department, Maurice? Are you the genius behind the rabbit thing? Not a stroke of genius because many rabbits who survive Myxomatosis will be inedible." Ivy scowled at the spymaster across the table. "That means the scum will want more protein from the marts, just when we won't have any extra from the rabbits caught on farms."

"I didn't authorise the operation. As far as I understand Vanna now has the research team responsible in her care?" Maurice raised an eyebrow at Vanna, who smiled.

"Apparently the team were given the job by Nate before he had his misadventure." Her thin smile showed quite a bit of malice. "They've had their own misadventure."

Maurice chuckled. "Just so. Will you be able to control the Myxomatosis, Henry?"

"Not now. If the idiots had bothered to ask anyone in the farming community we'd have told them not to bother." Henry sighed in resignation. "The disease would have re-appeared anyway if the population rose too high. Right now most of the rabbits will still be resistant from the last outbreak so a good few will catch it but survive. Unfortunately they'll be scarred and nobody will want to eat them."

"The infection is taking hold already and we're too late to stop it?" Ivy glared at both Maurice and Henry. "We need another source of protein because there's very little frozen pork left. I really did mean what I said about fish. Starting and then stopping fresh fish will cause more trouble than shortages."

Maurice consulted a report. "Sorry but the team didn't seem sure about the actual results. We'll know the full effect better in the spring because I'm told the disease spreads in crowded burrows when all the young are born."

"There'll be a big plus if the protein problem can be sorted out because rabbits eat a lot of crops which is why we trap and shoot them." Henry scowled. "Which is another reason the idea is stupid because the crops in London will grow better."

"I'm sure there'll be enough protein for the rest if we close off another city, only now that is essential rather than a desirable experiment." Owen moved his gaze to Maurice. "Are you sure stopping the tea, coffee and beer will trigger an attack? After all, the animals have both London and this failed attack as examples."

"We'll stop chocolate as well. That and some encouragement from local assets will do it." Maurice smiled. "Assets who'll make damn sure they aren't on the attack. The attack will be an attempt to stock up with food before breaking out. It'll look exactly the same as this last one."

"Excellent. As long as they don't actually break out except where and when Joshua wants them to. Please keep us in the loop if you decide to get a little experimental in the future, Maurice. News like that mart attack disturbs my digestion." Maurice nodded acceptance of the rebuke. "Now, if the broad business is complete, let's deal with specifics." Owen opened another file.

As the rest left Vanna, Maurice and Grace hung back. Owen smirked. "Your people worked out well with regard to Nate. That solution won't work again because everyone will beef up their personal security so I'd like to go a little further. Maurice has pointed out that Joshua has all snipers which is a problem if we want to remove someone the Army don't feel they should kill." His lip curled in a sneer. "At least one general comes to mind. We can't train up proper snipers but I'm told we don't need them, just people taught some hand to hand for emergencies and to shoot very, very well."

Maurice chuckled. "No learning to blend in with a hillside or trekking fifty miles over mountains and all that rubbish. They'll be driven to the base nearest the target, go into the ruins to shoot a target at a time and place arranged, then be driven home. We do need special people in one way, broken people." He tapped his head. "If they've been badly traumatised in certain ways, we now have people who can rebuild them into perfect killing machines." He shrugged. "There'll be a couple of our people just behind them, in case."

"That sounds risky, giving the scum skills like that." Vanna frowned. "That could backfire."

The spymaster shook his head. "No, we have been experimenting on the examples collected up to date. The idea is for them to have no other useful skills and little or no motive left to develop any. The proposed conditioning almost amounts to programming. Though unfortunately many of the experiments were to destruction, so we have very few lab-rats left. We will need a good few candidates because the ones we want must have a certain something, I'm assured, simply to be able to shoot that well. Find me plenty of broken men or women, because we'll use the others to actually learn how to cure Joshua's soldiers." Maurice looked at the women expectantly.

"Can you do that, Vanna, Grace?" Owen smiled at the nods. "Good. These will be our personal aces so keep this very close." He nodded towards the spymaster. "Meanwhile Maurice can look for the source of propellant because there really did seem to be a lot of ammunition." As the three left, Vanna and Maurice exchanged glances and smiled.

Chapter 7:

Gifts for Good and Bad Children

Ten days of hard work and fierce trading later, Harold knocked on the forge door and waited until Liz let him in. "Luckily I know I'm totally unworthy, or I might be trying to buy your favours." Harold hopped up to sit on Liz's bench. "It's a bit chilly in here anyway."

"Because I never have enough charcoal to get a good bed of coals. I'm even having a job working up a decent sweat. I check the trees daily but they're just not trying to grow." Liz poked with a hammer at a piece of flat iron. "I'm using brute strength rather than heating and there's no finesse in that."

"Oh well, I'll take my offerings elsewhere."

"Yes where, exactly? There are vague rumours about you showering without locking the bathroom. Worse than that the rumours are so vague I can't figure out who started them." Liz sniffed disdainfully. "Starting rumours is my job because I know everything, but not this time and it's ruining my reputation." She narrowed her eyes. "Just what pathetic treasure did you think I might be impressed with?"

Harold grinned. "Charcoal. Big clean pieces without any chemicals. Bags of the stuff from the Geeks, with more coming from the GOFS. I've got oodles of propellant because I traded some machetes, knives and single shot pistols as well as lots of repairs, so I allowed them to persuade me to take charcoal." He raised his arms across in front of his face. "What sort of thank you is that?"

Liz stopped beating on his arms with her hands. "You, you soldier you! Where is it?" Harold pointed at the door. "Ooh. I should…" She went to the door and looked out. "Cripes, you should have made that offer. I might have overlooked your wimpy physique." Liz went outside and her voice floated back. "Come on then, give me a hand."

Harold did, and soon the small bags and sacks were stacked in a corner of the garage used as a forge. "There is a price, more hardened rods for reloads."

"Do they work?"

"The people fell over, though maybe soft lead would have done the job?" Harold shrugged, smiling hopefully. "Better safe than sorry? Surely the bribe is big enough."

"Just about." Liz looked at the charcoal. "I've lots of straightening to do, crossbow points to make, and fettling for the gnomes as well as your unreasonable demands. Though with luck there'll be enough here to get back to my tempering experiments. Hah, when I get that right, I'll be receiving all sorts of offers in return for my wares." Liz smiled brightly. "I'll be singing without even a hint of sooty passion."

"Singing and all that stuff. Casper is still not happy. I'm worried." Harold frowned and shrugged uncomfortably. "He seems to have got over Fury and the Holly thing, but he's not the same idiot."

"Neither are you. Casper got over the first euphoria about coming out as gay, but then he had a couple of hard knocks. That's it. He's happy with Amber and he's still a complete burke with the kids." Liz sniggered. "Unless you can find him a lumberjack I reckon he's as happy as the lump will ever be."

"I've tried. I thought we'd have ended up with another gay bloke or two by now."

"Maybe we have, but not the right one. After all look how many impressionable women are fluttering lashes at you without a result?" Liz pushed Harold towards the door, then picked up her music player. "Now go. Soldier off. I've been recording from some of those old CDs. Heavy Metal music, music with a beat for beating, from the likes of Motorhead and Nuklea Hamma." Harold got out while his eardrums were intact.

*   *   *

Though Harold only went as far as Barry, where his eardrums were assailed by one-year-old Violet. "Cripes, Barry, how do you live here with that?"

"That'll be for about five minutes before she goes to sleep. I ended up babysitting Matti and Doll while they were little so this is barely annoying." Barry finished putting on his coat. "We are leaving anyway, since I don't play with chemicals near children."

"Ah, that sort of news, more pipe bombs." A short walk to the detached garage later Harold looked at a tube with a fuse. "That looks the same as the others."

"Except, as requested, these don't use sugar. That pipe bomb will be much hotter when it goes off though maybe it won't throw shrapnel as far. Fasten that to a container of that old petrol or diesel mixed with oil out of old engines to make a Molotov plus. Better yet, that fuse is in thin plastic tube with an added extra, so once the flame goes in there even water won't put it out." Barry gave the usual resigned sigh when he had to make chemicals burn or go boom. "I thought about how the TV kept showing your truck, and all the scroats out there who might decide to armour up as well. If the Russians could kill early tanks with Molotovs, a car with a bit of plate welded to it should burn easily."

"That's handy in another way, because glass containers for old-style Molotovs are getting scarcer. The red stripe means burn?" Harold reached out to tap the red band painted round the short length of pipe but thought better of it.

"No, that means a hot boom because the contents get hot very fast which means they expand until the tube bursts and throws the shrapnel. This other one really will burn, which means it'll be much nastier if it goes off near people." Barry rubbed at his head and then his face, clearly ill at ease about the tube marked with yellow and blue bands. "I'm still not certain about making those. There's aluminium filings and some other unpleasant this and that in there. When it bursts those bits will fly out, burning anything they hit. The next part is what really worries me." Barry hesitated a long time, but Harold left him to decide. "They're hot enough to stick to skin, and they'll keep hot long enough to burn deep, or burn through clothing."

"We won't use them except to defend Orchard Close, Barry. Then if burned skin slows some up, there'll be fewer we have to stop coming over walls. After that we may have the luxury of deciding to either kill or treat a burned survivor." Harold looked at the first one. "We could do with smaller pipes fitted up like that one, then they can go inside plastic containers full of flammable liquids." He saw Barry wince. "You already may have saved some of us, Barry. You saw them on the TV coming around the flanks, and while you weren't there your bombs stopped them. One bullet from the flank could have killed Lenny, then Doll wouldn't have made it."

Harold knew that would have been unlikely, even if they'd been flanked, but he got the right reaction. Barry straightened and nodded. "Without Lenny she wouldn't have survived. I'll make them, or at least show Bernie how to." Barry still felt uncomfortable with making bombs so he showed Bernie how to do it, and Bernie actually made them.

"I promise we won't just throw them about without good reason Barry, but you know that. Look on the bright side, your fireworks were a success?" Harold smiled at him.

"Oh yes. Messing about deliberately burning things reminded me of all the pretty colours if some materials just burn instead of going bang." Barry smiled properly at the memory. "My Dad used to point out that early fireworks did that, without having to explode. He said they were called Volcanoes and Silver Rain so Guy Fawkes night used to be pretty without being as noisy." He gestured at the pipes. "Those will be pretty, just don't be near when they get noisy."

"Cripes no." Though Harold had a candidate for one or more very hot bombs. Caddi had been trying to jump the queue for repairs, again.

*　*　*

Several times during the fortnight after the mart attack Harold considered sending Caddi a dangerous firework or a bullet to stop the stream of demands. Caddi didn't like having to wait his turn for Soldier Boy to fix his captured weapons, sending someone to ask almost daily. Eventually Harold sent the last weapon back to the GOFS and the following day Charger turned up as a hostage, so Harold drove over to The Mansion. Chevy rushed him through the search and Caddi himself opened the door to let Harold in.

"Cripes Caddi, don't you ever take a break? You've been whittling on about a visit since the smoke cleared. I'm still repairing what we took, and anyway the Geeks and GOFS came first. It was their turn." Harold looked over the heap of weapons on the desk, studiously ignoring the auburn-haired young woman stood in the corner. The Virginia experiment with willing women had finished because this maid had cane marks across her upper legs. "Didn't you get enough action at the mart?"

"Yeah, more than enough but I made sure we took plenty of loot as well. We should charge the rest of the city for stopping that." Caddi waved at the weapons. "Free repairs?"

"Not a chance. That was pure self-interest." Harold frowned. "You lot were definitely a bit slow shooting."

Caddi shrugged. "We thought you'd be all right in that armour and if they went for you that would make it easier on us. We had an outbreak of common sense because there were enough to swamp you. Then that mob would have your armoured division. It's a pity the Army hogged most of the weapons." He scowled. "I notice you got all the glory. I'll cane the next stupid shit to mention the blonde, or Patty or that fucking Emmy. We lost a lot more people."

"You've got more to lose. We did our bit but can't afford our losses any more than you."

Caddi grinned, volatile as ever. "The Ferdinands really got thinned. Pussies. They're crap at hand-to-hand and didn't have enough guns." He smirked. "Probably because of how many we took off them. The bastards coming our way went for them, the weakest spot, then the rest of us hit the arses from the side."

Harold frowned and glanced at him. "Did any actually break out? Are we likely to see any survivors from that mob running about?"

"No, none broke through. I left people until the Army were done bulldozing the bodies into a heap and so did the Baggies, just in case someone decided to lie doggo. Do you want more coffee, or anything?" Caddi raised an eyebrow, glancing at the woman.

"No thanks." Harold sipped his coffee and didn't look towards her.

"You can fuck off since he's not interested." Caddi sniggered because Harold still didn't look up as she left. Though Harold suppressed a small smile because Charger had passed on a bit of news. Roller watched the film and liked Virginia's willingness. Since Caddi didn't want her after she couldn't trap Harold into an indiscretion, Roller claimed the young woman. Virginia really did like polite and dangerous according to Charger, which left Roller looking both smug and haggard.

"I hope you don't want this lot in a hurry. It'll be nearly Christmas before they're done, maybe later for the difficult ones." Harold waited patiently for Caddi to take the piss or complain.

Sure enough. "Yeah but you'll have time to stop for a fucking party. What the fuck do your lot do? It's not like you have an orgy, is it? Bloody frigid, your lot."

"Just fussy. Fussy and carrying sharp stuff to remind visitors about their manners." Harold smiled at him. "We can be a lot of fun once the gates are locked."

"Yeah, right, though you don't seem to be able to take a joke these days. Have you taken in any more runners?" Caddi never stopped at one complaint. Harold thought he must have a list someplace.

"I've got a great sense of humour but not if some arse pulls a knife. I slap those down good and hard but your men never seem to learn. If something breaks that's hard luck." Harold grinned. "I take refugees not runners. There has been an increase in those looking for us after the TV publicity." He smiled happily because Caddi hated the next part. "You know I have more because we close the borders for a day each month for a welcoming party. Now, do you want to deal or are you going to keep trying to wind me up? It won't get you a better price." It wouldn't. If the harassment became too bad, Harold added something to the bill.

"All right, smartarse. I suppose you want more powder? You can have reloads?" Caddi grinned because he knew the reply.

Or thought he did, because this time Harold wasn't as short of propellant. "I'll want propellant, but I also want charcoal. Only clean charcoal and my metals man will check every bag." All the charcoal meant Liz had finally fired up her forge properly again and swore she nearly had tempering sorted. Harold wanted that since if Liz could finally make tempered blades, she could make the slimmer, pointed machetes he wanted. "Your reloads are rubbish and so are any you found. I know because I've got a lot of them."

"Why? What's wrong with them?"

"You expect me to tell you? Not a chance. If you ever get ambitious all our rounds will fire and our guns won't jam, while yours might blow up. Why would I do you the same favour? That one is past repair." The weapon might not be completely useless but Harold had just 'fined' Caddi a badly rusted shotgun as a way of dealing with the crap. "I'll take it as spares."

"Right, then you'll repair it for your lot." Caddi claimed Harold repaired all the ruined weapons. "How many big rifles have you got now after getting that one from the General?"

"At least three, and several really good shooters in addition to me but I'm not saying how many." Harold grinned despite Caddi finally learning about his extra rifle. "My extra shooters might practice when your men go home?"

"That isn't subtle." Caddi scowled. "Telling them they'd better go home because hanging about after you close the borders can be fatal? That's a neutral road."

"Yes, but out in the dark, without any friends coming to pick them up? Something terrible might happen." Harold smiled sunnily. "We'd be tucked up partying and never hear them scream."

"Yeah, right, at least you only party once a month these days. What do you know about Myxomatosis? The rabbit disease?"

"Very little. The usual on the TV which is probably crap because our rabbits are fine, tasty even. We'll sell you some burgers without any rat in them?" Harold frowned at the switch because something must have tweaked Caddi about rabbits.

"I've heard that some of the rabbits further over on the other side of the M5 have something wrong with them. The result is gross, a lot like bad mange with something else mixed. Even some of the live ones have disgusting marks and scars. I've stopped buying rabbit meat from outside, especially after the TV warning, and I'm hoping the canals stop it spreading." Caddi frowned, looking at Harold's hands. "What's the matter with that one?"

Harold had been frowning about the rabbits, but now he put down the pistol he'd been inspecting and shrugged. "That'll be expensive."

"They all are. Right, let's get these sorted out for delivery seventh of December at the latest?"

"Fourteenth, maybe." Harold settled down to haggle.

On the way back to Harold's pickup, Caddi stopped and chuckled. "I might have found an answer to those nasty bitches of yours. Watch her." Caddi pointed to a young woman who looked a little bit gaunt. At about five foot seven or eight with black hair that looked as if it had been hacked rather than cut, Harold couldn't see why Caddi had picked on her. Then he realised the young woman wore at least four knives and a machete over her short black skirt and white blouse. More significantly, the Hot Rods were steering clear of her.

A smile grew on Harold's lips. "An armed woman Caddi? You're taking a chance, and ruining your reputation."

"I've reassessed some of your bitches after one of my lot saw that Patty swinging a machete. Maybe I've tried your method of recruitment?" He pointed at the young woman. "Nobody is allowed to touch her." Caddi sniggered. "That's if they dared. I've had to stop her taking part in crossbow practice since she's as good as that bitch of yours and goes for the same targets."

Harold watched the gangsters rather than the woman. Those coming towards her avoided her eyes or contact while those behind eyed her up, smirked, and made jokes. "Cripes, is she actually allowed to cut them?"

"Fingers, hands, ears or nuts depending on where she's groped. There's a list. Put a hand on her ass and find out. Everyone is allowed to ask her?" From Caddi's little half-smile he already knew Harold wouldn't.

"Not my thing." Though on the way back home Harold wondered what sort of woman could walk around The Mansion without the Hot Rods daring to touch her. He worried about someone sending a woman like that to infiltrate Orchard Close, because Harold knew he was a sucker for refugee women.

Harold also worried about the reports of diseased rabbits, because rabbit supplied a high proportion of the meat eaten in Orchard Close. He'd have a talk to Rabbit Bob to see if his tame ones could catch this Myxomatosis since those TV reports seemed to be true.

Then Harold wondered how much hassle the shoppers would get from the new soldiers on the bypass. From experience the squaddies would be suspicious and probably downright belligerent for a while. He didn't like the soldiers thinking of the Orchard Close people as animals and scum, but it took time to get the difference across. After that Harold spent the rest of the trip worrying about Christmas and the New Year, because he couldn't see any Happy about either.

*　*　*

Harold had barely finished stashing Caddi's repairs in his workshop when the bullhorn on the by-pass started asking for Soldier Boy. Nobody worried because every new sergeant called Soldier Boy up there, to explain this enclave were getting no favours and should watch their step. Harold took off all his weapons, then walked out of the gates and along the road to the edge of the exclusion zone. "Hello the Army." He took off his jacket and turned to show he had no weapons. "Can I put my coat back on, please?" Despite the cold Harold expected a no.

"Yes, but come up nice and steady and keep your hands in view." A surprised and grateful Harold did, keeping his hands well out to the sides. Newly arrived soldiers tended to want him down to shirt and jeans for a first meeting. "That'll do. Turn round for the search." Harold did while a squaddie came through the sandbags and ran a wand over him. He asked about Harold's pocket, but accepted it was a phone without patting him down. The soldier retreated. "Come in closer."

The face looking over the sandbags looked serious but not unduly suspicious or antagonistic, which made a pleasant change. Harold smiled. "Hello sarge. I'm Harold Miller."

"We know. A brave and honest citizen, bloody but unbowed." Harold stared and the sergeant smiled slightly. "Yes, you and that thing down there are stars of stage and screen. Though that leaves me with two questions." The smile went leaving a very serious-looking sergeant. "First off, what is that armour made of?"

"The strongest parts are half inch cold rolled steel, but some is three-eighths and some is softer. Your rifles or any round with a steel core will no doubt go through any of it." Harold shrugged. "Most of the ammo down here is soft lead reloads and most gangsters skimp on propellant."

Sarge seemed to relax. "How were your people hit?"

"Eight rounds punched holes in the steel. Two hit people, and one got shot through a loophole. The other casualties were stood up behind a plate using a crossbow or went hand to hand. I tried putting us on an angle to shed any hits." Harold smiled. "One bloke tripped over a brick."

"There's always one. So the armour worked, or nearly, because there seemed to be a hell of a lot of incoming. We only saw the action on TV last night which prompts my second but less official question. How is that blonde lass? This lot can't sleep for worrying." Sarge might be smiling but didn't seem to be taking the piss, while the nearest soldiers did seem very interested.

"Doll is alive and with the best medic around here. You'll know when she comes back if you see a blonde in a Stetson and maybe cowboy boots." Harold smiled. "She might even bring up some chips or soup if that's allowed."

Sarge indicated with his head for Harold to move along the sandbags, further from the squaddies, though as he did he answered in a loud voice. "The lads would love that. They'd be the envy of the entire barracks." He lowered his voice. "Then I'd have to arrest her so the government could give her a medal."

Harold kept his voice down. "Seriously?"

"Very seriously. I would have to invite her to a medal ceremony and not take no for an answer. That came in writing that I have seen but I'm not allowed a copy of, which makes me just a little bit twitchy. Though anyone else with chips or soup will be safe." The last came with a wry smile. "Sergeant rumour says both are delicious."

Harold spoke louder. "I'm afraid she's very ill as yet, but someone else might come up to keep your lads updated?"

"They'd appreciate that. They've already taken pictures of that paintwork to show off." Sarge lowered his voice. "Careful lad. Your lot have been set up, and some asshole will try and knock you down."

"Thanks. We'll try very hard to keep on being," Harold smiled, "battered but unbroken."

"Good. I'll see you mart day no doubt. That'll liven the day up since very few use the bypass now and no, I really don't want to know how you manage."

"With difficulty." Harold hadn't expected this response, but he might as well take advantage. "I know this is an odd thing to ask, but can I show you a phone picture of a bloke? I just want to know if he's survived because his missus worries."

"Go on, but carefully." The sergeant tensed, then relaxed as the phone came clear. He looked at the picture. "No, but I'll mention it very unofficially. Why was he arrested?"

"He's a gardener, a good one, but a scroat injured him and he needed a medic." Harold shrugged. "We knew he wouldn't come back but it was that or die."

"He'll be all right if he's a gardener. We see them sometimes, a gardener with a dozen assholes in orange suits following him and a guard to keep the animals under control." Sarge grinned. "Now you'd better get back to being law-abiding."

"Always Sarge." Harold lifted a hand to the squaddies in farewell and walked back down with a bit of a bounce in his step.

As he walked through Orchard Close Harold told half a dozen people about both the medal thing, and how friendly these soldiers seemed to be. He made a point of telling Emmy about how gardeners were treated. Finally Harold explained everything to Sharyn over a drink and discussed the recent trip to Caddi. When Harold told Sharyn about the number of weapons Caddi had scored, more than the Geeks, her eyes narrowed. "Geeks. Wellington. What was it about Wellington? When we were watching TV."

"Wellington? Cripes, yes, hang on." Harold went to look in the pocket of his long leather coat, the one for disguising rifles. The front of the envelope said Soldier Boy in looping script. Harold took it back through. He explained the strange conversation, then had a look at the contents. The short letter shocked him, especially coming from a Geek.

'To anyone reading this, the young woman known as Ly Thien or Thien has been given permission to leave the Geek Freeks compound and live wherever she wishes. Signed Wellington – Geek warchief and senior manager.'

"Cripes. The rest of the Geeks keep making jokes about him and his woman, even the Barbies do. Now he's given her a free pass, because Wellington told me she'd be carrying another copy." Harold smiled. "Einstein will choke if she comes here and I wave this." Harold's smile widened. "With luck he'll call me a liar so I can kill the little shit."

Sharyn read the letter. "She's got to get here first."

Harold's smile never faltered. "He's their general or warchief so I'll bet she's got a way out, one that gives her a running start." He smirked. "Did Gayle really inject Wellington with decency and good manners when she fixed his teeth?"

"Maybe. Now who do we tell? Just in case you aren't here." Sharyn paused rather than mention her brother might be dead. "Shopping or something?" She brightened. "Shopping will be easier for you since our new soldiers had a good look at the battle bus and saw us on TV." Sharyn might be happier but nothing like as relieved as Harold. All the soldiers must have seen the news report so they were less likely to think of the people in Orchard Close as animals.

"We tell Umeko for starters since they're friends. Then Emmy, Alfie and Casper because one will be on duty at the gate, then Patty, Matthew and Bess in case she comes across the fields. Liz because otherwise she'll beat on me. Who else?" Harold looked at the letter again. "I'd nail this to the dance house door but someone would say something to wind a scroat up. Then the Geeks would find out."

"I'll choose a couple of the Coven, and maybe another couple of the girl club. We'll cover it." Sharyn smiled happily. "That really has cheered me up, because apparently miracles can happen." Harold debated briefly, then left the rabbit news until the following day, when he went to the expert first.

* * *

Harold found the expert tending to rabbits, of course. "Hi Bob. Do you prefer Bob or Rabbit Bob?"

"I don't mind. The Rabbit Bob name stopped confusion with another Bob but he's with the Barbies now." Rabbit Bob closed a hutch and came out of the garage, carefully changing his shoes so one pair never came outside the door. "Now why did you want me because it wasn't about my name?"

"No. It's about that Myxomatosis warning on the TV? I've heard disturbing things. I'm even more worried after seeing the shoe shuffle." As Harold explained, Rabbit Bob's worried frown deepened.

He thought for a few moments. "We can start by keeping each garage separated, with different food stock, different keepers, the droppings on a different compost heap, the full bit. Do you have any spare mesh?"

Since Patty had salvaged every scrap of net curtaining or mesh fencing within two square miles, Harold thought there must be some spare. "Some, for fruit trees and bushes or bee hats?"

"We could rabbit fence some areas to grow food for these? Otherwise the wild ones might leave infections." Bob scratched his head. "It's a pity we can't raid a vet's to look for drugs."

"After the crash I stripped a few vet's practices because Patricia could use some of the medicine, but I didn't know which." Harold smiled. "She should have the rest someplace because we don't throw much away."

Rabbit Bob brightened. "In that case your vet, er, doctor might have something for rabbits?"

"We can but ask. If not I'll try the Barbies in case the pet shop had vet supplies." As they walked to the hospital Rabbit Bob went into more detail. Harold zoned out while the breeder went through all the vet supplies with Patricia. "Well?"

"Good news and bad, of course. There's injections for both Viral Haemorrhagic Disease and Myxomatosis but not enough for more than the breeding stock. The ones being raised for meat will always be at risk." Rabbit Bob shrugged. "We'll tighten up all round, but protecting food supplies will be hardest. Can you get any more rabbit pellets?"

"Maybe. The Barbies were really nosy about the last lot. Worse, I'm not sure how much they've got left." Harold hoped the Barbies wanted more bespoke knitwear in exchange because he still didn't repair guns for them. He'd been tempted but if the GOFS hadn't mentioned it there might be a reason. Harold wasn't keen on the news spreading anyway because that could attract unwelcome attention. "You'll want to talk to the boss gnome, Emmy, about fencing and all that."

Harold left Rabbit Bob and Emmy deep in a discussion about rabbit fencing and which areas to protect. He sent a message to the Barbies, not hard just now since one or another of their fighters visited every couple of days to update everyone on Doll. Harold encouraged that by giving the first each day a free beer.

Three days later Chandra turned up. "Doll is fine, but no visitors allowed. Doc says she's definitely out of danger. Do I get the beer?" Chandra took a swig from the free bottle she'd already received as a visiting leader. "Cy should survive though he'll take a bit longer. So far neither is up to anything more than exchanging a few words. I'll let you know if she needs her chastity belt."

"Give her a cane and he'll get the message." Harold grinned. "If she chucks the cane away cover your eyes. Speaking of chastity leads me to rabbits and their lack of it, sort of. Have you any more rabbit pellets?"

"For your pet rabbits who might be lunch rabbits?" Chandra held up a hand. "We know you've got some. That bloody great load of bunny food you traded was a big hint. We've had a lot of fun trying to get details but so far it's tantalising hints. Anyone would think your lot enjoyed the questioning." Her eyes narrowed. "Have you raised wild ones, because we're considering that before the Myxi gets here? Is it right that makes them fatter, as someone hinted?"

"First you'll give us pellets for lessons in how to keep your bunnies safe because I've got an expert. Then I'll answer the other question and you'll give me more of something we want." Harold had just decided to trade a few live baby bunnies to the Barbies, just in case all the ones here were wiped out.

"Hah, you've always got an expert." Her eyes widened. "F... Cripes, the expert came with those refugees because that's when you suddenly wanted the pellets." A big smile spread across her face. "Some of the ones we took will know."

"They'll know why we wanted pellets, but they won't be experts." Ten minutes later Rabbit Bob wearing a balaclava came in with Mopsy and a twelve week old prospective dinner.

Five minutes after that Chandra had been convinced that the whole idea would work at Beth's. "I will have to talk to Christie or Malibu because of the secrecy and price?" She grinned. "I could just take this bloke and these two bunnies back with me in the morning to help explain?"

"Naughty. Play nice." Harold frowned. "Are you staying over?" He hadn't registered how late Chandra had arrived, but dusk had definitely started to gather.

"Yes but hard luck, you aren't my type. I've been told about these wild parties once the gates close at night?" Chandra giggled. "Even if you won't throw one, I might get lucky?" She held up both hands. "In the rules I promise. I'll just slip into something more comfortable so I can relax."

Harold burst out laughing. "You're only wearing a pair of curtains, or you are since you took off your jeans and knickers for the search."

"I wanted to welcome Alfie back on duty." Chandra grinned. "Anyway, this is uncomfortable. The laces leave marks everywhere. Patty could check and let you know?" Afterwards several people told Harold about Chandra turning up in the canteen to relax over an evening meal. She wore a white knitted dress that fitted like a glove but with all the holes looked more like a colander or net curtain.

Within the week a deal had been arranged for a baby buck from Mopsy and Rocket Man, and a pair of baby does, one from each of two other breeding mothers. Breeding pairs having the same daddy didn't matter with rabbits, Rabbit Bob assured both Harold and the Barbies. The bunnies, with some warm woollens instead of lacy skin tight versions, would be exchanged for another load of rabbit pellets once the weather allowed. That proviso had been added since a light covering of snow had fallen, and if more fell there were no snowploughs or gritters.

* * *

Just before the bunny pellets arrived Harold saw a lot less happy coming up this Christmas, at least for some. He'd just come down after Daisy-story. Sharyn headed for the kitchen to get a drink, then froze.

"Not all local citizens are as public-minded as those we showed previously. Here they combined with the scum to overwhelm the mart guards and Army post."

Both of them rushed for the settee to watch. Onscreen a repeat of the attack on the London mart played out. The background and detail were different, but once again the attackers overwhelmed an Army post then surged over the fence around the mart. No locals turned up to help, no helicopters or grenades or lorry loads of squaddies arrived in the nick of time. Smoke arced through the air from the mob, explosions ripped through the guards and the armoured car burst into flame before exploding.

Sharyn took Harold's hand. "Where is it Harold? Is it here?" With the light snow over everything, neither of them could see any distinguishing features.

"I can't tell." Harold tried to see something, anything, then he blew out a long breath in relief. "I just saw snow on steep hills in the distance. There's no deep snow here or hills like that. I'm sorry for the poor sods up there, but relieved because that's got to be a good way north."

"Thank all and any gods."

"Amen."

They sat watching as the mob ransacked the mart until the artillery crashed down. The survivors scattered while flames blossomed in the battered store. While the fires took hold, a convoy of lorries and an armoured vehicle with a cannon pulled up. Riflemen poured out to engage anyone attempting to leave the city.

"These residents of Glasgow have shown that they are allied to the criminals and revolutionaries. After such unprovoked murder and destruction SainsMorr Mart have closed their outlets, followed by all the other marts around Glasgow. The government supports them in this action, and have advised the marts to remain closed until the situation has been assessed. We will investigate to see if this is an isolated incident, or if the city has risen in rebellion. Be confident that your government remains vigilant in your protection."

Harold kept very quiet about the ancient armoured car that burned too easily, a museum piece he thought. He didn't wonder aloud about the difference between two lorry-loads of squaddies at the local mart, and the convoy that arrived in Glasgow. A total lack of close-ups didn't help alleviate Harold's paranoia.

*   *   *

The news subdued the excitement in Orchard Close during the run-up to Christmas but didn't completely depress everyone because the fairies, or their lights, were back. Now that the bare winter fields stretched away over a quarter mile in three directions, bereft of cover, the residents decided they were safe enough to put up their Christmas lights again. Many people had a string of coloured bulbs they put up inside, but now they brought out the large coloured bulbs and illuminated santas, reindeer and snowmen found in attics and sheds as they scavenged.

The first time Roy came home to find the place alight he stood for a long time at the gate, slowly shaking his head in sheer disbelief. The fairy glows were usually used to warn the sentries that returning scavengers were friends. Now various residents, especially the girl club, wore them as festive jewellery. They were used as hair decoration, or worn by the soup and chips women when they went up to see the soldiers. By the time the four men left to go back on duty Roy had been inveigled into wearing a string of glows though he had to leave them at the gate.

Both Finn and Trev were pressed into service to repair wiring or control boxes. Finn even ran a wire out to the potential forest so two of the baby Leylandii could twinkle through the night. The sergeant wondered if someone with a rifle might target the residents, but after two nights of illuminations agreed the plethora of moving, twinkling and flashing colours would probably confuse any marksman.

In quieter moments many of the residents discussed Glasgow. Nobody could work out what sort of lunacy had possessed the attackers for them to do that? Nor could anyone understand why the Glasgow locals allowed the mob to succeed without even trying to stop them? Worse, were there idiots elsewhere in their own city who might do the same? Every city now lived with that same threat, that one set of lunatics would leave them starving, because nobody expected the Glasgow marts to open again.

Perhaps because of those thoughts, rather than romantic ones, the Christmas Eve dance had more slow numbers. Even the fancy dress reflected that, with long dresses and suits for most to follow an older, more Victorian or maybe Edwardian theme. The usual suspects went as elves and fairies but even those were quieter, the modestly dressed versions.

Christmas Day brought another reminder of how much had been lost, of how life had changed. Every single Christmas card had been handmade or re-used, as had the wrapping paper. Most of the little extras and luxuries found during the first two years of scavenging were gone. Instead, gifts tended more towards homemade items, often decorated or personalised with more enthusiasm than skill. Kerry had her own elves now, the sewing and embroidering type who wanted to learn more.

Many residents parted with a few coupons to have their own efforts finished or decorated properly as Christmas presents. Others were attempting knitting while both a crochet and quilting club had started. Several men turned to making small gifts such as ear muffs or even mittens from white rabbit fur, while the more ambitious went for making doll houses or even little stick dolls and animals. The first attempts at colouring the white rabbit fur turned up Christmas morning.

Not all the presents were home-made or decorative. "Will you stop that!"

A totally unrepentant beaming smile showed around the kitchen door before Daisy raced in to scoop up her arrow. "I have to practice. Patty says if I want to be a proper Bat to protect against scroats I have to practice. Emmy says I have to build up the muscles to reload, and Fergie says I have to practice creeping up and pouncing." She stopped for a moment, frowning. "That might have been about boys." The miniature assassin crouched, moving towards the door with her crossbow at the ready. "Shhh, Uncle-Harold is coming in."

"Good, serves him right." Sharyn kept her voice down now and a smirk appeared on her face, because Harold had given Daisy the crossbow for Christmas.

A shout of alarm and peals of Daisy laughter meant she'd found a new victim. "Cripes, Sharyn. Isn't anywhere safe these days?"

"Come into the kitchen, Liz, it's an arrow-free zone." Sharyn raised her voice. "Because the next arrow coming in here gets baked into Daisy's apple pie." A wordless protest from the other room died away as Daisy went hunting for more victims.

"Which benighted fool gave her that? My heart can't stand that sort of welcome." Liz frowned as she came in. "Now I know why Wills grinned when he let me in." An outburst of excited barking meant Daisy had found another victim, one who wouldn't mind being hunted as long as fuss and play were involved and maybe a treat. "What is that arrow made of anyway because it nearly had my eye out?"

"No it didn't. The arrows are foam so to be honest they'll not last two days. I worry a lot more about what Daisy replaces them with. That is a child's crossbow, a real child's version not those vicious things the scavengers found just after the crash." Sharyn sighed. "Uncle-Harold gave her the damn thing as a Christmas present, then went out to check the walls."

"Ooh, sneaky. Where the hell did he find that?"

"The scavengers looking for boarding that can't have been infected by a wild rabbit are taking the floors out of lofts, since rabbits don't climb ladders. Harold told me that crossbow turned up hidden in a loft. I can guess why. Somebody must have been treated to this sort of onslaught." Sharyn did a double-take. "What are those?"

"These are earmuffs so that my delicate ears aren't ruined by the noise when I'm beating iron. They're from a secret admirer." Liz took off the pair of rabbit-fur pads on a headband that probably came from a pair of earphones. "Look, rainbows and a heart."

Sharyn looked at the brightly coloured stains on the white fur. "If you say so. Your secret admirer obviously never paid attention to your musical preferences. Harold reckons that drowns out the metal beating when it's turned up."

Liz preened. "I don't care, I've never had a secret admirer before. I'm more the drag 'em into the bedroom type. These might not stop the noise but they'll keep my ears warm which will come in handy when my charcoal runs out again. Anyway, stop changing the subject, or rather stopping me from changing it. Has Fergie been lurking?"

"No, why?"

"She's incredibly smug, and making cryptic comments about private personal training from the real expert. What is really intriguing is that I just saw her going into the dance house with your little brother, our revered leader." Liz sniggered. "That look says its news to you as well."

"This look says I'm going to slap his ears, because he said he had to do Soldier Boy things. That's why I'm peeling sprouts on my own." Sharyn glared at the bowl. "I might cook his with the mud on, just as a penance."

"That wouldn't matter with those disgusting things. Hmm, last night and tonight the sprout fiends switch with those who have taste, so we aren't stunk out. I'll have to check where Fergie is supposed to be sleeping." Liz beamed. "And then if she does actually sleep there tonight."

"Cripes. I don't mind him finding a girl, but that'll be lively. Fergie has already been giving Daisy advice about sneaking up on boys."

"Cripes. Well if you don't know, I'm off before you start to cook those." Liz curled a lip at the sprouts and headed for the door, then yelped. "Daisy!"

Sharyn laughed. "Blame Harold, Patty, Emmy and possibly Fergie, at least."

*　　*　　*

Despite several not particularly subtle attempts to find out more, Harold swore he had only been supervising a training class with machetes. Worse, Liz confirmed that Fergie stayed out Christmas night, but Sharyn knew Harold slept at home in the study. Sharyn realised she might be going over the top when she checked the snow outside the study window to see if there'd been a midnight visitor, so she let it drop. The snow stayed as a light covering, not enough for snowmen and barely enough for the occasional snowball. Clear paths soon appeared down all the common routes.

Hopes of a repeat of the New Year snowman competition faded after Christmas Day, a disappointment to those like Roy's squad who had heard about the last one. Roy and his three friends had all been found places where they could have a proper festive holiday and Christmas Dinner. All four were startled by the mistletoe at the Christmas dance, then again when Santa left them presents. Roy in particular still found the dances and decorations surreal after the last few years, though he now took a number from the hat at the dances.

Harold, through Liz, knew that some of the women traded to get Roy's number for the last dance. He didn't find out if they wanted Roy because he would be a safe walk home or the opposite. Liz just gave a knowing smile and pointed out that Harold didn't even know for sure why they used to trade for him. When Chris, one of Roy's men, walked Celine home at Christmas the gossip radar went on high alert, but interest subsided when there didn't seem to be any follow-up.

*   *   *

The day after Boxing Day the SUV driving very slowly along the road from the traffic island with the horn blaring and four white flags flying came as a complete surprise. The alarm gong from the front gate and the phones ringing all over Orchard Close meant that a crowd gathered even as the vehicle stopped at the bottom of the access road. Harold smiled quietly as Alfie brought the box out of the guardhouse so Soldier Boy could see over the closed gate. Wellington climbed out of the vehicle to give a slow turn with his hands holding his coat open to show there were no weapons in sight. "Can I talk to Soldier Boy please? Sorry about Christmas but this is very urgent."

Harold answered. "Come on up. Who is with you?"

"Just guards and I'll leave them here. No need for hostages." Harold could hear someone in the guardhouse relaying the view. A ripple of comments greeted Wellington's reply, because ranked visitors from the Geeks and Hot Rods were meticulous about exchanging hostages.

"All right. Do your men want to come inside to keep warm?"

"We won't be here long enough. Thanks anyway." Wellington had already started walking so Harold quietly asked for someone to open the gate enough to let him in.

As he came through Harold waved away a search. "He's not suicidal." Harold pointed. "Quick visit or not, we'll go into number three." Wellington nodded, following Harold along with Emmy and Casper.

They'd barely sat down when Wellington started. "We are almost certain the General will launch an attack across the flooded cutting in the next day or two." He debated for a few moments. "We know he's been moving up men, and where, but expected to stop them as they crossed the water. Now we've seen what he'll use." Wellington sighed. "We might need help."

"If he's let you see, maybe that's a feint and he won't attack there?" The General didn't seem the careless sort to Harold.

"He's made up boats, or rather floats, and boards faced with thin steel or maybe aluminium to put over them to make pontoon bridges. He won't know we saw them." Wellington sighed. "This is an ace of ours, but I've got to convince you because I need your help. We have a drone. A small one, a toy with cameras, and it can't go far or we'll lose it." Wellington shrugged, producing a hideous smile. "No Satnav now and all the radio interference means if it goes too far, the damn thing won't come back. We lost one like that and the Army shot another down when we were nosy, so we look after the last one."

"If you know where he's coming, why do you need us? Surely you'll just slaughter them as they cross?" Harold frowned. "Just a flat roadway, not covered?"

"The roadways aren't covered but there's a steel contraption with loopholes and wheels and a roof lurking at both crossing points. We reckon he'll put rifles on the far bank where it's higher than ours, with more behind the shields as they cross. We need more rifles our side." Wellington glanced at Harold. "The ballista team will be shot from the high ground while trying to rewind so we can't use it here."

"What about the catapult?" Harold frowned. "That threw bombs in the demo."

"It's an Onager and yes it does throw bombs, but not exactly accurately. Glass bottles and jars are getting scarcer and more to the point, if they hit people they won't break. Most plastic containers with bombs attached will bounce off a flat surface and the attackers can just kick the rest into the water, and that's if we don't miss the walkway completely. Then either the water will put out fuses, or the blast will be muffled. That's why we need a lot more bombs. There's a better chance of some exploding where they'll do some good and every one that goes off on the bridge will help."

"Maybe you should get some bombs from the GOFS as well? Extras." That would mean Harold needn't part with as many.

Wellington shook his head. "It has to be you because the General might have enough people to try attacking the GOFS as well. They and the Barbies have to stay in place and fully armed, and I've sent a message suggesting they get ready, really quietly. That way he might be tempted to go for both. If we can stop him hard enough this time, especially if the bastard loses his shields, he'll not try again."

"That's why you want bombs, but why do you need more rifles? I know you've got three big ones and at least three smaller calibres." Harold smiled. "Everyone could count them on the TV but I reckon you probably left one at home."

"You borrowed one from Caddi. Seven were shooting from your vehicles but I'll bet you still left a couple of smaller ones at home." Wellington sighed. "I'm sure nobody took all their rifles, the same as they only brought about half their fighters. We really would appreciate your big rifles and especially accurate shooters. The General has all those rifles from the MiB so he can put too many snipers on the high ground for ours to stop, and they'll target anyone shooting at the men crossing. We've got enough pistols, bows and crossbows to make the crossing expensive if our men aren't pinned. If possible we want to stop them getting onto our bank, but if we can't we have to thin them out."

"This might all be gospel, but forgive me for being a bit suspicious. You want our big rifles and best shooters for a sleepover in your backyard?" Harold had a dilemma, because he wouldn't put it past the Geeks to do this to kill the shooters and capture the weapons but daren't ignore a possible attack by the General.

Wellington sighed again. "We'd be suicidal to start a war with you at the same time, but to prove it Galileo and Nobel will come here as hostages for you and yours. They'll both mind their manners. Hawkins won't swap Nobel or probably Galileo for your weapons or your shooters, even including you."

"Why not?" Harold shrugged. "Two managers to get the rifles and take out our shooters makes sense, militarily speaking."

The Geek shook his head, firmly though a smile hovered on his lips. "Not these two, though I'd make that swap for Einstein and Darwin in a heartbeat. Nobel, chemist, made dynamite? Nobel is our bomb man. Galileo is our artillery and crossbow inventing and refining man, or him and Tell between them. We can't afford to lose them and whoever else you'd kill." Wellington hesitated. "I'll stay with you all the time, unarmed, so I'm one of those you kill?"

Harold had to respect that as a guarantee. "I hope you haven't upset Hawkins or this is a golden opportunity."

"I've explained it all to Hawkins. Fighting you while the General is just over the water is suicide. On top of that I pointed out you won't bring all your fighters, bombs, or the smaller rifles and you've got at least three of those. Even Einstein finally got the message, because Hawkins has threatened to hand him over to your women tied hand and foot if he starts trouble." Wellington looked at the three of them hopefully. "Well?"

Harold thought frantically. "Give us ten minutes. You'll get help, it's just how much."

"I'll wait in the car so you can swear at each other." Wellington's ruined mouth twisted in a smile again. "Will you be bringing the armour?"

"No point for this. That truck is really slow and not manoeuvrable. The General will either avoid it or have an answer." Harold smiled. "I've got the answer if he has another one armoured like that. Get you gone then, so we can get on with the shouting."

The shouting mainly concerned having to help the Geeks, but even Emmy conceded that the Geeks were better than the General as a neighbour. Harold headed for his gun room to cast a few special bullets. While the lead cooled he went to see Barry, about using pipe bombs to help Geeks because they were a lesser evil than the General. Eventually Harold persuaded the ex-fireman the General had to be stopped any way possible. Some of Barry's paranoia over Geeks looking for his grandchildren had gone, especially since Doll and Matti dyed their hair back to their natural colours and none of the Geek visitors commented. Harold collected four boxes of bombs from Bernie's garage, including all of the latest types, though he wouldn't allow Bernie himself to come along.

Emmy, Roy and Alfie didn't take long to organise their weapons and back-up once the decision had been made. Patty, Billy, Louie with a bandage still on his ear and Chris, one of Roy's friends, came as personal bodyguards because those with big rifles would be preoccupied. In the chaos someone like Einstein might give in to temptation. Thirty Orchard Close fighters, men and women including the other two of Roy's friends and all four of the refugee fighters, came with handguns, machetes and some shotguns. Harold delayed everyone while he went to marry the new rounds to the right brass, then hurried back with his special Christmas present for Wellington. The small force crammed into two transit vans, along with the padded boxes containing pipe bombs.

* * *

Within minutes of being escorted to the Geek front line, Harold sat watching the grainy images on the Geek TV with real interest. They weren't very good quality but Wellington had told the truth. The tracks in the light snow were clear from the air but invisible from the Geek side of the flooded railway cutting. The tracks and footprints showed where men and equipment had been moved up in two of the places where the opposite banks had a gentler slope to the water. The clincher for Harold was the rough punt shapes sealed across the top, which had to be floats, and the metal faced boards stacked alongside. He had a quiet word with Wellington who chortled and went off to collect old petrol and oil in plastic containers.

Darwin stayed away from the Orchard Close contingent as did Marconi and Einstein. Hawkins confirmed he'd given them other jobs in case one of them opened his big mouth near Emmy or Patty. Hawkins seemed torn between feeling disgusted he needed Orchard Close, and grateful they'd come. He left Wellington and Tell to deal with Harold's contingent as much as possible. Tell, the Geek bowyer, came for a discussion with Wellington because they would each command the defence at one crossing. The bowyer took one look at Patty's crossbow and a big grin split his face. He spent some time with Patty, experimenting with her weapon.

The Orchard Close party split up. Emmy and Harold covered one crossing with Patty and Louie to watch their backs, with Roy and Alfie at the other. The rest of the fighters split with them to meet the two attacks. The Geeks provided houses for Harold's party, with blow heaters but no running water. Their fighters stared at Emmy and Patty, and the women among the fighters, then gave them a wide berth as Hawkins had promised. After a long, restless, but undisturbed night Harold, Emmy, Wellington and Hawkins looked at the overnight pictures from the drone.

"F...ferkit, they must be f... freezing in there." Hawkins glanced at Emmy and Patty, then back to the screen. "The roofs are still covered in snow."

"I don't care how tough they are, he can't keep troops in there for long." Wellington grinned. "Though I hope he does because they'll not sleep well. The cold will sap their strength so after a few days of that they'll be knackered."

Harold nodded agreement. "Can you put the drone back up, to keep an eye on them?"

Wellington shook his head. "Not this morning, it's too clear. We only need one of them to look up and notice the odd-shaped birdie up there. The General ain't stupid, he'll know we're watching and call the whole thing off." The Geek gestured at the screen. "This infrared stuff is easy to get at night, but as you can see the actual camera pictures at night are crap."

"Enough to see these though." Emmy tapped a shape on the screen. "That's the same as on the daylight pictures you got, though the detail on this is worse." She frowned. "If the shield is still there, he's not coming right away."

"No but this was an hour ago, because we took the drone down at first light. We can't tell if it's on the move now." Wellington tried to sound hopeful. "At least we'll spot him moving up for a night or dawn attack."

"Though an attack could be any time today." Harold stretched. "I'll let my people know to relax, but keep their gear ready to go." By late morning most people started to think the attack might not be today, since the attackers would want plenty of daylight to consolidate any gains.

* * *

Perhaps the General tried to catch everyone out because the attack started early in the afternoon. "Go, go, go. The bastard is coming." The Geek stopped, mouth open, visibly mentally repeating what he'd said when he saw Emmy.

She smiled. "We're coming." They were, already picking up weapons before running towards their positions. Gunfire started from the other side followed by screams this side warning everyone the incoming shots were accurate. Wellington waited at the Orchard Close firing position, an arc of bricks six thick backed by earth, with slots at intervals to fire through without looking over. Patty moved to one side with her binoculars and settled in while Harold and Emmy each chose a slot to fire through.

"Not yet." Wellington picked up a field telephone, waving the hand-piece. "Marconi fixed these up when he heard about yours." He held the receiver to his ear. "Have you got them spotted?" He paused for an answer, then chuckled. "Fire." The GOFS general gestured to the slits. "Take a peek." On the far bank four strips of metal, railway lines when Harold looked closer, now led from a sandbagged and steel covered structure. A long line of floats and boards came out of the shelter and slid down the steel into the water. Down at the water's edge three sections were already floating, moving further out as another pushed into the water.

Lines of smoke curved in from behind Harold, in two clumps. They landed at two different places along the opposite crest of the cutting, high points. At one location two men with rifles stood and started to run; at the other the victims must have opted for keeping low. After the ripple of explosions Harold doubted either action made much difference. The lack of any more shooting from either spot confirmed his thoughts. "That's careless." Harold couldn't understand why the General put men in range of the catapult.

"Not really. Galileo used coil springs from railway wagons to make these onagers so they are much more powerful. Up to now I've only used our older version, just once or twice against patrols to give the arses a false idea of our range. The original can't throw even a single bomb that far uphill." Wellington's grotesque smiled flashed. "My bad." He shrugged as more explosions and screams sounded in the distance. "Twice. We'll drop some more where the other rifles were firing from, though they seem to have got the idea already." More bombs arced across the gap followed by more explosions. No more rifles fired from the high points on the opposite bank.

"What are you expecting them to do now?" Harold guessed that Wellington and the General must have a plan B, both seemed to be that sort of person. He looked back through the loophole as more explosions sounded. A few bombs straddled the floats entering the water without appreciable effect.

"Something like your tank, probably adapted to have those loopholes rather than the original version, with maybe a roof to deflect pipe bombs. Possibly armoured with thicker steel which had worried me until you handed out the first Christmas presents." Wellington glanced across the water. "I'd hoped to blow the tyres at least though even that would be a bitch to manage if the driver kept moving. If we immobilise the damn things I intend throwing petrol and oil in bottles with wicks. Original Molotovs."

"The tyres won't blow. We have bullet holes in ours but they're filled with foam of some sort and still work perfectly. We've got those tyres you can run after a puncture on the trailer, but the foam is a better idea." Harold looked over the water as well. "How good are your riflemen at this end? Seriously, I need to know."

"As agreed, our best pair with the best rifles and one bloke with a two-two are backing your other pair of shooters. They can hit a man at five to six hundred yards. My other big rifle is about thirty yards along this bank with two more little rifles, but the shooters aren't that accurate. Neither are the rifles, which is why they're just backup for you two."

Harold frowned. "They won't be able to hit a loophole but can they hit the cab of a truck?"

"One should, and occasionally the others might." Wellington laughed. "The rifles might do better now that you've brought those piercing rounds. Hawkins was f… bloody annoyed you knew what rounds to bring until I reminded him you repaired the bloody rifles." He sobered. "The riflemen know if they use those rounds without my personal say-so I'll cut.. hurt them a lot."

Emmy nodded towards Patty. "We appreciate the effort with your language." She grinned. "If you do slip, we are on your patch."

"Yeah, but not everyone thinks that'll make any difference." Wellington smirked, waving a hand along the line of Geek troops. "Worrying about their language around your women will stop the men worrying about the General." He laughed. "Though if I'd put a couple of them in sight of Patty the idiots would have forgotten the bloody General altogether. They're sort of frightened but fascinated."

Harold watched the floats slide down the far bank one after the other as the line of fifteen metre long boards stretched out towards this bank. The General would need fifty at least to cross the seventy-odd metres of water, though the sections were sliding down in rapid succession so that wouldn't take long. "How far are you letting that bridge come?" The line of sharpened stakes the

Geeks had put in along the waterline might slow up men coming out of the water, but it wouldn't affect anyone running across a bridge.

"After seeing your new toys and plotting with Einstein and Darwin, I've got a wee bit more ambitious. The bridge can come all the way because I want him to send that shield. We'll let that get past halfway with all those nasty fighters following, then break the bridge. We may as well take the opportunity to thin them out a bit." Wellington chuckled. "It only seems fair after they've made such an effort. Though to stop the General from being suspicious we'll try to destroy the bridge before then." Wellington sighed dramatically. "We'll fail. So sad." Even as he spoke a few bombs sailed through the air. Most bounced off the floating walkway or landed in the water, while those that exploded didn't damage the metal sheeting.

Harold looked at Wellington. "Oops?"

"Oh yes. Now we'll frantically dash about. Oh dear, what can we do?" Behind him Patty tried not to burst out laughing because she didn't want to spoil Wellington's deadpan delivery. "We'll probably take three or four minutes to come up with something?" He made a small bow towards Harold. "Your extra bombs will let us bait the trap a bit, waste a few."

Four minutes later a mixture of bombs and plastic bags full of dark liquid arced up. The bags flew further since they weighed less, splattering on the bank and the nearby bridge sections. The bombs landed nearer, most of them landing in the water or bouncing there. Once again, those exploding on the metal sheet did no discernible harm. The next bombs were smaller, overshooting the plastic bags to explode beside the railway lines and the roadway inching down it. The dark bags splattered across the bank again. "Those floats will be damaged but not enough. We could destroy the first floats coming down those rails by dropping bombs around them but would use up all our ammo. Then he'd send more floats."

Emmy scowled. "Why isn't that stuff on the bank burning?"

"Nobel reckons that stuff shouldn't catch even if an ordinary bomb drops near." Wellington rolled his eyes. "Oh, disaster." He grinned. "Though once something hot enough spatters over the bank and sets it going, it'll be a stone bitch getting off the bridge without a serious hotfoot. The stuff is a sort of sticky jelly."

"So the idea is to trap some men on the bridge. Will our hot bombs set that jelly off?" Harold started worrying since the Geek seemed certain, despite never seeing one explode. He couldn't have since Harold believed Barry and never wasted one to see.

"We already have something to do the job. Tell has a, er, blasted great big fancy bow to deliver his. He reckons that bloody great crossbow will do the same for us without exposing the shooter, which saves our blokes poking their heads up over the bank to do it." He nodded towards Patty but then Wellington's face sobered. "I don't want those f..er, er, lipping shields getting back off that bridge. I want them either at the bottom of that water or tucked up safe on this side." He looked through a firing slit as a few more bombs mixed with a lot of bags arced overhead. "Now we know why he put up those buildings in six places. We thought they were just guard posts at low spots on the bank and the rails might be to launch boats."

"Something's coming, Welly. I just heard vehicles." The Geek with binoculars further along the bank raised a hand. "They've stopped."

"Probably the armoured trucks for when the men move onto the bridge. It won't be long now." The front of the bridge had passed the three-quarter mark as the last sections came clear of the construction shed and started down the slope. Wellington used the field telephone, listened, then reported. "There were engine noises at the other bridge as well. I hope that thing won't support a heavily armoured vehicle."

"Not a chance. There's over a ton of plate on our truck and we'll shoot clean through that thickness from this range." Harold pointed. "Those floats are half-submerged already. I can't see them taking that sort of extra weight let alone something with thicker steel. If they don't sink, they'll flip if it's only a bit off-centre. Why don't you take a peek with the drone now everyone's busy?"

Wellington's wry smile looked odd with his scars. "I told you, I daren't because the skies are clear. That smartarse over there would call it off and be sneakier next time or worse, someone might shoot it down." Wellington peered out of the viewing slit again. "Brace yourselves. Those fuses really are waterproof?"

"So I'm told." Harold thought crossing his fingers might not help Wellington's nerves.

"Goody. Contact. The bridge has reached this side." He made a call on the phone. "The other one is about fifteen feet short yet." Along this bank, Geeks were coming to the lip and lying behind slots or just the bricks and earth with firearms or crossbows ready. Behind them men with bows stood ready to loft arrows over the crest. Wellington worried at a thumbnail. "He's got to have something to keep our blokes from opening up on his men as they cross. Otherwise, even at this range the sheer volume of pistol rounds and crossbows will cause serious casualties." He sighed. "We can destroy the bridge now, but I really want to kill a shitload of his men as well." He glanced at Patty.

She grinned. "I'm good with that sentiment, however it's put." They all waited, and worried.

*   *   *

Even as the field telephone reported the other bridge had reached this bank, a Geek nearby called out to let everyone know he could hear engines again. The tops of two armoured trucks came into view, covered trucks with sloping roofs and loopholes. "Armour to protect the covering fire. That's a relief in some ways because Galileo and Nobel reckon they could rig up mortars. We daren't because of the RAF reaction to rockets, but I worried the General might risk it." Wellington really sounded relieved but Harold added that to his own list of worries for the future.

The vehicles kept coming until the drivers turned parallel to the cutting, either side of the attack on top of the high ridge in plain view. Harold looked at the curious pattern of small metal shapes over the rear section and driver's door, almost like scales, and wondered if they worked better than big plates. Wellington answered the field telephone. "There's two more at the other crossing."

"Here they come." Patty pointed and the rest looked through the firing slits. A steel plate with three loopholes moved out of the construction shelter, quickly sliding down the rails to the water, helped by pushing fighters. Then it slowed, presumably due to its weight since the bridge definitely dipped as the contraption moved onto the first floating section. The fighters ducked down under a steel cover extending back from the top.

"Ask your man to shoot at it with a special, but move bloody quick afterwards because those armoured things are waiting for a target." Harold put his sights on the steel plate and frowned. The shape tugged at his mind but he couldn't place it. A shot rang out echoed by a loud clang and then two return shots, one from each vehicle. "Is he all right?"

"Yup. Laid flat and trying not to swear loud enough for us to hear. What happened?" Wellington smiled. "I kept my head down."

Harold moved his sights along the shield and grimaced. "No penetration. All I can see is a bright mark. The shape looks familiar."

"It's from a grader, one of those giant earthmovers with the blade in the middle, though that one is cut short. Maybe one cut in half?" The man who spoke up shrugged. "I worked on building roads for a bit."

"Look on the bright side." A Geek with binoculars looked over with relief showing in his voice and face. "They've just poked gun barrels out of the slots but they're shotguns, not rifles. No, er, effing good until they get closer."

"Plan C then, or is it D?" Wellington glanced at Emmy. "Oh dear, help, we can't stop it. We'll just try to shoot the nasty gangsters following it." He winked at her. "Could you shoot those nasty people in the trucks before they shoot our men, please? I'd pretty please but that bit broke."

Emmy laughed. Wellington's humour was definitely helping everyone to cope with the stress. "My pleasure. Harold?"

"Count of three from Wellington when he's set with the onagers. Take the truck on the left first. We'll go for the first two loopholes in the back and the Geek rifles go for the driver." Harold glanced at Wellington. "Remind your people. Duck and move."

"I'll get the rifles at the other crossing to shoot at about the same time." Wellington spoke on the field telephone, and waited until someone confirmed the others were ready. "Ready?" Harold and Emmy confirmed without looking away from the scopes. "Three, two, one, fire." The two rifles rapped out almost as one and both Harold and Emmy rolled sideways away from their slits. Moments later so did everyone else even if they hadn't fired, all hugging the dirt. "Holy shit!" A pale-faced Wellington glanced at Patty and did his best to shrug while lying flat. "Sorry, but two automatics?"

An equally white-faced Patty tried to smile back. "Sometimes cripes doesn't quite cover it. What the hell are they, Harold?"

"Like Wellington said, automatics, machine guns." Harold glanced along the defences to where two Geeks lay spread-eagled and another huddled up, nursing a shoulder. "Some sort of machine gun, but not a heavy one or it'd probably chew right through our cover."

Wellington recovered enough to use the field telephone, speaking to his men further along the line and those opposite the other bridge. "There's two automatics at the other crossing as well, in the trucks. We lost three men there and another further along here. There's several wounded, but your pair are safe." A single shot cracked out and a man further along the defences flew backwards and laid still. Wellington raised his voice. "Keep down, there's snipers as well. Anyone see how the bombs did?"

A man raised his hand on the other side of the dead one. "That shot came from the back of the truck. The damn thing moved as soon as the fucking bombs went over so we missed. Er, sorry."

"Which means the bullets bounced." Harold eased up carefully to look out of a different slit. "Remind your men to keep the rifle barrel well back in the slit, not poked through." He looked at the loophole he'd fired at through the scope, then the driver's door. "Your blokes hit, Wellington, but the rounds only left a bright mark. Those plates are very hard, maybe real armour plate hard."

"Which means we can't stop the damn things. Swear, swear. Though they can't hit the onagers even with automatics." Wellington frowned. "Most of the fighters will get back off the bridge when we break it since we can't really open up. Not with bloody automatics targeting anyone who tries." He glanced at Patty and then at a row of men with missile weapons stood behind a high wall. "We'll get some with bows and crossbows, by lofting the shafts, but their shields will stop most arrows."

"Maybe we can still get the trucks. Tell your men to target the engine on the one on the right because the bonnets aren't armoured with the same plates. We'll do the same, because with luck the specials will break the engine block or at least chew up the wiring. Throw a few bombs just the same, but send over a couple of your Molotovs or ours mixed with them." Harold put another hardened round in the Blazer. "If we stop the engine whoever is in the back won't want to roast."

"Oh yes, a plan E, or F for flipping heck? Count of three again?" Wellington used the field telephone to the team covering the other bridge, then spoke to the onager operator. "Three, two, one, fire." The shots rapped out and again automatic gunfire raked the defences while everyone ducked.

Patty peeked. "Crap, it moved just far enough to avoid the bombs. Now a lot of fighters are coming out of the shed thing and running down to the bridge. Why have both trucks started moving again?"

"Not crap, hit the engine again." Wellington had the telephone to his ear and a big smile. "The one opposite the other bridge stopped."

"Be quick Harold, they're trying to turn." Patty stayed watching as Emmy and Harold took aim.

"Duck Patty. Emmy, three, two, one, fire." The automatics lashed out again straight after the shots, but further along more shots rapped out and a man cheered.

"It's stopped! It's stopped! The fucking truck has stopped!" The Geek dived flat as he realised his waving hand would have shown above the earthwork.

Wellington spoke rapidly on the telephone and grinned. "Roast sniper coming up. We've just straddled the stopped one at the other crossing with bombs and Molotovs and it's not moved. The onagers here are loading with just Molotovs. What about the other truck?"

Harold moved five slits along to look. "Crap is right this time. They're parking with the rear facing this way, and the rear is wider than the bonnet. Even if we moved further along we might not get penetration at an angle. On the good side, there's only one loophole in the rear." He moved to the side to see the damaged truck as both onagers fired. Molotovs fell on and around the vehicle bathing it in flames. "Watch for the back door opening on the burning one. Use soft lead bullets." The nearby Geeks passed the message along to their riflemen.

"You've lost the onagers, Soldier Boy. We've got to use them to break the bridge now."

Harold barely heard Wellington. He fixed his attention firmly on that door, visible because the truck had partly turned away before the damage stopped the engine. The loophole in the rear door spat automatic fire and the other truck joined in to lash the defences, but further along from Harold. The gunfire from the burning truck stopped, the rear door and driver's door flew open, and a rifle cracked from further along the Geek line. The incoming from the automatic in the undamaged truck shifted to suppress that rifle, giving Harold all the time in the world.

Even then he didn't shoot the man trying to get out of the rear because another shot rang out, and the man carrying the distinctive shape of an AK flew back into the truck. Harold snapped off a shot at the driver before ducking.

This time Harold stayed down as the remaining automatic worked over his section of the defences. He watched the next two loads sail up and over him from the onagers and one bomb seemed to stay up there. Harold blinked. "Is your drone up, Wellington?" Then Harold realised this one flew too high and had wings, unlike the circular plastic toy the Geeks used. "It's an Army drone, smile everyone."

"Let's hope they really, really don't like automatics. Annoy that truck enough to keep the bloody thing firing, will you?" Sheer glee sounded in Wellington's voice but Harold wasn't happy. That automatic sat under six hundred yards away, which seemed a bit close for artillery when the Army were only working from a drone camera. Still, Wellington had a point so as soon as the weapon stopped firing, Harold did his best to stick a round through the loophole. So did Emmy and the three Geek riflemen, though when that became two Geek riflemen the other shooters became even more keen on moving quickly and erratically.

Harold had annoyed the gunner over there again and lay keeping his head down when he saw Patty open the long box a Geek had brought her. She pulled out a longer crossbow bolt, with the last four inches being made of thicker tube with a fuse. Patty saw him looking and waved it. "A little something from Tell because he says my old crossbow is the only prototype left. The newer ones are lighter and handier, but mine has more brute power." She smirked. "That means I can loft this into the target at this range, without sticking my fragile head above the parapets." Patty's expression morphed into a snarl. "I'm going to burn off the end of the bridge so Wellington can kill those bastards on it."

The Geek soldier stayed, holding a lit candle in a jar. Patty knelt, loaded the arrow, nodded for him to light the fuse, raised her crossbow and sent the missile up at a steep angle trailing a line of smoke. The Geek scuttled forward to look through a firing slit, before ducking again. "Just over a metre short."

Patty cranked her crossbow again and reached for another arrow. "Wellington? The next shot should hit." Wellington raised a hand to acknowledge her before speaking into the phone. Patty let the next shaft go and the Geek confirmed she'd hit the wide strip of liquid on the far bank.

More bombs sailed over, but every time anyone with a gun tried to target the men now on the bridge the rifle or automatic in the truck would open up. Arrows and crossbow bolts flew up and over while a couple of Geeks peered through firing slits to call out corrections. Harold rolled away after another attempt at the loophole and then yelled in pain and rolled again. He twisted to look for the reason his ass felt as if it had been set on fire. The spreading bloodstain on his jeans gave him a hint. "Watch out!" Emmy and Patty looked over. "There might be more rifles."

Wellington sent a query up the line. While he waited for replies Harold stuffed a pad down his jeans to try and stop the bleeding. "Yes, at least one rifle on top of the bank but I can't spare an onager to sort it out. Our riflemen will try to keep the bastard's head down." The Geek warchief sighed. "We might be in trouble. We're trying to sink the bridge at yon end but even that might not be enough."

More bombs went up and over. The automatic moved on to targeting someone else allowing Harold to take a quick look. The bombs landed on the far end of the bridge but as far as Harold could see the men kicked them all off. More men jumped onto the bridge, through the line of flame on the bank where the dark liquid had ignited. "They kicked them off!"

"Good. Those are some of yours in plastic tubs of metal scrap. Einstein suggested cutting the fuses long. With luck they'll rupture the floats when they explode in the water." Wellington looked decidedly unhappy. "We need luck."

Instead of trying for the truck again Harold fired at the men now coming over the grader blade. Molotovs might have bathed it in flame and stopped anyone pushing but men were still coming up and over, running for the Geek end of the bridge. "They're coming across." Harold looked back at the fifteen of his fighters with pistols and shotguns. "Get ready. Keep your heads down between shots." At eighty yards the water's edge lay a bit beyond accurate range, especially with a lot of incoming fire. Bess nodded, a relief to Harold because she'd be the one most likely to forget to duck.

Harold fired at the truck again, then rolled. A bullet came in through his loophole but missed him. As he peeked out of the next one, someone further down the line shouted "Now!" Harold glanced over and saw a Geek pouring liquid into a tube. He looked back at the men now leaping onto the bank and the numbers following, raising his rifle again. If it hadn't been for the covering fire from the bloody truck the attackers would have been sitting ducks. Someone shouted "Ignition!" Harold aimed at a man with a shotgun but before he fired the entire water's edge erupted!

The grass along the edge of the water flew skywards and the whole end float and bridge section flipped back onto the men on the bridge. The water itself burst into flame, and so did the wrecked end of the bridge! Harold lifted his aim to shoot a man who had stopped, frozen in shock even as he climbed over the steel shield. He waved the Orchard Close fighters forward. "Aimed shots, first option, three at a time!" Geeks were popping up above the earthworks to fire at the men on the bank before ducking again.

"Five." Fergie, Tilly and Chris, one of Roy's men, dived forward to the loopholes. Chris emptied his double-barrelled shotgun while the women each fired four quick shots down the bank then rolled back. "Three." Another team of three did the same but further along. Harold had told Matthew to use random loopholes, and hoped the redhead didn't drop into a pattern. No chance, because Matthew was throwing dice! "Two."

"Keep still." Patty yanked Harold's jeans down far enough to tape a pad over the hole in his ass, then pulled Harold's jeans back up. She crawled back to her crossbow and started lofting shafts again, though not the burning ones. Harold moved back up to a firing slit since the automatic had stopped, and tried to hit that bloody loophole again.

"Crap, they're bringing more bridge down to replace the sunk bit at yon end!" Patty moved back and cranked her crossbow frantically. "They'll bring more men across."

Harold moved to another firing slit and shot a man on the bridge before rolling away as a bullet hit the bricks nearby. More of the attackers were risking the flames this end to get onto the bank, then lying down to shoot at the Geeks. The defenders were being pinning by the General's rifles and automatic while the attackers gained a foothold on this bank. More bombs flew over and screams sounded after the explosions so Darwin hadn't used long fuses this time.

Harold's firing positions were quiet again so he picked one for another go at the truck. The line of smoke coming in and hitting the vehicle arrived without noise, but everyone heard the explosion as the cab disintegrated and the entire armoured back flew off! Harold's eyes automatically followed the line of smoke back to a rapidly swelling dot as another line of smoke went past and out of sight towards the other bridge. Harold saw the two black dots dropping from the plane as it grew larger and flattened himself. "Down! Down! Down! Get down!"

All firing from the men on the bridge or the Geeks stopped when the Eurofighter screamed by overhead. Moments later a thumping noise and a whoomph rather than an explosion left Harold feeling much happier, because he'd been worried about fragmentation. The wash of heat confirmed just what the jet had dropped. A quick look confirmed that whatever the automatic weapon had been, nobody would be using it again. The two parts of the vehicle lay off-centre of the sea of flame, but not enough off-centre to escape. A rattle of exploding ammunition confirmed just how damn hot that fire must be. On the other side of the attack a dull thud sealed the fate of the other truck as its fuel tank finally went up.

Wellington's voice rang out in the stunned silence. "Now kill the fuckers, kill them all!" With a roar the Geeks threw themselves forward, standing along the defence line to open up with every weapon that could be brought to bear on the crowded bridge. The section of bridge next to the far back had now completely sunk and flames covered the stretch of water, widening the wall of fire on the bank. The onagers bombarded the men still coming down the bank beyond the flames, the vicious explosions ripping into those waiting to cross and the replacement bridge sections.

The fifteen from Orchard Close all moved up to the slits, firing single aimed shots with their handguns. In contrast the Geeks were standing up above their defences, blazing away as fast as possible. The men still on the bridge were about a hundred and fifty yards away, but the Orchard Close rounds were probably hitting the group. After the battle at the mart Harold experimented, then all his shooters had practiced hitting a group as large as the attackers on the bridge at these sorts of distances.

The shield hadn't moved, stuck three-quarters of the way across and still bathed in flame. Those who had jumped over and run towards the Geeks' end to leap onto the bank reeled as bullets and shafts tore into them. More men surged up and over the steel, through the flames, running straight into those trying to get back and chaos reigned as the Geeks poured more gunfire and arrows into them.

"Charge! Let's get 'em!" The Geeks surged up and over their earthworks and charged down the bank. Any surviving attackers at the water's edge died in a few frantic, bloody minutes. The Geeks opened fire on the bridge again, but from much closer now. Someone on the other side still fired back, because Geeks started to fall.

"Harold. On top of the bank. I just saw a rifle firing." Emmy pointed. "There's no firing slits up there away from the burning areas so he has to show himself to fire." She put her eye to her sights. "With luck he'll show himself long enough."

"Damn, I forgot the General's other rifles. You take the stretch to the left of where you pointed." Harold settled his sights on the right of the spot and waited.

For a while the fire and fury raged on barely heeded, then a rifle shot cracked out. "Gottim!"

A startled head popped up near Harold's sights to look across so he re-targeted and shot the man. "Maybe got the spotter." Harold looked at the bridge, swallowing hard as his gut churned. This end and the water around it were ablaze, while bodies and wounded cluttered the unburned section back to the shield. Nearly thirty feet of the other end had now slipped underwater, leaving the water in the gap and the bank beyond burning furiously. Even as he watched, Harold saw squat shapes landing in the water around the far end of the bridge. He winced because he knew exactly what they were, one gallon plastic tubs full of petrol and oil with a Barry special. Even as that section and the water exploded in flame, adding to the inferno, the second onager dropped bombs into the men crowded on the bank.

"Emmy? If nobody is aiming this way, shoot the men who are burning. Mercy shots."

Emmy's quiet reply contrasted sharply with her elation of moments before. "Yeah. That's not a good way for anyone to go." Her rifle cracked.

On the bridge the trapped men behind the steel barrier were maintaining discipline even as they were slowly whittled down. They held their shields up above them to deflect any bombs and arrows, partially protected by the burning digger blade while shooting back at the Geeks. A few tried to swim back through the wall of flames to the bank, but most swimmers stopped and started thrashing and screaming as the flames bit deeper. Their comrades were shooting the ones who made it to the bank out of sheer pity. Harold concentrated on killing those still shooting or anyone with a shotgun.

"Burn, baby, burn." Wellington's voice sounded above the background noise. Harold looked up, then at the middle of the bridge as two loads of bombs fell towards those under the raised shields. Harold barely registered the lines connecting the missiles before they dropped onto the men and instead of bouncing off the shields, wrapped around the group for long seconds. A few screamed when they realised the bombs were tied together in a big web, but then the explosions started and they all screamed. Harold winced and looked away, but he couldn't shut out the sounds. Wellington had found an effective use for Barry's skin burning bombs.

The disciplined group came apart as frantic fighters ran for the water, even the burning patches, or rolled in agony as the fire bit deeper. Nobody stopped to help the wounded because everyone who could move tried to run away, in many cases beating at the flames sprouting from their clothes. Harold shifted to mercy killing as those still mobile threw themselves into the water to get to the bank, any bank.

Even as he did the onagers lifted their fire again to ravage those retreating up the far bank with a mixture of explosives and more of Barry's incendiaries. Men rolled around screaming, torn by shrapnel or frantically beating at the smoke and flame sprouting in their clothes and hair. Down by the water's edge many Geeks had run along the bank each way to shoot past the wall of flame. Some poured fire into any survivors on the remaining floating section of bridge, stranded in the middle of the flood. Others concentrated on anyone swimming along the cutting to try and get clear of the flames.

"Suck on this, bastards." A deep twang followed Wellington's words. The streak of smoke disappearing into the construction shed showed that Wellington had brought up the ballista now the General's covering fire had gone. Three more missiles and flames licked out of the front of the building as fire took hold inside.

By that time the onagers had stopped. Even the Geeks took the time to aim now because the targets were fewer, and more interested in escape than fighting back. Eventually the last attacker slipped below the water, ran over the opposite hill out of sight, or died screaming in the flames. Relative silence descended as the shooting slackened and then died away. Almost silence, because on the far bank some wounded still whimpered or cried out for help above the crackle of flames. A few Geeks cheered, but most of them looked shocked at what they'd done.

* * *

Behind the firing positions everyone stood up, taking in the scene. "Cripes." An arm slipped around Harold. "Really cripes Harold." Emmy came up on the other side and Harold propped his rifle up against the bricks to put his other arm round her.

"That worked better than expected. Better than the other end but we got the other shield and killed," Wellington gave Patty a tired smile, "a shitload." His pale face didn't look particularly triumphant. He looked up to where the drone still flew and raised a hand to wave at it. "The RAF made the difference in the end. Well, sort of." Wellington seemed to be rambling a little, with his eyes skipping here and there over the scene below. "The bombs in the bank did a bit. Your extra bombs did a bit. The extra rifles did as well. Those dinky bullets helped. The onagers worked well. The waterproof fuses added a bit. Those fire bombs...." He shook his head. "Even then, with those automatics still firing the result wouldn't have been so...." He looked over the scene. "Conclusive." The Geek warchief took a deep breath. "We'll replace anything you need."

Harold shrugged. "Only sugar really and some propellant but we didn't use much." Louie had gone to help the other Orchard Close fighters applying dressings and bandages or picking up their brass. To Harold's relief the wounded were all mobile and conscious, and the wounds seemed to be all in arms. "How did it go at the other bridge?"

"We lost twelve men there, and fifteen here, most of them when they ran down the bank to get nearer. There were a good few of ours wounded when they were lined up on the bank but by then the General's men weren't taking the time to aim. Yours are all alive, though some are wounded." Wellington pointed towards the burning shed on the other side of the water. "The ballista will move along the cutting and burn all those huts. Just to make sure there'll be no repeat." The Geek swayed a little unsteadily. "I've been in fights. This is different."

Patty held out her other arm. "No other Geek, but I reckon I'm safe with you?"

"Really?" Wellington put an arm round her. "True though... Oh. You know?" He looked over at Harold.

Harold glanced round but nobody stood near enough to hear his lowered voice. "I spread the word a bit in case I'm not about if the time comes. Umeko is very happy."

"I'll pass that on." They stood for a while watching as Geeks brought some kayaks down to the water and paddled out to the surviving bridge sections. A few screams rang out as machetes flashed in the weak sun. Some men began to prise the burning section of bridge with the shield free of the rest, while the kayaks came back to ferry men to the other bank.

"It won't make such a good shield now. Heat will knacker the steel I'm told, though it's still thick." Harold raised his head to look at the top of the opposite bank. "The same with the metal on those armoured trucks, thank all and any gods."

"Amen. One of my men at the other bridge recognised the shapes. They're hardened steel targets for shooting ranges. He used to blast away at them with shotguns." Wellington grimaced. "I really hope that's all the General has got, had got."

"Probably or he'd have covered the bonnets as well." Harold frowned. "What the hell did you do at this end of the bridge?" Harold had just remembered the men pouring something into a funnel.

"I mined a wide section along the bank to be sure of getting this end of the bridge. We did it under cover of putting stakes opposite all those huts he put up, once I saw those pontoons. Unfortunately I needed over half of our bombs to be sure of getting the two bridge ends, and that's why we wanted more from you. We buried a couple of lengths of plastic downpipe at the same time so we could pour oil and petrol down them into the water." Wellington spat as if getting rid of a bad taste. "That's worse than I expected, people burning like that."

"This is cosy." The four of them parted, turning to face a grinning Hawkins. "Watch out Welly, or you'll be in trouble back home. You'll be nagged. You'd better hope she's not found a cane."

"Not really. Patty is a lady so I'm barely bruised." Wellington seemed used to the comments about his home life, and not particularly bothered. "We were just wondering what the General will do next?"

"Beat his head bloody against a wall? I suppose it's too much to hope the bastard came in one of those trucks?" Hawkins looked at the burning shed. "That or he was lurking in there? Though I doubt we'd be that lucky. What do you reckon, Soldier Boy?"

"I keep being told he's a computer General so maybe he doesn't get up the sharp end." Harold grinned wolfishly. "If he does, I'll bet he needs a power-up pretty damn badly." Everyone laughed at that, the mood starting to lift.

"Welly is a computer general as well, but his power-up didn't work right." Hawkins tapped his lips.

"Is that right?" Harold looked over at the carnage. "I guess you won the title and the cup or posh certificate."

"Ah well, I played paintball and D&D as well as the one on one computer tournaments and shoot-em-ups. I learned to combine different skills in a team of real people, and that people don't obey or react like computers. Though never in something like this." Wellington wasn't joking at all now. "None of them stink like this, and even the best simulations don't scream like real people." He looked out over the scene again. "I guess we're about done. Whatever the loot is, I'm sure even this tight-fisted sod will send you some if you want to get home?"

"Good enough for me. Tammy will be missing her mummy." Harold smiled innocently. "If you let me have the bombs you didn't use, we'll get off."

Hawkins stared. "How do you know there's any left?"

Harold chuckled. "Ours explode with pretty colours, didn't you notice? Whichever of your people saved a few of our bombs, tell him hard luck. Roy will have been counting at the other bridge." Harold had no idea if anyone had done any such thing but thought it highly likely.

"Don't piss Soldier Boy about, Hawkins, because that also means the arses stopped firing while they had some left. I'm not really impressed by that. If Einstein or Darwin have been cute and saved a few, tell them to give or I'll shove one someplace inventive." Wellington waved a hand to encompass the scene. "Without all the bits of this and that, the extra bombs, different bombs, bullets, the RAF and whatever, the result would have been closer and nothing like as cheap." He grinned at his gang leader. "Nobel will work out how they're made from the colours, just to avoid the shit he'll get from you."

"Don't grin like that in daylight, not without a mask. I've just eaten." Hawkins shrugged. "I'll let them know, with the 'or else' bit as well. After all, taking one apart might be a bit dodgy." The Geek boss swept the Orchard Close fighters with his eyes. "Are you leaving now, or has Wellington invited you for a sleepover?"

"It might be a bit crowded. Besides, we should get our beauty sleep before New Year." Harold frowned. "Only a few days now."

Hawkins sniggered. "Oh yes, party time, though misery won't come to ours any more. He's a home boy now." Wellington shrugged and smiled, before beckoning over a couple of men to escort the Orchard Close party home and bring back the two hostages. Within half an hour the thirty-eight of them, eleven wounded but none needing a stretcher, were getting into the transit vans and pickup truck. A Geek delivered four padded boxes, each containing two unused bombs.

"How did you manage that, Roy." Harold inspected the pad bandaged to Roy's head.

"I moved after shooting like you keep saying, but I'm a bit lazy and didn't move far. The bastard put a round through the slit and it ricocheted off a brick." He touched his head, wincing. "I hope my headache is gone by New Year but I'll still be wearing this. Fancy dress? Wounded hero?"

"That could work." Patty inspected it. "You'll need a bit of red on the bandage, and you should practice a brave smile as if you're in agony?"

"I am in agony. Maybe I can get my hand held? My head kissed?"

"You've more chance of getting your wound kissed than Harold has." Harold left Roy and Patty verbally sparring about who might get what kissed better and checked everyone else. Wellington had told the truth. The wounds were painful and bloody but not life-threatening, and with a bit of luck not crippling. On the way back a subdued Emmy, worried about Tammy, complained that she really needed to get back. Tammy had enough milk for another three days if necessary because Emmy had built up a reserve in case of mishaps, but she worried anyway. She cheered up a bit by teasing Harold about needing to cut down on burgers so his ass didn't stick up.

Emmy soon lapsed into talking about the bloody mess they'd just been in, and both agreed a war with the Geeks could be very nasty. Despite Caddi's opinion, with Wellington's brain directing them the erstwhile shop assistants were a force to reckon with. The drone gave Wellington an edge but he had exploited that ruthlessly, folding in every tiny extra to deal the General a crushing blow. Despite both of them liking the Geek warchief, if a war started Wellington would be top of the sniper target list.

Harold pointed out that the marks he had seen on the truck showed that the Geek rifleman were getting better. Emmy thought the onagers could be more dangerous than rifles. She suggested knocking down any cover out to at least seven hundred yards from the walls of Orchard Close. Those walls looked both impressive and very welcoming when the vans arrived home. A crowd of anxious residents descended on the party, while Patricia and Lenny swooped down on the wounded and set into cleaning and inspecting and patching.

Chapter 8:

A New Year, a New Start

The days to New Year seemed a little unreal to Harold and probably the other thirty-seven who had been to the Geeks. As with the previous fight the rest of Orchard Close had seen nothing, and this time there were no fatalities. Apart from Harold and the long graze that had just missed the top of Roy's ear all the rest hit arms. The only conclusion had to be that shooting from cover and aiming two-handed, their arms were the biggest bit exposed. Orchard Close had been remarkably lucky. Roy thought that the General's men had targeted Geeks because they were easier targets, especially at the end when the Geek fighters charged and lined up on the bank. The General's rifles on the ridge certainly had because apart from Harold and Roy, the Orchard Close wounds were all from underpowered pistol reloads. Even Harold only had half the ricocheted round in his ass when Lenny dug it out.

The contrast between the slaughter on the bridges at the end and the happy, smiling faces preparing for New Year kept catching Harold out. The knowledge that the General would be licking his wounds for a while yet might have been one reason for the bright smiles. Another reason might be Harold's ass. Harold didn't mind the hilarity about his wound, because he'd got off light according to Lenny. He wouldn't be sitting comfortably for a while, but the angle meant the fragment went from top to bottom of Harold's buttock, only hitting muscle.

The residents who had hoped for a snowman competition decided they didn't need snow, just a competition. The theme for New Year's fancy dress should be snow. Harold's bee suit had little white snowflakes or possibly snowballs all over instead of yellow strips, with one red one on his ass of course.

Celine's white dress made her a snow-lady with some frills on the shoulders and her head to represent snowfall. Those competing for the mystery prize seemed to think either the snowflakes, snowballs or bits of white rabbit fur or lace snowfall worked just as well more or less on their own. The dance itself turned out to be lively and cheerful, and Harold found that New Year had a lot more Happy than he'd expected.

Even the car delivering a dozen pistols, two small calibre shotguns, a small bag of ammunition, some machetes and bags of sugar for bombs didn't spoil Harold's mood. Hawkins had definitely stiffed Orchard Close over their share of the loot but right now Harold didn't care. The General had been knocked back, and none of Harold's people had died.

*　　*　　*

In the bunker the atmosphere definitely bordered on festive. "Glasgow worked well, Maurice, Vanna. I really did worry." Owen smiled happily.

"I'm definitely relieved because we don't have to feed or even guard Glasgow any more. The extra protein meant for an entire enclosure can be spread elsewhere and will make a real difference to the other forty-three." Ivy raised a hand. "I'd toast you if these meetings weren't dry."

Owen laughed. "Not as dry as Glasgow. Maurice arranged for the breakout to go in exactly the right direction and persuaded almost all the population to join in. A few guards will still be needed, but there's no way what is left will become another London."

"I spent hours trying to work out why the fools did that, ran off into the snow." Ivy, the redhead in charge of the marts, frowned. "Why did the fools do that?"

"Rumours were spread of stockpiles at Fort William. More rumours followed that the Navy had pulled out of Fastlane nuclear submarine base but some of the stores and all the accommodation blocks and generators were intact." Maurice spread his hands, smirking. "The blizzard had been predicted but we didn't tell the inhabitants of Glasgow." Maurice paused for effect. "Then we cut the electricity and water."

Ivy smiled. "Nicely done. They all left to get to a place there would be food and electricity."

"Exactly. We sacrificed some of the less reliable mart guards to man the overwhelmed posts. That motivated the civilian contractors sent in to clear the docks for you, Gerard. They will clean up the rest of Glasgow when the weather is a little better." Joshua grinned. "The real Army were waiting with artillery once the mob were out in the open, and with armour and rifles at Fort William in case they got that far."

"Did you get them all?" Henry, the bearded farms manager, shrugged. "We don't want them over on the east coast of Scotland where the farms are."

"Any survivors fled into the mountains where they'll be under metres of snow for another two months." Joshua laughed. "The weather up there is so bad even the sheep have come down to the lowlands or died. Better yet, the survivors left in the city will mark their own positions by burning wood to keep warm. We'll plot the smoke and areas where heat has melted the snow, then the civilian contractors can stroll in and collect them before spring."

"That business about cutting off the electricity to drive them out takes one item off my agenda." Grace used the control to show Orchard Close ablaze with coloured lights, then moved on to show other enclaves that had similar decorations lit up. "I know the wave generators, wind farms, Solar Panels, Hydro and nuclear are more than enough now, but I'd been going to suggest rationing electricity to stop this sort of wastage." She mock-bowed towards Maurice without getting out of her chair. "Now I can see that keeping the scum firmly tied into electricity as a reliable source of heat and light is useful, for the effect when we do cut them off."

Henry settled back and relaxed. "Good point. Now what about that other business, the brave citizens and all that rubbish. Will you use that again when you show Glasgow?"

"Definitely, as a contrast. We've more footage now, of another battle and this time they killed real scum, a lot of them. Annoyingly, the wrong scum but the propaganda will be a consolation prize. The Army drones even have pictures of more women fighting, that one with a crossbow again for God's sake. The same one who showed up on the footage of the first battle. Ah, there might be a problem." Maurice frowned, looking over at Faraz, the RAF liaison. "Do you have the proper sequence of events leading up to the Eurofighter strike?"

"The request came from the Army, a properly authorised strike mission against automatic weapons." Faraz shrugged. "The mission brief didn't specifically mention Army personnel being under fire, but did ask for speed which is why control sent a jet. The pilot received co-ordinates and clear pictures of the targets from the forward controller. He hit them both as instructed. Textbook."

Maurice looked at Joshua. "The Army?"

"Drones moved to investigate the firing of automatic weapons within two miles of the bypass. Since the fight seemed to be between two gangs, the operator left the situation until the maximum scum died and then would have sent a helicopter." Joshua looked at Maurice with a rueful smile. "Reading between the lines the operator recognised the woman with the crossbow, and decided that the bloody but unbowed should stay that way. I can't argue because those trucks were properly armoured which might have been a nasty surprise at a mart or Army post."

"No they wouldn't, because I knew about them. Never mind. Though I'll have to put some serious thought into how I can get those maniacs to attack again." Maurice laughed. "One setback is insignificant because elsewhere the plans for eradicating democracies are starting to succeed. These particular maniacs already wiped out two."

The chairman frowned at the spymaster. "You might have known about that armour, Maurice, but Joshua's and Vanna's people didn't. Telling them after one of our posts had been slaughtered would have been too late. Perhaps you will share this sort of news another time? You tend to keep everything to yourself, but that isn't always the best way."

Maurice looked at the two frowning faces, and the other unhappy ones, and sobered. "A valid point. My apologies Joshua, Vanna." Both nodded acceptance of Maurice's apology, though Joshua's came grudgingly.

Owen smiled. "Excellent. Actually in this case preserving the women might be more important than the army getting protective, if we can truly exploit them." Joshua looked over at Grace, then Vanna. "Has there been any word?"

Maurice interrupted any reply. "Yes. The blonde has survived but we could be waiting months to get to her because she's been shot through a lung. I'm surprised they managed to save her life, and a bit annoyed she didn't end up asking the Army for medical help. The Army, or the squaddies in particular, would have been overjoyed to rescue her." Maurice smirked, obviously recovered from his rebuke. "We have sources near enough to keep track."

"Why don't we invite that whole enclave out of the city, and give them a farm up on the Scottish Borders. Then we'll have willing candidates for your propaganda machine." Boris the diplomat looked at Vanna. "Why arrest her? It won't make her more inclined to help us."

"No mission creep. Those innocents just slaughtered two attacking forces and are unlikely to make obedient little drones." Owen glanced at Maurice. "We don't want that blonde happy and smiling, we want her defeated, injured and desperate if possible. If she has been badly abused and we rescue her, that works even better. The propaganda will prime the Army and stop them sympathising with anyone inside the enclosures." Boris subsided, frowning.

"Don't worry, I'll motivate her regardless of her condition when she arrives. When will you tell the other cities about the breakout from Glasgow?"

Grace glanced at Vanna. "We don't want unrest or similar breakout attempts elsewhere unless there are extra forces in place."

"Later, let the animals enjoy New Year. Then we'll mix shots of the honest citizens elsewhere enjoying New Year with the foolish residents of Glasgow dying in the snow. Our blonde and her friends can help with the contrast, since they're one of the enclaves with Christmas lights up." Maurice smiled happily. "The general opinion in the other cities is that the local idiots should have stopped the attack on the Glasgow mart. We'll just reinforce that, especially with the latest fighting. Those few gangs, and especially that one enclave, are developing into a handy propaganda tool."

"Don't get carried away with clever propaganda, Maurice. We don't want more squirrels. More spam or possibly some help from Argentina would help more than pretty pictures?" Ivy raised an eyebrow at Owen and then Gerard. "Or has some other problem come up?"

"No problems. There'll be beef for our people and Corned Beef for the scum very soon. The ships will be here more or less as the last snow south of Scotland melts, either just before or just after Valentine's." The youngest cabal member smiled. "If it's before then Corned Beef might be more popular than a card or chocolate as a gift." The cabal members laughed and Gerard rapped on the wooden table with his knuckles. "For luck, because we seem to be finally getting the situation here under control." Several others rapped the wood for luck as well.

"What about elsewhere? Is the rest of the world starting to settle down, Boris?"

Boris shrugged. "Not exactly settled, but nothing really worrying. According to my reports the Chinese Army splintered once the national leadership were removed. After a generation of obedience brainwashing, the soldiers simply transferred their loyalty to their commanders and now each general is trying to carve his own empire. The Chinese navy are more interested in defending their bases than getting ambitious."

Boris moved those reports to one side, clicking to alter the view and highlight the Chinese-Russian border. "The Russian and Chinese forces facing each other on the border both believed the other had launched an attack and called up reinforcements. Both were ordered to attack again and are badly mauled with their munitions depleted. Both sides desperately need resupply which won't arrive. The allied navies based in Australia and New Zealand have control of the southern Pacific."

"I'm more interested in the Atlantic, or rather the countries with fleets that might interfere here?" Victor the Navy liaison shrugged. "Purely as a practical matter, the Pacific doesn't really impact us here."

"My apologies, those will be next. Though first there's the land border with Europe since that might also have some impact." The view shifted to the eastern borders of Europe. "The entire area is chaotic. Some of the armed groups have armour so we must be ready if they combine and strike west."

"The Russians?" Henry held up his hand. "Sorry, I always worry about the Russians."

Boris laughed. "The remaining Russian forces along that border have withdrawn to the Crimea where they have cover from the fleet. They are launching air strikes at any of the armoured groups they can find." He glanced at Victor. "Like all Russian naval units the Black Sea Fleet are still obeying orders, not least because that protects their home bases and families."

The map changed again and several of those present sighed. "The USA. Now those ships I really worry about. One of their fleets putting to sea would drive a coach and horses through all our plans." Victor grimaced. "We would be forced to ask our colleagues in Russia to arrange a confrontation and the whole affair would spiral out of control."

"No need, Victor. The US Navy also have orders keeping the ships tied up so the crews can help to maintain law and order round their bases. Most of the remaining US Army are trying to deal with the people from the population centres, who are spread across the country and stripping it bare. Our allies are stirring race hatred, religious hatred, and sheer bloody-mindedness to keep everyone fighting their neighbours." Boris smiled. "That encourages the Navy to look after their bases."

He changed the schematic to show the USA land forces. "The country is regressing to States, each using their own National Guards to try and impose order and defend food stocks from their own and neighbouring irregulars. Every private army and nut group are in on the act, and the number of American soldiers abroad when their transport failed to arrive has helped." He chuckled. "The chaos following the death of pretty much the entire top tier of American government still hasn't settled down. The survivors are all our people."

"Any time scale on the chaos settling down, Boris?"

"Not really Owen. There is no chance of the US refineries being repaired until all the fighting dies down. There's plenty of oil of course, but burning refineries is now a national sport." Boris highlighted various places on the map. "Actually an international sport which might be awkward in time."

"We can shoot those problems when necessary." Owen started to smile.

"But we can continue on the assumption that no major force will suddenly interfere."

"Yes Owen." Boris rapped on the wooden table. "For luck of course, but we can get back to dealing with our own problems." The discussion that followed, about the increased quantities of foodstuffs and the first shipments of refined fuels, kept the atmosphere cheery for the rest of the meeting.

Vanna and Maurice both hung back without any prompting. Maurice spoke first. "The air strike to support civilians is worrying. If the Army are going to be picking favourites, eradicating some enclaves could be a real problem."

"Both the Army and RAF might be a problem. The pilots are downright triumphant about who they saved because someone let them know." Vanna frowned. "What happens when we authorise the final clearance of an enclosure where the Army have local favourites? They may not attack, or the RAF might get cold feet."

Owen frowned thoughtfully. "Perhaps we should send a few weapons into your watching posts, Maurice. They are manned by Vanna's people, so there'll be no leaks to the Army or the scum. We could send something capable of killing a tank or two, or blowing a pilot out of the sky when fired from one of those innocent enclosures?"

"Oh yes, that should concentrate minds." Vanna smirked. "We can always use the same weapons to remove other problems nearer to home if required?"

"Looking for silver linings again, Vanna? I will look through the lists of munitions the refugee armed forces brought with them. Both the types you'll need will probably be among the shipments from Brest." Owen glanced at the exit with a half-smile. "You had better catch up. I'll let you know where to collect the items."

*   *   *

Nearer to Orchard Close, Vulcan also wore a half-smile when he saw Harold for the next trading session. "You've been holding out on us, Soldier Boy. That's mean after I let you have that rifle."

"You couldn't shoot it properly anyway." Harold thought hard. "What have I done to you now?"

"Bunnies. You've always got what you reckon is clean rabbit meat, and your lot are truthful about that sort of shit. One of the Barbies let slip you'd fixed their rabbit problems. Lust and booze has a terrible effect on some people." Vulcan grinned. "Then one of our new tenants asked what happened to the rabbits, the big yummy ones?"

"We've got them." Harold grinned. "Definitely yummy."

"How much?" Vulcan sighed. "You must have an expert because you always do, and I'll bet your rabbits don't get the Myxi. How much for rabbits and what we need to do to keep them safe?"

"You could buy them from the Barbies?" Harold had wondered if the Barbies were selling any on, to recoup the cost.

"I tried and no sale. I reckon they haven't got enough because Christie didn't even try to bargain. Not only that but their advice would be second-hand." The GOFS frowned. "We haven't a lot of spare coupons, but I'm sure we can sort something."

Harold relaxed because spreading the bunnies around made sense. After all, if the rabbits in Orchard Close were infected and died, he could buy some from either the GOFS or Barbies. "All right. You get three, two does and a buck, and instructions on breeding them up. There's another set of instructions for keeping them safe and if you short-cut you'll be buying more rabbits."

"Three? That's not much of a start."

"Breed like rabbits? They'll push out a litter every two months, and if you let the first few litters mature?" Harold shrugged. "Rabbit Bob reckons ninety pounds of meat a year off each doe."

"How much will this cost us?" Vulcan grinned. "Bearing in mind I sent you that poser rifle."

"Bloody expensive considering I still had to buy it, and I shot your sniper. Though if I have to buy some rabbits back, I'll pay the same price you do." Harold grinned back and they started serious negotiations.

* * *

When he arrived back Harold called for the cauldron and the usual suspects. "The GOFS are buying bunnies. Just three and the information. How do you feel about selling live ones elsewhere?"

"I don't mind the GOFS too much. After all they'll probably sell us some back in a disaster." Emmy's lip curled. "Geeks, however?"

"The GOFS will sell some back, as part of this deal. I've been thinking about the others. I reckon we should sell some to the Hot Rods and Geeks, just three to each and all the information." Harold frowned because he'd prefer not to sell to either. "Otherwise either of them might try to infect ours, steal some, or they'll get some from elsewhere anyway."

"True, but I just don't like doing them any favours." Patty looked as if she was about to spit. "The Hot Rods tried to cheat on the last deal for knitting, putting spoiled coupons in the middle of the bundle."

Harold let a big smile come. "Who mentioned doing them any favours? Hawkins screwed us over the loot after stopping the General. I reckon I can even up for that." He laughed. "Even Caddi will have to pay up, because this is something he can't get anywhere else."

"What do we need from those two? More Geek crossbows would be handy." Patty smiled at Harold. "A lot more, unless you want more firearms?"

"No, we're all right for pistols now and we can make ammo for crossbows easier and cheaper than getting propellant." Harold looked around them. "What do we want from Caddi?"

"More of that good charcoal. Either he did steal some trees or someone else has plenty of timber." Liz scowled. "Our trees are still slacking. There's not a single stick big enough yet."

"We should sell a few more rabbits to the Barbies, to help them build up. Not many, but maybe another three does?" Elizabeth smirked. "Nobody will steal from them and my money is on them having a good safe place to keep theirs free from disease. No wild rabbits will be hopping into Beth's."

"If the GOFS keep theirs safe for a few months we can sell them a few more, since they seem civilised. If there's a shortage and a fight breaks out, I'd rather team up with them and the Barbies." Casper shrugged. "They seem better neighbours." The discussion went on to what they wanted from Caddi and Hawkins, then what price the Barbies might pay for another three does.

Over the next ten days Harold sold the Barbies three more rabbits, with a definite arrangement to sell some back at the same price if Orchard Close had a real disaster. He also closed deals for three rabbits to each of the other gangs. Each rabbit traded came with reams of advice, and warnings about the draconian precautions Orchard Close took. That extended to never giving the rabbits any scraps from veg bought at the mart, since wild rabbits had probably been all over them. The GOFS were told they could buy another three does if their first attempts were successful, and agreed to the buy-back idea. The price Harold screwed out of Caddi and Hawkins almost sparked off a party among the few who knew.

*　　*　　*

The TV did eventually show the breakout from Glasgow, two weeks into January, and the fairly happy start to the year in Orchard Close evaporated. Everyone in Orchard Close stayed glued to the screens as a massive horde of armed gangsters, followed by non-combatants, women and children, ran straight over two guard posts. The cameras showed long processions of people streaming across the city to funnel out through the gap.

"The Army have been caught completely by surprise due to the sheer size and ferocity of this assault. Now the soldiers are battling to prevent any of these scum spreading south or east to threaten the farmlands or Edinburgh. Forces are being rushed into place to deal with the threat, but that will take time."

Onscreen small groups of troops with armour fought to turn back the mob as it tried to veer to, presumably, the east or south. More views showed a long column trekking up snow-choked roads and then alongside a wide stretch of water.

"The Army have diverted the breakout northwards, west of Loch Lomond where the water will help to keep them away from other populations. We believe they will try to capture the submarine base at Fastlane, and the nuclear weapons there, so drastic steps must be taken."

"Not a nuke. Please, not a nuke." Sharyn clenched her hands together.

"They'll never get to Fastlane let alone capture a nuke." Harold sighed. "Look at them. They're freezing to death or will when night falls. What the hell possessed them to go north?"

"No Harold, I meant the government using a nuke." They stared at each other, horrified because both thought it possible after what had already happened.

A banging on the door shook them out of it. Harold went to answer. "Liz, Emmy, Finn, and Patty? What on earth do you want, what's the matter?"

"We have a nasty question that needs an answer, Harold." Liz pushed him in the chest. "Now move out of the way and let us get warm." Behind them Casper appeared, looking grim.

Harold moved for the five of them to come inside, then headed for the kitchen to get something for everyone to drink. This would be a small beer sort of discussion according to Patty. When he came back into the room everyone had found a seat and sat watching the screen. Sharyn patted the settee. "Sit down Harold. The TV has flipped forward from morning to midday and now to dusk so it's another of those doctored reports. There's a storm coming in looking at the way the snow is blowing now and the drifts look deeper."

Harold sat and took in the views of driving snow. He shook his head. "Why are they trying to march anywhere in that weather?"

"The horde is still marching north, and now darkness is falling. The Army cannot risk losing touch during the night in case large numbers arrive unexpectedly at the nuclear base. The commander on the scene has been instructed to stop these savages now while they can still be found. Artillery units have been rushed into place because aircraft still can't operate due to the conditions."

"But camera drones can?"

"Hush Emmy. Just the usual mushroom food because the Army can see in the dark better than bats, or Patty." Harold felt a nudge from Patty but everyone's attention stayed on the screen.

Bright flashes were all the warning the straggling horde received, as a ripple of explosions swept from one side to the other of the steep-sided pass. Some struck the ground but most exploded in the air over the heads of the leaders, lethal because the fleeing mass had no shelter, not even vehicles. The next ripple of flashes were a little further south, then the next a little further and now the mass heaved and surged, fighting to get back away from the next salvo. Again and again the bright flashes rippled, leaving dark, still forms scattered across the snow. Some of the crowd turned on each other, exchanging gunfire as they attempted to break clear. Several determined groups broke west and east, and headed into the steep hills.

Eventually the artillery fell silent, and night covered the carnage. Nobody in Harold's house spoke for a while because that had been a massacre, pure and simple. Sharyn finally broke their silence. "Is that how they intend to kill us, in the end?"

A long pause followed until Patty spoke. "No Sharyn, because Harold will never lead us into someplace like that. Will you Harold?" Her short laugh sounded harsh and contained no humour. "That's a slightly modified version of our nasty question, would he ever expect us to break out like that?"

"No to both questions, but we might be driven out and then into a bad place. Though after this I think the clear lesson is to stay in the city if at all possible." Several voices objected but Harold raised a hand to stop them. "House to house in built-up areas, even with tanks in support, will be bloody if they come to get us. Especially since the enclaves have all been fighting for a while so they aren't amateurs." He forced a smile. "After all, if the Army come to get us there'll be Wellington, Caddi and even the General all working on the nastiest possible surprise they can come up with."

"Not a thought I ever expected to be happy about." Liz shook her head. "Now explain why those idiots left the city in a blizzard." Harold couldn't come up with a sensible answer. The rest also tried to work out why the hell the idiots had gone north, into the mountains, but couldn't come up with a reason for that either. They eventually gave up and went home still wondering.

*　　*　　*

The phone call three days after the Glasgow breakout sent Veronica outside to disturb Harold as he stacked pipe fittings behind the library. "Harold, the gate said that Big Mack and three Hot Rods are walking down the road."

"Walking? I'll go and see what's up. Maybe they've broken down?" Mack ranked high enough in the Hot Rods to have a private vehicle, a transit mini-bus because he had trouble fitting in a car. By the time Harold arrived, Mack had started up the access road to the gate. Harold noticed that one of the others wore the overalls that were a uniform for top Hot Rods, which puzzled him even more.

"Eyup 'Arry. Can we come in?" Mack's big smile contrasted sharply with the scowls on the other three.

"No problem Mack." Once the four had been searched and disarmed, Harold led Mack and the new man, called Dodge, to the embassy. Alfie and Emmy followed as guards, and behind them Gayle brought a bag containing four pistols.

"How come you walked, Mack? There's barely any snow. Has Caddi started a new fitness program?"

Mack laughed. "Yeah, or summat close. I don't mind walking but this lot need toughening up. You could take them on a march with big packs full of rocks, like the Army does?" Mack turned to the scowling gangster. "This is Dodge, and 'e's ere so you lot know 'im next time 'e comes."

Harold inspected the young man, a typical muscular Caddi-style recruit. "A new one? Is Caddi recruiting?"

"Always, just in case 'e loses one, careless-like. You can go and get stew and beer now Dodge. I've 'eard the stew is real good, and the beer definitely is." Mack watched the man leave, then turned back to Harold. "Caddi is saving on diesel, just a bit. 'E reckons if we 'ave a power cut, The Mansion can be warmed up with it. There's only those four pistols to fix so I just stuck 'em in my belt and walked."

That also meant Caddi jumped the queue but four pistols weren't worth an argument. "In that case do you want some stew? We'll go down to the canteen to chat so you can eat up and get home before dark."

"I'd better. Something terrible might 'appen to anyone walkin' around in the dark near Orchard Close. Our blokes up near the island 'ave mentioned it." Mack smiled, confident it wouldn't happen to him.

They talked about Glasgow while Mack ate. After the big man had eaten his first bowl of stew and asked for a second, Dodge joined Harold and Mack. "Does this stew have them giant rabbits in it?"

"Yes. Though it also has herbs and plenty of veg." Harold smiled. "You'll be able to make your own soon."

"Hah, maybe, if Caddi don't eat them himself as fast as the er, bloody things grow." Dodge scowled. "He reckons we won't get any for months yet."

"Not until they've bred up a bit. You'll want to keep the first litter or two if possible to boost the numbers." Harold gestured towards the kitchen. "Until then you can come and get some here."

"I doubt we'll get any then. He'll be selling them to the other gangs to get the price back." Dodge sighed. "Which means I'll be back because this is good stew."

Dodge switched to talking about what turned out to be the armed woman Harold had seen on his last visit. The woman had become a true Hot Rod, called Mercedes, though she wore short skirts or tight jeans rather than overalls. Dodge seemed to be a fan. Allegedly Mercedes had arrived armed to the teeth and wearing a necklace of human ears, and demanded to see Caddi. After the meeting she pointed out that anyone trying to get into her pants without permission would contribute his ears to the necklace, since his nuts would shrink after she cut them off.

More than that, Caddi agreed, and added that anyone trying to rape her had better hope Mercedes killed him before Caddi started carving. Harold stared. "Really? Does he mean it?"

"He does, and she does. She cut the first man before word from Caddi spread." Dodge grinned. "I saw it, before I got promotion. She came in and went up to the bar for a beer. This youth put a hand on the back of her leg and started sliding it up to go under her skirt." The Hot Rod shrugged. "Don't get me wrong, she wasn't much of a prize then, kinda rough looking with scruffy clothes and hair and cuts and bruises. I reckon he did it more as a reflex, with the short skirt and all that. To be honest I hadn't noticed the knives myself."

About what Harold had expected to happen at The Mansion. "What did Caddi do?"

Both Mack and Dodge laughed. Dodge recovered enough to answer. "Nothing. Mercedes grabbed the bloke's wrist, slapped his hand down on the counter, and nailed it there with a knife. She tried her beer and pointed out it tasted bloody awful. Then she told him and the rest of the room that the wound was the penalty for touching her leg. If he'd gone up her skirt she'd have cut the whole hand off." He sniggered. "She pulled out the knife, wiped it on the bloke's shirt, and wandered off to sit down with her beer. Half the men there fell in love on the spot." From his voice that included Dodge.

"What did he do, the one she stabbed?" Harold couldn't see a Hot Rod standing for that treatment from a woman.

"You mean once he'd been to get the bleeding stopped?" Dodge laughed again. "He found out about the ears and thought himself lucky. He shows the wound off now and then. The t.. idiot will probably have 'Mercedes did this' tattooed on the scar afterwards."

"Caddi mentioned a list of penalties and asking." Harold felt relieved in an odd way, because this Mercedes had made herself visible rather than slipping quietly into Orchard Close as a refugee and causing trouble.

"Yer. She ain't a dyke, 'Arry. Mercedes reckons anyone can ask and she might say yes, but if she says no they better listen. She killed the first one who wouldn't take no and took 'is ears." Mack wasn't smiling. "A lot 'ave asked but nobody got a yes, and some 'ave got scars where they touched after a no. Caddi just laughs at 'em."

"Is she Caddi's woman?" Though Harold couldn't see Caddi with a woman who used knives, not the way the Hot Rod boss treated women.

"No. She's nobody's woman which is driving some of the blokes crackers." Mack smiled now. "She does jobs for Caddi and brings back ears."

Harold realised this Mercedes must be Caddi's assassin. He scowled. "Warn her to stay half a mile clear of here then."

"Caddi says her methods wouldn't work 'ere, but 'e didn't say what methods." Mack shrugged. "I'll mention it to 'er anyway." He looked round. "Where's the blonde woman, the one on the TV? We knew Emmy, Patty, that Fergie and some of the others when they showed up on the screen. Caddi is mad as 'ell because you got all the publicity again."

"Yeah, too true. One of the blokes drew a heart and I lust Patty on his Tee. Caddi had the poor sod caned." Dodge sighed. "Lusting after that dirty minded, er, woman on Barbie Radio was safer, but now that's stopped." He smiled and shrugged. "Though if Caddi was in a bad mood, getting caught listening could be painful. On top of that woman commenting and the music, they let us know how the blonde was getting on." He frowned. "They called her doll. We thought it was because they're the Barbie Girls, right, but someone said that's her name?"

"She is called Doll. With luck she'll be coming home soon." Harold hesitated, then decided the news might make Caddi mad at someone else for a change. "There's another patient at Beth's, a GOFS, and he'll be going home once he's cured. Now there's a legend in the making."

"Ooh yes, too true." Dodge smiled happily. "Maybe it's a good job Barbie Radio is broken, or Caddi would burst something. The Barbies will brag what the bloke got up to and worse, the GOFS will just add to it."

"Did you get anyone 'urt at that fight with the General, 'Arry?" Mack would be fishing for information to tell Caddi so Harold gave him enough to hopefully make Caddi cautious without feeling threatened. They both had a laugh when Harold confessed he'd perched half on the table because his ass hadn't healed. The three of them chatted about the General for a bit while Mack finished his second bowl of soup. The big man decided if he had a third he'd not fancy the walk home.

Harold watched the four of them walk off up the road with a slight frown. Apparently Orchard Close wasn't the only place short of diesel, unless Caddi just wanted to make sure he stayed warm. The bastard would probably use a car engine to keep his lights on as well while the rest shivered in the dark. Harold's slight frown also had to do with the young woman walking around among the Hot Rods with a gang name, knives and a machete. Harold wasn't going to underestimate a woman.

He didn't underestimate the Barbie women turning up for a beer and making casual enquiries about the radio repair man. They asked what could he repair, could they check out his workshop, could they have a chat to him about their big radio? Allegedly, the standard recruiting procedure for Barbies tended towards kidnap so Trev started to look decidedly haunted. He stayed firmly locked in his workshop if Barbies visited, and actually seemed happy to have Thandia laid outside the door. Outside now because the Mastiff wrecked a partly repaired radio just by being too big in a small space.

Within a week the Barbie visitors brought a pale-faced Doll home. Her lung had healed, or well enough to be allowed home if she took it easy. Unfortunately she wasn't well enough, Doll pointed out, for the Barbies to put chaperones in with her and Cy, the GOFS casualty. Cy would still be a guest in Beth's for a while. He could count himself a very lucky boy and not just because of the number of nurses. The Barbie doc had fought a long hard battle to stop an infection in his gut wound before finally beating it. Now Cy's internal embroidery had to heal well enough to stand the trip home. Doll reckoned the GOFS soldier might delay going home just to sample the aftercare he'd been promised by his Barbie nurses.

* * *

In early February, luck ran out for the bunnies in Orchard Close. Despite all the efforts put in by the bunny-keepers, Myxomatosis made it over the wall. After a quick talk to Rabbit Bob, Harold ended up stood outside a garage wearing thin disposable overalls, plastic jam-bags over his oldest trainers, an old pair of gardening gloves and an impromptu balaclava made of thick curtaining with wraparound sunglasses. Casper handed him a machete and a bucket of bleach, while Rabbit Bob opened the rear door of the garage. Harold went in.

Ten minutes later he came out, placing the bloody machete in the tray full of strong bleach before standing in it. Harold stayed in the bleach while picking up the nearby bundles of fodder and bedding, throwing them into the garage. He followed those with two buckets of old petrol, throwing the liquid as far into the interior as he could. Then he began to strip off the possibly infected clothing, throwing it into the garage. Stood only in his boxers, Harold picked up a length of wood with soaked cloth around the top and Casper lit it. Harold hurled the flaming brand inside, slamming the door with a whispered, "Fare thee well."

The compost heap out in the fields where the used bunny bedding from this garage had always been taken would become a bonfire, and hopefully a pyre for any infection left. Meanwhile Rabbit Bob, George and Maryam were comforting the two people who had cared for this garage of rabbits. As Harold padded away in bare feet and his boxers to get dressed, the flames sterilised everything inside the garage. The solution might be dramatic and probably more than necessary, but sacrificing one garage of hutches and rabbits to make sure the rest remained uninfected made a good trade.

A small crowd with buckets and hosepipes, supervised by Barry, wet down anything nearby that might receive sparks once the roof went up. Rabbit Bob had no idea how the infection got in there with all the netting and precautions. Maybe a single flea or gnat had come in on someone's clothing, because this had been the only garage infected. Considering that the disease now ran rampant through the wild rabbits outside the walls, that could be counted as success. Rabbit Bob thought another three garages should be turned into giant breeding hutches to spread the risk. The carpenters could use timbers scavenged from lofts, where no wild rabbit could have infected them.

Harold resisted steady pressure from other gangs to part with more rabbits, pointing out that they would have to breed theirs up because his people needed the food. The home-bred rabbits had become the only source of meat outside the chew sticks and paste since the last mart trip. Harold hadn't been able to bring any spam because although the shelves were still labelled up, they were bare.

* * *

All the gangs eased off on using motors, though the Barbies came to Orchard Close on foot anyway. According to the GOFS, Gofannon wasn't sure why Caddi had stopped his people using as much diesel but wanted to play safe in case the bastard knew something the rest didn't. Despite that a steady stream of GOFS walked or cycled the two or three miles to either flirt with the women or eat uninfected fresh meat. Visiting Doll had now gone onto their list of reasons and the influx of visitors gave the Orchard Close businesses a welcome boost in income. The lack of Geeks might have been saving diesel, or they were worried about Harold's reaction to Hawkins short-changing him. Though one Geek made the trip, walking the three miles to buy Patty a beer and pay to have his picture taken with her.

The majority of Hot Rods walked or cycled now. "Eyup 'Arry." Harold looked at the eight Hot Rods walking behind Mack, including E-Type, and they were all smiling.

"Cripes, has Caddi pulled your car keys as well, E-Type?" Harold watched the Hot Rods being searched. They were in tremendous high spirits, laughing and cracking clean jokes. "How come you need such a big escort Mack?"

"Those idiots? E-Type is 'ere because Caddi makes one of 'em come with me in case I come over faint or something." Mack glanced at the rest. "The rest 'ave 'eard that Doll is 'ome."

"Yes she is. How come you know?" Harold laughed as he realised. "We've had GOFS visiting so you had to find out."

"The GOFS were braggin' of course. A few of 'em have pictures on their phones, stood or sat with 'er, so these grinnin' idiots 'ave all brought a phone." Mack shook his head. "That lass is the nearest thing to a film star these days."

"She's still not very well." Harold grinned at the idiots in question. "Her rules for pictures are simple. If you buy a beer for her and yourselves, and then do business with anyone else here or pay a fee, she'll pose for a photo with you. No hugging, no kissing, but she'll wear her Stetson." Doll didn't drink the beers, just collected the coupons and paid half to the Coven because she reckoned she couldn't work for her keep just now. Harold shrugged. "Patty will be there if anyone gets frisky."

Mack shook his head. "Oh, the idiots know and they've all come prepared to spend their coupons. Some want Patty in the picture as well. Idiots. Caddi will skin 'em if 'e finds out."

E-Type laughed at the last bit. "They won't care as long as he doesn't wipe the phones. The silly f.. idiots want to brag to the other gangs, especially the Ferdinands since she spanked some of them." The gangster rolled his eyes. "The soft, er, Ferdinands are actually bragging about that now."

"As long as your new pinup, that Mercedes, doesn't get jealous." Harold stood aside for the pair of them to go into the canteen first. "We'll sort out the repaired weapons once Mack has had his stew."

"Too true. Them rabbits of yours make it dead meaty. I 'ope more of ours grow up soon." Mack waved to Elizabeth. "Stew please, with a bap?"

She scowled, because Elizabeth still hadn't forgiven the Hot Rods for her son dying. "It'll be a slice of bread. We're only baking loaves just now because we're a bit short on flour."

"That'll do, ta."

"There's a lot of things getting a bit scarce in the marts now." E-Type frowned. "We don't do too badly, but some of the civvies are getting really short." He glanced towards the door and the fields beyond. "Someone said you might be growing wheat next year for flour."

"Emmy would like to grow wheat, barley and hops, but we'd need a lot more land." Harold shrugged. "If she ever gets any seed, we'll see."

"That'd be a sight to see."

The conversation moved on to gossip, and then to Mercedes since E-Type wanted to brag about her new trick. Paddy, one of the top Murphies, had visited the Mansion for an overnighter. He'd expected Mercedes to be available to warm his bed since nobody else seemed to be using her. E-Type almost choked on the next bit. "She said yes, she'd warm the bed all night but he couldn't touch her. Caddi offered them a bedroom in The Mansion, though he didn't mention the sound and vision."

"She slept with him?" Harold thought that might be the beginning of the end for the woman. Once one had, the rest would expect to and she'd end up passed around.

"Sort of. She warned him, upfront in front of his bodyguards, that anything that touched her she'd cut off." E-Type sniggered. "Paddy said all right." The gangster shook his head. "Paddy didn't make it up to midnight. Once they were in bed he insisted on a lot more than touching - all on film." He frowned thoughtfully. "Mercedes must have known about the cameras because she never even showed her bra and knickers, just a long nightshirt." E-Type's grin came back. "Mercedes needed a shower and a new nightie, the bed needed a new mattress, and Paddy needed a new set of nuts and ears and about eight pints of blood."

Harold blinked, startled, because that meant Paddy had bled out in the bed. Considering the size of Paddy, and the size of Mercedes, she must be handy with a knife and probably stronger than she looked. "What did the Murphies say?"

"The bodyguards were shown the recording of the slice and dice, and they'd heard the rules laid out and Paddy agreeing. The Murphies had to hand the hostage back, which came as a relief for Dodge." E-Type sat back with a big smile. "Caddi has set her up with a room in The Mansion for repeats."

"Repeats? Who the hell will go for a repeat?" Harold looked from one to another.

"Anyone who gets the offer. Mercedes made it very clear, 'Arry. If Paddy kept 'is 'ands to 'imself there'd be no trouble." Mack shrugged. "Caddi is going to get her to offer a few top people, ones 'e'd like killed or took down a peg. After all, if they back down they're scared of a woman."

Harold winced. "Better than bleeding out."

"Yeah, but if they sleep in her bed but keep their hands to themselves, they'll save their rep. Well, not sleep." E-Type chuckled. "After all, they wouldn't want anything to sleepwalk and join the necklace."

"Cripes. How does he pick victims?"

"Dunno 'Arry, but I reckon 'e's got a shit list someplace that 'e'll work down." Mack smiled at Harold. "I dunno if yer on it, 'Arry."

"I'll be there, but I don't know what number." Harold grinned and made the expected gang boss type response. "If I'm not I'll have to try harder to annoy him." The other two laughed.

"She kills a few who don't come anywhere near our place. Don't accept offers from strange women in dark alleys, Soldier Boy." E-Type frowned. "To be honest we don't know how she does it. Mercedes killed two Hot Rods who caught her alone and tried it on. All we know is they were armed but never managed to cut her, and she took their ears."

Mack shook his head. "Caddi even 'as a way to make a profit out of 'er now. Someone dared one of the blokes to lie down so 'e could see 'er knickers an' she said what knickers." Mac grinned. "Though she put 'er 'and on 'er knife so 'e didn't try to see."

"Yeah, there's betting now. If anyone gets the chance to see if she's got knickers or a bra on, a clear chance, he gets a third of the bets. Caddi gets ten percent and the winners of the day's betting get the rest." E-Type laughed. "A few actually asked if they could look but she said no. Others tried too hard to find out and a few have scars but nobody has collected the commando or knicker bets. A couple have seen a bit of bra and won that, but nobody has confirmed braless either."

"What about cameras? I know Caddi has them all over the place." Harold couldn't see how the young woman could keep it up. Someone would film her in the shower or the loo.

"No cameras are allowed in her bathroom and nobody else will try after the first bloke she found drilling the wall." E-Type moved on to describe a list of scars that Mercedes had inflicted on the driller and various other gangsters and why.

*　　*　　*

Mack left after paying in coupons for the repairs, and a crate of beer because he didn't mind carrying that. The men with him were in good spirits since Doll had put on her boots as well as her Stetson for the pictures, one with each. Two had even more expensive pictures with Patty stood holding her crossbow at the other side of them. Harold waved the group goodbye before changing into his gardening jeans and wellies.

Emmy had started making gardening noises, even though there weren't any plants to go out in the fields. She insisted that if more ruins were knocked down because of the Geek onager, the ground may as well be dug over. The conservatories were already filling with baby this and that so perhaps she'd actually fill the extra acres. Despite the digging, Harold found as much time as possible for training those who wanted to be a bit more dangerous.

"Oops, sorry. Hang on, what are you doing?" Liz put her hands on her hips. "Well that was a waste of time."

"What was?" Both Fergie and Harold grinned at her.

"Finding an excuse to wander into the dance house all accidental-like when you two had snuck in here. You do realise the pair of you have been driving us crackers?" Liz glared from one to the other of the pair of sunny smiles.

"Why? When someone asks I tell them exactly where I've been and what I was up to." Harold smirked. "It's not my fault if people have dirty minds."

"I always tell the truth." Fergie clasped her hands in front of her and fluttered her eyes bashfully. "My mummy said I should."

"Oh yes, I've heard your truth. Hints about personal, private lessons with big rough soldier types, then trotting off alone with one certain soldier." Liz glowered some more, but it wasn't working. "Now I come in here and find you actually are practicing with blessed machetes. Cripes, nobody will believe me even if it's the stone cold truth." Her glare moved to Harold. "How come Fergie gets these personal private lessons?"

"Bribery." Harold started laughing.

"Truly." Fergie managed not to actually laugh. "I want to catch up with all the real fighters like Patty and Emmy and Doll, so I traded."

"Traded what? Or is that going to be worse than not knowing." Liz rolled her eyes. "I'll never live this down. I'm supposed to know these things."

"But we told the truth. I said I had been supervising practice, and Fergie said she'd been practicing. We just didn't mention one-on-one. Fergie found something I wanted, and not her body despite what some nasty-minded people think. In return she wanted extra lessons, one-on-one, with a machete and a pistol." Harold shrugged and brandished his wooden machete and stick. "I don't even kiss her bruises better." He left it a few moments, until Liz nearly burst with impatience and opened her mouth to ask. "She traded Daisy's Christmas present, the little toy crossbow. I don't go on those sorts of scavenges much these days but Fergie does, and she didn't have any use for it."

Liz stood while that worked its way in, then rounded on Fergie. "Getting my eye poked out is your fault?"

"No, blame whoever suggested that Daisy could use little sticks once the foam arrows were ruined." Harold sighed. "She barely hit your eye and lost a week's archery practice. Now she can only use the durn thing on targets unless someone finds more foam suitable for arrows."

"Now clear off because this is my practice time, and I haven't many lessons left." Fergie sighed dramatically, pushing out her chest. "If I don't learn enough I'll have to find something else he wants, and lock the doors before we practice."

"Cripes, don't spread that idea. He'll be in permanent hiding or too knackered to spank any scroats that need it." Liz turned towards the door, then chuckled. "I'm not going to tell anyone, not until after Valentine's. There's a book on if you pair end up walking home together, and where you end up. I'll make a killing." Fergie and Harold watched her go, both wearing big smiles.

"Ow."

"You said to strike while my opponent is distracted."

Harold shook his head. "I'm not sure you need any lessons for that." They both set themselves, wooden machetes and sticks poised. "Ready?"

*　　*　　*

Doll wasn't up to machete practice yet, but she felt much better by Valentine's. Doll insisted on coming to the dance, wearing her Stetson and boots, but bowed out of any competition this time. The Barbie doc had warned her to take it easy because although Doll's lung had healed well enough to be up and about, she hadn't to strain it yet. Lenny blushed when Doll announced that the first time she strained herself, he would be the lucky boy. Then he had to suffer the teasing when Doll explained she only meant a dance, though if the dance went well?

Liz wore a big smile when Stewart Baumber walked Fergie home because the fifty-eight-year-old ex-caretaker would definitely be a safe escort. Harold walked Louise to her home, not Fergie's. By now everyone had worked out that men didn't float Louise's boat, but at least one Barbie Girl did. Though how the quiet thirty-one-year-old graphics designer had managed to land the exotic, flamboyant Chandra, or the other way round, kept speculation alive. The gossip radar did go on alert when Celine agreed to Roy walking her home. Celine swore Roy wasn't in any danger, or not until her skirt hem strayed a lot higher, at least above her knees.

Somehow having Doll back, teasing at least one man, cheered everyone up. They had felt better after the General had his nose bloodied, the high spirits persisting through January even while the food at the marts grew less and less. The new refugees were particularly happy about the number of Bloods who died. The newcomers were rapidly being absorbed, and had already been infected with the cripes. Now some were experimenting with all and any gods, dressing up and competing at the dances, or finding new gnome names for their new hats. A few joined in learning new ways of using a machete, and how an iron bar could make them much more dangerous.

The proof that their fighters really were dangerous meant many residents began to feel more secure. The neighbours were finally starting to treat Orchard Close as a true enclave, a force to be reckoned with. Some of the guards on the gate even started to swagger, just a bit in front of the visitors. Harold suggested stopping them, but his advisors reckoned the gangsters expected that from real fighters and would actually respect Orchard Close more. Harold knew hand-to-hand would be much worse than defending from cover, and concentrated on making sure the fighters could back their swagger up if the worst happened. The rest were enjoying the peace, but Soldier Boy didn't expect that to last.

Characters in Branching Out

ORCHARD CLOSE ENCLAVE

Harold (Harry) Miller - 22 - ex Corporal pay clerk with CGC Conspicuous Gallantry Cross.

Abigail - 24 - refugee from the north

Alfie - 17 - Probable orphan since his Mum disappeared. Living with Betty.

Alicia - 23 - Small dumpy woman from the original flats.

Barry - 63 - Ex firefighter - ran from Geeks with granddaughters - designs bombs

Bernie - 28 - original resident - Bomb maker (under instruction)

Berry - 18 - daughter of Nigel. Taller, stronger, and also a brewer.

Bess - 21 - Ex- girlfriend of gangster, now Matthew's gartered wench

Betty - 61 - Oldest woman - an original resident

Billy - 18 - original resident of flats

Casper - 22 - big well-muscled gay man who becomes Harry's friend

Celine - 27 - from burned flats - slim redhead. Shy - rape victim.

Christopher - 29 - refugee from north - Gnome on the Range

Conn - 24 - short slim man, prematurely bald

Curtis - 26 - original from flats, short and stout, amateur gardener

Daisy - 6 - Harold's niece

Doll - Dolly - 21 - Barry's eldest grand daughter

Elizabeth - 36 - from north - Pricilla's mum

Emmy - 23 - Jamaican - tall, well-built woman, from burned flats, Curtis' gartered wench

Faith - 37 - short, stout, light brown hair. Her son Toby died defending Orchard Close

Finn - 50 - Electrician, original from flats

Gayle - 20 - Dental trainee and now Orchard Close anaesthetist

Georgina - 9 - Zach and Olive's daughter

Hazel - 16 - orphan, from burned flats

Hilda - 43 - ex clerical worker, loves collating lists, original from flats

Isiah - 36 - reclusive - redundant telephone engineer, original from flats

Janine - 36 - Laundry assistant.

Jeremy - 20- from north

Jilli - 14 - Jillian - bought in trade

Joey - 8 - Pippa and Robert's son

John's Pat - 37 - from north - Philip's mum

June - 39 - looks early twenties at first - ex-trophy wife.

Kerry - 34 - Shy - Isiah's wife - seamstress and sold embroidery, original from flats

Lenny - 27 - Nearly qualified paramedic

Lillian - 21 - tall overweight woman who moves in with Conn

Liz - 23 - 5' 11", arts and crafts in iron and bronze - now the smith, original from flats

Louie - 20 - Fleeing from north

Louise - 31 - quiet - small time graphic designer on internet, original from flats

Matthew - 26 - red haired ex Traffic Warden.

Matti - Matracia - 19 - Barry's younger granddaughter.

Nigel - 43 - brewer, widower

Olive - 31 - part-time cleaner - Zach's wife, Georgina's Mum, original from flats

Patricia Elliot - 28 - Trainee nurse. From burned flats

Pat's John - 38 - from north

Patty - 26 - demon knitter who wants to have a crossbow

Phillip - 19 - from north - John's Pat's son - No Place like Gnome

Pippa - 27 - Genius baker

Pricilla - 13 - from north - Elizabeth's daughter

Rob - 38 - divorced - Short and portly Plumber, original from flats

Robert - 28 - Pippa's husband

Rory - 3 - Abigail's son

Sal - 28 - blonde woman - original resident

Seth - 24 - trainee brewer - original resident

Sharyn - 27 - Harold's sister - widowed

Stewart Baumber - 58 - caretaker, original from flats.

Sukie - 6 - Suzie's daughter.

Susan - 33 - divorcee, original from flats

Suzie - 23 - Sukie's single Mum - her sister died in fighting - Asian

Tim - 24 - Refugee with nothing but his fiancée, Toyah

Toyah - 21 - Refugee with nothing but Tim

Umeko - 18 - Asian girl rescued from Geeks brothel

Veronica - 16 - quiet - daughter of Isiah and Kerry

Violet - Abigail's baby girl
Wills - 4 - Harold's nephew
Zach - 34 - ex-office manager, original from flats

94 residents - January Year 3

Bethany - 21 - Gnome Sweet Gnome
Charlie - 32 - home appliance (washing machine) repair man. refugee from General
Chris - 28 - fighter with Roy, refugee from General
Theo - fighter with Roy, refugee from General
Fergie - 20 - From ? - Wants to learn to fight - joins knicker competition
George - 43 - rabbit breeder. Maryam's hubby - refugee from General
Maryam - 41 - rabbit breeder. George's wife - refugee from General
Max - fighter refugee from General
Nathan - fighter refugee from General
Rabbit Bob - 35 - Rabbit breeder with buck Rocket Man - refugee from General
Roy - 31 - fighter who has already been driven from his home by the General - twice
Stu - 28 - fighter with Roy, refugee from General
Tilly - 18 - refugee from ? - 'Omeless Gnome-lass'
Wade - 23 - refugee from? - amateur carpenter
William - 27 - amateur mechanic - refugee from General

46 arrivals fleeing General, including Roy's five, and four escaped fighters
22 other refugees
Less two dead and Curtis

159 residents - March Year 4

1 acre and can theoretically feed 8 people if the meat is from elsewhere. Potatoes are a very good crop - food value vs space

Orchard Close fields are now 51 acres. More acres to be added at each end, plus all the gardens inside the walls. Will grow enough for at least 200 despite being inefficient.

OTHERS

The Bunker – UK cell of global cabal

Owen - Chairman

Boris – small slim dark-haired man - Foreign Office

Faraz – RAF liaison

Gerard - Youngest of the dozen cabal leaders - transport incl. distribution of food

Grace - tall spare grey-haired aristocratic woman dealing with work camps

Henry - Portly man with thick black hair and beard in charge of farms

Irina - slightly obese woman with short black hair. Ex prison officer, in charge of brothels

Ivy - Stout middle-aged redhead in charge of food preparation and sale

Joshua - Army liaison. Spare, balding man

Keris – Falklands operation

Maurice – Spymaster. Bland, unassuming, mousy-haired and medium size and build.

Vanna - tall Asian woman dealing with special facilities and private military forces

Victor – Navy liaison

IN THE CITY

Hot Rods – ex car thieves - gang to the south of Orchard Close - wear overalls as uniform

Cadillac - gang boss

Big Mac - 7 foot bodyguard - named after trucks

Bugatti - senior gang member

Cooper - short for Mini Cooper - second in command

Charger - senior gang member

Chevy - senior gang member

Dodge - senior gang member

E-Type - senior gang member

Porsche - senior gang member

Samuel - man with shotgun, loses a finger when Harold shoots him

Mercedes - only female who is a gang member with car name

GOFS - Gods of Fire and Steel - gang to the west

Gofannon - gang boss, has a genuine pre-Crash sword

Vulcan - senior gang member - warchief

Wayland - gang blacksmith

Hephaestus - Heff - senior gang member
Ogou - senior gang member
Cy – Gofs soldier

Geek Freeks - ex- shop assistants - gang to the north – wear smocks with name badges
Hawkins - gang boss - senior manager
Darwin - manager - (senior gang member) Amateur gardener
Einstein - manager - collects rents and women
Galileo - manager - builds crossbows and other weapons
Marconi - manager, builds field telephone and repairs some radios
Nobel - manager - chemistry student
Tell - aka William Tell - gang bowyer & archer
Wellington - manager - warchief
Ly Thien or Thien - young Vietnamese woman now Wellington's companion
Mathias - Geek soldier

Barbie Girls - all-female gang beyond GOFS - based in 'Beth's' shopping mall, leaders wear blonde wigs and are named after dolls
Malibu - Senior Barbie leader wears twinset and pearls, and a machete
Christie - Senior Barbie leader - African ethnicity
Ken - Senior Barbie leader - Large and dresses as a man - warchief
Chandra - Asian Barbie in 'dress' slit right up both sides
Splash - Staffy X sold to a Barbie

Ferdinands - based in American Football stadium - heavily influenced by Mad Max films
Bull - leader - overweight - a bad look with skin tight pants.
Snoop - coach (lieutenant) - big muscular black youth
Slash - coach

Trainspotters - border the city centre exclusion zone. Wear anoraks
Franco - leader with red dreadlocks

Bloodsuckers - Bloods - Mixed race gang, notoriously savage assault fighters for General.

The Generals - Gang to the north-west
The General - Leader - champion strategic games player
Patton - bosses the bloodsuckers, the Bloods

MIB - Men in Black - Ex city trader trainees. Wear black suits and shades.
Near city centre
Branson - Leader
Jones - senior MiB
Scrooge - senior MiB

Professors - mixed race and mixed sex leaders - allegedly from University
Prof - Leader - old professor in a suit and robe
Celeste - Dance teacher

Bargees - have steel houseboats - surrounded by old canals. Sell fish
Skipper - gang leader
Smiley - senior member
Goldie - fighter

SIMs - mixed sex commune, - use wicked short-range rockets keep others
at bay.
Bert, Julie, Maisie and Stevie - fighters

Baggies - ex-football fans. wear black and white stripes. Based south of
TesdaMart
Boing - leader
Throstle - a senior gang member

Murphies - wear a shamrock - gang west of Caddi
Paddy - leader

Precinct 19 - enclave led by ex-police - West of M5 Motorway - use short-
ened ID numbers
Sarge - No. 33 - retired police sergeant - now the leader
Sergeant Koos - No. 15 - senior fighter, ex police firearms squad
David - No. 613 - constable leading a squad of ten
Javed - No. 229 - constable leading a squad of ten
Simeon - No. 814 - constable leading a squad of ten

Benny - No. 518 - marksman
Samuel - No. 277 - marksman
Sue - Sarge's granddaughter

Sinners - London gang controlling school playing fields, based in a library
Sinner - gang leader
Nita - senior gang member
Preacher - leads nearby enclave
Kermit - leads nearby gang
Imam - Zaid - leads nearby enclave
Hans - leads nearby gang

This ends Book Three of
The Fall of the Cities.

Find out what happens next!
Book 4
A Mercedes for Soldier Boy
will be available soon!

VANCE HUXLEY

Vance Huxley lives out in the countryside in Lincolnshire, England. He has spent a busy life working in many different fields – including the building and rail industries, as a workshop manager, trouble-shooter for an engineering firm, accountancy, cafe proprietor, and graphic artist. He also spent time in other jobs, and is proud of never being dismissed, and only once made redundant.

Eventually he found his Noeline, but unfortunately she died much too young. To help with the aftermath, Vance tried writing though without any real structure. As an editor and beta readers explained the difference between words and books, he tried again.

Now he tries to type as often as possible in spite of the assistance of his cats, since his legs no longer work well enough to allow anything more strenuous. An avid reader of sci-fi, fantasy and adventure novels, his writing tends towards those genres.

www.ingramcontent.com/pod-product-compliance
Lightning Source LLC
Chambersburg PA
CBHW061312170626
46817CB00001B/151